MW00629404

WILD
GROUND

RANDOM HOUSE • NEW YORK

GR

WILD BOUND

EMILY USHER

A NOVEL

Wild Ground is a work of fiction. Names, characters, places, and incidents are the products of the author's imagination or are used fictitiously. Any resemblance to actual events, locales, or persons, living or dead, is entirely coincidental.

Copyright © 2024 by Emily Usher

All rights reserved.

Published in the United States by Random House, an imprint and division of Penguin Random House LLC, New York.

RANDOM HOUSE and the HOUSE colophon are registered trademarks of Penguin Random House LLC.

Originally published in hardcover in Great Britain by Serpent's Tail, an imprint of Profile Books Ltd, London, in 2024.

LIBRARY OF CONGRESS CATALOGING-IN-PUBLICATION DATA
Names: Usher, Emily, author.
Title: Wild ground : a novel / Emily Usher.
Description: New York : Random House, 2024.
Identifiers: LCCN 2023052129 (print) | LCCN 2023052130 (ebook) | ISBN 9780593731291 (hardcover ; acid-free paper) | ISBN 9780593731307 (ebook)
Subjects: LCGFT: Bildungsromans. | Romance fiction. | Novels.
Classification: LCC PR9619.4.U74 W55 2024 (print) | LCC PR9619.4.U74 (ebook) | DDC 823/.92—dc23/eng/20231117
LC record available at https://lccn.loc.gov/2023052129
LC ebook record available at https://lccn.loc.gov/2023052130

Printed in the United States of America on acid-free paper

randomhousebooks.com

9 8 7 6 5 4 3 2 1

First U.S. Edition

Book design by Debbie Glasserman

For all the friends from those days

WILD GROUND

tell myself that the memory comes from nowhere. Not a memory exactly, but not a dream, either. More like a series of fragmented scenes, playing out behind my eyes in the space between asleep and awake. I haven't thought of it all in years. I spend most of my time trying not to think.

I am back there, in that place they sent me to. Caged within the walls of a sprawling building on the edge of a spa town known for middle-aged women in cashmere twinsets and quaint cafés that serve overpriced cream teas. Except it isn't a spa. It's a unit, intended for people like me, people with dead eyes and messed-up heads and teeth falling out of faces.

Whenever anyone asks me what my name is, I say the same thing. Chrissy. My name's Chrissy. The nurses exchange a look, pat my arm, scribble something down on their clipboards. I know it isn't my name, of course I do. But every time I look in the mirror it's her I see. My mam. And then, inevitably, I lose it, lift up my fist, smash it against the woman staring back at me. The mirror doesn't crack, Chrissy just stays there, mocking us both. So I fling myself at her again, fling anything I can find, until eventually there are arms on mine, lifting me up, out, down, sinking a sedative into my skin.

The memory shifts so that I am in the common room, sitting in a semicircle with the other inmates. Except they don't call us that. "Service Users" is the term they use, as if we have any say in being there. Some look near enough normal, like they might not seem out of place ordering a scone and an Earl Grey only a stone's throw from where we're all locked up. Others are in a bad way, their features swollen, their skin sallow, ravaged by the life they've led.

The telly is on, as it always is. We stare at the screen, but I am the only one watching it. A documentary about a rainforest, far, far away, plants of every size and color.

You know, I say out loud to no one in particular, a quarter of all medicines start off in the rainforest.

No one says anything back, although a few shift uncomfortably in their seats, cast nervous glances my way. Someone behind me clears their throat.

Almost every drug on this earth comes out the ground.

All right, Jennifer, the nurse sighs. Quieten down, please.

I ignore him, set my attention on the lass sitting to my left. She can't be much older than me, her skin gray, the inside of her elbows covered in tracks that she doesn't bother to hide. It's a seed, I say, nodding at the marks. It starts with a seed.

She edges away from me, folds her arms over her chest. I

smile to myself, turn back to the telly, watching a utopia of reds and yellows and blues unfurl on the screen, soaring trees and mad fauna.

Papaver somniferum. The flower of joy.

The lass looks up at me coldly. What yer goin on about, yer crank?

Poppies, that's all they are. Same flower everyone sticks on as a paper pin fer Remembrance Day. When the petals fall away, I say—lifting my hands in the air and then letting them float down to my lap—they leave behind a pod, and inside it there's a black, sticky gum.

That's enough, Jennifer. The nurse presses a hand firmly on my shoulder. My eyes move back to the screen, but still I am talking, remembering.

And they take that and they mix it up, mix it with all sorts of chemicals and shit, I carry on, shaking the hand off, addressing the room now. Sell it on and then sell it on again, until eventually it reaches us lot, people like us, who've got nowt else to live fer.

The nurse moves around to my side of the sofa, grips me hard by the elbow. I try to pull away, but another one has joined him now, dragging me to my feet.

See, they say green is one thing, I call over my shoulder as the two of them lead me out of the room by force. They say it's white and brown and all that other shit that'll put you in t'ground. But it's bullshit, see? It's none of them things. What hurts is *people*. People you love, you know what I'm sayin? They're the ones that can mess you up. They're the ones that will ruin. Your. Life.

I open my eyes with a start, my lungs empty, my mind swirling in a terror thick as tar. Squeezing my hands between my knees, I begin to count. To ten at first. One hundred, one thousand. I count the movements of each of my limbs as I climb out of bed, count the steps to the bathroom, the turn of the shower tap, the cracks in the tiles on the wall. The tip of my tongue runs along the surface of each of my teeth, counting, counting. Tallying and calculating, filling my head with nothingness.

That same day, I see Denz again.

don't recognize him at first. Or perhaps that's not quite right. Perhaps it's more that I hope he is someone else. He hovers in the doorway of the caff, watching the blood drain from my face. The familiarity of his outline turns me to stone. The broadness of his shoulders, the thick neck. The scar under his eye that cuts across the dark plane of his right cheekbone. Danny used to think it was the shit, that scar.

Minutes pass, or maybe just a split second. Fionnoula must have been talking to me because the next thing I know, she's there in my ear.

Jen. Je-e-en? Are you still with us, love?

I steady myself on the counter, clear my throat. Sorry, Fi, what was that?

Denz is walking toward me, although I can't bring myself to meet his gaze again. Instead I act as though he's no one, except we both know it's too late to play that game. It's only when I take over the tea he ordered that he looks straight at me and says it out loud.

Cheers, Neef.

He uses that name like a weapon. A lifetime has passed since anybody called me that. But there he is, saying it like nothing has changed at all.

We don't speak again, but I can feel his eyes on me. When he leaves the caff that afternoon, I have to hold myself back from following him, letting him lead me like the Pied Piper toward the person I used to be.

He comes again the next day, walks right in like he owns the place, puts a fiver on the counter, asks for a tea and then sits down, doesn't even wait for the change.

Still like to act the big man, I see, I say as I slide the three pound coins back across the table to him. I put his tea in a paper cup but he doesn't take the hint to leave. Instead he looks at me steadily, a spark of something dancing in his eyes. Denz always hated me, could see right through me, knew what I was before I had even become it.

Still got as much mouth as you always did, he shoots back.

I ignore him, go back to the counter, pretend to be busy even though it's dead in there. The minute the clock hits four I turn the sign on the door to Closed, make a big show of it so he can't pretend he hasn't seen. That's when he stops me.

Neef, can we talk?

For a second I freeze, steadying myself against the door-frame. There isn't anyone here by that name, I say, enunciating my words, not dropping a single *t* or *h*. So I suggest you fuck off elsewhere.

He does nothing more in response than give me the same slow nod that I despised all those years ago. Then he leaves without another word.

Danny would be ashamed of me if he'd heard how I'd spoken to him. He's still my dad, he would say, his jaw set, his eyes scalding. Whatever you think of him, he's still my dad.

Yeah, I'd bite back, but he's no one to me. He never was.

The caff I live above isn't mine. I don't even run it, just work there, six days a week with Sundays off, and only then because it's closed. I've tried to talk Fionnoula and Ali into keeping it open, seems daft to close it on a Sunday, all the extra trade we'd get from people passing through Streatham on a weekend. But Fionnoula won't hear of it. Sundays are a day of rest, she says.

Fionnoula goes to Mass every week, but still calls herself a bad Catholic. It's like a private joke between her and Ali. The Bad Catholic and the Bad Muslim, they'll quip, exchanging this look that's only for them. They've been together for years and years, longer than I've been alive, she likes to tell me. But they've never married. Mostly because they couldn't figure out where to do it, and besides, who would come? She laughs when she says that but I know it hurts her.

It was hard for them at the start, being together. Too hard for their families, Fionnoula says, although that's her being kind, trying to forgive. It's better now, down here at least. People from all corners of the earth walk past the caff every single day and still there are some who don't like it. Folk can be strange like that. But at the start, she says, it was terrible. All the looks, the names, the turned backs. They got a brick through their window once, with a note tied to it. She's never told me what it said. It doesn't surprise me, though, how tough it was. It would have been strange to see the pair of them together even when I was a kid, round our neck of the woods at least. I just have to think of all the ways Danny used to get it, growing up in that pallid town where barely anyone looked like him.

The only reason I walked into the caff all those years ago was because I saw the hunched-over bloke with the ripped-up shoes and dirty coat go in before me. I figured if they let him in, I might be all right. That bloke's got different shoes these days, but he still wears that same old brown coat. That's why we call him Sandy. No one knows his real name, no one's ever asked. He drinks tea with milk and two sugars and if you put a coffee in front of him, he'll sip it slowly with a downturned smile, but he'll never tell you he doesn't want it. Some days he'll have a bit of toast; most, he doesn't bother. He's as thin as a rake and Fionnoula would happily feed him more if he'd have it, but he'll only take what he needs, he has his pride. I don't know his story, how old he is, where he comes from. All I know is that he's there every day. Him. The old lady with the scarred face and the limp who works down the corner shop. The night cleaner whose empty eyes never seem to close. The shy musician with the long, graying dreads that fall all the way down his back. We're all the same. A flock of silent souls circling around each other day in, day out, safe among chosen strangers. None of them know me, either. Not even Fionnoula and Ali, not really. They'd be disgusted by me if they did. They call me Jennifer, Jenny. Jen, sometimes. I don't care which. They don't know who I used to be, that I've spent almost half my life pretending to be someone else.

Fionnoula thinks I'm a dreamer but Ali knows better. Not that he's ever said anything. It's just the way he moves around me on those days when he catches me staring, unblinking, at the steam curling out of the kettle, or turning circles with a damp cloth on the same patch of table over and over again. Mostly he'll leave me be, but every so often I'll feel his hand on my shoulder, warm and heavy, a reminder that he's there. It brings me back somehow, when he does that.

Fionnoula has another tack. She'll swipe me round the back of the head with the corner of her tea towel, or wave her hand around in front of my eyes. He-llaaaaw? Anybody home, Lady Head-in-the-clouds? she'll trill, her accent still so singsong Irish no one would guess she's lived down here all this time.

And then I'll snap out of it, come to. Sorry, I'll say. You caught me at it again.

It's easier to let her think it's a daydream, but in fact it's the opposite of that. It's doing anything I possibly can for it not to be a dream, for my brain not to get carried away with itself and take me to the places I want to stay away from. Sometimes it's a song, a lyric on the radio, or a flat vowel that sounds like home. Other times it's the gap between a stranger's front teeth, the way someone shifts their weight, the cadence of a laugh.

When I first arrived in London, I'd see Danny everywhere. On the back of every bus, the corner of every street. But as the years passed, I got better at blocking him out. Sometimes months would go by without me having that sense of him, the feeling that if I were to turn around he'd be there, within arm's reach. Just the other day I followed a lad all the way down the High Road, hoping that when he turned it would be Danny's face I'd see. I caught myself in time, the foolishness of it. Turned around and walked the other way.

I didn't have any choice in the end, knew that if I had any chance of pulling through I would have to forget all of it, the bad and the good. But still I have these moments, these days when thinking gets the better of me. Because there were parts that were bliss, there were parts that were full and faultless and laden with joy. When Danny and I were kids, when we were innocent and daft and just the sight of each other, the split second of a look, could make us keel over laughing. And then later, in that middle bit. Fuck, that bit. It was beyond. The way everything we did, everything we felt, we did, we felt together. The way we loved and loved and loved each other. The way we loved each other.

've all but convinced myself that I imagined Denz's visit to the caff, that me seeing him was a sign I'm going mad all over again. I've been waiting for it to happen. But then he shows up a few days later, asks me to go for a walk with him, like it's the most normal thing in the world. I tell myself to say no, but when I open my mouth that isn't what comes out.

We make our way toward Streatham Common in silence, like the strangers we've become, or maybe always were. Denz doesn't look all that different from the version I've tried to bury in my head. He's not as big as he once was, and there is a heaviness around his eyes, his mouth, that wasn't there fifteen years ago. But he still has that same feel, the same foreboding air.

He stops at a bench, tries to make small talk while he rolls a spliff; a comment on the weather, another about a fat

Labrador chasing something up a tree. I sit as far away from him as I can, stare straight ahead until he turns to look at me.

You're not an easy girl to track down, you know.

I wasn't hiding, I say.

He pulls a lighter from his pocket, sparks up. It's taken time, man. These days you can find near enough anyone just by typin their name into a computer.

Wouldn't even know how to turn one of them on.

Denz smiles as though I've made a joke but I keep my face blank. You angry? he says. That I'm here?

I count to ten silently in my head, wait for the feelings to go, but they are still there and so I go again, all the way to twenty, thirty, forty this time and then . . . No, I say. I don't care.

There is a long pause and even though I don't look at him, I know that he is watching me. I heard you'd left, he says eventually. Disappeared, that's what they told me. It didn't surprise me much. We're all good at disappearin, aren't we? You and me. Chrissy.

My eyes smart at the sound of my mam's name and I cough, shove my hands deep in my pockets.

I haven't been back there in years.

He doesn't need to explain that he is talking about the little town I once called home, all pretty on the outside until you break it open and see the rot and the darkness underneath.

Lived all over since I left Leeds, he carries on. Few years in Manchester, few in Spain.

I yearn to ask him about Danny but pride or fear bite my tongue and I stay quiet, press the toes of my trainers into the dirt.

Ended up down here for work, stayin with me cousin. You'll remember him. Lewis.

I shrug like I don't, but I do. Of course I do.

Yeah. Well. He's been here a while. Got family in London from his dad's side. Sorted me out with a job. Security.

Something in his voice makes me look at him then, and I see the regret pulling at the corners of his mouth. You don't like it? The job?

Denz blinks, rubs his chin with his palm. Been doin it years, it's all I know, he says. Always told meself it were just temporary, that I'd get back to studyin at some point. I were gonna be an engineer, once upon a time. He shifts in his seat as if to reset his thoughts. But it's good money, a decent gig. That's what it comes down to. Pays the bills.

He offers me the spliff but I shake my head. The smell, that smell. I close my eyes, breathe in his smoke.

First time I saw you were here, he is saying. I were out, walkin, can't even remember where I were goin. I like it, me—just goin for a mooch on a night. Space to think, innit? And I saw you, from right across the other side of the grass, runnin. I had to look twice, to be sure, and even then. You're fast, man. Proper fast. It were like you were bein chased.

He pauses, takes a few slow draws.

You'd disappeared before I got anywhere near close enough for a proper look. I shouted after you, though, and I thought I saw you slow down, but it were only for a second and then you were gone.

A memory comes to me. A sound, a voice, catching in the wind. A name that doesn't belong to me anymore.

I came back every day for near enough a week before I

saw you again. That's when I followed you back to t'caff. You've hardly changed. Looks-wise at least. But your eyes. Your spirit, man—

I cut him off. What do you want with me, Denz? Why were you looking for me?

He takes one last pull of the spliff before flicking the roach into the grass.

It weren't you I were lookin for. Not exactly.

What?

I were . . . He pauses, rubbing at the joints of his jaw with his knuckles as if to relax the muscles. I were hopin you could tell me where Danny is, he says at last.

It takes me a moment to speak again, but when I do, my voice sounds strange. I don't understand, I say.

Denz turns his face toward me, looks at me for a long time. I ain't seen Danny in nearly two years. And I had this idea in me head, see. That mebbe he'd come lookin for you.

Well, he didn't, did he?

You tell me.

I get to my feet, not wanting to be here anymore. I've worked so hard not to let my mind go there, to travel back to a time of Danny and Denz and Chrissy and all the other ghosts of before. They don't exist, they never did. And yet here they all are, their names, their faces floating around in front of me, as though Denz has picked up the past and poured it out into the air.

I have to go, I mumble, but Denz puts out a hand to stop me and, when I look at him, I see the pleading in his eyes.

You'd tell me, wouldn't you, Neef? If he'd been in touch?

A beat passes before I take a step back, another, another.

And then I turn, walk, run as fast as I can away from him. Cold air cuts at my cheeks as I cross the common, past the hairdresser's, the chemist, the supermarket on the corner. Past the kids in their gaggles, dawdling home from school, their ties hanging loose round their necks. I run toward the crowds, dodging and weaving and searching face after face after face. I run until it feels like my legs will give way, until the tiredness knocks me dead, takes me back to the caff, forces me down on my bed.

Danny is missing. Danny is lost.

5

Some memories are easier than others. Like if I go right back: way, way back to when I was really little, in the flats, only me and Chrissy. Before there was an us, a Danny and me. It's not that those times were perfect, idyllic, anything like that. It's just that the memory of them slices a little less deep.

I never thought of where I came from as anything other than normal, living in those Lego towers with all of us stacked on top of one another. The walls in those flats were so thin you could hear the flushing of every bog, the whine of every telly, the tremor of every slammed door. Chrissy used to say that was its beauty and its curse. You never had to explain anything, never needed to say what had happened to that fella you'd been seeing, or why her down the way wasn't speaking to you, or who'd made your face swell and burst like a bag of jewels. I only realized later what other people thought of it, when I'd tell them where I'd spent the first twelve-and-a-bit years of my life and I'd see the kids' eyes shine with awe and the grown-ups' fill with pity.

We never had a family before we left the flats. I don't know that I ever craved one especially. We weren't any different from any of the other kids I used to knock about with. But I reckon Chrissy wanted one. To be part of one, somehow. Plenty of people would disagree with that. They'd say Chrissy never gave a shit about anyone or anything other than herself, and maybe they'd be right in a way. But there's a difference between wanting to be my mam and wanting to belong somewhere.

Chrissy barely spoke about anything to do with her life before I came along. She'd been in care since she was a little kid, I knew that. Passed and parceled from one foster family to the next until social services decided she was old enough to stand on her own two feet. Some were better than others, she told me, although that was as far as she ever got. There was one lady that had been the nicest of the lot, Margaret or Marsha or something along those lines. We went to her house a few times. I remember Chrissy sipping tea awkwardly on the sofa, and me playing with a box of old toys on the floor while the lady fussed around us, trying to make small talk, passing me little bags of dried apricots and raisins that made me retch when I tried to swallow them. I'd spend the whole time burying the bits of chewed-up fruit in among the toys when she wasn't watching, so that on each visit I'd unearth more of it than on the last, molding and rotting between the joints of a Barbie doll's legs or inside the wheel of a Fisher-Price car. One day there was a row about something, an envelope that had been on the side ready for the cleaner to pick up. Chrissy lost her temper and ended up smashing her teacup against the living-room wall. The visits stopped after that.

Chrissy was smarter than a lot of people gave her credit for. Book-smart, the type that would have done well at school, given half a chance. She never had boyfriends when I was really little. We didn't even have a telly, she used to read all the time instead. Tattered paperbacks from the charity shop, newspapers, magazines. Anything she could get her hands on. For a while she had a library card, we both did. It was only round the corner from us but to me it felt like another world. The building had a graceful type of beauty, all ornate sandstone and red brick, with a great big clock on the tower. I used to pretend we were royalty when she took me, climbing up the steps to our castle, our own private fortress of books. Most days it was only the two of us in there and we'd stagger up to the counter with our arms full, before loading our finds into an Asda carrier bag for the walk home. If Chrissy was still in a good mood by the time we got back to the flat we'd sit on the bed together and she'd read aloud to me, encourage me to do it myself, sounding out the big words, holding my hand in hers to trace the shapes with the tip of my finger. We had the letters of the alphabet stuck up all over the flat, written out on scraps of paper in fat black marker. F for Fridge. B for Bed. M for Microwave. Chrissy would set me spelling challenges that she'd mark out of ten, rewarding me with a Push-Pop or maybe a bag of Wotsits if I did well.

By the time I was five or six I knew my way around words better than most grown-ups. Chrissy was proud of that, she was always getting me to read stuff out loud if she knew we had an audience. Now and again we'd make up stories together, put ourselves in the middle of the books we loved. Annie, the Little Princess, Pippi Longstocking. It was our favorite game, to imagine ourselves in a different life.

WHEN I WAS SEVEN, CHRISSY GOT A BOYFRIEND. I DON'T REMEMber all that much about him, only that he used to take the piss out of her always having her head in a book. What you wastin yer time fer? he'd gripe. D'yer reckon it meks you look clever? Reckon knowin a few big words meks you better'n anyone else?

The fella didn't last long, but his words did. Up until him, my mam had dreams. She wanted a job, wanted to do one of them courses. She might like to be a teacher, she thought. He laughed so hard when she told him that I hoped he would choke and pass out. For a moment Chrissy stayed silent, but then she started laughing too, pretended she was having him on. I don't know what happened between them, only that by the time he was gone she'd lost interest in books, started putting all her efforts into men instead. I missed our stories, tried my best to bring her back, but when I'd start on telling our tales in front of one of her fellas she'd shush me like she was embarrassed, like it might put them off if they got an inkling that either of us was smart. Stop showin off, Jen, she'd hiss. No one likes a cleverdick.

I couldn't get my head round what had changed and so I'd kick off, cry and shout and make a scene, until in the end she'd drag me out of the room, or sometimes the fella would do it for her. Eventually we stopped going to the library, she said there were better things to be doing with our time, although she never told me what. The books got lost among the chaos of our lives and we racked up so many late fees that I was too embarrassed to show my face in there again. I never doubted that Chrissy loved me when I was little, but the bigger I got, the less certain of it I became. On some days she'd talk to me about everything, anything that popped into her head, wittering on about an article she'd read in a magazine, or so-and-so down the way, or did I think this pair of jeans looked good on her, that top, this eyeshadow? She'd call me her little marra, her little mate, and I'd bask in those moments, those hours, nodding along, saying the right thing, trying my best to keep it going, keep her happy and talking, knowing that soon things would change.

There's probably a name for it now. A label, a condition. A name for all those days when she was silent. Cold, long stretches that seemed to last forever, when she'd stay in bed for hours, so still it was as though somebody had switched her off. I'd talk to her, make up stories about the two of us finding a pot of gold buried underneath the flats, a long-lost auntie who'd left us a million quid in her will. I'd grab her shoulders in both my hands and shake her, and still she'd stare at me with such emptiness that I'd convince myself something terrible had happened to her brain, a stroke or a seizure or some other nameless thing that would leave her devoid of personality, a vegetable for the rest of her days.

The thing is, I could take all that. I could handle it just about, because Chrissy was there, she was solid and real. Nothing was as bad as the times when she'd disappear. Really, physically disappear. Often I could sense it coming, as though she were preparing to untether, readying herself to float away. The thought of it happening was almost worse than the event itself, that I might go down the park and, when I'd come back, she'd be gone.

I never knew how long she'd be away for. Sometimes it was only a night, often longer. At the start she'd arrange for someone to take me, one of the neighbors usually, although she never told them she'd be gone for as long as she was, so that in the end she'd burned all her bridges and no offers of help came her way anymore. But by then I was ten or so and I suppose she thought I'd be all right on my own. She'd usually leave me a fiver or a tenner maybe, and a note, always a note, full of long, flourishing words and madcap descriptions. The adventures she was going on, the things she would see. Don't worry, Little Marra, she'd sign them off, I'll be back in a bit.

She did come back, in those days at least. Except by then I would be chewed up with nerves, panicking when I didn't have her within my reach, clinging to her like shit to a shovel. For a while the guilt would soften her and she'd pull me in close, let me crawl onto her lap and press my cheek into the crook of her neck. But within weeks I would sense it coming again, feel the itch of her feet, the need for me to be out of her hair. It would make me physically sick, my stomach hurt and my head pound, and she'd get angry, say I was faking it, attention-seeking, didn't I get it, couldn't I see? That she just needed some bloody space?

Often she would turf me out, tell me to go and play, make some mates. I was getting too big to be hanging around her legs all the time, she'd say. I did as I was told but I never made any friends, not really. Not until I met Danny. I could hold my own with the kids from the flats, could give as good as I got, pretend I was like them even if I didn't feel like I was. I'd taken to carrying a little notebook around with me by then, writing my imaginings down instead of trying to share them with Chrissy. There must have been hundreds of stories and poems in there, all of them different but each of them the same. Me and Chrissy living another life.

Writing wasn't what kids did round my end, and so I'd shove the notebook in the waistband of my trackies every time I caught sight of them, act the little gobshite, put on a front. The ones my own age never bothered me. It was the big ones that got under my skin, the lads especially. But I learned soon enough that they weren't interested in my words. All they cared about was winding me up over Chrissy.

Oi, where's yer mam? Tell her to come down here and open her legs fer us!

Bet she'd do it fer a fiver, but she's fit though, innit? Tell her I'll up it to a tenner, the dirty mare.

She'd do it fer nowt, that one. She'd do us all in one go. Not long before you're old enough to join in, either, eh?

I worked out quickly that what I saw as beautiful in Chrissy was the same thing that men saw as theirs to stamp on, that they took the way she looked as permission to grab and paw and whistle at her, as though she were a stray dog let loose in a park.

It was because of them, the handsy men and boys, that I learned how to fight. A thousand of their leers loaded into each of my fists. I'd knocked a girl in my class clean to the floor when she called Chrissy a prossie, said she'd slept with the fella that was married to her mam's sister. When I told Chrissy she'd looked puzzled, cocked her head to one side, her thinking face. What's his name? she'd said, taking a long drag on her cigarette. As though she couldn't be sure, like one just faded into the next, like yes, maybe she had, but she was buggered if she could remember any of the details.

6

We used to share a bed, me and Chrissy, except when she had a fella on the go, which was a fair amount of the time. That's when I'd have to go on the mattress in the front room. Now and again when I had nightmares she'd let me drag it through to the bedroom, but that was worse. I'd lie there, pretending not to hear the grunts and moans of bodies rolling together above me in the bed, my bed.

The bloke Chrissy had right before we finally left the flats had been the worst in a while. I was twelve when he turned up. He only lasted a couple of months, but in that time, everything shifted. He had this way of looking at Chrissy like she wasn't even human, like she was meat, or prey that he could hunt. When he spoke to her his words came out on a knife edge. Get me a drink, or give me a cig, or get that little shit out from under my feet. The worst part was that Chrissy did as she was told. I don't know if it was fear or thrill or just that she was too stupid or weak to do anything else, but she'd always say the same thing in the end.

Go play, love. I'll come find yer in a bit.

I knew what was going to happen as soon as he'd arrived that day, all jerky and frantic, his eyes scattered, his pupils too dark. Chrissy put herself between the two of us, shielding me as he paced up and down like a caged animal in our tiny front room. I hadn't wanted to leave, tried my best to make excuses to stay, but Chrissy wouldn't have it. Go play, love, she'd said, but I stood rooted to the spot. Jen, go play. I'll come find yer in a bit.

In the end she took me by the hand and led me out into the hallway. I kept twisting my head to catch her eye but she wouldn't look at me, pulled herself loose from my grip and closed the door behind me. When I tried the handle, it was locked.

It didn't take long for it to start. The pounding of fists, the splitting of skin. The sound of my mam screaming. I ran to the next flat, banged on the door, but no one came, so I tried the next one, and the one after that. I knew they were home, the cowards, the fucking cowards.

I was at the end of the footbridge when I saw him leave. He was calmer now, his movements controlled and smooth, like kicking the living daylights out of Chrissy had left him soothed. At the last doorway he passed me, glanced at me like he'd never seen me before, and I caught a glimpse of his swollen hand, the dark, sticky stain on his upper lip.

We added another bolt to the door once Chrissy got out of hospital. She rang the council from the phone box at the bottom of the car park to ask them to change the locks, but they put her on hold for so long she ran out of coins. The lad in the hardware shop must have felt sorry for us because he sold us the biggest one he had for half the price on the ticket. Either that or he fancied Chrissy, except I doubted it, looking at the state of her.

She told me after that that she was sworn off men for good, and for once I believed her. I didn't see her with another fella for a good two months. But then there was Barry.

I don't know where she met him, maybe some bar or club in town, although I couldn't imagine him knocking around anywhere like that. Chrissy brought him to the flats after a couple of weeks. I'd been sitting on the floor writing in my notebook when they came in. I hadn't understood why he was there at first, thought maybe he was from the council coming to check on us, they did that sometimes. She offered to make him a cup of tea and as she walked past, Barry patted her backside. It made me sit up straight, him doing that. I didn't like men touching Chrissy. She hadn't seemed to mind, though. She never did. I'd heard one of the other mams say that was half her problem. There were always men round at the flat by then, always laying their hands on her, talking to her like she belonged to them. But they never looked like Barry, with his bulging belly and basset-hound face and hardly a hair left on his head.

I didn't take my eyes off him the whole time he was there that afternoon. It must have made him uncomfortable; but it didn't stop him making an effort, trying to make conversation, calling me "the famous Jennifer." Chrissy kept telling him not to mind me, that I was funny with strangers, that I'd come round soon, talking about me like I was a difficult puppy instead of her kid, even though she knew why I was the way I was. After he left she tried to avoid me, but I cornered her that night when she was in the bath.

You said you didn't want another fella. Not after last time.

She'd laughed, told me to mind my own, that she was big enough and ugly enough to make her own decisions. And besides, I didn't know how hard it was, bringing up a kid on her own. It was about time she had some adult company. I'd rolled my eyes but bitten my tongue. There was nothing else to say, I never liked to row with her.

Early one morning a couple of weeks later I was in our bed, not quite asleep but not awake, either, the way I always was when Chrissy hadn't come home from her night out. I heard the keys in the lock but the door stuck fast, she must have forgotten about the bolt. She swore, dropped her bag so that its insides spilled and clattered. I rolled over, hoping she'd go round her mate's. I hated talking to her when she was off her head. But she didn't give up, started tapping at the window, then banging harder with the flat of her palm, her silhouette distorted behind the makeshift curtain she'd made by pinning up an old sarong to the frame. Jen, she said in a hoarse whisper. Let me in. I've got summat to tell yer.

She crawled into bed with me after that, still fully dressed, tucking the cover around us so that our bodies were pressed together tight. I buried my face into her neck, our hair tangling so that you couldn't tell where I ended and she began.

We're movin to the country, Jen, she whispered into the top of my head. Barry's asked us to move in with him.

'd spent so long imagining another life and yet, when the time actually came, I would have done anything to keep the devil I knew. At least I never had to question where I stood, at the flats. I knew Chrissy would always come back to me in the end.

Chrissy was oblivious to how I felt. She'd promised that we'd have a nice last night together, watch a film in bed and get an early one, so we could be fresh and ready for the move, but at the last minute she decided to throw a party, a "leaving do" she called it. In the end I'd woken up on the sofa in the flat downstairs, the Nintendo I'd been playing with the girl who lived there still plugged into the telly. The music was still going at ours, the doosh-doosh-doosh beat of it thumping against the ceiling, the sound of furniture scraping and footsteps charging about. I wanted to go up but I'd made that mistake before when Chrissy'd had one of her dos. They'd all been off their heads, white-faced and black-eyed, sweating and gurning and carrying on like they hadn't realized it wasn't still the night before.

It was the first time I'd been in the flat downstairs, they'd only moved in a few weeks back. The layout was the same as ours, though. Sitting room, kitchen, bathroom, bedroom. Each doorway no more than two or three steps from the next. The girl I'd been playing with was asleep on the bed, a toddler wearing a fat nappy in the cot beside her. I didn't know their names. Whoever else lived there must have been upstairs.

I found a half-eaten box of Coco Pops in the cupboard and leaned up against the window, eating them straight from the packet. I remember being impressed with that, we never had anything like Coco Pops at ours. An empty cig packet was blowing across the tarmac outside and I watched it for a while, twisting and whirling before coming to a standstill next to a bent-out old bike with a missing front wheel, something translucent and slimy-looking trapped underneath the handlebars. It didn't seem possible that this could be the last time I would see that view. The car park I'd walked across every day of my life. The playground where I'd swung on the swings, watching the big kids pass tiny packages hidden in handshakes.

After a while, I heard keys jangle in the lock. A woman came in, stumbling onto the sofa with a can still in her hand. She didn't notice me there, her eyes already half closed as the drink slipped from her fingers, the piss-colored liquid hissing and frothing onto the carpet. I slid past her out of the door and up the cold, hard metal of the stairwell.

Our door upstairs was propped open with Chrissy's battered old boombox. Someone had had the sense to switch it off at least, but Chrissy's body still jolted to a beat no one else could hear. She had her back to me, the distance between us littered with the wreckage of the party. I hung back, watching for a moment, and then I went to her, wrapped my arms around her ribcage, pressed her bones against my cheek. She didn't hug me back, just stood there, then pulled away and cupped my face in her hands, the chemicals still sparkling in her eyes.

It's today! she said to me, her voice hoarse and scratched but still so giddy that it made me wish I could feel even some of what she did. She didn't notice that I didn't, or maybe she didn't care. She just grinned, spun me round in a circle to the sound of glass splintering under our feet, laughing at the expression on my face, making a gesture with her shoulders that said who cares, who cares about this place, this shithole, we won't be back here, it's not our problem anymore. Stop worryin, love, she said, passing me a roll of plastic bin liners. Just pack what yer can't do wi'out. We won't need much. He'll get us whatever we need.

WE WAITED FOR BARRY IN THE BUS SHELTER OUTSIDE THE FLATS for what seemed like hours. Chrissy was all right at first, strolling up and down the pavement, easy, languid, like she was only moving to pass the time. But the longer we waited the faster her steps got, until she was almost marching, except more frantic, more urgent than a march. Up and down, up and down, her ankles quivering in her stilettos, the wet tarmac splattering the whites of her bare legs gray. She'd bought those shoes down the market a couple of weeks before, knock-offs of a pair she'd seen in a magazine at the doctor's. I remember thinking how they didn't suit her, how daft she looked wearing them first thing in the morning. I never said anything, though.

I was sitting on the wall, my head down but my eyes following her. Occasionally she stopped to take a draw of her cig, stretching up onto the tips of her toes so that her heels slipped out of her shoes, twisting her neck to get a better view of the road. My cheeks burned brighter with every minute that passed, not daring to turn around, convinced I'd see them all peering through the blinds at us, a tower full of eyes, floor upon floor of snarled lives. They'd love this. It'd give them something to talk about for days if Barry didn't show up, especially after the carry-on Chrissy had made about leaving. The thought made the blood behind my eyes pound so that I had to squeeze them shut, say a prayer to a god I didn't believe in. Please come, please come, please come, even though it was the last thing I wanted really. Almost the last thing. Anything would be better than hearing that lot gloat.

I tried to make the time go quicker by kicking my feet against the wall, telling myself he'd be there once I reached five hundred, seven hundred, one thousand kicks. The soles of my trainers rubbed against the bin bags at my feet, until in the end one of them ripped and sagged open. Two bags for her, one for me. That was all our lives had added up to.

After a while Chrissy came and sat beside me, picking off the plastic fingernails she'd stuck on the day before, asking me if I thought he'd changed his mind, lighting each new cigarette with the end of her last. I didn't answer, too busy worrying that the rain was going to ruin my shoes, stain the stiff white leather and the big pink swoosh glittering on each side. Barry had turned up with them the weekend before. He'd seen me sitting on the steps at the back of the flats in bare feet, said he'd been worried about all the smashed glass on the floor.

Danny liked those trainers. It was one of the first things

he said to me in fact. He told me, in that throwaway manner he had, that they were cool, and I'd sneered back that they were shit, that I was only wearing them because I felt sorry for Barry, the sad old bastard, wasting his money on crap that I didn't even like.

Chrissy spotted him first. She jumped up, waving her arms about: he's here, he's here! And there he was, in that clapped-out BMW that had seemed so posh to us at the time. Swinging his door open, clambering out, looking all flustered, sweaty, his face a patchwork, a roll of flesh spilling over the top of his trousers. He was apologizing, a stream of half-formed sentences, like he was out of breath even though he'd only been sitting behind the bloody wheel. Something about the delivery from the brewery, a burst barrel, traffic on the A1. Chrissy didn't notice. She was that relieved to see him that she almost knocked him off his feet, despite the fact she weighed close to nowt wet through. His face lit up then and he wrapped his arms around her gauntness. I looked away, trying to unsee the yellowing stains under his pits, but Barry must have noticed me standing there like a spare part because he let go of Chrissy more quickly than I think he'd have liked to.

Hello, love, he said, reaching out as though to ruffle my hair and then thinking better of it, pausing halfway through the action so that his hand hung suspended in midair between us. He drew it back, resting it awkwardly on his hip. I followed his eyes to the bin bags at my feet, watched him glance around as though he was looking for the rest of our stuff. Chrissy was already in the passenger seat by then. I slid past him, climbed into the back.

8

I am wiping tables in the far corner of the caff when Denz strolls in. It's only been a few days, but he smiles at me and lifts his hand in a wave, like he's forgotten how our last meeting ended. He walks to the counter where Fionnoula takes his order, but my eyes don't stray from him for a moment.

Why are you still here? I snarl quietly as I take over his tea, my back to the counter so no one can watch our exchange.

Denz shifts in his seat. I just want to talk, Neef—

Don't call me that, I snap, raising my voice without meaning to. I know, without looking, that Fionnoula is watching us now.

Shit. Sorry. Jen. I just . . . I want to talk to you.

About what? I don't know where your son is. I haven't spoken to him in fifteen years, since I was a bloody teenager,

Denz. I told you already, I can't remember anything from those days.

He sighs, but I can see by the look on his face that he's not going to let it go. Look, I know a lot went on back then. But if you would . . . if you could talk to me, that's all I'm askin. That we go somewhere. Later, when you finish work. To talk.

I glance over my shoulder, my eyes meeting Fi's.

You okay? she mouths, her brows knitted. I smile tightly, nod my head, then turn back to Denz.

Okay, I say. Fine. Okay.

WE MEET OUTSIDE THE CAFF AT THE END OF MY SHIFT AND ALI watches us, eyeing Denz from behind the counter with a wariness that makes my heart swell.

D'you fancy a drink? Denz asks and I shake my head, burrow my chin into my scarf. Summat to eat then?

I make a noise that could mean yes or no, and Denz looks up and down the street uncertainly. I know I'm being diffi-cult. I take pleasure in it.

We end up in the McDonald's on Brixton Hill. Denz buys me a Diet Coke, orders himself a Big Mac meal, although he doesn't take a bite.

You ever think about goin back up north? he asks me as we sit across from each other on the red, shiny seats.

No, I tell him honestly. We are quiet then and he toys with his burger, picking out the gherkins, moving them to one side. You ever been back to the pub? I ask.

He looks up at me, surprised. Relieved, perhaps, that I have opened my mouth. The pub went under, he says. You know it were never the same, after Chrissy left. It int even a pub anymore. They've turned it into a charity shop now.

I pick up my Coke, suck hard on the straw. I don't know how I feel, hearing that.

I pass through the town now and again, he carries on. Not that I keep in touch with anyone.

You never did have many friends there.

Something like amusement plays across Denz's face. No, he says. Not many could stand the sight of someone like me, could they?

Behind Denz a little girl dressed in a dirty school uniform rips open her Happy Meal, squeals with delight at the plastic toy and waves it in front of her mam's face. The woman bats her hand away, her eyes glued to the screen of her phone.

You sure you don't remember Lewis? Denz says.

I look up then, my eyes locking with his. Are we here to talk about your cousin? Or Danny?

Denz carries on like I didn't even open my mouth, and I see again how little he has changed.

Tall bloke, wore his hair in locs. Used to come round mine a lot when you and Danny were kids. Moved to London after he got sick of all the aggro from t'pigs.

I shift in my seat and Denz's eyes narrow like he's losing patience. You and Danny used to say you'd do the same, soon as you were old enough. Reckoned you'd make your fortunes down here. Proper little pair of Dick Whittingtons, you were.

Did we?

Yeah. He leans forward in his seat, his eyebrows raised expectantly. Yeah, you did. You used to talk about it all the time, you must remember that?

I don't remember much, I lie.

Well, he says. Looks like you found your way here.

A current of anger shoots up my spine, making me sit up straight. Get to the point, Denz. You asked me here to talk, and I'm here, aren't I? You say you weren't looking for me, and yet somehow you found me. So let's get into it. What is it you want?

Denz leans further across the table toward me, his voice measured. I can understand why you're angry. And I can understand why you wouldn't trust me, why you wouldn't want to tell me . . . He catches himself, tries again. I just know, in me gut, that the reason Danny disappeared is because of you.

Really? You're really going to sit there and blame me—

No. No, I didn't mean it like that. Please, Neef. Hear me out.

I bite my lips between my teeth. Denz takes a deep breath, lets it out slowly.

Danny were always a bit of a lone wolf, you know that. Never really had any mates, anyone he were close to, not since . . . He glances at me uncertainly, clears his throat. Well, you know. He spent a lot of time on his own, used to go off by himself, few nights here, few nights there. He never said where, and I knew better than to ask. We had this big blow-up in the summer about two years back, over summat of nowt really. We were always rowin, mind, but this time it were enough for the pair of us to need a bit of space, you know?

Then round Christmas I thought I'd give him a bell, make peace, except when I tried ringin him the number were disconnected. I got in touch with his landlord, but he couldn't tell me owt other than Danny had moved on at the end of his lease a few months before, and the lads he worked with hadn't seen him in time. I couldn't even say if there were summat that triggered it. All I know is that for the last few years he were so angry with me.

Why?

Denz seems to think this over for a while. Danny never understood, he says eventually, why I wanted so badly to keep you apart.

No, I shake my head vehemently. That's not why he left, Denz. If that were true, it would be him sitting here now.

Like I said. You're not easy to track down. The only reason I figured you might be here were because—

Because what? Because of the plans Danny and I made? You don't think he could remember those too, if he tried?

Denz studies me carefully. Lewis reckons he saw him. Danny. Reckons he spotted him a couple of times. Round here.

What?

That's what he told me. Once in a crowd at the station. Another time getting on a bus up Brixton Hill. Says it's always just been a glimpse, and both times he's lost sight of him before he could get close enough to be sure. I had me doubts, to be honest; he still smokes too much, our Lewis. But I'd been thinkin of comin down here for a while, I always had this feelin about Danny and London. Except I didn't find Danny, did I? I found you.

It takes me a moment before I can speak, takes everything I have to keep my voice steady. Listen to me, Denz, I say to him. Danny isn't here. He's never been here. I haven't seen him since I was eighteen years old, and I haven't seen Chrissy in even longer. And you know why? Because you took them away from me. Because, for some fucked-up reason, you were hell-bent on keeping me apart from the only two people I've ever cared about. You told me to leave Danny alone. You said that. You told me I would ruin his life, and I believed you.

Neef—

Don't call me that, I yell, pushing myself back from the table with force. The little girl and her mum are staring at me, the toy discarded, the woman's phone hanging limp in her hand. My chair teeters for a moment before crashing to the ground and I cross the floor, yank the door open. I want to be far away from my memories, from Denz, but he follows behind me, beside me, in front of me, blocking my path. I will not look at him, my breath sharp and ragged.

Look, he says. I never expected you to be glad to see me. But I just want us to keep talkin, please. I know I have no right to ask, but . . . please, can you take this?

He thrusts a scrap of paper at me, a row of digits already scrawled on it as though he's been preparing to give it to me all along. If I don't hear from you, you have me word, I'll leave you alone. But take it. In case you change your mind.

I stare at the phone number in his hand, swallow the hurt in my throat. I don't want it, I don't. But despite myself, I take the paper, shove it deep into my pocket. He nods at me slowly.

Thank you, he says.

I watch him walk away.

very brick of the town that Danny and I spent our teenage years in is still imprinted on my memory, whether I like it or not. The pubs, the chippy, the Chinese takeaway that shut down and someone started a rumor that it was because they'd been using rat meat instead of chicken. The drive from the flats was short, less than an hour, but the landscape changed quickly from black and white to color. A tapestry of fields, cows, sheep, houses, bigger and bigger at every turn. It seemed impossible to me back then that my childhood home could exist just a few miles down the road from that picture-book place, full of bustle, everybody moving with reason, with purpose. Mams out running errands, old boys on their way to the pubs for opening time, those funny little gaggles of out-of-towners eating picnics by the river, shivering in their shorts and T-shirts under the watery sun.

The Lamb and Lion didn't look like the pubs from round our way with their barred-up windows and piss-streaked doorways. Danny used to take the mick out of me, said I always had a way of making everything sound more romantic than it really was. But there was something almost human about Barry's pub, standing there proudly in the middle of the high street. Those shiny black planters overflowing with flowers that I learned soon afterward were Danny's handiwork, the polished brass letters above the doorway. That sign, the fierce-looking beast watching over the little white lamb.

Barry pulled into the car park behind the building, stopped in the spot nearest the back door. I took it all in. The beer garden, the cut grass, the wooden bench-tables shaded by parasols. The boy.

He was hunched over two empty beer kegs at the far end of the car park, a cap pulled low over his face, although I could tell he was watching us by the angle of his shoulders. Barry called toward him, made a crude "oi" sound, asked if he was going to say hello. It was then that our eyes locked. I took in the clear, dark depth of them, the high cut of his cheekbones, the gold of his skin. But then he turned his back, pulled himself up onto the wall that circled the car park and jumped out of sight.

It seemed to set Barry on edge, him disappearing like that. He started making excuses, telling me he was a funny lad, a loner really, a head full of strange ideas, the corners of his mouth turning down as he spoke. You'll see a fair bit of him, though, he said. His nana, Mary, works in t'kitchen.

I was only half listening, my eyes on Chrissy as she climbed out of the car and walked toward the building, trailing her fingers along the rough brickwork of the pub walls. She was smiling, chattering on about wasn't it gorgeous, and doesn't it look like something out of a magazine, and can you believe we're going to live here? To anyone else she would have looked happy, ecstatic even. But to me there was already an uncertainness in her eyes, as though she was lost, or thinking about something far away.

Barry stepped toward her, put a hand on her shoulder and she leaned into him, stroked his cheek with her fingertips. I felt my stomach harden and he cleared his throat, peered in at me, sitting awkwardly in the backseat.

So are yer comin in then?

I turned my head toward the spot on the wall that the boy had jumped from, feeling it already. The something between us.

Yeah. I nodded. I'll come in.

I WAS SITTING IN THE BACK BAR WHEN I SAW HIM AGAIN, LEANING over the kegs at the far end of the car park. I could see now that they were filled with soil. Piles of plants were heaped on the ground around him, downy ferns and bottle-green grasses and flowers as wild and varied as a tub of pick-'n'-mix. Every couple of minutes he'd crouch, hold a shrub up to the light, then closer to his eyes, turning it over in his hands. Then he would either cast it aside or try it this way and that against the growing arrangement, his hands gently folding the roots into the damp earth.

That's me grandson, Danny, I heard Mary say behind me, and I jumped, felt my cheeks flush with shame that she'd caught me staring.

Mary was a big woman. Tall and broad, with an awkward limp that made it seem as though her hips couldn't quite manage her breadth. She didn't look anything like Danny, her skin mottled pink, her ashy hair pulled back in a wiry bun. I'd met her that morning, when Barry had ushered us in through the back door. Ever since I'd woken up that day I'd been putting on a face like none of this upheaval had even touched my sides, and so when I saw Mary I kept it up, made out as though just standing there being introduced to her was a chore. She'd seen right through me, though, like she always did. Told me to go sit myself down in the back bar, that she'd bring me something through to eat. I liked that, the way she spoke to me as though Chrissy and Barry weren't even there.

Mary laid a plate of chips and a sausage butty, glistening with fat, onto the table in front of me and eased into the chair opposite. We both pretended not to notice Chrissy standing at the other side of the bar, fawning over Barry, giggling, putting on a show.

Nodding her chin in the direction of Danny, Mary grimaced. Does them daft barrel-things fer Barry fer t'fun of it, she said. Obsessed with plants, he is.

I thought I'd heard her wrong at first. There he was, this boy in his trainers and trackies, a swagger in the way he carried himself. He didn't look like someone who'd sit around making flower arrangements, being obsessed with plants. And what sort of a thing was that to be obsessed with anyway? Lads our age were meant to be into footie, girls maybe. Not plants, not bloody flowers.

Why's he like doin it so much?

I dunno, love, she said, her gray eyes tinted with worry, or confusion maybe. He's a funny one, my Dan.

Mary got up, started tidying away the stacks of empties littered across the tables, and I sat there like a lemon for a while longer until Barry noticed, pried himself away from Chrissy and took me upstairs to show me the apartment. He'd had the decorators in, wanted to smarten it up for us, he said, the smell of fresh paint and bleach and something chemically floral cloying in the air. It was three times the size of our old flat at least, stretching across the entire top floor of the pub, with a big fancy living room that looked out over the high street below. Danny thought it was fancy too, when I first took him up there. All that fake antique furniture, polished wood and brushed velvet. Neither of us were used to that kind of stuff.

Barry wanted to show me my room first, said he knew I must be excited to have my own space at last: a big girl like me. I kept quiet, followed him down the hallway to a door decorated with silver letters that arched like a rainbow. I stared at them, spelling out the word in my head as though I'd never seen it before. J-E-N-N-I-F-E-R. My name, and yet it didn't look like it somehow. Not up there, not like that.

It was a little girl's room really, meant for someone much younger than me, although it stayed like that for all the years I slept there. The only thing I took down in the end was a framed picture of two yellow bears holding hands, because Danny said it weirded him out, to have them perv over us like that.

I could tell Barry was waiting for a reaction, standing there behind me, rocking backward and forward on his heels. I kept my back to him, walked toward the window at the opposite side of the room and smoothed my hands along the glossy windowsill until he couldn't take it anymore, his words coming out jilted and stuttering.

We can always change it if yer like, I heard him say as I gazed out through the glass, taking in the car park, the beer garden, the section of the river where the little bandstand overlooked the water. My eyes came to rest on Danny, still holding flowers in his hands.

I just thought . . . well, it were one of t'lasses that comes in actually, she's got a daughter 'bout your age and she thought this sort of thing would be nice, the colors and that, but if you don't like it . . .

It's nice, I said, turning to face him. Ta.

Oh good. He beamed, nodding his head up and down, making the flesh underneath his chin dance. Good, good. Good stuff.

We stood there awkwardly until Chrissy appeared, her arms wrapped around one of our black bin liners. She smiled at me without meeting my eyes, said something about getting ourselves settled in, before dumping the bag onto the bed. It rolled onto the floor, spilling the contents out onto the carpet, but she didn't react, just leaned into Barry, tilting her face up to him and planting a kiss on his ruddy cheek.

Come and help me unpack, will yer, Baz? she said, tugging at his hand like a child.

There wasn't much in that bin liner. A few T-shirts, a hoodie. A dress that Chrissy's mate had given me when it got too small for her kid. I don't know how long I sat there, on the floor with my face buried in them, knowing that as soon as I stood up I'd be letting something go, shedding a skin that would never fit me again. I remember not wanting to move and yet doing it anyway. Folding everything carefully, meticulously, putting each item away in those wardrobes that took up an entire wall of the room, laying them out onto the endless shelves, trying to fill the space, rearranging everything again and then for a third time, before pulling it all out, abandoning it where it fell. I slid the door shut, my fingers leaving a smear on the glass, and then I walked out of the room, took the back stairs down past the kitchen and into the car park.

10

G ot any cigs?

Danny barely glanced up, still crouched over by the beer kegs. I don't smoke.

Neither do I.

Not unless I can blag em off someone, that is.

I grinned. Same.

He looked up at me then, his eyes squinting against the sun as he took me in, but nothing he saw seemed to impress him and he turned back to what he'd been doing. I took a few steps toward him, perched myself up on one of the wooden bench-tables.

What you doin?

What's it look like?

Looks like nowt I've ever seen before. Looks mental in fact. But I like it, still.

I sensed him smile then and he stood, moved toward me, pausing before pulling himself up next to where I sat.

See this? he said, twirling the stem of a leaf between his fingers. I nodded. Ivy. He lifted it so that it was level with our noses. Bet you don't see a lotta this where you're from, do yer?

They've got bushes in Leeds, yer div.

He laughed. Yeah, but not as many as round here.

Danny's interest piqued, and he tilted his face up from under his cap as though to get a better look at me. I kicked my legs back and forth, exposed under his gaze, aware of how much more he knew about me than I did about him. I'd felt like that earlier too, when Chrissy had stepped forward in the kitchen to give Mary a stiff hug. It had dawned on me then that I was the only stranger in the room. That Chrissy knew all these people already, that her life here had already begun.

What you starin at? I snapped in the end.

Nowt, he said. Just seein yer.

I pulled my legs into my chest, trying to cover the freckles on my knees, the dirt on my forearm. The smile in his eyes unnerved me and I reached forward, tipped the cap back from his head so that it fell onto the table behind him. Danny's lips stretched into a grin.

There y'are. You can get a proper look at me now, and all.

It irked me, how cocky he was. I wanted him to feel some of the discomfort I did and so I screwed up my nose. Your hair's messy.

A flicker of self-consciousness passed across his face as he ran his hand across the mass of tight black coils. I shave it off usually, he shrugged, pulling the cap back on, but lower this time so that it was almost covering his eyes. But me dad said if I grow it, he'll take me to get it done.

Looks long enough to me.

Yeah. He kicked the heels of his feet against the bench below us. Just dunno when he's comin back.

I leaned back against the rusted umbrella pole that pierced the center of the table. Someone had carved the words *Si Dudley '98* into the wooden slats of the bench where the varnish was peeling away in strips. Where's he gone? I asked.

Who, me dad? He's busy, man. Got a lot on, innit?

I nodded, rolling a strip of varnish between my forefinger and thumb and flicking it out of sight into the grass.

Mine too.

WE STAYED OUT THERE TOGETHER UNTIL THE END OF MARY'S shift and, when Danny left, I headed back upstairs to the apartment. Stretching out on my new bed, I pulled my notebook from the waistband of my shorts, scrawled a story about a boy who had magical powers and could talk to plants. The minute I'd finished I ripped it out, shredded it with my hands and threw the scraps into the purple plastic bin in the corner of the room. Up until that moment, Chrissy had been the only person I'd ever written about, the only person who mattered to me. I didn't understand what it meant, to feel for anyone other than my mam.

The next morning I woke early, crept over to the window, my stomach flipping at the sight of Danny already there. Quietly I padded down the stairs and outside, chucked him a cig as I walked past. Danny frowned.

Where d'you get this from?

Chrissy's bag. I shrugged, sparking up and passing him the lighter. He took it, toying the flint with his thumb.

Chrissy? he asked, puzzled.

Yeah.

Danny kept his eyes on me for a moment longer, then threw the lighter back without using it and turned to the kegs again.

What you doin? I asked after a while.

Same thing I were doin yesterday.

We were quiet then. Danny's mood was hard to read and the silence made me fidgety, uncomfortable. I wasn't used to it. Where I came from, there was always noise. I started chatting on, mithering him with so many questions about what and why and how that in the end he sighed, beckoned me over with a nod, told me I might as well come and look with my own eyes rather than peck his head all day.

At the beginning I would just watch Danny, the way he handled the roots of each plant, how he'd consider every leaf and stem and then marry them together, pairing upright stalks with trailing leaves, blending and tinkering like a shaman casting a spell. But as the days wore on, he began to talk, teach, using names and terms and language I'd never heard before. Me, who considered myself better with words than any kid I'd ever met. Chlorosis. Begonia. Ericaceous. Clematis. In the beginning I took the mick, tried to make out he sounded daft, but only because I didn't know what else to do. Before long I had quietened, his manner drawing me into silence, listening intently. I was enraptured by all the things he knew, how clever he was. And I could tell he liked me being there too.

What's that? Danny asked one day not long after we'd first met as I peered over the kegs. I looked down, saw my notebook poking out of the waistband of my shorts. My cheeks flushed and I shirked back, yanking my T-shirt over the top of it.

Nowt, I snapped and he drew back in surprise.

Whoa, all right. Keep yer knickers on.

It's just summat I like to do, I mumbled after a while. Summat weird. Like you.

What d'you mean, like me?

Like you. With yer weird plant stuff. I like . . . I dunno. I like writin stuff down.

What sort of stuff?

I dipped my head. Stories, mostly.

About what?

About . . . all sorts really. Different things. Like what it would be like to be someone different. To live a different life, be a different person.

The silence fell between us, longer this time, and I didn't dare look up for fear of what I might see on Danny's face.

That int weird, he said eventually. I like that.

t was the second-to-last summer of the nineties when we arrived at the pub. School was closed for six weeks, and most days when I woke up Chrissy and Barry would be in bed, too hungover to surface. Sometimes I wondered if they even bothered coming up from the bar at the end of the night, or if they just stayed down there, passed out on the green velour benches behind the pool table until Mary knocked on the next day.

I was in awe of the pub when we first moved there. The sports lounge at the front where all the old fellas would sit, the big dining room that doubled up as a disco on a night, and the back bar with its pool table and view of the beer garden and the little snicket that led straight through to the wonderland of Mary's kitchen.

The kitchen was my favorite, with its wide-mouthed

freezers and the huge, blistering fryer. And all those pots and pans, I couldn't get my head round them. At the flat we had one knackered old frying pan and a tiny little saucepan that Chrissy occasionally used to make dippy eggs in, or minute noodles if the leccy was off and we couldn't use the microwave. But at the pub there were all sorts. Minuscule, mammoth, some with lids and others without, nearly every one of them filled to the brim with something different. Potatoes, carrots, soup, gravy, some sort of white sauce that Mary told us was called béchamel, and me and Danny pissed ourselves laughing at her for trying to sound posh.

Mary never seemed to be out of that kitchen. Stacking triangular sarnies on trays; peeling petals of potato skin into the sink; bent down low with her head in the oven, one hand on the base of her back and the other prodding at a joint of meat.

I'd never known so much food before we moved into the pub. Full Englishes and butties and lamb roasts. Chips on the side of every meal. How we both stayed so skinny I'll never know, Danny especially, shoveling his in and then starting on mine. Mary would go mad when she'd catch him, standing over us with her hands on her hips telling Danny to have some manners, and did he think he'd been dragged up, and the-way-yer-actin-people'll-think-I-aren't-feedin-yer. But he'd carry on anyway, face like a hamster, ketchup stains on his lips.

After Mary had done breakfast for the lorry drivers passing through on their way up to Edinburgh or down to London, she'd call us through to the back bar. The telly in there was meant for sports, but Mary would put on the kids' shows for us while we ate breakfast and we'd sit there, the pair of us, swallowing plate-loads of toast and eggs and beans and bacon, watching episodes of that game show where kids got gunged and raced round in go-karts looking for prizes to the sound of a cockerel crowing. There were these twins, I remember, assistants to the mullet-haired presenter, all springy and clean-looking. Danny told me once that he thought they were fit. I hated that game show after that.

I would have liked to spend more time with Mary at the pub, but Danny's mood always turned sour around his nana. He'd moan about her nagging; it did his head in, he said. The way she was always going on about when to be home for dinner, or what time to be up in the morning, or asking where he'd been all day, and with who and doing what. I nodded along with him, agreeing, rolling my eyes behind her back whenever she started chirping on. But in truth, I was jealous. I would've killed for Chrissy to ask me just once how I spent my days.

I GOT WIND FAIRLY EARLY ON THAT BARRY DIDN'T THINK MUCH TO Danny. People were always making comments about the flower boxes out the front, the kegs in the garden, how unique they were. Barry took the praise, although I never heard him mention Danny's name. Instead, he made it known that he didn't like Danny hanging around in the car park once the pub opened. Makes the place look untidy, him sittin about out there. Punters don't like to see that sort of thing, he'd say.

It set me on edge when Barry came out with those barbed remarks. I'd come to see that the town wasn't like the flats, where languages intermingled on the stairwells, Bengali with Portuguese, French with Urdu. Where skin tones spanned from bone to ebony. But I didn't understand what the sameness of everyone in that town might have meant for a brown-skinned boy like Danny. He never gave Barry the satisfaction of showing that he cared, though. He'd just finish up what he was doing, make himself scarce, and I'd trot after him like a little lost dog.

Danny was almost a year older than me, although the way our birthdays fell meant we would have been in the same school year. But the childhood I'd had, the things I'd seen, often made me feel like the older one.

We hadn't known each other long when I lifted a few bits from the Co-op in front of him. We'd gone in to get a drink and his eyes got all big and round when he saw me slide the bottle of pop up the sleeve of my jumper. I never thought twice about stuff like that, it was easy at the shops round the flats, no one batted an eyelid. It didn't occur to me that it might be different in that fancy little town. I started showing off then, shoving bags of crisps and packets of sweets in my pockets, getting a kick out of the look on Danny's face. I didn't notice the posh-looking fella wearing nice shoes and a button-down shirt. It was only when I started making for the door that we heard him yelling. Hey! You two! I suppose you'll be paying for those items?

We bolted then, quick as we could. I could keep up with Danny just about, but I didn't know the town, nearly lost sight of him when he took a sharp right toward the old church. I followed his lead, passing through the wrought-iron gates that led onto its driveway, snaking through grass up to our knees, jumping over mossy gravestones until we reached the far side and he stopped, slumping down against a crumbling mausoleum, both of us out of breath.

What did you do that fer? Danny asked.

I curled my lip. Fer t'laugh.

Me nan would've made you summat to eat. If you said you were hungry.

I'm not, really.

Danny fell silent then, not looking at me, and I scowled, feeling embarrassed without knowing why.

Bit creepy down here, innit?

I like it. All the flowers and that.

I wrinkled my nose, unconvinced as I pulled out my haul, laid it in front of us like a banquet while Danny watched on, his face blank.

She is yer mum, int she? Barry's new bird? he asked after a while as I ripped open a packet of Haribo.

You know she is.

Why don't you call her it then?

Dunno really, I said, pulling at a jelly snake with my teeth. Just always called her Chrissy. It's not like she walks about callin me Daughter, is it?

He looked away, scratched his neck. I don't have a mum. It's only me and me nana. And me dad, sometimes.

I nodded, not saying anything.

You don't believe me, do yer? About me dad?

What about him?

You think I've made him up.

I don't.

Ask anyone round here. They all know. Ask em, you'll see.

I don't give a shit about yer dad.

I didn't mean it to sound harsh; it was true. I hadn't given a second thought to Danny's dad, or lack of one for that matter. Plenty of the kids I'd known before didn't have dads, me included. There's no great love-story, Chrissy had said to me flatly, the one time I'd asked. It was just a fling, happened not long after she left care, although when I did the maths I could never make it come out without a crossover. She was six months gone before she even realized she was pregnant, it's not like she had a choice in any of it. Even as a kid, I could read the subtext behind those words.

Beside me Danny tensed, scooping up a handful of pebbles, aiming one at a row of rickety headstones. Must be strange, he said, the tone of his voice changed. Livin upstairs at t'pub.

I didn't reply, prodded my tongue into a lump of gelatine that had caught in my back teeth.

Can't remember Barry havin a bird before Chrissy. Bet he thinks he's scored with your mum, mind. Lads in t'pub'll think she's well fit.

He was goading me now but still I stayed quiet. The chewed-up sweet came loose in my mouth and I spat a wet rainbow onto the grass.

He must be nearly as old as me nan, y'know. Bit weird, innit? He int even that rich. If she were after someone with money, she could've done better'n that.

There was an itch in my knuckles, the skin on my face growing hot, but still he went on.

But the lads in t'pub . . . He let out a low whistle. They'll love it, seein her every day. Watch, it'll get loads busier now, people just comin in to ogle her and that. They'll all be after a go on her—

The crack of my fist against Danny's jaw made him fall

back and I jumped to my feet. I wanted to yell at him, tell him it wasn't my choice to move there, to that bloody pub and that stupid bloody apartment, with its stench of paint and bleach and too much air freshener fighting to cover up the stink from downstairs. That this wasn't what I meant, all those times when I wished that we could leave, all those stories I wrote imagining another life, another way. This wasn't how it was supposed to be; this was all Chrissy's idea, and so let them, let them ogle her all they wanted, see if I cared.

But I didn't. Instead I spun away from him, heading any-where but the pub, the apartment. Apartment. Such a stupid bloody word. Whose idea was it to call it that, like we were living in some big swanky city or something? It was just a flat, as far as I could see. Bigger and posher than ours, but still a flat, not deserving of some elaborate name that made it sound better than it was. I should have kicked off, thrown a proper fit, dug my fingernails into the doorframes and told Chrissy there was no way I was moving anywhere with some fat old numpty she'd known less than a month.

I heard footsteps behind me but I kept on going, faster now. Danny caught up, doing a double-sidestep so that he was a couple of strides ahead, then turning to walk backward, facing me. I hoped he'd trip over.

Yer jab's not bad, fer t'size of yer. He grinned, and I could see the bruise already blooming under his skin. I tried to pass him but he blocked my way, dancing to the left and then to the right, mirroring my moves.

Get out my way, I said, pushing at him with my arm, but he blocked me again. I stopped, looked him in the eye. Get. Out. Of my way.

He laughed, but with a note of uncertainty, then stepped

aside, making a big show of it, bowing down and waving me past with his arms. I carried on, not wanting to admit I had no idea where I was. Danny didn't follow.

The street came to an abrupt end, but rather than go back the way I'd come, I scrambled up a shallow hill that overlooked the dual carriageway, the cars thundering below me. I stared down at them, my head pounding. Chrissy said it would be different here, and I'd wanted it to be true. Wanted people not to look at her like they did back there, hoped that maybe they'd see us as more than that, better. Except now I understood. All that talk was nothing more than childish fantasies. Nothing was going to change.

12

Danny wasn't in the pub the next morning when I came downstairs, and despite myself I felt my stomach sink, hated how much I'd grown to look forward to seeing him each day. For a while I skulked around in the kitchen, but Mary was in a foul mood and so I made myself scarce, wandered into the car park, dragging the soles of my trainers along the tarmac.

Oi!

The sound of Danny's voice made me jump, but it took all my effort not to skip toward it. He was sitting on the other side of the wall, his back leaning up against the stone.

What you doin down there?

He looked up at me then and I cringed. One side of his jaw was swollen and violet, an angry welt where my fist had landed. Shit, I said. Were that me?

Danny shrugged. I deserved it. But me nan's on one. Reckons I been fightin. Best I stay out her way today.

I glanced in the direction of the kitchen, then slid down the other side of the wall, landing beside him on the damp earth.

He looked at me nervously. Are you pissed off with me still?

I shrugged, non-committal, but my insides fizzed with the thought that he cared. My face must have given me away, though, because he smiled shyly.

I've got summat to show yer, he said.

What you on about?

Come on. You'll like it. He stood as if to go but I stayed put, too stubborn to relent so easily. Please, he said, crouching to take both my hands in his. Please please please?

I couldn't say no to him, even then, and so I let him pull me to my feet. We ran down the bank together, turning up toward the main square, past the supermarket, the town hall. At the crossroads almost at the other side of town Danny led me through a narrow laneway that opened onto a housing estate. We passed through the houses until we came to a wide dirt track, the earthy ground dappled by leafy trees that Danny told me were horse chestnuts.

The old railway line, he said. Used to go all the way to Leeds, years ago. Up near where you're from, I think. And if you keep goin that way, he pointed in the direction we were looking, you get to a castle. Or the ruins of one, any rate.

Is that where you're takin me?

Nah, he shook his head. Somewhere better'n that.

We walked in silence and I tipped my chin up to gaze at

the canopy of leaves shading our path, the calmness belonging to a world that wasn't mine. I like how it smells, I said,
breathing it in. Like the Sunday dinner yer nana makes.

Danny raised his eyebrows knowingly, walking over to
the side of the path where clusters of tiny white flowers grew.
Carefully he plucked a bunch of the heart-shaped leaves
from their stems, crushed their ragged edges between his
fingers, then held them up to my nose. Smell this, he said. Is
this it?

I nodded.

Garlic mustard. He smiled, letting the leaves fall to the
ground. The roots taste like horseradish, sort of. That's why
it reminds you of a Sunday dinner, I bet.

We carried on a while longer until Danny paused at the
side of a grassy bank.

Up here.

A path of sorts wound up through the shrubbery and
gnarled tree roots and I followed as he climbed upward, his
feet finding familiar footholds, glancing over his shoulder
every so often to check on me. When he reached the top he
turned, stretching his arm down to take hold of my wrist,
helping me up the last few feet.

I stood, gazing at the little clearing in the trees where two
railway lines once split, the sound of my breath dimmed by
birdsong. Gingerly I stepped forward, spun in a slow circle,
taking in the wildness, the way every inch of the space stood
thick with life. Plants and flowers, grasses and thistles, hidden
all around by the treetops, reaching up and over us from the
bank below.

It's good, innit?

Yeah, I breathed.

I've never taken anyone else up here.

We looked at each other and grinned.

IT WAS A SPOT THAT TIME FORGOT; NO ONE ELSE KNEW ABOUT that place but Danny. He'd found it a few years before, on an old map of the town in the library. They used to call it Devil's Claw, he told me, but he didn't like that name.

Nah, me neither. It sounds like the sort of place bad things would happen. I can't imagine owt bad ever happenin here.

He smiled at me. Exactly, he said. That's exactly what I think.

We stayed up there for hours, looking at the plants, mucking around. Doing whatever we could to make each other laugh. It started to get dark, but still the bruise around Danny's jaw was visible, the sight of it making me wince. Why didn't you tell yer nan? That it were me that did that t'yer?

He tugged at a handful of grass, the blades snapping in his palm. I dunno. She'd've jumped to the wrong idea, knowin her. Probably thought I'd tried to rip the knickers off you or summat—been on t'blower to the cop shop before I could blink.

What?

Danny laughed then, but the sound of it was all wrong. I just mean . . . she jumps to conclusions, does me nan. When it comes to me, at least. He cleared his throat uncomfortably. Sorry I said that yesterday, 'bout yer mum and that. It's proper shite when people say stuff like that, I should know. You pissed me off is all. But . . . well, yeah. Sorry.

I lay back in the grass, tilted my face up to the sky, could see now a gap in the leaves where the stars shone through. Chrissy reckoned it'd be better here, I said. But it won't be.

Better how?

She reckons Barry'll look after us, turn it all into a fuckin fairytale. It's all bollocks, though. It'll be just the same.

Danny didn't say anything, rolled onto his belly beside me.

That's the thing about me mam, see, I carried on. She used to act smart, but these days it's like she's livin in a film or summat. And I get it, sort of. Cos she is special. She's got summat that other people don't—that thing that all them Hollywood lasses have, what d'you call it . . . ? Star power or summat. Only problem is she's never known how to use it. I reckon that's why all them men are always after tryin to steal a piece of her. They try and smash her up and break her, cos they want a piece of her to keep. They all want to own a little piece of a star.

As soon as the words had escaped from my lips I had the urge to grab hold of them, shove them back into my mouth, swallow them whole. I sat up quickly, pinching my fingernails down into my palms, waiting for Danny to laugh at me, readying myself to take it.

Danny was sitting up now too, although it took me a long time to build up the nerve to look at him. When I did, his face confused me even more. There was no sign of mirth. Of reproach or laughter or mockery. Instead, his eyes were full of something else.

I were worried, yesterday, he said. That I'd got you wrong.

What d'you mean?

After you nicked all that stuff from t'Co-op. I started thinkin mebbe you were just like everyone else, all the other divs round this town that don't give a shit about anyone but themselves. But you're not, are yer?

I blinked, bit down on my lip.

I ain't never heard anyone talk like you, he said quietly.

No, I scoffed. No, I bet you ain't. I talk a load of old shit, I know I do—

Danny shook his head, cutting me off. Nah, nah. Don't say that.

He traced the tip of a leaf along the veins on the inside of my wrist and I stayed as still as I could, afraid that if I moved he might stop.

This town, yeah . . . it's so full of dickheads, so full of people who think there's only one way to be and that if you're not like them, if you don't think like them, then you're wrong, that there must be summat wrong with you. But it's them that are the wrong'uns. It's people who think differently that can make the world good.

Something sparked inside me again and for a moment the two of us were quiet.

That stuff in the shop. Don't do it again, all right? It int worth it.

Okay. I nodded. Okay.

DANNY SAID DEVIL'S CLAW MADE HIM FEEL LIKE HE COULD HAVE been in a forest, a jungle even, anywhere in the world. There wasn't a plant in those woods he didn't know the name of. Cow parsley and traveler's joy and sea holly. The difference between a dead-nettle and a stinging nettle. How the buddleia that I loved so much, with its tiny purple flowers and honey-like scent, wasn't a real Yorkshire plant but instead had been brought over from China almost a hundred years before. He knew when they'd flower, when they'd die; which animals liked them and which ones they would poison. He knew so much. He filled me up.

Within a few weeks he'd taught me the names of every tree and wildflower in that spot, all of them still tattooed on the underlayers of my brain. I'd try and catch him out, pulling up shrubs from the ground and waving them in front of his nose. Bet you don't know this one, do yer? But he did. He always did.

Often we'd stay there until late and although I loved it too, the walk home made my spine shiver. Danny told me the railway line was haunted and I said I didn't believe in any of that crap, but he went on and on about it anyway, telling me all them daft stories about the young girl who'd gone missing years ago and how she still wandered the tracks, trying to find her lost love.

People say they still see her sometimes, at night, cryin and searchin. People say they still hear her wailin, he'd say, and I'd tell him to shut it, knowing he was winding me up.

One day a crow came hurtling out of a pine tree toward me, with a look on its face like it was possessed. I almost shit myself then and it wasn't like me, screaming and running a good twenty yards before I calmed down. Danny killed himself laughing for years after that, just with the memory of it.

Fuck's sake.

What I'd give to hear that laugh now.

t's Sunday and I'm alone, as I am every Sunday. I wake too
early, lie motionless under the thin duvet and try to fool
myself that I'm still asleep. By the time the sun comes up I
can no longer bear it, drag myself to the little bathroom and
stand under the shower, let the water scald my skin and my
scalp, the way I used to at Mary's, in those months when
Danny and I would call her home our own. For a moment I
close my eyes and Danny is there, bawling at me from the
bottom of the stairs not to use up all the hot water.

Snap them open again.

Afterward I sit back down on my bed in the corner of the
attic, the piece of paper that Denz scrawled his number on
resting on my thigh. My phone is in my hand, my thumb
hovering over the digits. But in the end I text Fionnoula, ask
her if she'd like some help at the wholesaler's later, once
she's finished Mass.

She replies straight away. *Yes. U OK?*

Yeah, I tell her. *I'm fine.*

I've not gone with her before. She used to ask me all the time if I fancied it but I always said no. Even though her and Ali mean the world to me, I'm not sure if I can be on my own with her for that long outside of the caff. She likes to talk and I haven't been good at that for years, but I don't want to be alone today. Not with all these memories pulling at the edges of my brain.

We go there in their little beat-up transit van and although Fionnoula's driving is terrible, it's lovely, being inside it, like climbing into a piece of them both. Ali's tinkling charms hanging from the rearview mirror. A picture of St. Christopher taped to the dashboard. Sweet wrappers all over the floor, and pouches full of herbs or incense or something dotted around the various wells and nooks. I want to close my eyes and just soak it up, but the effing-this and bloody-that and whattheshittinhelldyerthinkyerdoingyerdaftbeggar every time she has to so much as change a lane means I spend half the journey with my knuckles to my mouth and the rest with my palms pressed between my thighs, bracing myself for what's to come.

Somehow we make it, and the pair of us potter around the wholesaler's like it's an everyday thing, chatting amiably about how-much-bread-will-we-get and do-you-think-one-slab-of-spread-or-two? We're in the queue waiting to pay when Fionnoula pats me on the arm.

Thanks for coming with me, love, she says. Ali doesn't like to do the shopping. He can't bear it, in fact. Probably because of me, wittering on and chewing his ear off about whatever comes into me head.

I feel bad then that I've never offered before to keep her

company for an hour or two. What do you talk about? I blurt out, and she looks at me in surprise. All these years I've been worrying that I wouldn't be able to think of anything to say, that Fionnoula will ask me a question I can't answer. And yet ever since Denz showed up, it's like my mouth keeps coming out with things before it's even run them by my brain.

Who, me and Ali?

I nod, even though I'm not sure myself if that's what I mean.

Oh god. Anything. Anything, really. I mean, he's a man of few words, isn't he, but you know me! She laughs. I'll talk about anything.

The woman at the checkout begins scanning our shopping and we busy ourselves with bagging everything up and paying and carting all the bags and boxes back to the van, stacking them up on top of each other in the boot. Once we're on the road, Fionnoula picks up her thread as though she'd paused only a second ago.

That's what Ali loves about me. How I talk. Or that's what he says, anyway. It was my accent at first, he reckons. Said it sounded like a cat purring, daft old beggar he is. And I liked the look of him, ha-ha, that's how shallow I am. Oh, but he was so handsome, Jen. So gorgeous. And his cooking, well, that's enough to win anyone over, I tell you what. No wonder I'm the size I am, ha-ha-ha. I was slim before I met him, you should see the pictures!

I'd love to see them, I tell her.

She smiles sadly. I don't have them, love. They were all at me mammy's, but she's long gone now. I'd been planning to move back there with Ali, see. To Ireland. Shipped a load of me stuff over, but we never made it in the end. Never even

bothered to get the stuff back, too much of a hassle. No doubt
me sister would have burned everything anyway, the old
wench. She was the worst of them, even though it made the
least sense, coming from her.

A car glides gently into the lane in front of Fionnoula and
she stops talking to lean on the horn, a tirade of curses pouring
from her mouth before she picks up where she left off.

You know, she lived over here for a time, me sister. She
left in the end, got chased out really, with all the Troubles
and that. She was the enemy, we both were—we all bloody
were, us Irish. She knew what it was like to be singled out
for nothing more than where you came from. And yet still
she could hate Ali with such vengeance, such passion. Even
though she doesn't know him. Doesn't know a thing about
him, in fact.

Maybe if they spent some time together . . . I mumble,
although it feels like an empty thing to say. Fionnoula shakes
her head.

Oh, they wouldn't. They wouldn't. My family never liked
it, the idea of it, me with a Paki. That's what they used to call
him, the eejits. Didn't make a jot of difference to them that
he's Iranian. I turned up on the doorstep with him a couple
of months before we were set to move back. Thought I'd
surprise them. It dawned on me, see, that maybe they should
know him a bit, before we went there for good. I knew they
had their funny ideas about people. But I never expected
them to have so . . . so little . . . feeling, you know? Maybe I
should have warned him, or them. Maybe it was my fault,
but I just thought, if they saw him in the flesh, saw the kindness and the goodness, surely they could get past their ideas,
the stupid ideas some halfwit put in their heads. And he was

so nervous, bless him. He had flowers for me mammy and he'd put on his best suit. He so wanted them to like him, he'd have loved nothing more, I swear. But they wouldn't even let him put his foot in the door, Jen. Wouldn't look him in the eye. Turned us away in the cold, told me to come back when I'd seen sense.

Her voice starts to crack, and in that moment my mind darts to Danny. The slurs, shrouded as banter, that he'd be expected to laugh off. The countless infractions I pretended didn't exist.

We were walking off back down the road, Fionnoula carries on, pulling me back from my thoughts. And me nephews, they were only ten, eleven or so, they started shouting at him out the window. Calling him all sorts of filth. The oldest one, he spat at Ali, straight at him. I could've killed them, honestly. But Ali, he just kept his head high, wrapped his arm around my shoulder. They're only kids, he said, it's not their fault. They don't know what they're saying, love.

It would have made another man run a mile, being treated like that. Humiliated. And rightly so. But he never let anyone see that it hurt him. Ali still made sure I rang me mammy every Sunday, even though we never had a word to say to each other. Every week she'd ask me if I'd got rid of him yet and I used to seethe with it, so I did. But still, he made me ring her.

It was the Twin Towers that did it in the end. The bloody Towers, thousands of miles from any of us, for crying out loud. My sister called me the next day. Gave me an ultimatum. Told me they would have nothing to do with me if I insisted on continuing to sleep with that type of a person.

Fionnoula slams the flat of her palm against the steering wheel.

That's what she said, those exact words. As if it was Ali who'd been flying that plane himself, as if he was the mastermind behind the whole bloody thing. I'd been with him close to twenty years by then. *That type of a person.*

She is shaking her head, her eyes shining. I reach across, put my hand over hers on the wheel, try to still its tremor.

I'm sorry, love, she says. It just gets to me, you know? All this hate, this nasty, insidious hate. It'll tear the world apart; I swear to god. It'll tear us apart.

14

Toward the end of that first summer living at the pub a heatwave hit the town. Seemed like no one bothered going to work for the best part of a week, topless lads and shiny girls packing out the beer gardens, each of them a different shade of pink.

The weather was too hot for Danny and me to face the uphill journey to Devil's Claw. Instead we rode his bike down to the river, where we lolled on the grass by the water, watching the little kids throw breadcrumbs to the ducks as their mams gazed on from the sidelines, looking bored. In the bandstand a knot of frail-looking oldies sat quietly, their faces creased to a point of blankness, their thin knees covered with blankets despite the heat, and further up a group of kids our age mucked around close to where the water met the weir.

Are they yer mates? I asked Danny, nodding in the direction of three of the boys, ankle-deep in the river. He looked up briefly.

Nah, he said, lying back again and closing his eyes against the glare of the sun. They go to me school, most of em. I know em. But not me mates.

I looked back across at the group, who were by now splashing two girls perched on the bank, squeals of high-pitched laughter pealing across the water to where we sat.

They're all divvies round here, I heard Danny say sleepily, eyes still closed and hands behind his head. They all end up goin the same way. Can't be arsed with all that, me.

Barry had told me that Danny was a loner on the very first day I'd met him. It didn't surprise me. He was an easy target, all that time he spent talking to plants. But it occurred to me then that maybe it was by choice, that it might have been him shunning everyone else rather than the other way around. I'd never given a second thought to where the kids I'd known at the flats would end up. They were just there, same as me. A crew to knock about with. It made me embarrassed, like I hadn't realized I could choose who I wanted to be mates with. It made me realize how deeply I cared what Danny thought of me.

The grass where we lay was strewn with dandelions and I plucked one from the ground, piercing its stem with my thumbnail and threading it through another, my back to Danny as though I was afraid he might open his eyes and see me for who I really was. A duck waddled toward me, curious, and I held out my hand in offering. It quacked loudly, lifting up its wings and bringing them back down again. Another one joined in, the pair of them flapping and shrieking as if they were trying to shoo me away. *We know you're not from here. Get off our turf.* Danny leaned up on one elbow, imitating them, and they jumped back in surprise, let out a noise that sounded almost like a telling off, before turning crossly, shuffling away like two little old women muttering to each other. The fattest one dropped a turd as if to have the last word and that set us both off laughing, finding it funnier than we should have really, in that way we always had.

All right, Flower Boy.

One of the lads from the river was standing over us, his calves still wet from where he'd been wading in the water. Danny stayed silent, wiped his nose with the back of his hand. The lad turned to me, lifting his cap so that I could get a better view of his face. Pockmarked and rangy, a tuft of ginger hair escaping from underneath. This yer mate, is it?

Still Danny didn't say anything, glanced at me, then looked away.

The lad's eyes narrowed. You're the lass who's moved into t'Lamb, aren't yer? He smirked. Yer mum's old Barry's new bird.

My neck prickled with shame at the way he said it, the sneer on his face. I couldn't think of anything clever to say, so I just nodded, tried to look bored. He glanced at Danny and then back at me again, something like amusement tugging at the corners of his mouth. Yous two comin up here? he said in the end, nodding his head back toward the group, who were by now all watching us from the low wall leading up the path toward the center of town. A girl in a neon skirt was laughing in a way that made me sure we were the brunt of her joke. I wouldn't have minded going, meeting them. But Danny made the decision for us.

Nah, he said, getting to his feet and pulling his bike upright. You're all right, ta.

Danny got onto the seat and I climbed on for a croggy, my hands gripped tight around the crossbar as he pedaled fast in the opposite direction from the way we'd come. Someone shouted something after us, their hoots and brays carrying across the water as we rode. For a second I wondered if they would give chase, but then we were gone, up the hill and around the corner, out of their sight.

DANNY AND MARY LIVED ON THE COUNCIL ESTATE UP BY THE HIGH school, a corner plot that faced out onto the main road. I hadn't been up there before; Mary didn't like Danny having mates over to his house. She don't trust me, he'd said with a shrug, when I'd asked him why.

It didn't look like any council house I'd ever seen, all neat and tidy with a brand-new PVC door and gaggle of gnomes smiling cheerily from the welcome-mat out front. Surprised they've not been nicked, I said, and Danny looked at me strangely before turning his key in the lock.

Mary loved those gnomes. Every couple of months she'd turn up with a new one, setting it down in the midst of the beautiful jungle Danny had made at the back of the house. Thought this were bonny, she'd smile obliviously, while Danny scowled behind her back and I bit my lip, trying not to laugh. A few days later he would find it a new home on the front doorstep, Mary seemingly none the wiser. The gnomes' eerie little grins greeted us as we arrived, their eyes following us as we walked through the door. Later, though, in the earliest days of lying on our bellies out the back, hazy and giggly, our thoughts cloaked with smoke, it became more fun to leave the dumpy little clay men where Mary had placed them.

Look at him there, with his little fishin rod.

And that one! Oh my god, look at that one! Leanin over on his side, with them come-to-bed eyes.

How come he's only got one eye? Or is that an eye there, just dead wonky?

And on and on and on, until our cheeks were wet with laughter, neither of us sure what was funny anymore.

That day Danny led me through the house and out the other side, onto the little plot at the back. I walked behind him slowly, taking it all in as we headed down the jigsaw path, framed on each side by a carpet of thick greenery and ornamental grasses dotted with old wooden crates, beer barrels and dented oil tins overflowing with flowers. Across the back fence the creepers hung heavy; cloud-like blooms knotting with trailing ivy and climbing rose bushes that teemed with bees and butterflies. I'd never had the slightest interest in anything to do with plants or flowers before me and Chrissy moved to that town. Then again, I'd never seen anything like the places Danny showed me.

Best one fer miles, this, Danny said over his shoulder, gesturing to the dazzling chaos around us. Even nicer'n all them big ones they've got at t'posh houses up the top of town.

It must have taken you ferever, I said in wonderment. I thought only people who owned their places bothered doin owt with their yards.

What d'you mean?

Nowt, just . . . seems like a lot of effort. When they might want it back.

Danny paused then, looked at me over his shoulder. Who?

The council. If they wanted to, like, move yer on. Re-house yer.

Naaaah. They can't do that. Me nan's been here fer years, he said. But I saw the look that passed over his face.

At the very bottom corner of the yard sat a tiny green-house. Danny showed me inside, pointing out tomato plants, runner beans, the herbs right at the back. It's mad, innit? he said, rubbing one of the leaves between his thumb and forefinger. How them little roots appear, how they just know to grow downwards. And then that speck of life pushes itself out toward the light. You could be anywhere, out in the desert or in some mucky city . . . and you'll still see flowers, fightin through the cracks in the pavement. It's like they know that this is it, this is the only chance they've got. And once it's gone, it's gone.

I ribbed him with my elbow. You're soft, you, I laughed, and he shrugged, turned away to hide the hurt that flashed in his eyes.

WE SAT WITH OUR BACKS AGAINST THE GREENHOUSE AFTER THAT, our legs stretched out in front of us, knees just touching as he listed each plant, explaining to me what it was, the soil it needed, when it would flower.

How d'you know all this stuff? I asked him eventually.

Danny pulled his knees up to his chest, resting his chin on them. Me nana got me into it, I s'pose. First memory I've got is of plantin tulips in t'dirt with her. It near blew me head off when the flowers sprung out the earth. But mostly . . . I dunno—I . . . feel it. He paused. I did most of this, mind. Me nan can't do that much now. She gets poorly, see. Sometimes. She's all right now but . . . sometimes she's not.

He rubbed his hands over his face, and for a moment we were quiet.

What about you then? With yer writing?

I'd barely written a word since we'd left the flats, bar the story about Danny that I'd shredded on that first day.

I ain't been doin it much. I shrugged.

Why not?

I didn't know how to answer and Danny must have sensed it because he let it go, plucking a buttercup out of the ground and tugging absentmindedly at its petals. I don't want to end up like everyone else, me, he said.

What you on about?

Like everyone else, everyone from this town. That lad from earlier, Ste, and all the rest of his divvy mates. I don't want to just finish school and get some shitty job at the call center, or paintin and decoratin or cleanin someone's mucky house.

Me neither, I said uncertainly.

Before the summer, Danny carried on, we had this lesson at school. Career Guidance, they called it. And they were askin some of the other kids, the ones that sit up the front, what they wanted to be when they left school. But they never asked me.

What would you've said?

It don't matter. What matters is they think I wouldn't answer, that I wouldn't know what to say. They think I'm thick, proper thick. But it's them that are stupid. They don't know that I'll make more of meself than the rest of that lot put together.

I reached out shyly, nudged his leg with my toe. It matters to me.

Danny considered me for a moment. D'you know what a horticulturalist is?

It's a gardener, innit?

Yeah, well, it can be . . . but I don't just mean mowin lawns and shit, it's more'n that. In the olden days they used to put em on the ships, the botanists, the horticulturalists. They'd go off explorin all round the world, huntin plants to bring back and make their own. You never hear about em, they're not in any of them history books you get at school. But they were heroes. They'd put their lives at risk, some of em, to bring back a good plant. And that's what I want, see? I want to know all the plants there are to know. Not only trees and grass and that, but everythin, anythin that grows, here on our doorstep as much as the stuff in t'jungles, the Congo Basin, the Amazon. Places people have never stepped foot in before. There's loads out there, man. We hardly know any of the plants on the whole of this planet and I reckon I'd be good at findin em, givin em names. He leaned into me gently. Mebbe I'd call one after you.

Would yer?

Mebbe. He grinned, flicking a tiny yellow petal so that it landed on my shoulder. If you play yer cards right.

His gaze stayed on me and I felt awkward suddenly.

So you gonna be a writer then? he asked.

Yeah, I said, clearing my throat and twisting a strand of hair between my finger and thumb. I am.

Danny smiled with a gleam of satisfaction. What will you write about?

I glanced at him out of the corner of my eye, then flung

my arms open wide. The famous horticulturalist, I announced grandly. Sir Daniel Campbell!

He laughed, a big, wide laugh that let me see down the tunnel of his throat. Then he did something unexpected; he flung an arm around my shoulders, pulling me in close, half hug, half headlock. I stayed very still, not wanting to break the spell.

Jennifer, he said. It don't suit you, that name.

Well, it's me name.

Nah. Nah, it won't do, that. You're no Jennifer.

I pulled a face. What am I then?

His hold on me loosened and he leaned back, scrutinizing me, his forehead wrinkled as he tried things out. Jen. Jenny. J? Nah. None of them.

Above us, clouds were gathering, painting the edges of the sky a soot-gray. Shall we go inside? I mumbled. It's gonna piss it down.

Neef! he said suddenly, sitting up straight like a switch had gone on behind his eyes.

I looked at him blankly.

Neef, that's what you are. Like nymph, sort of, one of them little fairy things, y'know. Jen-Neef-Fer.

Neef? What sort of a name is that? It don't even mean owt.

Yeah, but that's why it's good. Danny was pleased with himself, I could tell, settling back, elbowing me gently in the side. It's different. Like you.

I looked away then, burrowing my chin in the neck of my T-shirt so he wouldn't see my smile, so he couldn't tell how much I liked it, how it made me feel like I was his, somehow, even if I didn't know yet that I wanted to be.

Hardly anyone ever called me anything but Neef after that. Neef and Danny. Danny and Neef.

INSIDE, MARY'S HOUSE SMELT LIKE CIGARETTE SMOKE AND POT-pourri, and even though it was clean there were things everywhere. Knickknacks and doilies and china plates. Floral cushions, porcelain dolls with painted-on faces, an oval frame on the mantelpiece with *Love Makes a House a Home* embroidered across the center. And all those photos, all over the walls and crammed together on every surface, the same face staring out of almost every one. Danny as a chubby baby, his legs splayed out in front of him on the grass; Danny in a blue-and-yellow football strip, riding a little trike down a road that looked exactly like the one we'd walked along. Danny in a gray jumper, grinning at the photographer. Next to that one, another, faded and blurred with age: a girl in a school shirt, a gap between her teeth like his. When I looked closer I could just about make out the name along the bottom. *Kim Morris. Third Form.*

The more I looked, the more I could see her now, mostly in the background of the photos when Danny was very little. In all of them she was young; a kid, then a teenager, sometimes smiling, other times looking like she was in the middle of saying something, thinking something, her face a mixture of Danny's and Mary's all at once.

I picked up a frame from the row at the back, Danny in just a nappy, wrapping paper scrunched around his feet. His hair was Afroed up around his head like a halo and he was grinning, holding something toward the camera in his hand—a car or a train, maybe—two tiny white teeth poking out of his bottom gums. She was on the sofa behind him, but there was something about the way she was sitting, curled over, her hair hanging lankly over her face, that unsettled me.

Danny came up behind me, took the frame out of my hands and put it back, at a different angle now, so that it was facing away from us slightly.

Don't be lookin at all them baby photos of me, he said, trying to sound light, jokey. Something hung between us and he walked away, flopped down on the sofa, pulling out a Game Boy from behind the cushions.

I can hardly remember her, he said, turning the console on so that it sang its funny little tune. Wanna game?

tell myself to forget about Denz, to put him back in the part of my head that's stayed locked for all these years. But hard as I try, I can't shake the thought of him. The scent of him.

They say the part of your brain which stores memory is so intertwined with your sense of smell that it's impossible to separate the two. I've struggled with it all these years, how the warm, homely stench of a place, the nauseating stink, can pull me back to somewhere I don't want to be. Most other things I can find a way around: music and thoughts and feelings. But the smell, the molecular aroma of a person or time or place, I still haven't figured out. It's one of the reasons I don't drink, although it's not the only one. Pubs smell too much like when we were kids. Cigarettes and chip fat and beer-stained carpets, Danny and I at the table in the back bar by the window pretending to do homework, keeping an eye on the punters to see if any of them were far enough gone that we might be able to lift their cigs, sneak the change they'd left on top of the bar. Spray-on deodorant and alcopops and cut grass in the beer garden. The pair of us sitting on the bench out the back, minesweeping half-empty drinks, smoking dock-ends out of the ashtrays, laughing at all the pissed-up idiots stumbling over each other and throwing punches they couldn't land.

Those years living in the pub turned out to be the happiest of my whole life, although I couldn't have known it then. All those afternoons in Barry's apartment, Danny sneaking up the back stairs with a school bag full of scratched CDs that he'd play on the old stereo while I lolled on the cushions of the overstuffed sofa, watching him move to beats unfamiliar to me. Smiley Culture, Bunny Wailer, Jimmy Cliff. Reeling off the names, looking at me incredulously when I'd shake my head blankly. All we ever listened to at the flats was dance music, Liquid and Strike and Livin' Joy blasting out of Chrissy's boombox night after night.

Every so often Mary would yell from the bottom of the stairs, checking on us, making sure we weren't up to no good. You're to stay in the front room, don't be slidin an inch off that sofa, the pair of yer, and no disappearin off into the bedroom, d'yer hear? she'd bawl, wise to us before we were even wise to ourselves.

Much later, in those early years of discovering one another, we found ways to sneak under the covers of my bed, despite Mary's warnings. It was easy when she wasn't around—Chrissy didn't care, and Barry was mostly too pissed up to notice. We'd lie there together, amid the pink and the lilac and the glitter, exploring each other, taking it in turns to gasp up at the glow-in-the-dark stickered ceiling, our bodies barely out of childhood, already entwined.

I've never felt anything for another person since Danny. I pretended, once, just to get under his skin. To hurt him the way he'd hurt me. But it was a lie and he knew it, I hope. Danny is the only person whose touch I ever welcomed.

16

The first time I met Denz I was sitting on the wall outside the pub, wondering when Danny would show
up. He usually came with Mary at the start of her shift on a
Saturday, but she'd arrived alone that morning. When I
asked her where Danny was, she shooed me away, but not
before I'd seen her wipe at her damp cheeks with the corners
of her apron, her eyes red and her mouth downturned.

There was no missing the car that turned up late that
afternoon. Music blasted from the open windows as it cut
across the top of the mini-roundabout outside the pub,
swerving into the car park to a chorus of blasting horns.
Danny was sitting in the back, his elbow resting in the frame
of the open window, but I didn't move, sat there scratching
my nails against the gritty sandstone.

Danny got out first and I could tell he was trying to act

slick, the extra swagger in the way he moved. He didn't come over, just looked at me and nodded, leaning against the back door waiting for whoever else was inside to show their face. He was wearing new trainers. New clothes too, and his hair had been pulled back into tight canerows, each finished with a black bead at the nape of his neck.

The driver got out of the car next. Skinny and tall, swamped in a denim jacket, locs poking out from underneath a New York Yankees cap. His eyes scanned the car park and then the beer garden as though he was checking for something, then he leaned down, spoke to someone sitting in the car. The passenger door swung open and another figure emerged, dressed all in black, a hood over his head and a cap pulled low over his eyes. He was shorter than the driver but broad, heavyset, his hands thrust deep into the pockets of his hoodie. I could tell just by the way he moved, the way Danny stood up that little bit taller at the sight of him, that this was Danny's dad. Denz.

After that first row we'd had at the graveyard about our parents, I'd let Danny fill my head with stories about his dad. I didn't believe much of what he said, certainly never thought this person—this fantastical storybook character—would actually materialize into something real. As far as I was concerned, Danny's dad existed in the same way mine did. In the depths of our imaginations, a figment of whatever tale we chose to tell that day.

I hadn't noticed until then that Mary was standing at the back door, the roundness of her pale face now pinched and tight. She was leaning against the doorframe, her arms folded across her chest. I don't want you comin in here, she said, her eyes fixed on Denz.

Nan—

It's all right, Denz cut in. Something stirred inside me as he placed a hand heavily on Danny's shoulder, set his gaze on Mary. We were just gonna have a beer, Mary. Been a long drive.

There are other pubs. You don't need to come in this one. Mary stood firm but there was a catch in her voice. I wondered if she might cry. Denz must have heard it too. He paused, looked over at the driver, then back at Mary before lowering his hood. I saw the scar then, dark and raised, cutting a line across his cheekbone.

I got the same right to drink in this pub as everyone else.

Danny bowed his head low, his weight shifting from foot to foot, and my stomach hardened with dislike for Denz. For talking to Mary like that, for making Danny look so unlike the boy I knew. I wanted to say something but I didn't know what. Denz turned to the driver.

Come on, Lewis.

The two of them sidestepped Mary into the pub and we watched through the window as they walked up to the bar, none of us looking the other in the eye. It was Mary who spoke first.

You have fun then? she said, a sigh in her voice.

Danny bit his thumbnail, nodded. Yeah.

New clothes?

I lifted my chin to look at him but he didn't answer his nana, skulking the dirt with the toe of his new trainers. She watched him for a second, then turned, walked in that heavy way she had back into the kitchen.

The weight of the moment hung between us, neither of us sure what to say. Danny sidled over to the wall, leaning next to where my legs dangled.

What you been doin then? he said eventually.

I shrugged. Nowt.

You missed me? He cocked his head to one side, resting it there on my arm and then lifting it again, playful, a smile in his voice. I prodded him back with my heel, glad to feel him next to me. D'you wanna come and meet him then? Me dad?

I wanted to say no, to act like I didn't care. To ignore the niggling fear that someone might matter to Danny more than I did. We'd only known each other for a few months by then, but my desperation to have something, someone who was just mine, was thirsty. And yet I couldn't ignore my curiosity. I did want to meet Denz, Danny's make-believe man. I wanted to see if he was real.

THEY WERE PLAYING POOL WHEN WE WALKED IN, THE POUND coins lined up on the frame of the table, Denz bent down low, taking a shot.

Here he is! Denz's cousin, Lewis, walked over, grabbed Danny in a headlock. Brought the lady in to meet us, is it?

I live here, I scowled, and Denz looked at me with vague interest, told Lewis to buy us a drink, but Barry wouldn't have it.

I'll take care of these kids, pal, he said darkly, pushing two half pints of Coke across the bar at us. They won't be needin owt from you.

I thought Denz might kick off then, but he didn't. He just shrugged, carried on with his game while two of the locals glared at him from across the bar. I didn't want to be there, didn't like the way it felt. The pub wasn't a place for outsiders.

Come on, let's do one, I said, pulling at Danny's arm. Let's go up the chippy and get summat to eat.

Me nan'll make us summat to eat.

I'm bored, though, I whined. Let's see if we can swipe some cigs from the old fellas in the sports lounge, go have one round t'back.

I don't want a cig.

I gave up, sat there sulkily, sipping Coke and watching music videos on the telly above our heads as the three of them played pool. It irritated me, how much Danny wanted to be around Denz. It was only later that I came to understand how afraid he was to let his dad out of his sight. He never knew, when Denz left, if he'd be coming back.

We'd been there a while when Chrissy turned up. I could tell by the looseness of her laugh that she was half cut. She came in through the main doors at the front of the pub and I heard someone whistle, someone else make a crude comment, before Barry told whoever it was to pipe down. Chrissy didn't mind, though. She carried on with that laugh, a blank sound that filled the space between her and me. I heard her say something, crack a joke and then another peal of laughter, hers and someone else's, dirty and cheap.

By the time she came through to where we were she had a drink in her hand, the liquid sloshing in her glass as she walked. Her eyes took Denz in before she'd even realized I was there and I saw the change in her, the wing's-beat falter in her step. Seeing him made her bring herself back together somehow, and she leaned against the end of the bar, angling herself so that her chest rested just above its wooden edge, running her fingers through her hair and fanning the bleached tendrils over her shoulder.

All right, Chrissy, I heard Danny say beside me. I would have punched him if no one else had been looking.

Chrissy's eyes lit up at the sight of him, her way in. It was only then that she noticed me. Hiya, Neef, she purred, all over-the-top as she tottered over, leaning down to kiss the crown of my head so that I could smell the booze on her breath. I glared at her, my eyes narrowed with suspicion. She'd never called me Neef before.

Denz barely looked up and I liked him and loathed him for that, all at the same time. It was Lewis who started fawning over her, giving her the eye, fumbling to light her cig, offering to buy her another drink.

You don't need to be buyin me drinks, babe, she purred. This is my pub.

She was trying to show off and maybe it would have worked on Lewis. He'd have at least pretended to be impressed, even if he knew she was bullshitting. But Denz wasn't up for playing her games.

No, it's not, he said, and Chrissy looked up, surprised.
What?
This. It's not your pub.

She shot him a smile. That smile. She was so beautiful. More mine than it is yours, she said.

His eyes sparked. Yeah. I'll give you that.

Denz put down his cue, walked over to the jukebox and started feeding coins into the slot. I wondered if Chrissy would follow him, but then Lewis asked her if she fancied a game of pool and she turned her attention back to him, said yeah. He let her win twice and he would have done it a third time, had it not been for the two blokes who walked in.

I recognized the taller of the pair as one of the pigs that

came in the pub a fair bit at the end of his shifts, although he wasn't wearing his uniform that day. He was friendly with Barry, turned a blind eye to his lock-ins and, in exchange, Barry never charged him for his drinks. I didn't know the other fella, though. They stood at the end of the bar, neither of them taking their eyes off Denz, who was still at the jukebox with his back to them.

Everythin all right, pal? Lewis had spotted them too, taking a step toward them, unsmiling. Denz turned then and a look of recognition passed over his face. The men ignored Lewis, their eyes still on Denz.

Not seen you round here in a bit, fella.

A nerve in Denz's jaw twitched. I've come to see me lad.

The pig lifted his chin. Not causin any trouble, are we?

Nah, mate. Not unless you are.

The four men stared at one another, the air in the room thickening.

Not my place to cause trouble, pal. But mine to do away with it. As, and when, I see it.

There was silence and then Denz made a sound like a laugh through his nose. Don't worry about it, he said, shaking his head slowly and pulling up his hood. We were leavin anyway.

The men watched as Denz walked past us, punching Danny lightly on the arm.

See you later, yeah, he said, and I felt Danny slump back against the wall. Denz didn't say anything to Chrissy, but I saw the look he gave her as they left, the look she gave right back to him.

The pig shook his head, leaned over the bar. Scum, he muttered to his mate. Don't need folk like that round here.

Damn bloody right. Nowt but trouble. Tell you what, you go through Leeds these days and it's like drivin through t'bloody Cari-bbeen.

Damn shame, that's what it is, the pig grimaced. Damn shame. Chrissy, love, get us a couple of pints, will yer?

Chrissy didn't even look at them, tipped her head back to drain her glass, then got to her feet, stalking out of the bar and letting the door close behind her with a slam.

17

Summer was almost over by the time the subject of school came up. Danny was out with Denz somewhere, and Mary had come upstairs looking for Barry when she caught me writing in my notebook at the dining table. I'd had more time on my hands since Denz had come on the scene. I slammed it shut as though I'd been doing something I shouldn't and Mary looked at me strangely. What you got there, love?

Nowt, I mumbled. Just some . . . schoolwork.

She laughed. In t'holidees? That reminds me in fact, she said, waving the tea towel that she was holding in my direction. I've got an old school jumper of Danny's you can have, I'll bring it tomorra. Has yer mum filled in t'forms and that? Fer t'school?

. . .

CHRISSY HAD BEEN EXCITED WHEN I WAS LITTLE AND FIRST starting school. I remember her geeing me up about it for ages, telling me how much I'd love it, how I'd learn all sorts and get to read and write and show everyone that I was clever. She bought me a Sylvanian Families lunchbox and a polka-dot raincoat to wear on my first day, kissed me on the cheek at the gates, stood there waving till I disappeared in the sea of kids through the entrance. But school wasn't what I had expected. I don't remember all that much but I know there wasn't a lot of learning. Just feral kids and too much noise, and a teacher who had a face on her like she wasn't sure how the fuck she'd ended up in that place.

After a few weeks Chrissy requested a meeting with the head teacher, a middle-aged man called Mr. Babington who wore a permanent sneer on his lip. She wanted me to learn, she said. Wanted to make sure he knew how smart I was, that I'd been reading proper books since I was knee-high to a grasshopper. She wanted them to see what potential I had. She wasn't going to let me slip through the cracks.

We went in there together after school one afternoon, and when the head opened the door to his office, Chrissy marched straight in, looking like she was ready to fight. I felt so in awe of her in that moment, but when I saw Mr. Babington glance at her then exchange a smile with the receptionist as though they'd just shared a joke, a hot wave of shame washed away my pride.

Chrissy wasn't in there long. When she came out, her cheeks were flushed a high pink, her mouth set in a thin, chastened line. You'll just have to try harder, she'd muttered. And that was the end of that.

By the time we moved to the pub, school had long since stopped being a priority for either of us. The year before, my attendance had been so bad that they'd ended up sending some bloke round from the Department of Education, and Chrissy got all giddy like he'd come over to ask her out for a drink or something. He said all this stuff about social services and court, and I swear she didn't hear a word of it, just kept smiling and nodding and twiddling the straps of her top in a way that made his eyes wander down to her chest.

It hadn't crossed my mind that us moving would mean me changing schools. I'd assumed I'd carry on at the comp near the flats. But it was miles away from the pub. I don't know how I thought I'd get there, other than maybe Barry would drive me. Not that it was worth traveling to. Everyone knew the comp was shite.

That night after Mary mentioned the jumper, I told Chrissy that she'd need to get on with sorting something out. I was supposed to start Year Nine in a couple of weeks. She nodded vaguely, in the middle of painting her toenails petrol-blue at the coffee table in the front room, her club music blasting in the background.

Did you hear me? I said, turning it down. You need to sign me up fer school or you'll have the council after you again.

She looked up, annoyed. Yeah, I heard. Just get me the forms I need to fill in and I'll do it.

I walked round to where she was sitting and perched on the arm of her chair, making it tip so that her hand jerked, the varnish streaking across her toes.

Bloody hell, Neef! she yelled, fully pissed off now. Go get me a tissue.

Chrissy had taken to calling me by my nickname all the time since that first day we'd met Denz in the pub. It jarred with me whenever I heard it on her lips. We'd only been living there a few weeks and already it was like she'd forgotten who I was.

I don't know where to get the forms from, I snapped. You need to do it.

All right, Princess, Chrissy sighed, screwing the top back onto the little glass bottle and hobbling over to the kitchen, pulling a paper towel from the roll on the worktop and wiping at her feet. Fine. I'll figure it out. We can ask Barry, can't we?

Barry appeared at the door then, like a dog being called for a treat, a doltish grin on his face.

This one's on about what school to go to after the holidees, said Chrissy, jerking her head backward to me. A funny expression passed over Barry's face as he looked back and forth between us, patting his belly awkwardly, then clearing his throat as though readying himself to speak. Instead he walked over to the cabinet near where I stood, pulled open the top drawer and slid out what looked like a glossy holiday brochure. He placed it down on the coffee table. A group of girls smiled up at us from outside an elegant brick building, blood-red hats perched on each of their heads. Chrissy came up behind me, picked it up.

Boroughford Independent Ladies' College, she mouthed slowly, her vowels long and flat.

Barry started bumbling then, something about no pressure and just an idea, and me being such a bright girl, but my eyes stayed on Chrissy, trying to read her reaction, clock the speed of the cogs turning in her head.

Well, she said, her voice dense as she flicked through the pages, stopping now and then to take a better look. Well.

I moved toward her, peering over her shoulder. A classroom full of shiny girls, all of them looking like they were about to self-combust with excitement at the lines of chalky numbers scrawled on a blackboard. A photo of a swimming pool. Another of a girl on a horse. Barry was looking at me, and for once I met his gaze. He cleared his throat again, gave me an awkward half smile.

What d'you think then, love?

About what?

Well, he started and then paused for a minute, unsure what to say next. About, mebbe, goin there. To this school. They've a waitin list as long as me arm usually, but I've got a mate, see. On t'Board of Gov'nors. He owes me a favor. I've had a word with him already, as it happens. It's a good opportunity. A chance to get a better education, a good start in life . . . He trailed off and I tugged at a fraying thread on the sofa cushion, looked up at Chrissy. Her expression was strange, unreadable, but when she clapped the brochure shut, she beamed at Barry.

It's a lovely idea! Just lovely, she said with a twisted smile. Think how good she'd look in one of them hats!

Flinging her arms around Barry's neck, she kissed his cheek so that his face flushed beetroot. I wondered how long this was going to last, this clumsiness around Chrissy, like he couldn't quite believe his luck every time she was anywhere near him. I wondered if Chrissy sensed it too, if she liked it in fact. He'd have done anything for her.

So d'you fancy it, love? Barry said after a pause. This mate of mine, he can pull a few strings. We'd need to send yer last school report and meet with the headmistress. Mrs. Herrington, they call her.

I pulled harder at the thread, making it snap. I already felt like enough of an intruder in that town, the sort of person who could never fit in. At least I'd have a friend at Danny's school. I'd have no chance at somewhere like Boroughford.

Could I not just go round here? I mumbled.

Don't be daft, why would you go round here when—

Barry cut Chrissy off and I looked up, surprised, impressed even. Thing is, Neef, he said softly, kneeling down so that I couldn't avoid looking at him. I haven't got me own kids. Wanted em, don't get me wrong. But it never worked out, fer one reason or another. Me and yer mum . . . well, I'm very fond of her. And you, of course. So I want to do the best by you. By both of you. And these schools, well . . . they're good, they're bloody good schools, see. You get a great education, you could go to uni, get a good job and that . . .

And then, just as I was starting to warm to him, he changed tack, standing up and puffing his chest out like a peacock. Besides, he said, pushing his hands into his pockets and leaning back on his heels. I saw him look at Chrissy out of the corner of his eye, knew that the next point was for her benefit. I can afford it. Wouldn't be any problems there.

I HADN'T EXPECTED CHRISSY TO HAVE KEPT A COPY OF MY SCHOOL report, but it turned out she had. Not just one, either, there was a whole stack of them folded neatly into a shoebox that she pulled out from under Barry's bed, and beside it a plastic wallet filled with schoolwork that had been sent home at the end of each year. They can look at whatever they like, she told Barry. She's smart, is Neef. Money can't buy yer that.

It was true, what Chrissy said. We might have been skint

and there was no getting round the fact that my attendance at my old school had been crap. But I'd always done all right. Better than all right, in English at least. Still, even if that fancy-pants school liked me on paper, I knew I didn't stand much chance. This Mrs. Herrington would take one look at me and my mam and turf us out on our ear.

Barry wasn't dissuaded, though. He took it upon himself to deliver the report, insisted on handing it over to the head-mistress herself. The school called a few days later to set a date for an interview.

Tuesday, is it? Chrissy piped up from where she'd been sitting, flicking through a magazine in the corner of the room and pretending not to eavesdrop. I can't come, love. I've got an appointment.

I frowned at her but she wouldn't meet my eye. What sort of appointment?

At the dentist's, she lied.

I tried to think of something to say, but in the end I just nodded, my eyes pricking with the shame of my relief. The truth was I didn't want Chrissy there. The school had seen something in me, on paper at least. And although I'd never have admitted it, I was beginning to feel the tiniest glimmer of curiosity about that chance, that prospect of a different life.

BOROUGHFORD WAS IN THE MIDDLE OF NOWHERE, THE SMELL OF horse-shit seeping through Barry's car windows as we drove to the interview the following week, descending further and further into the countryside until we reached the sprawling buildings, set back from the road and surrounded by acres of green. A bead of sweat trickled down Barry's forehead as we pulled in, taking in the grandeur of the architecture, the immaculate grounds, the parking area filled with a glitter of cars.

They kept us waiting in reception for a good half hour before Mrs. Herrington swooped in, tall and thin and hawkish, her sensible heels clacking against the polished tiles of the hallway. She stuck out a hand toward Barry and fixed her mouth up into a hard, flat smile that showed a lipstick smudge on one of her eye-teeth. So very nice to see you again, she simpered.

The interview was held in a room on the top floor of the building, overlooking the grounds. It was the poshest place I'd ever seen, all polished wood and draping curtains, the walls covered with old paintings and engraved brass plaques. Mrs. Herrington talked for a long time, her voice clipped and sharp like the yap of a small dog.

It does rather go against protocol, you see, she said, clasping her hands together on the desk, her stare making me snap back to attention. To admit a student on the basis of . . . recommendation. But I must say, my colleagues and I were—how can I put it?—*intrigued* by Jennifer.

She tapped a thin stack of paper in front of her with a sharp, unpolished nail and I looked down to see a copy of the story I'd written the year before, about a little girl who became invisible. I'd got top marks for it, and the teacher had asked if I'd read it out to the school at assembly. I'd laughed in his face, told him there was no chance in hell I was doing that.

Obviously we're very different from the sort of schools you're used to, Mrs. Herrington said with a haughty little laugh. But it does seem you may have potential, Jennifer.

She was looking at me like she was waiting for me to say something and so I cleared my throat. Ta, I muttered.

Mrs. Herrington gave me another tight smile, leaned forward in her seat. We have an excellent English department here at Boroughford, so many wonderful resources. Is that something that interests you?

I stared down at the floor, nodded. Yeah, I said honestly. Very much.

THE ENVELOPE ARRIVED WITHIN A WEEK, LANDING ON THE DOOR-mat with a fat thud. I pretended I hadn't seen it, let Barry get to it first. Later that morning I heard him in the front room, hooting and cheering and carrying on. My stomach flipped, but whether it was with fear or excitement I couldn't tell.

They were offering me a place to start the following month, pending a hefty deposit and the first term's payment upfront. Barry was over the moon of course, waving it around like we'd just won the lottery. Chrissy didn't say much and neither did I. It was only when he'd gone downstairs that she picked up the letter herself.

Seems like money'll buy yer owt these days. She shrugged.

It were me writin they liked too, I said, my voice sounding more defensive than I'd meant it to.

Chrissy's eyes flashed. Don't be so bloody naïve, Neef.

18

Danny had already been at school three weeks by the time I started at Boroughford. The local schools went back earlier than the private ones. Barry had loved making a joke out of that, how he was paying all this money to get me a good education and I'd only be there for half the time. More fool you, Mary had muttered under her breath.

I can still remember the weight of the blazer on my shoulders, the heat of the woolen bowler hat on my head. Shoes like cement on my feet, slowing me as I clomped down the stairs that first day, terrified I would topple. And I remember everyone standing there at the bottom. Barry with his cardboard camera, my red-and-gold backpack at his feet, and Chrissy just behind him, her mouth smiling but her eyes confused. Mary looking like she'd rather be anywhere but there. And Danny at the back, his cheeks puffed out with the effort of not laughing.

I'd never had a uniform before. There'd been one at the comp, but no one had ever bothered wearing it. I'd caught Mary rolling her eyes the day we came back from town, Barry's boot stuffed with fancy carrier bags. Blazers and jumpers and regulation shoes. Charcoal-colored tights for the cold, white socks in the summer. A whole kitbag for sports—gym knickers and netball skirts, polo shirts, swimsuits, a rubber cap that Danny said made me look like a human condom. The only thing his school insisted on was a gray jumper with their logo on the front. Danny had a whole pile of them. Mary always managed to get hold of second-hand ones off the locals in the pub.

We stood around awkwardly for a while as Barry snapped photos, directing various poses that everyone ignored. As we turned to walk out to the car, I felt Chrissy grab at my arm, pull me away. She lifted a hand, touched my cheek, and I leaned back in surprise.

Good luck, love.

You not comin?

Me? She made a sound like a laugh that had hit the wrong note. Nah, not fer me, somewhere like that. Don't want to be showin yer up now, do I?

I looked at her then, really looked at her. Words spun in my head, a yearning to tell her that I understood, that I knew she only wanted to make things better. I should have told her I was proud of her, that she was cleverer than anyone I knew, that nothing she did could ever show me up. But instead I just nodded. See yer later then, I said.

BARRY AND I SAT WAITING IN THE OVERHEATED RECEPTION AREA, sweat pooling in my pits, the box pleats of my skirt creasing under my knees as he fumbled blindly through a stack of paperwork. The woman at the desk peered at us over the top of her glasses, patting her pouf of blond hair every few seconds like a nervous twitch. She thought I hadn't clocked her staring, hadn't seen how she tugged at the neckline of her expensive jumper as she eyed us with bewilderment, scanning me up and down like she was looking for faults.

Eventually Mrs. Herrington arrived, smiled in that fake way, before checking with the lady at the desk that Barry's payments were up to date.

Yes, yes, all present and correct, Barry laughed jovially, rocking back on his heels. The two women eyed him with thinly veiled disdain, and I felt a strange rush of protectiveness flush my cheeks.

Well, it looks like we're all done here, yapped Mrs. Herrington. If you'd like to follow me, Jennifer, I'll escort you to your form room.

The two of us walked through the maze of corridors, her a few strides ahead and me trying my best to keep up. At one point I tripped, catching the clunky sole of my shoe with my other foot. She didn't react.

We stopped outside a large dark-wood door and she rapped on it abruptly before turning the brass handle. Thirty heads swiveled toward us, the sound of chair scrapes filling the air as each of the girls got to their feet.

Good morning, Mrs. Herrington, they chanted in unison. She nodded at them approvingly.

Good morning, girls. You may be seated.

The girls moved as one, quiet and deft and orderly, their eyes boring into me as I stared back, my chin high. They sat me next to a girl called Agnes, three rows from the front. She glanced at me with her lips pursed as I took my seat, her eyes snapping open and shut like a camera taking a shot, before turning back to the front desk.

My form tutor was called Miss Bell. A young, solid, bookish type with a soft Scottish accent and a deep dimple in the center of her chin. She made a big deal about introducing me, giving everyone this long spiel about welcoming new members of our school community, how much we can all learn from one another, how they were all looking forward to getting to know me better. Eventually she stopped talking, looked at me expectantly. I stared back at her mutely, unsure if she'd asked me a question.

Could you tell us a little bit about yourself? she asked, slowing her words as though addressing someone who spoke a different language, her gaze curious. The girls in the rows in front of me swerved round in their seats, watching, waiting. Do you live locally? In the village perhaps?

I shook my head. No, I said eventually. Leeds. Except then I remembered that wasn't true anymore, but by the time I could correct myself I'd become aware of the noises, the swallowed hiccups and nasal sniggers. Out of the corner of my eye I saw Agnes shift her books a few inches toward the other side of the desk, angling her chair away from me.

When the bell rang for the next lesson I hung back, watching as the girls stood up, filing silently toward the door and assembling themselves into an orderly line. I joined the end, behind a pretty brunette whose hair swung in a fat ponytail.

At break time I stood alone at the side of the yard, its edges framed by manicured lawns. There were tennis courts at the far end and what looked like the indoor-pool building from the brochure. At my old school, break had meant hanging round the back of the bike sheds, sharing half a cig between a bunch of you and talking about who fancied who, watching the occasional scrap or getting into one yourself. It wasn't like that here. The girls idled languidly in their cliques, all clean hair and straight teeth, swapping stories of summer breaks in second homes, holding out slender forearms to compare shades of bronze.

Three of them were watching me from the steps leading back into the main building, thinking I hadn't noticed. In the end I eyeballed them back. What? I mouthed. They seemed surprised at first, turning in as though to pretend they hadn't been looking. Only the brunette with the ponytail held my gaze. She must have said something to them because they made their way over to me, the ponytail flanked by a blonde with a sharp bob that swung round her jaw, and a wiry girl with narrow eyes and mousy hair pinched into a plait.

All right? I said as they reached me. The three of them exchanged glances, smirked. The blond one spoke first, her angular face fixed on me, her eyelids fluttering as she looked me up and down. Hello, she said. Jennifer, isn't it?

Yeah, I said. I get called Neef, mostly, but—

Pardon?

Neef. That's me nickname.

Silence.

But you can call me Jennifer, if that's better.

Another loaded glance, another round of barely concealed smirks before they remembered their bought-and-paid-for manners and introduced themselves. Eloise, Rebecca, Frances. I nodded at each of them and they gawped back at me.

Do you know anyone who goes here then? Eloise asked.

No. I don't.

You sound like you're from Leeds, she said, her ponytail swinging from side to side, a note of mocking in her voice.

I pressed my tongue against my teeth, trying to quash the tightness in my throat. That's cos I am.

She nodded at me slowly, taking me in with that sly smile, until Frances spotted another girl they'd not seen *all* summer, and hadn't she got *fat* and did you *hear* what happened to her *poor* mother and let's go and say hello to her, shall we? I watched them turn on their heels, forgetting about me in an instant. So poised, so sure of their place in the world, so gilded by the privileges bestowed on them.

19

No one asked me much about school once I started there. Not Danny, not Mary or Chrissy. Barry liked to show off about it, his "stepdaughter" going to an exclusive private establishment, him having the means to foot the bill. But he never asked me if I liked it, how I spent my days there, how I was getting on.

Maybe it was a good thing he didn't. I doubt my answers would have impressed him. I didn't much like it. Spent most of my days clock-watching, wishing they were over. I reckon they'd have turfed me out on my arse within a week if it hadn't been for Miss Bell.

The school decided I'd be placed in the lower sets for all the main subjects, said it was standard protocol, until they got a gauge of my ability. Less than a month passed before they bumped me up to the top tier in English, much to the astounded stares of the other girls in there. Miss Bell happened to teach that class, beaming far too brightly at the sight of me. I could tell she'd already earmarked me as her project. She had this habit of grinning inanely each time she saw me, nodding along over-enthusiastically if I ever opened my mouth. I reckon I could have come out with any old shit and she'd still have looked at me the same way, apoplectic with delight. After a couple of weeks she stopped me on the way out of class.

How are you settling in, Jennifer? she asked, all smiley and concerned-looking.

Yeah. Fine.

I know it's not always easy, moving to a new area. A new school. You can probably tell I'm not from round here myself.

I nodded vaguely, wondered how long this might take.

Have you ever been to Scotland?

Nah. But me mam had a fella from up there once.

Miss Bell blanched. Oh, really? What part?

Dundee.

I'm from Edinburgh. She smiled. But Dundee is lovely!

He didn't seem to think so.

No? Ah, well. Different strokes for different folks, I suppose, she said with an embarrassed little laugh. Anyway, Jennifer, I just wanted to have a quick word . . .

She reached across the desk and picked up her ring-binder, slid out an A4 plastic wallet. I recognized my writing straight away, an essay I'd written the week before on *The Catcher in the Rye*. I'd liked the book, read it in one sitting, up in my room over the weekend when Danny was with Denz. It hadn't taken me long to finish the assignment. Stuff like that never did. I wished now I'd taken more care with it, not because I worried about Miss Bell pulling me up, but because I had better things to do than stand there listening to her.

Jennifer, I have to say—she was beaming again—this was really wonderfully done. Don't get me wrong, there's some work needed on the presentation, and maybe some tightening up of the grammar. But the way you write, your understanding of the characters, the themes. It really is exceptional.

Oh, right, I mumbled, surprised by the direction the conversation had taken. Ta.

Miss Bell looked down at the essay, her eyes scanning my writing. I thought it was so interesting, your insight into Holden, she said, her brow furrowed. The way he alienates himself as a form of self-protection, how the only thing he really wants is to find someone who understands him.

I didn't know what she wanted me to say to that, so I stood there silently, feeling awkward until she put the essay back on the desk, smiled up at me sincerely.

I'm so enjoying having you in the class, she said. Really I am. You have such an aptitude for writing, a real talent. I've shown your work to the other teachers in the English department and honestly, we're all very impressed.

I could tell by the way she said it that impressed meant surprised, but I didn't pull her up on it, just waited for her to tell me I could go.

Are you enjoying it here at Boroughford? she said, leaning forward and studying me intently.

I shrugged. I'm not really one fer school.

Oh?

The second bell shrilled down the hallway and I could see through the glass partition in the door that Miss Bell's next class had arrived. Can I go now, Miss? I'll be late fer me lesson otherwise.

Yes, in a moment. I just . . . She trailed off, sighed. If there's anything you need, Jennifer. Anything you want to chat about, please don't hesitate to come and see me. I want to make sure you feel supported here. Really. I mean that.

I felt a bit sorry for her then, sitting there all earnest and benevolent. Thanks, I mumbled before shoving my rucksack on my back. I'll bear it in mind.

I HAD NO INTENTION OF TAKING MISS BELL UP ON HER OFFER. I didn't need her meddling in my life. Didn't need anyone really.

Autumn had set in by then, and it was dark by teatime. I hadn't been seeing much of Danny lately. Often I didn't get home until after Mary had finished her shift and the two of them had left for the day. At the weekends he was with Denz. I'd had to learn to rely on my words to keep me company again.

Chrissy didn't feature in my writing much anymore, barely featured in my life in fact. She was too busy putting in a performance as First Lady of the Lamb and Lion. For a while I wrote stories about Danny and me: him discovering a plant up at Devil's Claw that grew fruit so rare it was worth its weight in gold; me winning the big cash prize on a game show and spending it on first-class plane tickets for us both to the Amazon rainforest. But before long I ended up writing Danny out too. On the rare occasions I did see him, he'd spend the entire time melting my head about all the fun he'd had with his dad, the interesting people he'd met, the places he'd been. I'd yawn, act bored until he took the hint to leave, and then I'd pull out my notebook, replace Danny with childish fantasies about my own dad, someone I'd barely given a second thought to up until that point. He was a millionaire, a prince, that fella who Chrissy used to fancy off *EastEnders*. He was so many different people, all of them superior to Denz.

A FEW WEEKS INTO THE SCHOOL TERM, DANNY SHOWED UP AT the pub, a slump in his shoulders and a scowl in his eyes. Turned out Denz hadn't come to pick him up that morning like he'd said he would. As annoyed as I'd been with Danny, I still couldn't bear to see him sad. And if I were being honest, I was glad he was pissed off with his dad. For once he was completely mine, the whole of Saturday stretching gloriously ahead of us. I didn't understand then what was going through Danny's head. All the times that Denz had done this to him, let him down, disappeared for months on end. I was yet to witness the slow-burn devastation of his vanishing acts.

The pair of us wandered the streets aimlessly for a while until we found ourselves shivering in the bandstand, me scattering the air with half stories, trying to make Danny laugh. The DJ who'd driven his van into the wall of the pub last Friday, the keg of beer that had exploded in the cellar, the girl who'd fallen asleep in the toilet cubicle and only woken up the next day when Barry went downstairs to open the pub. Danny barely spoke, his face half hidden by the zip-up collar of his new jacket.

I saw the car before he did, watched it creep around the bend that led down toward the river. I willed it not to slow, to circle round the car park and then turn back the way it had come, leave Danny alone, with me. But it pulled up right in front of the bandstand, the music pumping from the stereo. Danny jumped to his feet, his face splitting into a grin as Denz wound down the window, asked us if we wanted to go for a drive, with no explanation as to where he'd been, why he'd turned up late.

Does Mary know? I asked piously as Danny made his way to the car. I could feel him rolling his eyes, even though I couldn't see his face. Denz took me in coldly.

Yeah, he said. She knows.

Danny had already got in the backseat by then, nodding his head toward me, signaling me to come. And even though I didn't want to, I wanted to be away from him even less. I was desperate for him not to have a life outside of me, even then. I wanted so badly to be a part of all of it. My stomach rolled at the memory of Chrissy's eyes on Denz that day in the pub as she played pool with Lewis. Denz was bad news. Everyone said so.

Denz drove us to a Caribbean takeaway place near his house, on the opposite side of Leeds from the flats where I'd grown up. I hung behind the two of them as they reeled off names of dishes I'd never heard of. Ackee, saltfish, plantains, jerk chicken, falling into easy chat with the woman behind the counter. In the end I went outside, leaned against the bonnet until Danny appeared, his arms loaded with bags of food. He piled them into the backseat next to me, their heat warming my thigh, the heady scent making my mouth water.

Denz's place was the first in a row of red-brick terraces,

with a large bay window that looked out onto the street and a door painted emerald-green. I followed him and Danny through the hallway, staring up at a row of photos; proud-looking women and sharply dressed men turning from sepia to color. In the front room, a huge sound system filled most of the far wall and an oversized leather sofa the other. A stack of weights in every shape and size took up one corner, and across from them stood a carving of a woman whose eyes held your stare and didn't let it go. There was art hanging up too, beautiful, brightly colored pieces. The Lion of Judah, Haile Selassie, Danny told me proudly when he saw me looking at them. Words I'd never heard before.

Danny sat straight down, his legs splayed open, shoveling forkfuls of mysterious food straight from the polystyrene box into his mouth while I perched at the other end of the sofa, trying not to look like I didn't belong. Denz paid no attention to me, spoke only to Danny. Question after question about school, what the other kids were like, how did the teachers talk to him? It made me suspicious, wary of Denz. It never occurred to me that it was normal to have a parent take such an interest in your day-to-day.

It's all right. Danny shrugged. The kids are divs. Teachers are and all. But it's all right.

Why divs? Denz pressed.

I looked at Danny, interested now. He answered with his mouth full.

Just are, man. Just are.

Do they give you any bother?

Nowt I can't handle.

Denz laughed, then tilted his chin toward me.

And what about you, eh . . . Neef? he said, the name

sounding uncomfortable in his mouth. You're from Leeds, aren't you? You and your mum?

He knew the answer, but I nodded anyway.

How come you moved?

I prodded at the creamy, yellow ackee with my plastic fork. Chrissy wanted to live with Barry. So, we moved.

Denz leaned forward so that his elbows were resting on his knees. Funny pair, aren't they? Barry and your mum.

I didn't know if it was a statement or a question, so I just sat there, quiet. He set his eyes on me as though he was about to ask me something else, then seemed to think better of it, changing the subject.

Danny tells me you're at some private girls' school out in the back of beyond.

Yeah. She hates it, don't you, Neef? Danny cut in. Proper hates it.

I didn't say anything, just nodded dumbly again.

Why you hate it so much? Denz asked.

They're stuck up. I shrugged.

You aren't stuck up?

Naaaah, Danny laughed, digging his elbow into my ribs. She's rough as they come.

I shoved him in the side but harder than I meant to, so that a forkful of rice caught in the back of his throat, making him choke. I laughed and he dug me back. We tussled, the pair of us, but Denz stayed quiet. I could feel him watching us, taking it in. The way we were. After a while he reached for the remote, flicking through the channels, before settling on the news. Danny and I fell silent, our attention caught by a clip that had been playing over and over that summer. A protest outside a building in South London, the sound of someone screaming, someone else shouting. Policemen in ridiculous hats, with no control. Shoving, yelling, crowds swarming and pushing, and then a reporter, a young bloke in a suit talking about public disorder, violence. Hot coffee thrown over a murder suspect. Danny stilled beside me as Denz leaned forward, the rims of his eyes red, watching five men dressed in cheap shirts and sunglasses strut past the baying crowds.

Five years, man, Denz muttered. Five years and those pieces of shit are still walkin around as free men. Five years and all they doin is *inquiring*? A fuckin *inquiry*? Bullshit, that's what it is. Bull. Shit.

An image flashed up on the screen. A young lad, not much older than Danny was at the time, his expression soft, a smile on his lips. Denz started talking again then, his eyes still on the screen, his finger jabbing toward it.

See what world we livin in, Dan? See this? Kids gettin killed in the street for nowt other than lookin like you and me. People gettin away with murder. You see this? You understand what is happenin here?

Danny leaned forward, dropped the takeaway box onto the coffee table in front of us. Can you turn it off, Dad?

Something inside Denz ignited then. Turn it off? he spat. You don't want to see this? Fuckin turn it off?

Danny looked away and Denz got to his feet, grabbed Danny's face in his hand, forced his eyes toward the telly. Look at this, Danny. You. Look. You see any of them coppers—any of them pigs—that look like you? Like me? You see anyone makin these decisions, that those bastards should walk free, lookin like *me*? No. There int no one decidin this shit that's like us. No one.

He let go of Danny's face and stood back, his breath heavy. There were marks on Danny's cheeks where Denz's fingers had pressed into the skin, and Danny rubbed at the bones along his jaw, his eyes to the floor.

Jesus. Sorry, Dan. Sorry. Denz leaned down, circling Danny in his arms. I turned my face to the window.

DENZ TOOK US HOME NOT LONG AFTER THAT, THE MOOD IN THE car somber. We didn't go back to the pub, neither of us wanting to have to deal with Mary's mithering. Instead we walked up the old railway line, headed toward Devil's Claw.

Are you pissed off with him then? I asked as we moved in step along the dirt path. Danny had barely spoken since we'd left his dad's house. He frowned.

He just cares about that stuff, man. It riles him up. He's only tryin to get me understand what it's like, fer us.

What you on about, "fer you"?

Fer us. He shrugged, awkward, uncomfortable. Because of who we are, what we look like. It's different to how it is fer you.

Something like panic surged in my throat. I didn't want to hear that Danny and I weren't the same, afraid of anything that might put a space between us.

Oh, all right then, Dan, I scoffed, my fear remolding itself into anger as the words left my mouth. Cos you and yer dad are so *special,* aren't yer . . . so *different?*

Danny shook his head. Nah, I don't mean it like that.

I stopped walking. What d'you mean then?

He sighed. You wouldn't understand.

Get over yerself, Danny, I snorted, shoving my hands deep in my pockets and turning back the way we'd come.

. . .

I TOLD MYSELF THAT DENZ WAS THE PROBLEM. HE WAS THE ONE driving a fissure between us, putting ideas in Danny's head. It was nothing to do with the tangle of my thoughts, my confusion around what Danny meant when he said things weren't the same for us. Nothing to do with jealousy, with the fierceness with which Denz protected Danny, how hard Danny loved him back.

For a long time I'd steered clear of Denz out of spite, acting like he wasn't worth my efforts, hoping that might make Danny see his dad the way I did, the way everyone else did. But after that evening on the old railway line I started tagging along, shadowing Danny whenever he'd go over to his dad's place, trying to stay close. Denz never complained, never mentioned anything in front of me at least. But I could tell he didn't want me there. Could see it in the way he looked at me, at us when we were together. I told myself I didn't care, that I was glad to rile him. But the truth was I liked being at Danny's dad's. The smell of yard food, the endless stream of friends dropping in for a smoke, a chat, a drink. The red-lipstick smiles of the pretty girls on the men's arms, the way they always made everyone feel like they were part of something.

Danny and I used to sit on the floor and listen to them talk, yarn, crack jokes that we were still too young to understand, soaking it all up, listening, listening. I could see, then, where he got his talent for storytelling. Almost always there were good vibes. Music playing and people laughing and life. But there were times too when there was anger, seething, dark, frustrated anger that I would watch play out with a wary type of awe while Danny stiffened beside me, his jaw locked, his eyes not meeting mine.

Rows would erupt over police breathing down Black necks; over any one of the young men in that room being stopped, searched, publicly humiliated for no other reason than a uniform not liking the look of them. Raised voices and clenched fists when yet another cousin or brother or friend was pulled over because the boys in blue deemed certain types of faces not worthy of driving certain types of cars. Fury over good people being made to feel like lesser-than, simply because their complexions set the pigs on edge.

One night Lewis showed up at the house wound up like a spring, pacing the room, his anger coming out in short, manic bursts that I struggled to make sense of. He'd been kept in the cells overnight, I understood that much. For Breach of the Peace this time. It was his third arrest in as many months; seemed like whenever he left the house in those days, the police were on his heels.

Pigs, man. Fuckin pigs, he said, collapsing onto the sofa and taking the joint Denz handed him. He put it to his lips with relief, nodding his chin toward Danny, who was sitting beside me on the rug.

How old you now, kid?

Fourteen next month, Danny muttered, not looking up.

Lewis grimaced, turned back to Denz. You gotta keep an eye on him, bruv. He's gettin to that age. They'll be all over him soon.

Danny cast a sidelong look at Denz and we both waited for him to reassure us, tell us Lewis didn't know what he was talking about. But he didn't. Instead he spoke about Danny as though he wasn't even there.

Innit, he muttered. That town's worse than anywhere. I should know. Least round here there's a community. But what can I do—you know the way the old lady is. He'll find out for himself, no way round it. Just gotta be there when it all falls down.

No one noticed when I stood up, walking away from words that I didn't want to hear. I made my way to the little bathroom at the back of the house, leaned against the door, my eyes closed. Denz's words spun in my head. *When it all falls down, all falls down.* Don't let it then, I wanted to scream. Why are you going to let it?

When I got back to the lounge the mood had lifted, a buzz of conversation, beats playing. There was a girl draped over Lewis's lap, the pair of them laughing. She took the joint from between his fingers and I watched, entranced, as she put it to her lips, her eyes half closed, her mouth a perfect O. Her gaze met mine as the smoke curled up in front of her face and she winked, stretched her hand toward me.

Here, girl.

I stepped forward, took the joint. Sucked on it hard, and then again, and again. The girl laughed without malice, a light, tinkling sound, and then Lewis too, telling me to take it easy, slow down. I looked at Danny, watching me still from our spot on the floor. He nodded and I knelt, passing it to him. We grinned at one another, a look that was just for us.

Danny and I had never smoked weed before, although we'd been around it plenty of times. For a while we sat there, passing the joint backward and forward, the conversation and laughter floating over the tops of our heads until the roach burned our lips. Wordlessly, we wandered out into the yard at the back, both somehow aware of the need to be by ourselves, away from adult judgment, self-conscious of our stonedness. The minute we got out there, our eyes met and it was like something went off inside us both, making us laugh at nothing, tears rolling down our cheeks, bent over double. We found ourselves lying on our backs, our heads touching, unperturbed by the cold concrete slabs beneath us as we stared up at the sky, watching clouds become giants and dragons and kingdoms.

Only once the sun had dipped below the city's skyline did we stand again, both ravenous, ducking back into the kitchen, raiding the cupboards for anything we could find. Cereal and cheese and leftover pizza, Pot Noodles and bread and fizzy pop. When Denz came in, he found us huddled together on the floor in the darkness, our faces illuminated by the blue glow of the fridge as we scavenged inside. He chuckled quietly, said something over his shoulder so that the room behind him erupted in laughter. Then he left us alone again.

LATER, AS WE DROVE HOME, HAZY AND FUGUED IN THE AFTER-math of our first high, I saw Denz watching me in the rearview mirror, glancing at Danny, then me, then back to Danny again.

You all right, Dan?

Danny turned to him dozily. Yeah, man.

That feel good?

I fiddled with my seatbelt, pulling it back and forth away from my neck, and Danny glanced at me uncertainly, neither of us sure how to read Denz's mood. Yeah. Yeah, it felt good.

Denz nodded slowly and the three of us were quiet.

I don't mind it, me, he said after a while. You know I don't. There's a lot worse people can put in their bodies. But this . . . this int gonna harm you, not really. Nobody ever got in a fight from smokin bud, did they? No one ever went home and beat up their wife, murdered anyone, raped anyone, just off a smoke. He paused then, tapping his hand on the steering wheel. But that's where it's gotta end, innit? That's where you gotta draw the line. He threw me another glance in the rearview mirror, then looked at Danny again. Remember that. Dan. Danny?

What?

Denz reached across, cuffed Danny lightly over the top of his head. Listen to me, man. Listen, I'm serious. Green is one thing, yeah? White and brown and all that other shit, you stay away from that. That shit will put you in the ground. And if it don't, it might as well have, you know what I'm sayin? That shit will ruin your life. He shook his head emphatically, then repeated himself, slapping the steering wheel with the palm of his hand on the beat of each word. Ruin. Your. Life.

Danny and I stayed quiet. Awkward. Embarrassed, somehow.

And you do it under my roof, yeah? Denz continued a few minutes later, as though he'd been mulling it over. I aren't never gonna give you the shit that makes you go crazy; the stuff I give you'll wake you up, you get me? Don't be buyin any old hash from them lowlifes at school, smokin dirty shit. You do it with me, you understand that, Danny? You only do it when I'm there.

20

D'you ever wish you were someone else?

Danny and I were upstairs in Barry's living room, the telly on, a packet of Scampi Fries ripped open in front of us. I glanced at him curiously. I used to, I told him. I used to all the time.

He frowned. What changed then?

You, I wanted to say, but I pushed the thought away. It were just one of them things I'd do when I were a kid. Stories I'd write and that.

I still think about it now, and I'm older'n you.

Who would you be then?

Danny picked up a Scampi Fry and threw it in the air before catching it in his mouth. I dunno. Someone who fitted somewhere.

Well, at least you don't have to stick out like a sore thumb at a divvy school like mine.

I stick out everywhere, Neef.

What?

He shook his head, straightening his back against the stiff sofa cushions. Nowt, he said. What's it like then? Yer posh school?

I shrugged. Posh. Proper old and fancy, and everyone walks about like they've got a stick up their arse. Leaning forward, I pressed the pad of my thumb onto the foil of the crisp packet, licked the orange crumbs from my skin. The grounds are nice, mind. There's some decent plants and that, near the woods at the bottom, you'd like it down there. I found this old bench, half hidden in the bushes, so's it's good fer skivin. It's rotten in parts and I reckon someone would've chucked it out if they knew it were there, it don't fit in with owt else in that place.

You not made any mates then?

Nah. I screwed up my nose, turned my gaze back to the telly. I aren't bothered, though.

There wasn't any getting around the fact that I didn't fit in at Boroughford. Most of the teachers acted like I wasn't even there, and I couldn't blame them, I spent all of my time wishing I wasn't. Mrs. Herrington had been right about it being a different school from what I was used to. Even when I did understand something, I knew better than to say so, knew that there'd be a line of girls waiting to snark a clever comment about the way I talked. And there were so many rules, stupid, stupid rules. Rules for rules' sake, rules that I still don't understand, and penalties that came with them. Bloody *penalties,* they called them. Penalties for not asking if you could sit down, for taking your blazer off without being told. Penalties for dropping t's and h's, for wearing the wrong-color tights or not-quite-the-right-length tie. Penalties for rolling your eyes, for looking away, for this, for that, for every time I opened my mouth and every time I didn't.

Miss Bell never pulled me up on any of those things, though. She was too hell-bent on becoming my savior. I could see it upset her that I wasn't up for her rescue attempts; holding me back after the morning register to "check in," or calling on me to join in during English class. The more she did it, the less I gave her. I didn't want anyone nebbing into my business.

I hadn't tried to make friends, didn't see the point in wasting everyone's time. At break I'd sit at the back of the library, or if it was dry out, I'd go down to my secret bench and scrawl in my notebook. I rarely did any homework, but I always wrote stuff for Miss Bell. Not because I cared what she thought. Just because I liked writing.

I was down there skiving one afternoon when I felt the graze of a pebble bouncing off my neck. There was a movement in the woodland behind me, maybe some pervert coming to get his kicks off all the posh girls in their uniforms. Unlucky for him he'd got stuck with me.

I didn't stand, didn't want to give whoever it was the satisfaction of looking like I was bothered. I only jumped to my feet when the predator let out a low growl, making me back away with a gasp. I heard the laugh then, a laugh I knew.

Bloody hell, Danny! I hissed, glancing over my shoulder and clambering over the low fence that marked the end of the school grounds, my skirt catching on the splintered post. He was crouched down in the shrubbery, his shoulders shaking, eyes creased. I reached out, shoved him so that he fell backward. What you playin at, you muppet?

Danny stood, brushing the soil from the back of his legs. Thought I'd come steal you fer a bit. He grinned.

I bit down on the inside of my cheek, tried not to smile. I thought you were some dirty flasher with a thing fer pleated skirts, I told him.

He laughed. Mebbe I am.

Danny took my hand and led me to a clearing a few hundred yards from the fence. I sat with my back against the damp tree trunks, but he tugged me to my feet again. Come on, he said, nodding his chin to the sky. Up there. I'll race yer.

He didn't wait for me to argue, scampering up through the branches while I scrabbled behind, following his lead. When he reached halfway he paused, resting in the crook of a tree limb to pull out a baggy from the inside of his sleeve. We'd been pocketing cut-offs of Denz's stash on the sly for weeks by then. I perched awkwardly on the branch below, scrutinizing the deft flicks of Danny's fingers as he skinned up. He looked down at me once it was done, spinning it in his fingers, a satisfied smile on his face. I held out my hand but he shook his head, put the jay to his lips. Roller's rights. He grinned.

How did you find me?

Bus. Then walked. Fer miles, man. This place is *rural*.

I laughed. They've done that on purpose. Makes it too hard fer anyone to escape.

Danny took a few tokes, passed it to me, and I closed my eyes, leaned my head against his calf, easing into the warmth that wrapped itself around us.

You were right about there bein some decent plants down here, he said. Good trees and all.

I stayed quiet, the sound of his voice soothing me.

D'you know, he carried on, trees've been on earth fer three hundred and eighty-six million years. *Three hundred and eighty-six million.* How mad is that?

Mad.

They reckon there might be one hundred thousand species of trees on earth. Reckon they ain't even found half of em yet.

I nodded, listening, listening.

This tree's older than us. Older than me nana, probably older than anyone we know. Imagine all the stories it could tell us, all the people it's seen, the secrets it's heard. If I could have one superpower, that'd be it. To be able to talk to the trees.

I smiled, looked up at him. Nice to see yer, I whispered.

Nowt better to do, Danny shrugged, but his voice was kind. For a moment we were quiet, listening to the sounds of the woods as we passed the joint back and forth between us.

Did you not bother with school?

I went this mornin, he replied. Meant to be doin a group presentation after lunch with all these divvies in me English class. Teacher says we've got to talk about our hero, stand up in front of everyone and talk about it fer fifteen minutes, man.

Sounds shit, I murmured.

Yeah, well . . . it wouldn't be so bad, 'cept all they want to talk about is Ryan Giggs and Eric-fuckin-Cantona. No one's interested in talkin about a hero, a proper hero.

Don't tell me . . . you wanted to talk about yer dad, did yer? I snickered cruelly and Danny tensed, inched away ever so slightly.

Course I didn't want to talk about me dad, fool.

Who then?

I dunno—a geezer who actually did summat decent with his life.

Like who?

Danny took a deep drag, let the smoke filter slowly from his mouth. You ever heard of a fella called George Washington Carver?

The president?

Not the president, you eejit. He were an American agricultural scientist. Started out enslaved, so no one ever thought he'd be able to do owt with his life. Probably thought he were thick as pig-shit. But he weren't. He were bright, man, Danny said, tapping the side of his temple with his index finger. Bright as they come.

Anyway, when he were a kid the Civil War happened, so all the whites had to get rid of their slaves. He got lucky, this George fella, because the people who had owned him—the slave owners—turned out they had a sliver of conscience after all and they decided to look after him. Raise him good and educate him, and that. He weren't allowed to go to school, though, bein Black, and so they taught him at home until he got a bit older and things changed and they found this school, miles away, that would take him. He ended up goin to live with another family then, so that he could get his education. Except one day he sees all these white fellas kickin the shit out of a Black guy. They kill him, right there in front of George, and course that messes his head right up and he decides to leave, but still it don't put him off learnin. He just keeps movin from school to school, doin what he needs to do, until eventually he gets his diploma. Happy days.

He thought he were on a roll then, gets a place at college. But when he turns up and they see what color he is, they send George off on his way. And fer a while he thinks he's screwed, but then he winds up claimin this bit of land, yeah, and he starts collectin all these plants and flowers and shit. And he's good at it, lookin after it and ploughin it and gettin the most out of all these crops. He starts growin stuff like rice and corn and fruit trees. But still, he wants an education. And so a few years pass and he gets a loan, to study art and piano, but his teacher sees his talent fer plants, fer botany, and she encourages him, tells him to apply to uni in Iowa, and he's not sure because he's been knocked down that many times before but in t'end he gives it a go, sends off his application, and y'know what? He gets in! First Black student they've ever had. And after that he's flyin, right. He's top of all his classes, he's gettin people wantin a piece of him from all over.

Then when he finishes uni, he starts teachin at this other place that's been set up, this institute that's especially fer Black students, and so by doin that he's givin all these other kids a chance. And not only that, he's a mint scientist, the best around, and by this point all the white farmers have ballsed up their farms because fer years they've just been plantin cotton, over and over, so the land's all knackered. But George comes up with all these ways of makin it better, plantin peanuts and that in t'soil to improve it. Crop rotation, they call it. And that means the farmers get another way to make cash, which is good fer everyone, innit? Next thing he knows even the president gets wind of it, starts publicly admirin his work, and then bloody Gandhi's gettin in touch, all the way from India, and he wants George to help him sort out all their agricultural problems. Mad thing is, no one thought George'd ever amount to owt. But he did. Didn't matter what they all thought. He did.

My eyes had fallen closed at some point while Danny was speaking, the insides of my chest vibrating at the sound of his voice. How d'you know all that? I asked him sleepily.

Me dad told me.

You'll amount to a lot of things, Dan, I said, lifting my head toward him.

For a beat he was quiet, but then he looked down at me. I don't need you to tell me that. He grinned.

DANNY STARTED APPEARING OFTEN AFTER THAT, GIVING ME ALL the more reason to skip my lessons. I didn't think anyone would notice, but I'd forgotten about Miss Bell.

She started getting on my case more and more, commenting on how tired I looked, how withdrawn I'd become. And some of the work you're handing in, Jennifer, she said to me one day. I mean, it's interesting, certainly. But it's not really related to the syllabus.

I just thought you'd enjoy readin it. I shrugged.

Miss Bell looked perplexed then, like she didn't know what to say. I could tell she liked that I shared my words with her, it fed into her savior complex. But it's true I hadn't been paying any attention to what we were learning about in class, the assignments being set.

It must be exhausting, she said at last, changing tack. Living above a pub. When I told her it could be a lot worse, she seemed confused, like she couldn't imagine how.

I can't remember what lesson I was in when I got the

giggles, only that I'd had a smoke in the woods with Danny just before I went in. The teacher sent me out in the end, everyone staring after me like I was unhinged, but still I couldn't stop. That afternoon when I got home, Chrissy got a phone call. They wanted her to come in, for a meeting. An "intervention," that's what Mrs. Herrington called it on the phone—I know because I heard Chrissy repeat it back, her voice thick with mockery. Ooooh, an in-ter-veeeen-tiooooon, is it?

The teachers were concerned about my disinterest in the curriculum, my inability to socialize, Miss Bell explained earnestly while Mrs. Herrington sat back, observing us with a bewildered sort of disdain. We were back in her posh office, my eyes fixed to a point on the fancy rug to stop myself laughing. What a sight we must have looked. Barry like a deer in the headlights, and me and Chrissy, two bored delinquents under the gaze of haughty eyes. I could have told them from the start that this would happen. Didn't matter how smart I was, how good with words. Someone like me could never do well at a school like that. More fool them for taking the chance.

It's our duty of care, to flag it up, Miss Bell was saying, a note of unease in her voice now. And there is *potential*. Really, there is. We would just hate for someone with such talent to fall through the cracks.

Barry nodded along, at least pretending to listen, but Chrissy made a point of looking disinterested, picking at her nails, letting her eyes wander. Every so often the room would fall into silence and the three of us would cast blank sidelong looks at one another, unsure what was expected.

After a while Mrs. Herrington decided to make her presence known, clearing her throat and placing a folder on the desk that had been sitting on her lap. Inside was a stack of A4 pages, all of them filled with my handwriting. I tried to catch Miss Bell's eye but she wouldn't look at me. This was a treachery from which there would be no going back.

Generally speaking, Jennifer has failed to stay on top of her work in the majority of subjects, Mrs. Herrington yapped. But in her English class the term started off very positively.

She pulled out the essay I'd written on *The Catcher in the Rye*, laid it before Chrissy, who swallowed a yawn, crossed and uncrossed her legs.

Jennifer handed in some exceptional work, Miss Bell cut in. She really seemed engaged. But lately the work I've been receiving, although interesting and certainly well written, well . . . it's completely off-topic.

Barry frowned, confused. What d'you mean by that?

Well, said Miss Bell, shifting uncomfortably, it's all very creative. Lots of short stories and imaginings. Some interesting poetry. But the themes are concerning. Domestic violence, drug use. Some rather unsavory characters—apart from anything, the work simply isn't in line with the assignments being set. Now, as much as we admire Jennifer's writing, there is a syllabus to adhere to—

Right, Chrissy cut in. So what you're sayin is, she's got wrong end of t'stick. About the work she's meant to be doin, is that it?

Not exactly, I—

So she just needs to get her head round what work's bein set, is that what it is?

Well, perhaps, but it's more—

Here's an idea fer yer, then. Chrissy was up on her feet now. Mebbe it's your job, as a teacher, to make sure she understands better. Whatever it is you're tryin to teach her. Because it seems to me like we're payin you a right lot of money fer not a right lot of teachin.

Miss Bell's eyes widened in surprise and Mrs. Herrington smiled thinly. I'm not sure—

Chrissy left the room before Mrs. Herrington had finished her sentence. I trotted after her, leaving Barry to mumble a stream of half-baked apologies.

Stuck-up cow, Chrissy muttered as she clip-clopped down the wooden staircase in her heels. And that silly bint wi t'glasses, did she get dressed in t'dark?

The school never called them back in again after that. I don't suppose they really cared about me falling through the cracks. So long as Barry paid the bills on time.

21

The first of Denz's disappearing acts that I was around for happened just before my first Christmas at the pub. We'd been over at his the day before, and the next morning Mary took it upon herself to go into Danny's room while he was still asleep, fish all the dirty clothes up off his floor, so she could put a wash on before she set off for her shift. It hadn't crossed Danny's mind that she might do that. That she might rummage through his pockets and find the little baggy we'd lifted from Denz.

Mary dragged Danny out of the bed, yelling at the top of her voice, eyes shining, threats of phone calls to the police, demands to tell her what was going on, what the bloody hell was going on, this minute, this instant, Danny. I'm not doin this again, she raged. I'm not goin through it all again.

They turned up at the pub not an hour later, Barry summoning me solemnly down the stairs to the back bar, where Danny stood bleary-eyed in the middle of the room like a circus exhibit, hands thrust deep in his pockets, eyes to the floor. The three grown-ups triangulated around him: Barry looking awkward; Mary with a face like thunder; Chrissy perched on a high stool by the bar, still in her dressing gown, a cig in her hand and an amused look on her face. I wanted to step forward, lean into Danny, rest my hand in the crook of his elbow, but instead I hung back in the doorway, curious as to how the scene would play out.

Come on then, Barry said, turning to me and crossing his arms over his chest in an attempt at authority that made me want to look away, embarrassed for him. Out with it.

What?

Tell us where you got them. The drugs.

I pressed my lips between my teeth to stifle a giggle, knowing that if I looked up at Chrissy she'd be doing the same. But it was Danny who let out a guffaw, leaning his head back to stare at the ceiling, smoothing his palm over his canerows in exasperation. Mary's eyes burned into him.

Think it's bloody funny, do yer, Danny? Eh?

Oh, come on. Chrissy took a drag of her cig and then blew out a stream of smoke, fanning it away with her hand as the rest of us turned to look at her. Bit of an overreaction, innit? Fer a ten bag of weed?

Barry rocked back on his heels awkwardly, his eyes darting from Mary to Chrissy.

Overreaction, is it? Mary said quietly, her eyes ablaze. Overreaction? Well, let me ask you this, Chrissy. She pointed at me, her hand trembling. Let me ask yer. Will it still be an overreaction when your daughter's life is destroyed by these people? When it's your daughter who ends up in the ground because of the shit they get her mixed up in? Because that were me once, in your shoes. But if I'd known, if I'd had the chance to see the warnin signs, trust me gut . . . well. Mebbe it would all be a different story.

I had only been half listening before Mary spoke, my mind flitting between the scene playing out in front of me and thoughts of food and a smoke, and how Danny and I would spend the rest of the day. But her words brought my focus back into the room and I looked around, confused. I was waiting for the lecture, the scolding, the unfolding of a petty melodrama that would be more of a box-ticking exercise in parenting than anything else. Instead there was something else playing out, something bigger and deeper and tentacled, somehow. My eyes went to Danny, his head bowed now, rubbing his toe into the worn carpet. I felt a chill on my neck, my stomach turning and sinking and turning again. I wanted to say something, but instead I just stood there, my tongue thick in my mouth.

Chrissy pulled a face. What you goin on about, Mary?

What I'm goin on about, she spat, is that his father, his piece-of-shit-of-a-so-called-father, and all the scumbags that come with him have been givin these kids drugs. Int that right, Danny?

Danny didn't lift his gaze from the floor, his shoulders tense.

Well? Am I right? Him and all his—Mary looked to me now, waved her hand vaguely—his *lot*. Am I right?

Jesus, Mary—

Don't you "Jesus Mary" me, Chrissy! I would know. I've lived through it once and that's enough. These people have different morals, different ideas. And it int right. It int *right*. I'll be damned if I'll stand by and watch it happen all over again.

I had the feeling in that moment of losing my balance, as though the floor below my feet had lost its solidity, the room itself suddenly off-kilter. Danny's words from that day on the old railway line played over in my head. *It's different to how it is for you.*

Danny was standing straight now, his chin lifted, angry. No, not angry perhaps. But defiant. Detached. I waited for him to speak but instead he just looked at Mary, a look that made him appear much older than his fourteen years.

Nobody called after him when he turned and walked out of the pub.

LATER, AS I EAVESDROPPED FROM THE TOP OF THE STAIRS, I heard the phone call Mary made, telling Denz in no uncertain terms that he wouldn't be seeing Danny again for the foreseeable; that if he tried, so much as *tried*, to get in touch with him she'd have the police all over him in a second. You know they'd be more than happy to pay you another visit, she said. I don't know what Denz replied on the other end but I was sure he wouldn't have liked being spoken to like that.

For a week there was no sign of Danny, no answer when I rang the house phone or knocked on the front door or threw pebbles at the closed windows. Mary turned up to work every morning with her eyes red and sore-looking, barely even glancing at me. Over her dead body was Denz seeing Danny this Christmas, I'd heard her saying to Barry. Not after what had happened with Kim.

. . .

THE SATURDAY BEFORE CHRISTMAS THE PUB WAS PACKED. BARRY had got the DJ to come in at lunchtime, the speakers cranked up, The Pogues and Roy Wood and Mariah Carey on repeat, the girls from the hairdresser's singing along tunelessly, their voices high-pitched and laced with booze. If Danny had been there, we'd have spent all day getting pissed on the dregs at the bottom of other people's glasses, but I'd lost hope of him showing up. Instead I hung around on my own in the back bar, watching everyone dancing about and acting daft. Someone knocked a pint of cider all over my leg and, as if to make up for it, someone else threw me up in the air and onto their shoulders, swaying about while they belted out the lyrics, wishing it could be Christmas every day, stumbling from left to right with each syllable. I was laughing, holding on for dear life, when I saw Danny come in, the hood of his puffer jacket low over his eyes. He shoved his way through the crowd toward the kitchen, ignoring the girl from the chip shop grabbing for his arm, the bloke who lived across the road from him calling out his name.

The fella who'd lifted me up on his shoulders seemed to have forgotten I was there and I slid down awkwardly, landing on my bum on the carpet. Someone trod on my hand as I scrambled up, clambering through arms and legs to get to Danny. I found him sitting in the hallway between the back bar and the kitchen, hunched over on the windowsill.

You all right? I said, not sure if he'd noticed me come in. He didn't look up. There was enough space for me to have sat beside him but I hung back, leaning against the wall instead. The song had changed now, a boyband. The video played on the music channels nonstop in the lead-up to Christmas, me and Danny pissing ourselves at the daft lads dressed in fluffy white anoraks begging their birds to stay. I tried to catch Danny's eye to see if he'd laugh, but they were fixed to a point on the floor. A blast of cold air ripped down the narrow hallway as a group of blokes lurched in through the back door, wrapped up in coats and scarves and hats, while their girlfriends tottered behind them, giggling and stumbling in their high heels and short skirts. I shivered, pulled my arms tight around my chest, taking a step closer toward the warmth of the kitchen.

Shall we ask yer nan if she'll make us summat to eat? When Danny looked up, I was shocked to see he'd been crying. I lowered my eyes, embarrassed for him. We weren't criers, me and Danny.

Me dad's gone to Spain.

Spain?

Yeah, he mumbled, his voice gruff. Been ringin him all week, man. To tell him about Nan, goin off on one. But he ain't been answerin and so I went over there. Got the bus up. No one answered the door and so I went to Lewis's and he told me. Got a job there, last minute. Be back in a few month.

I nodded uncertainly, kept my eyes down.

Where's yer mum?

Chrissy? I frowned, confused. In t'bar. Pissed up. Why?

A shadow of relief darted across Danny's face and he nodded.

What you wantin to know about her fer?

A shrug. No reason, he said.

You spendin Christmas with us then?

He looked at me, a glint in his eye. Looks like I ain't got a choice.

THE PUB WAS MEANT TO BE CLOSED ON CHRISTMAS DAY, BUT Barry decided he'd open up for an hour before lunch, so some of the old boys could come in while their dinner was getting cooked. He never said it, but I reckon he'd been hoping Chrissy might be in the kitchen doing the same for him. Course the offer never came and, in the end, he asked Mary if she'd help him out behind the bar, said he'd pay her double and a half for her time and then we could all have Christmas dinner together. That meant Mary cooking it, mind. She agreed, although she moaned about it enough. But I reckon she was glad really. She wouldn't have had much fun just her and Danny that year.

It might sound strange to anyone else, but that first Christmas at the pub was the best one I'd ever had. Most Christmases I'd known, Chrissy would either be hungover from the night before or getting on it with whoever happened to be living in the flats at the time. It was the same for most of us kids round there. A few did it properly, put up a tree and had a turkey and that for dinner. But it was never like Christmas in books or on the telly. By lunchtime there'd normally be a gaggle of us knocking about in the park or traipsing the footbridges, the bigger ones hoisting the bairns on their hips, copycatting the voices of the grown-ups around us. *Who does she think she is, dirty slag? I'll knock er head off next time I see er.* Staying out of the firing line while the real adults took their feelings out on the neck of a bottle.

That year was different, though. Barry let us deck the whole pub out at the start of December with tinsel and flashing lights, and when Danny and I had gone foraging in the cellar we'd found a great big plastic tree buried under a load of old crates. It didn't matter that it smelt like stale beer, and the stand was rusting at the bottom; once we got all the baubles and lights on, it were beautiful.

Danny was still in a mard when he got there on Christmas morning, but I'd snuck us half a bottle of rum from the bar and that seemed to cheer him up for a bit. The locals took forever to bugger off, the phone was ringing off the hook all morning with peeved wives trying to track down their already half-cut husbands. It was Danny and me that got tasked with answering it, yelling out the messages across the bar.

Terry, Sue says if you're not home in the next ten minutes, the dog's gettin yer dinner!

Nigel, Lisa says she's had enough; her and the kids are off to her mam's, and you're not invited!

Peter, Janet says she don't give a flyin fuck if it's Christmas, she told you HALF AN HOUR ago to get yer arse back, and you're takin t'piss now!

We'd fall about laughing after each one, the messages getting more irate with every five minutes that passed, until finally the last punter had stumbled out of the door, the threats of his missus still ringing in our ears. It was midafternoon by the time we sat down around the dining table in the front room of the apartment. It felt strange, us all being up there. Good strange, though. We'd have looked like a proper little family to anyone that didn't know us. Barry and Mary the doting grandparents, serving up the food and one-liners. Danny and me their spoiled grandkids, the pair of us both done out in new tracksuits and trainers. And Chrissy. The auntie maybe, or their moody grown-up daughter, pushing the food around her plate, refilling her glass twice as quick as anyone else. Every so often I'd catch her gazing out of the window toward the river and the main road, and then she'd see me, look away quickly, try and pretend she was laughing along to one of Barry's endless crap jokes.

I don't know how it came to it that Mary started crying. It seemed like one minute we were all having a laugh, the alcohol finally seeming to have lifted Chrissy's mood, Barry trying to persuade each of us to have a turn on the karaoke machine he'd dragged up from downstairs. And then next thing I knew, Mary was crying, proper crying with her shoulders shaking and her head in her hands.

We seemed to all notice it at the same time, except for Chrissy, who by now was over at the window, swaying hazily to the music, her arms weaving shapes in the space above her head. Mary kept saying she was sorry, she didn't want to make a fuss, it was just the time of year, always hard at this time of year. Barry nodded along, making reassuring noises, patting her awkwardly on the back, while Danny sat there at the dining table, his elbows on his knees, eyes to the floor.

I just miss our Kim so much, Barry. I really do.

That was when Danny stood up, grabbed me by the wrist and dragged me to my feet. Come on.

I didn't argue, followed him out of the room. He took the stairs two at a time, past the kitchen and out the back door toward the beer garden, so fast that I had to run to keep up. The tables were scabbed over with frost but he pulled himself up to sit on one anyway. I moved in beside him, tried to huddle in but he was tense, his body rigid, so I inched away, dragged down the sleeves of my tracksuit to cover my hands. From his pocket Danny pulled out the rum, took a slug and then passed it to me, our mouths curling as the liquid burned our throats. It was late afternoon but already it was dark, the steam from our breath lit up by the fairy lights at the back of the pub. I could see Chrissy's figure silhouetted in the glow of the living room, swaying still, oblivious to Mary's tears.

She always does this, Danny said after a minute or two, nodding his head up toward the window. Every Christmas. She gets pissed, and then she cries.

I didn't know what to say and so I sat there mute, the silence stretching out between us. When Danny spoke again it was muffled, his chin burrowed into the collar of his hoodie so that I had to strain to hear him.

You know she hates me dad, don't yer?

I scuffed the soles of my feet across the surface of the bench, making a scratching sound on the ice. Don't seem to be many round here that like him, Dan.

Danny made a noise at the back of his throat. No, he said. There int.

We passed the bottle back and forth between us and Danny lifted his face to the sky, his eyes searching the stars. He went to school round here. Me dad. Did you know that?

I was surprised. Denz always seemed like an outsider when he came into the town. No, I didn't know, I told him.

Yeah. He nodded. He were a year older than me mum, same difference as there is between me and you, pretty much. Told me that he used to see her when he were gettin off the school bus, walkin down t'street with her mates. Said there were summat about her that caught his eye, a look she had that made it seem as though she were always halfway through crackin a joke. He said she were pretty too, nice hair. Dark but red, sort of, when the light caught it. But that weren't what he liked the most about her. He liked her cos she were smart.

I took another swig of the rum, drunk now, half spellbound by Danny's voice; half hoping he'd be done soon, so we could go back upstairs.

When she were in third year she won the prize fer Science and had to go up onstage in front of the whole school to collect it, he said, taking the bottle from me and toying with it absentmindedly in his hands. Me dad liked her even more after that, because Science were his favorite subject too. He'd always thought he were good at it, even though none of the teachers did. He'd wanted to talk to her then but he lost sight of her when they all walked out the hall, and then it were summer and he lived in Leeds, and her just round t'corner from the high school, in me nana's house. My bedroom used to be hers, in fact.

Danny brought the last of the rum up to his lips and then launched the empty bottle into the beer garden. It must have landed in the grass, though, because we didn't hear it smash. I let my head fall against his shoulder, my eyes half closed as he carried on.

Me dad said there weren't a minute of that six weeks he didn't think about her. Said he made his mind up that when he went back after the holidees he'd say hi, strike up a conversation, ask her if she fancied meetin up with him one weekend, to go to this museum he knew in Bradford mebbe. But when he finally caught sight of her on that first week of school, up behind the bike sheds havin a smoke, it were like his mouth dried up. He just stood there feelin shy and lookin awkward and thinkin how lame it were, to offer to take this girl, this lovely girl, to a bloody museum of all places, in bloody Bradford, which might as well have been a different country then.

Anyway he's standin there, loiterin about, and she sees him—me mum. Except she weren't me mum yet, then. And so she asks him, are you after a cig? And he turns round and goes—Danny chuckled incredulously, shook his head as though the memory were his own—nah, I don't smoke, not them anyway. And so she laughed and said what you doin round here then? He says he got embarrassed then, all her mates standin there givin him dirty looks, and he were just about to forget it when she walks over to him.

When they started talkin, me dad said it were like they couldn't stop. They talked the whole of that lunch break and he would've carried on all afternoon, except she didn't want to skip her next lesson because it were double Science, and he understood that. He asked her if they could meet after school instead, before he caught the bus, and she said yeah. Said she liked the way he looked at her. Liked the way he looked.

Danny quietened, took a deep breath and I felt the shudder in his ribs. Christmas always reminds me nana of me mum, he said. Cos it were Christmas time. When she died.

I sat up straight, made a point of looking up toward the window. I wanted to go back inside, pretend this bit hadn't happened, return to the Christmas-card vignette we'd been playing out upstairs.

Don't you wanna know the rest?

I bit my lip, my face still turned away from him. A moment passed and then I nodded, said yeah, for his sake more than mine.

She went to a party. With me dad. And she never came back.

I waited for more but Danny was quiet. I only asked him because I knew he wanted me to. Where did she go?

She didn't go nowhere, he said flatly, his voice drained of emotion now. That were it. She went to the party. And then she died.

It was half a story, not even that. I didn't know if Danny knew more, if that was all he wanted to tell me. Or if that was all he'd ever been told, all the details anyone had ever given him. But I didn't care, didn't want to find out. Perhaps I was afraid, but mostly I was selfish. I didn't want to talk about it, didn't want to turn the day into being about his dead mam or what his dad had to do with it or any of that stuff. I just wanted to carry on play-acting. For one day I wanted it to feel like we were normal, like we were a family, all of us, having Christmas like people are supposed to. I jumped down from the table, wrapped my arms around myself.

It's freezin, I said. I'm off back inside.

Upstairs it was almost like nothing had happened. Chrissy had climbed up onto the sofa cushions now, the palms of her hands slapping against one another, missing the beat of the music, while Barry and Mary watched glassy-eyed, singing along halfheartedly, lit cigarettes dangling from their fingers. I climbed up onto the cushions, took Chrissy's hands in mine and she stumbled, giggled. Barry pulled out one of his throwaway cameras and Chrissy and I posed together, paper crowns perched on our heads, blowing kisses and pulling faces until the film roll ran out and we collapsed on top of one another, the weight of the day pressing down on us.

22

I am downstairs in the half dark of the caff, trying to straighten my thoughts and rid myself of them, all at the same time. More than two hours have passed since we closed, since I waved Fi and Ali off and watched them cross the street hand-in-hand. Denz has kept his word, hasn't been in touch since the day he gave me his number, and I'm glad of it. I am. I swear I am.

A migraine pulls at the back of my head, drawing my vision into my skull. I crave sleep, but I know it will evade me. Still, I drag myself upstairs, sit on the bed heavily, but instead of lying down I slide open the bedside drawer, retrieve Denz's number for the millionth time. It takes me forever to type the text into my phone, but in the end it is brief.

Let's talk.

Denz replies straight away, knows it's me even though I

didn't sign off with either of my names. By the time he arrives, the rain has begun, pounding against the pavements
in hard, wet sheets. We sit inside the caff with the blinds
closed, the telly off for a change. I put the kettle on, make a
pot of tea and he watches me with a strange look in his eye.

It's good to hear from you, Neef, he says as I stand at the
counter with my back to him. I weren't sure if I would. First
few days I were checkin me phone every two minutes, it
were sendin me mental. I nearly came here again, to t'caff,
but . . . well, I promised I'd leave you alone until I heard
otherwise. I weren't gonna go back on that.

Denz's voice, the shape of his words, hasn't changed, and
the warmth of it chills me. For years I've tried to shake off
my accent, the certain melodies and intonations. But listening
to him, I can hear it rising up in me again. That familiarity,
that terrifying comfort. He has been talking fast, too fast, but
now he pauses, hesitates.

I've been away in fact. Had to get out of here, only got
back last night. I been up north.

I turn to look at him and our eyes meet.

To see me daughter.

At the mention of her, my breath catches in my throat.
Nia? I hear myself say, although my voice doesn't sound
quite right.

He nods. Yeah.

Slowly I walk over to the table, pull out the chair across
from him. Do you have a picture of her?

Denz looks at me warily, his lips moving ever so slightly
as though he is about to say something. But then he pulls his
phone from his jacket pocket, scrolls his thumb across the
screen and passes it to me. I rest my chin in my hands, the

nerve in my temple pulsing against the pads of my fingers as I look down at the young girl staring back at me, her arms wrapped around Denz's neck, her cheek resting on his shoulder. How well I once knew the set of that jaw, the curve of those cheekbones, the clear, dark depth of those eyes.

She's not a baby anymore, I say, pushing the phone back toward Denz.

He nods. Sixteen this summer. All grown-up.

She live in Leeds?

Denz keeps his eyes on the screen. Yeah. Yeah, she does.

I want to know more, but I don't know if I'm ready. The silence between us feels loaded, the sound of the clock ticking on the wall like a grenade. What's she like? I ask at last.

The corners of his mouth turn up as he thinks over my question. She's tall, he says. Plays basketball for the school. Mad on sport. That and not much else. Never got into ballet, like a lot of the girls in her class. Her mum took her once when Nia were about three. She wouldn't even go in t'door. Insisted we took her to karate instead.

Denz picks up the phone, puts it in his pocket. Her and Danny look so alike, man, it's mad, he says, his eyes clouding. But they're different. With Nia, what you see is what you get—you can take one look at her face and know everythin she's thinkin. But with Danny, everythin runs so deep.

There is a piece of loose skin around my bitten-down thumbnail and I pick at it with my fingers, before bringing it up to my mouth, pulling at it with my teeth. Denz watches me.

He never changed, y'know. Danny. All he ever wanted to do were learn. When he were small he'd sit and listen to me teach him about all sorts, and he'd remember it too. Head like a bloody encyclopedia, that kid. But in the end, there were nowt I could tell him that he didn't already know. Plants, history, geography—

What about her mam? I say, cutting Denz off. Nia's mam? You still with her?

Denz makes a face, half smile, half grimace, shakes his head. Didn't work out. I've given up on women. I can never make it work.

Because of Kim.

Kim?

Because you never got over Kim. That's why you couldn't make it work with anyone else.

For a moment Denz is still, then he leans back, rubbing his hands over his face. Kim were years ago, Jen. I were a kid—we were kids.

Doesn't mean you didn't love her, just because you were kids.

No. No, it don't. But it don't mean I never moved on, either. I ain't hung me whole life up on a relationship I had when I were sixteen years old. Life int like that. You get over it, you move on. That's what I never understood with you and Danny, see, he says, the tone of his voice harder now. Why the fuck couldn't you move on?

I pull at the loose skin, peeling away a thin white strip that curls down the length of my nailbed, a bead of blood springing up from the rawness underneath.

What d'you think I've been trying to do all these years, Denz?

He looks at me then as though realizing something, shakes his head, angry with himself. Sorry. Sorry, I didn't mean that. Me temper gets the better of me, Danny used to tell me that all the time.

He pauses, takes a breath before speaking again.

And that's why I'm here, why I wanted to talk to you, Neef. Jen. See, no one ever understood Danny like you did. I know it were a long time ago, I know you've built a different life for yourself . . . Denz trails off, looks at me questioningly.

What?

Well, have you? Built a life? I dunno. Do you have . . . friends? A partner?

That's none of your business.

No, I didn't mean—sorry, I just . . . He is embarrassed, tries again. Your woman that runs this place seems nice. Her and the Indian fella.

He's Iranian.

Right. Yeah. He nods awkwardly. And they look after you? They see that you're okay?

I'm a grown woman, Denz.

I know, yeah. I know.

But it would make you feel better, wouldn't it? If you knew I had someone looking out for me. Am I right?

Well . . . yeah, I mean—

Because it wasn't only Danny you took from me, was it?

Denz holds my gaze but he doesn't speak, and I see the guilt there in his eyes, know I am in control.

You want me to talk to you. But why should I tell you anything when there's still so much you've kept from me?

What you gettin at, Neef?

The air stills as I stare at him, the question I've been wanting him to answer for all these years burning the tip of my tongue. Tell me what happened to my mam.

He shifts in his seat, his eyes sliding from mine. When he looks back at me, he is the old Denz again. Guarded, dis-

dainful. A cut above me and everyone else. What is it you
want to know?

Were you in love with her?

Silence.

Well? I push.

Well, what?

You were sleeping with Chrissy, weren't you? I say slowly,
trying to keep my anger in check.

Denz glances at the door as though readying himself to
leave. I'm not here to talk about Chrissy.

I shake my head in disbelief. It's all one and the same,
Denz, can you not see that? Kim. Chrissy. Danny. How can
we talk, how can I talk to you if—

Fine, he says, shrugging. Yeah. Me and Chrissy had . . . a
thing.

A "thing"?

Yeah. For a bit. She were a good-lookin girl, you know
that.

Heat courses through me and I press my nails into the
flesh of my palms beneath the table. Chrissy was a drug ad-
dict, I say quietly.

Denz frowns. Yeah?

You know she was. And you always said you hated drugs.

I did. I do.

So why her?

For the briefest of moments, it feels as though at last
Denz will help me to understand. But just as quickly, it
passes.

Like I said. He shrugs. It were nowt more than a thing.

I know what he is doing. He is trying to make me believe
Chrissy never mattered, that we were all so much better off

without her. I want to bring my fist down on the table, slam it hard. But I will not give him the satisfaction and instead I take a breath. Fine, I say. If you won't tell me about my mam, tell me about Danny's. Tell me about Kim. The party you took her to. How she died.

A look comes across him then that is sad and regretful and angry, all at once, and I know I have got him now. I know he feels things too. Denz wipes his palms down the length of his face as if to rid himself of his thoughts. I aren't gonna talk about that, Neef. Let it go.

He scrapes his chair back, pauses for a moment before walking to the door. The bell overhead jangles as it closes behind him, and I have the urge to throw something at it. Our every interaction is futile, a never-ending circle, and I am sick of it, the back and forth, the tug-of-war over history's secrets, the invasion of my life. Only Denz could expect so much from someone and give so little in return.

I walk toward the cupboard under the stairs where Fion-noula keeps the old vacuum cleaner, drag the heavy contraption from its depths with a clatter and shove the plug into the socket. My hand shakes as the machine whirs to life, but still there is not enough noise and so I switch on the radio, the telly too. Turn the volume up, up, up. Sink down with my back against the wall, drowning in the noise, the din, the roar. Too loud to hear myself think.

wo days later, Denz sends me a message.

I'm outside, it says.

I want to ignore him but I'm too far in to walk away now.

We catch the bus to Brixton Market, packed with kids just out of school. Their voices carry across the rows, their brashness making Denz's jaw tighten. A boy of fourteen or fifteen plays drill music loudly on his phone, yelling to someone at the back of the bus, plans to link up later on. The driver takes a corner and the boy stumbles into Denz, who shoves him back harder than is necessary. For a moment it looks as though it might all kick off, but the heat in Denz's stare stops the boy in his tracks.

We get off outside the station and although I know the market well, I let Denz lead the way. He chooses a Colombian café on the corner, offers to go inside to order a drink.

Beer? Wine? he says.

Just a Coke.

When he returns he seems distracted, his mind elsewhere.

It's changed a lot, this place, he says, looking around the market, taking in the artsy boutiques, the hipster diners where the price of a hot drink feels like a joke at the expense of anyone on the minimum wage. Brixton used to be about community, Denz grimaces. Used to be about feelin like you belong.

Is that what you thought about the pub, too? I say, wanting to bring the conversation back to us, to why I'm here. That you didn't belong?

He laughs humorlessly. That weren't about belongin. They just straight up didn't like me.

Because of what happened to Kim.

Denz sits back in his seat, exasperated. Come on, Neef. What?

You really think that? You think that's the reason they gave me such a hard time?

I stare at him in silence, the discomfort of what he is saying taking shape before the words have even been spoken.

You ever see another bloke that looked like me in that pub? A Black fella? Apart from me and Danny?

That's because there was hardly anyone Black in the whole town—

Well, there you go then. There you go. He holds up his hands, palms open, as though there is no further need for explanation, but it irks me, how simple he makes it sound.

It was wrong, the way people acted in that town, I say. But

it wasn't me treating you—treating Danny—that way. And don't you think I felt it too? Don't you think they judged me, made me feel like I didn't belong?

Denz picks up his fork, taps the tines against his plate irritably. You still don't get it, do you, Neef? he says.

We are interrupted by a waiter, a young man with an impossibly pretty face and the energy of an eager-to-please puppy. He slides a plate of steaming tamales in front of us and sets about describing them in excruciating detail. Denz nods along at first, but I can see he is losing patience.

All right, mate, you can leave us to it now, yeah?

The waiter looks taken aback, scurries off with chastened eyes.

Place is full of out-of-work actors, innit? Denz mutters, leaning forward to peel back the banana leaves, prodding at the contents with his fork.

You always did have a short fuse.

You sound like Danny. Plenty alike, me and our Danny. Apart from our tolerance for fools.

Danny was nothing like you, I snap.

Denz raises his eyebrows. I wish that were true.

I want him to explain what he means, but I am too stubborn to ask him. Instead I watch him cut his food into chunks, chew it slowly.

You know, Danny . . . He were very down before he disappeared, he says at last. And not just then. I could see it for years, creepin up in him. Not all the time, mind. On and off. But that's what it's like. I should know.

There is a labor to Denz's speech, as though each word is trying. He wipes his mouth with a napkin, the slow precision of the gesture somehow betraying his nerves.

See, you might not think Danny and I were all that alike, but there's a lot you don't know about me, Neef. We all got minds. We all got feelings.

Danny had feelings too, did you ever think of that? I snarl. Ever think of how much it hurt him, all those times you let him down? Disappearing for weeks on end without so much as a goodbye?

I can tell my words have cut deep, feel a mix of triumph and guilt at the broken look on Denz's face.

I aren't makin excuses for meself . . . He stops, scrunches a napkin in his fist. This int an easy thing to admit. Not for someone like me any rate. But I ain't always been that well upstairs meself.

Denz takes a deep breath, and I realize I am holding mine.

They used to call it "the black dog" when I were young, but it weren't summat people spoke about, he carries on. Started after Kim died. I'd be all right for a while and then summat would trigger me—the tiniest of things—and I'd lose it, for months sometimes. They used to tell him I were workin away, because it were the kindest thing to do. I never wanted him to see me in them states. I'd rather let him think I'd abandoned him than find out I were a head case. It never crossed my mind that it might be in our blood, that he could feel the same way I did, one day.

Denz reaches for his glass, and I see that his fingers are trembling. It takes me a moment to absorb what I have just heard. The conversation hasn't gone as I had planned: toward Chrissy, toward Kim. And yet there is a feeling like the coming-together of things, a piece pressed into an unfinished jigsaw. I rub at my eyes, trying to adjust them to this alternate version of a man I thought I knew. I have the urge to tell Denz about

Chrissy, about when I was little, all the days she would stay
in bed, the emptiness in her stare. But before I can form the
words, Denz starts to speak again.

When you left—he looks up at me warily—when I . . .
when I asked you to leave, I started seein it in Danny, the
mopin about, the feelin sorry for himself, and it made me
angry. I wanted him to understand, to see I'd done him a
favor by gettin you out of his life—

Jesus, I mutter. Our moment of connectivity has passed.
The old Denz is back, his words iced with blame.

I aren't gonna apologize, Neef. I stand by it still. You don't
know how dangerous you were to a kid like Danny. I could
see it a mile off. I had no choice but to get him away from
you. And sometimes, yeah, he seemed to get it. He got stuck
in at college, set up his own business for a bit. He had his
own place, a little allotment the end of his street. I tried to kid
meself that he were happy but I knew he weren't, not really.
He used to disappear for these weekends all by himself,
never tell anyone where he were goin. Then he'd come back
and sometimes he'd be better, but sometimes he'd be worse,
much worse. Every time I'd try to talk to him about it, about
gettin a girlfriend or at least tryin to make some friends, we'd
end up in a row. There were plenty of times we weren't on
speakin terms, and I know that's my fault. I know I weren't
the dad I should've been to him, but I never thought he'd . . .
he'd just . . .

Denz looks at me then, and I see the fear in his eyes. I
don't know where his head were at, he says quietly. After we
lost touch.

I feel cold suddenly, my heart beating too fast. All the
possible scenarios of what Danny's disappearance might
mean.

Denz leans forward, pleading. Tell me, Neef. Jen. Please, be honest with me. Have you heard from him?

Denz. I am telling you. I haven't spoken to Danny in fifteen years.

His eyes stay on me for a long time. Do you think what Lewis said is true? Do you think Danny is in London?

24

I n the weeks that followed that first Christmas, Danny drew so far inside himself that I began to wonder if he'd ever come back. Mary brushed it off, said it was always like this when Denz pulled one of his disappearing acts. Danny would have the wind knocked out of him for a few weeks and then slowly, slowly, he'd put himself back together. But as soon as he'd found his feet, there would be Denz, pulling the rug from under him, breaking Danny to pieces all over again. I didn't point out to her that this time she'd been the one to make Denz disappear.

Danny stopped coming to call on me at the pub, said he didn't like the way it felt in there. I never asked him what he meant by that, I didn't want to hear the answer. Instead I would go to Mary's, where I would find him turning the ground in his little garden, doing everything he could to keep it alive despite the freezing cold. And always he would greet me with a grin, even if there was, by then, a little less light in his eyes.

He was suspended from school for the first time soon after Christmas. Mary blamed it on Denz, of course.

See what I mean? Messes with Danny's head, makes him act all out of character, all this comin and goin, so the poor kid don't know his arse from his elbow.

I was still on a break from Boroughford for the Christmas holidays when it happened. I'd walked up to meet him outside the high school at the end of the day. I knew a few of the kids by then, vaguely. Ste, Greeny, Donna, Chelsea and the rest of that raggedy crew, all of them dawdling out of the gates, a couple of them nodding in my direction.

Lookin fer yer fella, are yer? Ste hollered from the pavement on the other side of the road. Sorry, love. Tyson's already gone home.

They all fell about laughing at that but I didn't say anything back, just set off walking in the direction of Mary's house. I found Danny in the greenhouse, saw straight away the lavender blooms across his knuckles.

What happened?

Got in a fight, didn't I?

With who?

What does that matter?

D'you want some ice?

Danny glanced at his hand, gave a half smile. I hope I did worse to his face.

We walked into the house silently, the ground crunching under our feet from the January frost. The garden should have looked a state, but even barren, it seemed beautiful.

I found some peas in the freezer, wrapped them up in a tea towel the way I'd done for Chrissy so many times before. Pressed them onto Danny's swollen bones.

They want me to shave me hair off, Danny said after a while.

What?

This new teacher. Says it int policy. Says I've got to shave it off.

I looked up at Danny, confused, but his eyes were glazed, narrowed.

He pulls me up today, man. Outside assembly. What you come dressed up as? he goes. Snoop Doggy Dogg? Tells me it int school policy to have me hair like this. Danny gestured to the neatly braided canerows lining his scalp. Tells me to go to the bathroom and take em out. So I says no. And he says, you aren't special. Int no reason fer you to be able to break rules everyone else has to stick to. Go. Now. Take em out. So I says, it's gonna look a lot worse, sir, if I take it out. All right then, he says, go home. Shave it off. And I look at him like he's mad, and I says, you shave yours off, sir. But he ignores that, course he does. He just goes: go home. Don't come back until they're gone. Course there's a whole bunch of em standin there gawkin by this point, so I'm like, yeah, all right, suits me, man, and even though it's pissed me off, I'm keepin my cool, I start walkin. And then I hear em all laughin and I'm thinkin, what's so funny? And when I turn round I see what it is. He's behind me doin this walk, yeah, like he's carryin carpets or some shit. And fer some reason, I dunno . . . Danny took a deep breath. I lost it, didn't I? Lamped him.

Who?

The teacher, man. The teacher.

The incident marked Danny for the rest of the years he was at that school. Mary started getting calls from them two, three times every week, so many that in the end she didn't even bother answering. He's brought it on himself, she'd say. Why's he got to wear his hair like that, anyway? Why's he got to make himself stand out any more than he already bloody well does?

When the suspension came to an end two weeks later, Danny returned to a hero's welcome, his features sharpened, hardened by the black stubble cropped short to his skull. The school labeled him a bad influence, a troublemaker, a consistent catalyst of disruption, and yet belting a teacher had earned him a twisted sort of respect among his classmates. That afternoon I found him loitering outside the school gates, standing shoulder-to-shoulder with Ste. The pair of them were laughing at a girl with long, dark hair worn high on the crown of her head, one hand on her hip, the other moving around animatedly in front of her as she spoke. At one point she leaned forward, shoved Danny playfully on the shoulder. He caught her wrist and she squealed in mock annoyance, masking her delight while I hung back on the other side of the road.

At first it seemed as though Danny liked his newfound notoriety, the way Ste and the rest of them buzzed around him like flies to shit. He'd gone from being the loner, the outcast, to being one of the in-kids. Mary's words about trying harder to fit in, to not be so bloody *different* all the time, had sunk in, even if he had put his own spin on them.

It wasn't long before we started knocking about with them all, going down the river or up to the park across the bridge, past the leisure center toward the posh end where the big houses were. No one paid much heed to me, I was only there because of Danny. One or two of the lads had a crack early on, but they soon decided I wasn't worth the bother.

We never did much of anything other than just stand around, the girls flirting with Danny, the lads blowing smoke up his arse. Someone usually had cigs, and more often than not I got my hands on some booze from the pub. Danny didn't mind a drink, but he didn't have a taste for it like me. I liked the way it untied my tongue, let me make jokes that people laughed at, say things that sounded clever and witty and good. Danny said it made him feel aggro, said he was much happier when he had a smoke. I knew that meant he was thinking about Denz.

We were at the park by the river on the night when a couple of the lads started winding me up. I'd got tipsy too early, perched on a bench with a bottle of cider, pretending not to see two of the girls vie for Danny's attention over at the climbing frame. Ste and Greeny stood in front of me, bouncing a football between one another. I could tell they were watching me, egging each other on.

There's a rumor goin round about yer mam and one them Gyppos that were stoppin up by t'school, Greeny said after a while. My cheeks burned, but I kept my voice level.

Oh yeah?

Yeah. She's meant to be shaggin that tall one wi t'long hair. He smirked. Me dad's mate saw em down the lorry car park, said they were proper goin fer it. He peered at me closely, his greasy fringe hanging in his eyes. Ste let out a nasty laugh just as Danny looked up from the climbing frame.

Shut the fuck up, Greeny.

Greeny sniggered, tossed the ball toward a hoop a few yards from where I sat, but I saw Ste's face darken.

The sky dimmed and I got up to go for a pee in the bushes. It was only when I'd finished that I realized Ste was standing there. The sight of him made me lose my footing, so that I slid down the bank. A moment later he was on the ground with me, his face coming toward mine, a hand on the softness of my chest. It took me a second to understand what was happening, to lunge back and pull away. I tried to stand but he reached for my hips, locking me down, laughing like it was a game until I kicked him hard and he pulled back, yelped in pain, swore. But then he laughed again as he clambered to his feet.

Let's go back to the park.

It took me a minute to catch my breath, although I did as he said. Danny was watching us as we walked back into the group, his eyes moving from Ste to me and back again.

Come on, he said, standing up abruptly. I'll walk you home.

I didn't argue, let him lead me in the opposite direction to the pub without questioning why. For a while we walked in silence and then Danny pulled out a CD Walkman from his back pocket, passed me one of the headphones, put the other one in his ear. I don't remember what we listened to, only that the shortness of the wires meant we had to stay in step, close-close, our bodies touching. At the very top of the hill Danny broke away from me, his body moving to a tune I could no longer hear, but it didn't matter, so long as I could watch him there, dancing underneath the orange light of the street lamp, its shine bouncing off him, making him glow. I giggled, joined in, even though the music was only in my head, and we moved together, pretending everything was okay.

The song came to an end and Danny tugged at my hand, gesturing to a giant trampoline in someone's back garden. We crept across the drive, edging along the manicured hedgerow until we reached it, then lay down on our backs, gazing up at the beautiful house, its windows blacked out by heavy curtains.

Reckon we'll ever live somewhere like this?

Better.

Danny smiled, then rolled on his side, propped his head up on his elbow. You shouldn't ever take any shit from anyone, Neef.

I laughed, like I didn't know what he meant. What you on about?

People round here, he said, his eyes down. You can't trust em all that easy.

I prodded him with my toe. But I can trust you, though, can I?

Danny looked at me seriously. Yeah, he said. Yeah, you can.

25

The girls and boys at the park were always swapping and changing with each other, sticking their tongues down a different throat on every night of the week. I wasn't interested in any of that. I didn't care that the lads called me a dick-tease. I knew how dangerous it could be, to let boys mess with you. I'd lived all my life with Chrissy, after all.

By the end of my first year at the pub the kids had got into the habit of stopping there on the way to the park to see if I was coming out, angling after some free booze most likely. The lads would be standing there, trackied and capped and scruffy as hell, and Chrissy would appear at the back door with a cig, even though there was no reason for her to go outside for a smoke. She'd be leaning against the doorframe with her dressing gown half open in the middle of the day, her thighs bared, hankering for the flush of pink creeping out from the collars of their sports jackets, those teenage-boy stares proof to her that she was worth something. All right, lads, she'd smirk as I'd slide past her, ignoring the urge to fling my arms around her neck and kiss her cheek every time I left, my heart breaking for the way she was.

For a time, it seemed as though Barry and all the things he'd given Chrissy—the jewelry, the pub, the apartment—had anchored her. But after a while it was like the weight of them became too much and that wispiness came back, except with more lostness than before. Sometimes it felt like Chrissy had become a ghost of herself, an avatar, putting on a front while inside her head she escaped.

It was just small things at first. The way her eyes would cloud over whenever Barry leaned across the bar, droning out some long-winded story we'd all heard a hundred times before. The beat of a nerve in her jaw when he'd grab her around the waist and pull her close to him, showing her off to the locals: *look what I've got, look what's mine.* The way she seemed to be searching for a reason to leave the room every time he walked in.

I'd see her sometimes sitting at the bar, a drink in one hand and a cig in the other, surrounded by people. And she'd be smiling, laughing, flirting till the cows came home mostly. But I'd catch this look, this strange sort of blankness in her eyes, like her soul had poured out of them. Sometimes she'd notice me watching her and for a fleeting second she'd look almost ashamed, as though I'd caught her out. Then it would be gone, she'd look away, flash that smile, throw herself back into it all, so that I'd be left to wonder if I'd imagined it. If that absence, that hollowness, was simply a reflection of myself.

I didn't understand the things Chrissy got up to when I

was a kid, just thought it was part of being a grown-up. I knew she partied hard in the years before we moved to the pub, knew what the comedown train looked like when it hit her in the days that followed. There was none of that in our first year living with Barry. She'd started to look normal. Healthy, even. When she got dressed, the lines of the fabric would skim against the curves of her flesh instead of hanging from her, like they were still strung up on their metal coat hangers in Barry's cavernous wardrobes. The dark shadows under her eyes lessened, her hair came back to life. But by our second winter at the pub, that familiar look had crept back in. The sallowness, the skinniness, the jitter in her jaw. Barry noticed it too, put it down to stress, he said, and she nodded without looking at him, pulled out another cig and lit it with her shaking hand.

What you got to be stressed about then? I asked her one day, when the pair of us were on our own up in the apartment. Chrissy laughed lightly, like we were in on it together, rummaging through her handbag without meeting my eye. Really, though, I said. What's on yer mind?

She looked at me properly then, trying to read my expression, then sighed, slamming her purse on the table. What you gettin at?

I looked away, bit down on the inside of my cheek, but she stalked over to where I sat, grabbed the top of my arm tight for a second and then drew her hand back as though I had scalded her.

You don't know a thing, d'you know that? You at yer fancy school, in yer fancy uniform with all them posh nobheads bangin on about all the things you could be—

I never asked to go to that school, I yelled, angrier than I'd realized. Chrissy guffawed.

See? That's exactly what I mean. You get all this, she waved her hand around the apartment, her face contorted in fury. All this on a fuckin plate. And you can't even see it. Can't even see how we got here, *why* we got here. You know fuck-all. You think you do, but you don't. You've got no idea what it's like.

What's that s'posed to mean?

It means, she said, then paused, pressing the heels of her hands into her eyes. It means that sometimes I just need to take the edge off.

I didn't look up but I heard her walk out, heard the slam of the door and her feet on the stairs, running back down to the safety of the bar.

Chrissy stopped hiding it from me so much after that. I wasn't sure if it was because she saw me as complicit, or if she was doing it out of spite. I'd catch her nipping upstairs from the bar on a Friday night, her jaw grinding as she tapped the plastic baggy over the rim of her glass, winking at me or avoiding my eyes altogether, depending on how far gone she already was.

What is it? Danny asked me when I told him. We were lying on the sofa in the apartment, taking it in turns to play songs on Barry's stereo. Danny had brought me round a snide copy of a Sade CD that he'd got off one of Denz's mates, said it was full of soppy shite that he bet was right up my alley, and he was right.

Speed. Phet. Whatever she can get, I bet.

He'd shaken his head slowly. That's bad, man. All chemical shit. That's the stuff that messes you up, it int like green. That shit'll put you in t'ground.

I didn't say anything to that, pressed repeat on the stereo.

26

When Danny was fifteen, at the point in my memory when he is the most golden and boyish and tender, Lewis's prediction began to come true.

It's not as though Danny had ever been a stranger to attention. More than a year had passed since I'd met him, and I'd grown used to the way people would look twice as he walked through the town, the way the punters' eyes would linger on him when he came into the pub. I'd always thought it was because he was beautiful. I didn't understand the narrowness of their gaze.

We moved about like a pack by then, us kids. Down by the river or in the bus shelter or at the park, never arranging where we'd meet but always ending up together, always with the unwritten aim of oblivion. I couldn't stand to be at the pub anymore, around Chrissy and all the skanky new mates she'd taken to knocking about with, most of them barred from half the other pubs in town. Barry would have liked to do the same, I think, if he wasn't so terrified of upsetting her.

I was out most of the time, whether Danny was there or not. The ease with which I could get hold of drink had cemented my place in that motley crew, and the lads seemed to like how I was always up for getting wrecked. *You're a funny drunk, you are*, they would grin at me the day after the night before, and even though I could never remember enough to know what they meant by that, it felt good to hear it.

The police had had their eye on us kids for a while, although they made up their own minds about who was trouble and who wasn't. Didn't matter that Danny wasn't like the other lads, getting their kicks from putting shop windows in, chucking rocks at cars passing under the viaduct just for the laugh. It felt as though they'd only ever round in on us when he was there, snipering him with their questions: *where you been?* and *what you doing?* and *empty your pockets, please, Danny lad.* Pulling out their little notebooks, asking a few of us our names. They never asked his, they already knew it. Danny Campbell, right at the top of the list.

It was always the same, the way they spoke to him, with their look-at-me-when-I'm-talking-to-you and take-your-hat-off-I-can't-see-your-face-under-that-hood and what-did-you-say-speak-English-son. And then, when he did all of those things that were asked of him, when he would stand up straight and take a deep breath and look them dead in the eye, they'd accuse him of being threatening, tell him to wind his neck in, that they'd take him down the station if he carried on like that.

I wasn't there the night the garage got done over. Danny had been late coming to call on me at the pub and so I'd ended up drinking Bacardi Breezers in my bedroom while I waited for him, leaning out of the window, smoking Chrissy's cigs. When he finally turned up I was already pissed, could see by the look on his face as I stumbled down the stairs that he didn't like it.

What you lookin at me like that fer? I slurred.

He shook his head slowly. Pigs'll pick you up before we even get to t'park, state you're in.

Yeah, I snapped, if you're there they will.

Danny's jaw tensed and I wished straight away I hadn't said it, tried to link his arm, but he turned too swiftly, heading back onto the main road through the pub car park. I followed, quickening my step to keep up.

How come you're so late then?

No reason.

Well, that's nice, innit? Just couldn't be arsed showin up.

He stopped walking. What you bein such a bitch fer, Neef?

Sorry, I mumbled, his words stinging like a slap. I didn't mean to be.

Danny's eyes softened and he slung an arm over my shoulders. Mardy cow, he muttered, but not unkindly. We carried on walking, neither of us speaking. Me dad's come back, he said eventually.

I stiffened. Yer dad?

That's what I said.

Someone was calling Danny's name from across the street and I looked up to see Donna and Chelsea standing there. They could have passed for eighteen easy, the pair of them, looking more polished and uptown than I ever would. Donna was smiling at Danny in a way that made the hairs stand up on the back of my neck, and Danny unhooked his arm from around me. When I looked up, I saw that he was blushing.

Y'all right, Dan? she called.

Yeah. He grinned. You?

Yeah, yeah.

The four of us stood there for a moment more, Chelsea and I looking awkward, Danny and Donna seeming to forget that we were there.

See yer in a bit, Dan, yeah? Donna smirked.

Yeah. Danny nodded. Yeah.

My stomach hardened and Danny carried on walking. He didn't try to put his arm around my shoulders this time.

Where's he been then? I spat after a while, quickening my step to keep up.

Eh?

Denz. Where's he been all these months?

He frowned. He's been in Spain. You know that. Workin.

Doin what? He don't even speak Spanish.

So?

So he's been in the nick. That's what I think, anyway. But you won't ask him, cos you're scared of what he'll say.

Danny's face changed. He ain't been in the nick.

Oh yeah? How d'you know?

He stopped, looked at me properly. That's me dad you're on about.

Yeah and he's a scumbag, your dad, everyone says so. He deserves to be locked up.

The moment stretched between us, my words ringing in

both our ears until Danny turned away from me sharply, his strides long and wide and his hands thrust in his pockets. A hot rage coursed through me, a hatred that was all for myself. For saying those things, for kicking Danny in the place I knew it would hurt most. I wanted to go after him, but I stayed where I was, still and silent until he reached the corner and disappeared from view.

CHRISSY WAS DOWNSTAIRS WHEN I GOT BACK TO THE PUB, STAND- ing near the pool table with a scraggle of her dosser mates, clenching her teeth in a way that told me she was already off her head. I watched her for a minute. Ached for her. On my way up the back stairs, I helped myself to another six-pack of Bacardi Breezers from the entrance to the cellar.

27

The next morning Barry woke me up, told me to come downstairs, that we had a visitor. I thought it must be Danny there to make amends, didn't bother getting dressed, just shoved a dressing gown over my pajamas.

The pig was waiting in the sports lounge. He looked me up and down, then smiled in a way that made me tighten the toweled belt around my waist. Barry said he was there to talk to me about an incident at the garage the night before, that the police would like some help, please, with their inquiries.

What sort of incident? I asked.

The pig cleared his throat, told me that some kids had frightened the lady working behind the counter, threatened her with a concealed weapon, then nicked a load of stuff before running off. She didn't get a good look at them because they had hoods over their heads and scarves covering their

faces, but, by the sounds of it, one of them fitted the description of Danny.

What's that s'posed to mean?

Excuse me?

Well, if she couldn't see their faces, how could she tell it
were Danny?

The pig cleared his throat again, his nostrils flaring ever
so slightly. The description she gave us, he said, enunciating
his words slowly, matched the one we have on file. For Daniel
Campbell.

I curled my lip. Sounds like bollocks to me.

Neef—

Well, it does. And besides. It weren't Danny. Apart from
the fact he'd never do owt like that, he were at home last night.

And were you with him?

I paused, pulled my hair out of my collar. No. Fer a bit,
but . . . I know he were at home.

What time did you last see him?

I dunno. Eightish?

The pig raised his eyebrows. I see, he said. This particular
incident happened just after midnight.

I didn't say anything to that but he nodded smugly as
though I had, thanked me for my help. As soon as he was
gone I went upstairs, threw on some clothes, ran all the way
to Mary's.

Danny answered the door straight away as though he'd
been waiting there, but at the sight of me, his face changed.
Oh, he said. It's you.

Were you expectin someone, like?

He frowned. Why you so out of breath?

I . . . I dunno, I wanted to say sorry. About yesterday. I
shouldn't have said that about yer dad.

Danny leaned against the doorframe, his arms folded. Yeah. You shouldn't have. He gave me a half smile. But I'll let you off, seein as it's you.

He didn't make any move to invite me in and so we stood there awkwardly. Is yer nana home? I asked after a while.

She just left fer work. And I'm off out in a bit.

I wanted to ask him where he was going but something about the way he was acting stopped me. We've had the pigs down t'pub. Askin if you had owt to do wi t'garage gettin turned over last night.

You and me both. They came round first thing this morning, I've already had me nan flippin her lid at me. But it's fine. They know it weren't me now.

How?

He shifted his weight from foot to foot, not quite meeting my eye. I were . . . a few of us went over to Donna's. Fer a bit. And her mam were there. She works fer t'council, upstandin citizen and all that. Anyways, she rang em. Said I were there last night. And so they've left it alone. Fer now.

Fer a bit?

What?

You said you were only there fer a bit. But it were after midnight when it happened.

All right, Nancy Drew.

I didn't laugh at Danny's joke. Instead I stared at my feet, trying to think of what to say next, but in the end it didn't matter. Both of us heard the familiar snarl of the car engine at the same time, getting louder until eventually it cut entirely, right outside Mary's house. Denz was the last person I wanted to see in that moment.

I better go.

You all right?

Yeah. Yeah, why wouldn't I be?

I hoped I could get to the gate before Denz got out of the car but he swung open his door as I reached the footpath, making it so that I couldn't avoid him. It had been months since I'd seen him last. For a second he didn't say anything, just looked at me funny, as though he wasn't sure it was me. It caught me off guard and a moment passed before either of us spoke. He broke the silence first.

Easy.

All right.

You surprised to see me?

No more'n I usually am.

At that, Denz raised his eyebrows. How's your mum?

What?

Your mum. She all right?

Yeah. She's all right.

Another nod. Good. That's good.

I stared at him coldly and he smiled uncertainly. Did Danny tell you?

Tell me what?

Denz glanced toward the front door where Danny still stood, watching without making any move to join us. Nowt, he said. Nowt. He paused. Mebbe I'll bring him down t'pub later. Will Chrissy be about?

Mebbe, I replied, my eyes narrowed.

OUR CONVERSATION WAS SPARSE AND YET IT CLUNG TO ME, ALL of the unsaid like tinnitus in my ears. I wanted to act like I didn't care, but when I got back to the pub I found myself sitting in the back bar by the window, a ruse of school books spread on the table in front of me.

Danny and Denz showed up an hour later. It was midweek, so there was hardly anyone in and Chrissy was supposed to be looking after the bar while Barry did some paperwork in the office upstairs. We both heard the car pull into the car park. I knew without even looking up that Chrissy would be checking herself in the mirror, pulling her hair out of her face, readjusting her neckline to show another half inch of skin.

I kept my head bent low as they crossed the tarmac, didn't want Danny to think I was watching them, even though I was. My insides tightened at the way he mimicked Denz's walk, how he set his shoulders square, his hands slung lazily in his pockets. I tried to pretend I hadn't noticed when they walked in, but Danny came straight over, ruffled my hair like everything was normal. I pushed his hand away.

Get off. Don't mess me hair up.

He laughed, sat down across from me. Your hair's always a mess, Neef.

I kicked his leg under the table, looked up at him properly, my heartbeat quickening at the nearness of him. Where's Denz? I asked, realizing that we were alone.

Danny raised an eyebrow. Yer mum's probably tryin to work her magic on him, knowin her.

I stood then, more quickly than I'd meant to. Made my way behind the bar and through the passage that led into the front part of the pub. Denz was sitting on a stool in the sports lounge, Chrissy perched on the edge of the sink, her head leaning in toward him. They both looked up at me when I walked in, in a way that made me certain I'd interrupted something.

Oi! You're not meant to be behind this bar. Barry'll have a fit if he sees yer, Chrissy scowled.

I ignored her, set my eyes on Denz. What you two doin round here?

He held up his glass, swirled the syrupy liquid so that the ice cubes chinked against the side and smiled, then turned to Chrissy. She's growin up, int she? Not such a little girl anymore.

Chrissy blinked then peered at me, her eyes flashing as though something had suddenly occurred to her, a dark thought that made me want to back out of her sight. Then just as quickly, it was gone—she'd caught herself. She hopped off the sink with a little laugh, telling Denz to pipe down, waving me away dismissively with a flick of the hand.

You two kids go and play.

I could tell she'd chosen those words carefully. Chrissy's eyes locked with mine then and I took a step back, knocking my elbow on the pop tap as I brushed past it, so that it squirted a stream of brown sticky liquid onto my shoe.

Danny was waiting for me where I'd left him, his eyes a question. I marched ahead and out of the back door but he caught up, slowing me down with a hand on my shoulder. It surprised me, the weight of it there, the firmness. I crossed my arms over my chest, hugging my fingers under my arm-pits so that he wouldn't see them tremor. We walked in silence, side by side, and I noticed how tall he'd grown.

It's true though, innit? he said after a while, as though we'd been in the middle of a conversation.

What?

You. Us. We're not kids anymore.

So?

Nowt, just . . . He tilted his face up to the slate of the sky and I waited for him to say more, but he didn't.

At the bus station we sat down, the plastic of the benches cold, even through our clothes. Danny pulled a crumpled cigarette from his pocket, lit it. Twos?

When did you start havin cigs?

He shrugged, took a few drags then held it out to me.

What's goin on with you and Donna then? I asked, not looking at him.

He grinned sheepishly, dug his elbow into my ribs. Why? You jealous?

I stayed quiet, flicking ash onto the floor. Yeah, I said eventually and he laughed, swung his arm around my neck.

Neefy, the little green-eyed monster, eh?

Shut up, dickhead. With a shove I wriggled free of his grip, put the cigarette to my lips. She yer girlfriend then? I said, blowing the smoke out the side of my mouth.

He laughed again, leaned over and landed a kiss hard on my cheek. Nah. I'll never have a girlfriend, me.

What, never?

Nope. Never. Our eyes held for a moment and then Danny looked away, started jiggling his knee up and down, a nervous tic. You know Lewis moved to London, he said.

I frowned, confused at the direction the conversation had taken. Did he?

Yeah. He told me dad he's sick of Leeds, reckons the pigs up here've got his card marked. His uncle's sorted him out with a job down there, a flat in Brixton.

Nice one.

It's sick, is London—all me dad's mates say so. There are these gardens, I read about em in t'library, you should see the pictures. Plants from all over the world, more'n fifty thousand of em. Can you imagine? It'd be like travelin the entire planet in just one day. He paused for a moment, shifted uncomfortably. Still, though, he said. Me dad'll miss him. Thick as thieves, them two.

I rolled my eyes, leaned back against the wall. The Leeds bus was pulling into the station, its doors creaking open for a woman with thinning white hair and a cobra-head cane that shook every time she took a step. As she climbed on board, she glanced over her shoulder at Danny and me, said something to the driver that I couldn't make out. The two of them looked back at us, the driver shaking his head with disdain.

I think I might move in with him.

I turned my attention back to Danny, confused. What, Lewis?

Nah, yer div. Me dad.

Why?

Danny shrugged. Keep him company, I s'pose.

Him and Lewis don't even live together!

Not just that. Danny sighed, his leg still jittering. I dunno, it's just . . . feels like every time I step out the house these days someone's runnin back to me nana with a story about summat I done wrong. I know what they all think. Poor old Mary. Ending up with a grandson *like that—*

That's not true, I cut in, but Danny carried on.

Worst bit of it is, she's all too ready to believe it. You should hear the way she goes on. I've seen it all on t'telly, she goes. Drugs, crime, the sort of stuff that *kids like you* get into. And what hope have you got anyway, with a father *like that?* I'm sick of it, man. I've had enough.

One of the paving stones underneath my feet was broken, and I pried the corner of it loose with the toe of my trainer, pressing my foot down so that its jagged edges dug through the rubber. I thought about how it would feel to pick it up, launch it at the bus. Imagined it smashing through the windscreen, ricocheting off the driver's head right into the face of that stupid old woman. I hated her. Hated him. Hated the idiot pigs in that town, the bigoted teachers at Danny's school. Mary. Barry. Denz. I fucking hated Denz.

When? I said quietly.

Danny rubbed his palm over the back of his skull, the hair there still shaven down to almost nothing. Now, he said. Today.

My hand trembled as I brought the end of the cig to my lips, sucked hard. Please don't go, Danny.

He looked up at me in surprise. What?

Please. I just . . . nowt. I mean . . . My words trailed off and I sniffed, wiped my nose with the back of my hand.

You're not cryin, are yer? he said, almost in disbelief.

No, I said, shaking my head, pulling myself back together again. I just got smoke in me eyes.

CHRISSY WAS SITTING AT HER DRESSING TABLE IN HER UNDERWEAR when I got back, dabbing orange makeup onto her forehead with a sponge. I perched on the end of the bed, watching her. She'd be heading down to the pub soon until closing time at least, maybe later if the police turned a blind eye. I could never sleep until I heard her stumble up the stairs. When we first moved in, I used to go down early on in the night, sit at the bar with a Coke and a packet of salt-and-vinegar crisps. But it did my head in after a while, everyone half cut, trying to get me to dance with them, acting daft, kissing and cuddling me like they'd known me all my life.

D'you love him? I heard myself say.

Chrissy turned and looked at me, a mascara wand halfway to her face. Love who?

Barry. Do you love him?

She snorted, turned back to the mirror, her eyes wide and unblinking as she fanned her lashes out with the wand.

Well, do yer?

You gone soft or what?

I just want to know.

She didn't answer me as she got to her feet, walking over to the double wardrobe at the other side of the room and flinging open the doors. From one of the drawers, she pulled out a silver dress and held it up against herself in the mirror, then wriggled into it, tucking the straps of her bra into the seams. We'd be in a lot of shit, you know, she said, her eyes not moving from her reflection. If it weren't fer Barry. He helped us out. She paused, fixing a thick hoop into her earlobe. The pair of us. He really helped us out.

Yeah, I said. But d'you love him?

She sighed, turned back to the wardrobe, rifling through the shoe rack and retrieving a pair of sandals, high-heeled and plastic and glittering. Course I do, she said, her back still to me as she slid her little feet into the shoes, the straps gaping around her ankles.

Denz were askin after you earlier, before he came in.

Chrissy spun to face me, her eyes narrowed. When did you see him?

At Danny's. I shrugged flippantly.

What did he say?

I leaned back into the cushions littering the bed, pulled one onto my lap. It was velvet, dark purple like a blackberry, with gold tassels hanging from each of its four corners. There were three of them on the bed, then two smaller ones, round and quilted, all propped up against the pile of pillows. Chrissy had chosen them when we'd moved in. I don't think we'd ever even owned a cushion before that.

You not gonna tell me then? She was staring at me now, wrapping a section of her hair around a curling tong.

I wanted to test her, see if my suspicions about her feelings for Denz were true. He said he thought you were beautiful, I lied.

She bit her lip and I could see she was trying not to smile. Well, that's nice.

Danny's off to live with him.

With who?

Denz.

What?

Danny. He's gonna live with Denz.

Chrissy stood still for a moment, then cracked her neck from one side to the other. A look came into her eyes that I couldn't read and I trailed after her into the bathroom, watching as she sprayed aerosol onto her armpits, her face thick with makeup, the muscles in her calves pulled tight in her high heels. Part of me wanted to follow her, cling to her, block her from view so that no one could look at her. But I knew they'd ogle her regardless, that she'd soon forget about me, forget I was sitting on the high stool at the bar wishing I could lock her away where no one would find her. She looked at me, her face serious, and for a second I thought she had something to say. But then she turned on her heel, tottered out toward the stairs in the hallway.

28

The morning gets off to a bad start; food burnt and orders misheard and the wrong change given. But it is the hot tea I spill, almost scalding an elderly lady's hand as she reaches for it, that pushes Ali over the edge. He tells me to take a minute and I shake my head no, but the look on his face makes it clear it's not a request, so I skulk away, collapse down on the back step outside.

I feel like Denz is unpacking my head without my permission and I want to put all the memories back, lock them away like I have all these years, except it's like I no longer know how. I can't tell if I've buried my thoughts so deeply that they have become lost or if I'm just pretending, lying to myself. Because when I think about it, all of it, there are no holes, no gaps. Everything is still there. Even the parts I don't want.

You okay, Jenny *joon*?

I lift my head from where it has been resting in my hands, look up to see Ali standing above me, his dark brows knotted.

Yeah, I say. Yeah.

You don't seem okay.

My gaze moves to the lid of the bin in front of us, the way the wind makes it lift and fall, the tap t-tap-tapping of plastic on plastic. Ali stoops down, takes a seat beside me.

This *doost* of yours, he says after a while. Denz, is it?

Yeah. Denz.

Ali nods. You've seemed a little . . . preoccupied. Since he's turned up.

No, it's—he's just . . . making me think.

You care about him?

No, not . . . I mean. I thought I hated him, but I don't, I just . . .

Is he important to you?

No. I don't know. He . . . I knew him a long time ago. In another life.

I understand. And do you see him in your future?

I rub at my eyes. I can't imagine a future, Ali.

Ali frowns, considers what I have said. You know, Jenny, he says slowly. When I came here. To London. I was all by myself. I left a whole life behind, a whole other world. I didn't want to, but I didn't have any choice. And for a long time it hurt too much to think about it. I was so angry, so sad. The thought of everything I had lost hurt too much. I couldn't move forward, couldn't go back. I got stuck, see? And I'm not saying our situation is the same—I know it's not. But you have to understand, Jenny, that you're not the only one with a past. You just have to find a way to get unstuck from it.

Ali has always been a man of fewer words than Fionnoula, and there is something about that quiet, that keeping of secrets, that can make me feel as though the two of us understand one another in a way no one else does. I know little about what happened to him, to those he left behind. Only the crumbs I have garnered over the years: that as a young man he was forced to flee the only country he had ever known, that everything he once loved was lost. And yet that, somehow, he is happy. Somehow he has found a way to heal from everything that came before.

How do I do it, Ali? I hear myself whisper.

What did you say, Jenny *joon*?

I turn to him, and the gentleness in his face makes my throat hurt.

What can I do? I say. What am I supposed to do when I'm so afraid of everything that's happened, of where thinking about it might take me? What can I do?

Ali looks at me for a long time, takes my hand in his. I'm here, Jenny, he says gently. Fionnoula too.

I try to swallow the pain in my throat, bend my head, afraid of what might happen if my eyes meet Ali's. He says something in Farsi, squeezes my palm. Says it again, in English this time.

It doesn't matter how slowly you go, Jenny. Just so long as you do not stop.

didn't want to miss Danny, didn't want my head to be filled with him whether I was asleep or awake. I hated myself for being so pathetic, didn't understand my own feelings, why it ached the way it did.

Now and again I thought about calling him. Thought about taking the three buses to Denz's house to surprise him even. But every time I came close to doing it, I would remember the way Donna had smiled at him from across the road. Imagine him there, at her house. After midnight.

He'd only been gone two or three weeks when I started going downstairs, sitting in the back bar with Chrissy and her hollow-faced mates, sipping on pop, watching them gurn and talk too fast. Every so often I'd sneak off to the toilets, top up my glass with whatever I'd nicked from the cellar. On my way back I'd pass the entrance to the sports lounge where

Barry would be hiding away, serving all the old boys their half pints of bitter, watery eyes glued to the horses on the telly.

I'd only leave for the park when I was drunk enough not to mind the mithering from the other kids. I knew they'd all be asking if I'd heard from Danny, where he'd gone, when he'd be back. On the night of Greeny's birthday I got so carried away that I threw up before I even left the pub, wiping my mouth on the back of my hand, stopping at the garage for a packet of chewy.

It was teatime when I arrived. The rest of them were already there, draped across climbing frames and fences and benches, intimidating mums with their toddlers, dads trying to push their littlies on the roundabouts. I didn't bother trying to make conversation with anyone, just sat on the swing swigging vodka straight from the bottle, washing it down with mouthfuls of flat lemonade.

Ste was watching me, I knew that. He'd been different around me since Danny had gone. Bolder, more brazen, acting, sometimes, as though I were his. I could handle him mostly, but I wasn't in the mood that night, kept looking the other way whenever he tried to talk to me, pretended more than once that I hadn't heard him speak.

You're a right moody cow tonight, you, he sniped at me in the end. I didn't say anything back. He gave a snort, kicked the seat of the swing so that I jolted backward. How come yer mum's so fit and you're such a little scarecrow?

I kicked him back, my heel landing on his shin, and he stumbled, taken by surprise, then laughed, pulling the swing's chains toward him, scissoring my legs inside his. I'm only messin, giz a cuddle. Don't worry, Danny won't see.

I tried to wriggle free of his grip, but Ste held fast on either side of me, close enough that I could smell him. Lynx and sweat and boy. Anyways, he said with a smirk, I've heard Danny's got plenty of other girls he's keepin himself busy with, over in Leeds.

Aye, he's got a new bird, Greeny piped up from where he perched on the lower rungs of the climbing frame, Chelsea balancing on his knee. Int that right, Chels?

Yeah. Chelsea nodded, sounding bored. I ain't seen Donna for time.

I clenched my jaw, tried to ignore the blood pulsing behind my eyes. Well, he can do what he likes, I said, forcing myself free finally with a yank. Me and Danny are just mates.

Ste laughed. Yeah. But you wish you weren't.

BY THE TIME IT WAS DARK I'D RUN OUT OF BOOZE, BUT I WASN'T ready to stop. More kids had arrived, kids from the next town across, plenty of others that no one seemed to know. I was scavenging for another drink when I spotted a couple of lads leaning against the fence, a crate at their feet.

All right, Neef? one of them said to me as I stumbled over, a sly smile playing on his lips.

All right. I smiled back, doing my best impression of Chrissy. I recognized him vaguely, but I didn't know his mates. It made it easier to flirt with them, somehow. Turned out I was good at it, all that hair-flicking and laughing too loud. One of the lads gave me a can, and after that another one gave me something else. Before I knew it, we were sharing bottles of syrupy wine and cheap cider until there were outstretched hands and piggybacks and arms around waists and pulling onto laps. I could tell they'd already decided it was a competition and I was the prize. But they had me all wrong. I was a dick-tease, after all.

I don't remember the point at which we split off from the rest of the group. One of them had a car, I think, because I remember being in the backseat. Kissing and hands. Cold fingers on bare skin. I remember being sick and the lad who was driving swearing at me. And I remember running off, stumbling and laughter, but I don't know if it was mine or theirs, and a feeling like I was being chased.

We ended up at Devil's Claw and that's why I always thought it was my fault, that I instigated it. No one else knew about that place. I remember the scraping of branches and brambles and weeds on my skin, soil underneath my fingernails. And I remember me on my back, staring at the sky, the weight of body after body pinning mine.

When I woke up it was still dark but I was alone, my clothes damp, bruises on my thighs, a churning sickness in the pit of my stomach. I pulled myself up onto my knees, an ache throbbing through every inch of me, thumping behind my eyes. The pain seared between my legs as I stumbled back through the woods toward the pub. I couldn't bring myself to go inside and so I leaned against Danny's spot on the wall, staring out into the blackness of the river, the way it swelled and roiled.

I don't know how long I'd been standing there when I heard footsteps, looked up to see Chrissy walking toward me from the direction of the road.

Where did you come from? I said, my voice coming out harsher than I had meant it to. The sound of a familiar car engine rumbled from somewhere close by as Chrissy pulled a rutted packet of cigs from her pocket, her hand trembling as she fumbled with the lighter, illuminating the yellow stains on the tips of her fingers.

What? she snapped, seeing me looking at her. She was still dressed in her clothes from the day before, her hair drawn back from her face in a way that made the bones of her skull jut out in the half light.

Where you been?

She ignored my question, leaning with her elbows on the wall, tapping ash onto the ground.

It's quiet out here, innit? she said. Peaceful.

I watched her pull another cigarette from the packet, light it with the end of her first, her right leg jittering up and down.

Mam, I said quietly, and she looked at me as though she was seeing me there for the first time. I could see the clench of her jaw, the wildness in her eyes like she wasn't really there. But when she looked at me—when she really looked at me—it was like she knew.

Oh, Neef, she said. Neef.

stayed with Chrissy until the sun came up, the hours slipping by. I didn't tell her what had happened to me that night. I didn't need to. We sat in the darkness of the back bar, our glasses never reaching their end. Chrissy kept dipping her finger in the wrap she kept hidden in her bra and at some point she offered it to me, or maybe I asked for it, I don't know.

I don't remember it feeling good, only that I couldn't sleep for what seemed like days after it, even though I stayed in bed for most of the time. The only relief I took from anything was that Danny wasn't around to hear about all the filthy things I'd done. I didn't leave the pub that whole week, too afraid I might bump into one of the kids from down the park. Knew the rumors that would be flying around about me. *Three men and a mucky little slut, all this time tryin to act like she's got a lock on her knickers. The apple don't fall far from the tree, eh? Dirty slag, just like her mother.*

Barry kept on at me about school until Chrissy snapped at him that I wasn't well, to leave me alone. He piped down after that. Mostly I stayed in my room, feeling numb, but every now and then it would come back to me. The taste of warm beer and vomit, cold skin and hot saliva, thighs pried apart and shoulders held down and the feeling of not being able to breathe. But the part that sickened me, the part I hated myself for, was knowing that I let it happen. That I led them on, that I didn't fight.

Within a few days I was back downstairs in the pub. If you'd been half blind you might have thought it was nice, the way I reverted to spending most of my time with Chrissy. But that's not how it was, not really. Almost always we were off our heads.

Chrissy took to telling people we were sisters, even though everyone knew fine well we weren't. I don't know how Barry didn't see something wasn't right. Or maybe he did, maybe he was so terrified of losing Chrissy that he pretended not to notice what was going on right under his nose. I'd sit there, watching her dance and flirt and carry on all night, her eyes getting blacker every time she nipped to the loos, until in the end she'd wink at me, pass me a wrap and then it would be my turn to creep off into the shadows, dip my finger in and rub it on my gums. It never made me feel the way she did, though. Never made me get up and prance about and have a good time. It just made everything go so fast that I didn't have a chance to think or care.

Chrissy got whizz off a lad called Jody, introduced him to me as one of her best mates, the way she said it making my eyes sting. I couldn't stand him, couldn't bear how he put his hands on me. I might as well have had *cheap* stamped on my forehead, that much was becoming clear.

I could see the gears whirring in Jody's scrawny skull the first day he laid eyes on me. It didn't take him long to suggest I help him out, make myself a nice bit of pocket money. I know you kids like to have fun, he'd said, all matey. But I don't want to get involved with sellin to anyone underage. Wouldn't be responsible—you know how it is.

Chrissy got funny about it, for all of a minute. Reckoned she didn't want me getting mixed up in all that, although she didn't put up much of a fight. Jody told her it wouldn't be a big deal, just a few quids' worth, and that seemed to win her over. I told him I didn't know anyone, didn't have any mates, not really. He grinned at that. Don't gimme that bollocks. You private-school girls are the worst of the lot.

A couple of days later Chrissy had a word with me, said it might be worth going back to Boroughford soon or she'd have the council on her back again. Or worse, Miss Bell-end and that silly Herrington cow, she laughed, digging me in the ribs like we were in on a joke.

Since when were you bothered about that? I scoffed.

I just feel bad fer Barry. He's payin all that money. And you know how they're always bangin on about yer *potential;* it might do you good.

When I didn't respond she sat down beside me on the sofa, put an arm around my shoulders. Go on, love, she wheedled. It'd make Jody proper happy, like.

MISS BELL LOOKED LIKE SHE'D SEEN A GHOST WHEN I WALKED into the form room a few days later. Jennifer, she exclaimed, her eyebrows up in her hairline. You're here! She kept me back once the first bell rang, of course she did. Told me they'd been trying to get hold of my parents, that they'd all been very concerned.

There were a death in the family.

Oh. I'm so sorry, Jennifer.

S'all right.

Miss Bell cleared her throat awkwardly. Still, though. It would have been helpful to have had a bit of . . . communication on the matter. At least then we might have been able to offer some support.

I didn't answer, kept my eyes on the ground. In the end she let out a long sigh, told me I'd better get to class.

JODY HAD A POINT, AS IT TURNED OUT. THERE WERE PLENTY OF girls whose parents were too distracted with fancy jobs and gala dinners and booking their next skiing holiday to notice that the heiress to their throne was going off the rails. I started eavesdropping on conversations, skulking around in the background, taking advantage of my invisibility. Didn't take me long to figure out which ones saw themselves as edgy, rule-breakers, talking about wild parties while mummy and daddy were away, weekends filled to the brim with debauchery.

Word got around pretty quickly, so that before long those swinging ponytails would come looking for me at lunchtime. Is it possible to place an order, please, they'd simper through orthodontic smiles. The next day we'd meet up in the toilets down at the bottom of the sports wing, the cubicle right at the back, where they'd swap their crisp new notes for my tiny packages and I'd smirk to myself, feel the power balance shifting.

After a while, the invites to the parties began to come in. I wouldn't go for long, just enough time to drop off what I needed while Jody waited for me in the car out the front. Mostly, when I'd turn up, they'd already be paralytic on their dad's spirit cabinet, thinking they were cool as shit, acting like we were old mates. Neef! they'd say, all elastic arms and frosted kisses. How aaaaare you? It's been foreeeeeever! Any chance you can sort us out?

It made me laugh, the way they'd talk. Trying to roughen their cut-glass edges, when all they'd ever done was look down their noses at me. Rich girls wanting to dip their toes in the murky waters, play on the wrong side of the tracks before disappearing back to their upper-crust lives, growing up to juggle 2.4 children and a socially acceptable cocaine habit. But still, it was good for business. They were always looser with daddy's wallet when they'd had a skinful.

I never gave much thought to what it was I was doing. I just wanted to keep my head busy.

anny never once got in touch in the time he was living with Denz. I was certain it was because he'd heard what a skank I was, what I'd done with those boys, those strangers. How disgusted he must be by me, how revolted. Whenever he entered my brain, I'd put something in it to chase him back out again. Missing him was pointless. I'd never mattered to him, not really. And perhaps I'd got it wrong too, maybe he'd never mattered to me, either. If he had, I'd never have let those boys do what they did.

Four months passed before I saw Danny again, and by then I'd all but convinced myself that what we once had never existed. Already I was getting good at blocking things out. My heart was hardening, learning to protect itself. Scarred by the knowledge that nothing good could last.

He was sitting on his spot on the wall as Barry's car

rounded the corner on the way back from school, just like he used to do when we were kids. It felt as though a long time had passed since then, although it hadn't. Not really.

Barry went straight inside without even a second glance at Danny. Part of me wished I could do the same, but the pull of him was too much. He gestured me toward him with his chin and I took a couple of steps forward, still leaving a gap between us.

Come here then, he said, a smile playing on his lips. I did as he asked, walking slowly, staring at the ground. He reached over, took the bowler hat from where it still perched on my head. You look like a proper div in that uniform.

I didn't say anything and he stretched out his leg, tapped my hip with his toe. Oi! How's tricks? Danny's face changed as I looked up, worry settling into the lines of his frown. You all right, Neef?

I nodded.

You don't look all right, you look proper poorly.

I'm just tired, s'all.

His eyes searched mine, his face serious. D'you wanna come round mine?

Yours where?

Danny glanced toward the kitchen. I'm back at me nan's fer a bit.

I knew by the way he said it that something had gone on between him and Denz. But if Danny wanted to have secrets, I would let him. So long as I could have some of my own. Yeah, I said quietly. All right. Yeah.

DANNY DIDN'T MENTION DENZ, OTHER THAN TO TELL ME HE'D been giving him lifts to and from school most days.

I ain't been goin in much, though. Just been comin here while Nan's at work instead.

I stiffened when he said that, chewed the cuff of my school shirt, too afraid to ask him why he didn't come and find me on all those days he'd been less than a mile from the pub.

How's Chrissy been?

I looked at him strangely. What you askin me that fer?

He sniffed, looked away. No reason.

She's all right, I s'pose. Same old.

In truth, Chrissy had been getting worse. There never seemed to be a time when she wasn't wasted, but that wasn't what frightened me. In the past few weeks I'd begun to sense it again. That itch in her feet.

Danny and I didn't bother with school the next day, or the one after that. Before long, I had Jody on my back, asking what was going on with the orders. I fobbed him off but I could tell he didn't like it. Not that I cared. Danny being back made all of that seem like another world.

It was easy for Danny to skip school. The teachers had no interest in him and Mary was out at the pub all day, so he could come and go as he pleased without her ever catching on. My situation might have been trickier, had Barry and Chrissy not already retreated into their own fucked-up worlds. No one ever checked the post, and the pub phone rarely got answered anymore. Barry had always ferried me to and from school, but he happily swallowed the story I made up about a girl from my class who lived at the top end of town and whose parents had offered to give me lifts instead.

So pleased you're finally makin friends, love. He'd beamed with red-rimmed eyes. That's what yer need, see, friends in high places. That's the power of these schools—it's all about connections.

I smiled at him, carried on getting dressed up every morning in that silly uniform, pretending not to smell the booze on his breath as he drove me to the top of the hill and dropped me off outside a stranger's big detached house, day after day.

I COULD TELL, BY THE WAY DANNY WAS WITH ME, THAT HE DIDN'T know about what I'd done with those boys, where I'd taken them. He was like medicine, an alternative therapy, replacing all the shit I'd been taking to make me forget the weight and the heat and the stench of strangers' bodies.

Jody carried on hounding me, skulking around the pub waiting for me to show my face, but I didn't care, not even when he threatened to tell Barry I'd been skipping school. I'd laughed in his face then. Reckon I could tell him one or two things about you too, mate.

He quietened down after that and I made an effort to stay out of his way, steering clear of the pub as much as I could. It cleaned me up, being away from Chrissy, from them. To some extent, anyway. Danny had got pally with the younger brother of one of Denz's mates while he'd been staying over in Leeds. Turned out this lad dealt weed to most of the kids in the neighborhood. He'd set Danny up with an account on tick, which meant we no longer had to rely on Denz for our supply. But it also meant we were both smoking plenty.

D'you wanna see summat? he said to me as we lay on our bellies in the garden one morning, passing a jay back and forth. I looked at him curiously, watched as he got to his feet. Come with me.

The pair of us floated through the little garden and into the greenhouse, right toward the back where the herbs grew. Danny grinned at me over his shoulder, then parted the plants gently, exposing the slender-fingered leaves, rich and green, their sweet perfume mingled in among basil, lavender, peppermint neighbors.

It's just a start. He beamed, fiddling with the angle of the lamp. I'm only learnin but . . . reckon I've got the touch fer it, just about.

Why didn't you tell me?

Danny shrugged. You been busy, innit.

I swallowed, leaning forward to inspect the plants so that he couldn't see how his words had stung. You done it all by yerself?

Course I have, man. Got a few tips here and there, but mostly I figured it out. You think anyone could do this better'n me?

Despite myself I laughed, reaching a hand out to stroke the leaves. Danny stood behind me, chattering on about the scent, the effervescence. Nitrogen, phosphorus, potassium. Light schedules and pH levels and humidity optimization; how best to avoid stale air in the greenhouse, how to manage pests and mold and bud rot. Look at the crystals on it, man. Look, he urged, tilting the bud toward me, squeezing it gently so the stickiness came away between his fingers.

You're clever, you are, Danny Campbell. I grinned.

Danny had spent all that time when he was supposed to be at school nurturing those buds, turning the tiny space in the roof above his bedroom into a makeshift drying room, the branches hanging upside down from a coathanger strung up on the ceiling beams. Every couple of days he'd hoist himself up there, change the batteries in the little handheld fan that he'd positioned just so, check for the snap in the stems. We won't need to rely on anyone else soon. He'd grin. The stuff I grow'll be the best fer miles, you'll see!

The plants kept him busy, purposeful, although I could tell there was more going on in his head than he let on. Danny hadn't mentioned his dad since he'd been back at Mary's. But there was something different about Denz's absence this time. As though it were Danny's decision, for once, to stay away.

THERE WAS A SENSE THAT THE PAIR OF US WERE BALANCING ON a tightrope wire, keeping one another steady as we tiptoed over a world that was fragile. The in-and-outness of Denz from Danny's life, the brittleness of mine and Chrissy's existence at the pub. Our parents felt like unsteadiness, like danger. Maybe that's why I never told Danny about the day I saw them together.

I'd taken the long route back from Danny's, trying to kill some time before going to the pub, when I spotted the car, pulled over on a dirt path not far from the exit for the motorway. Denz must have seen me walking toward them because he got out quickly as though to block my view, but not before I saw Chrissy in the passenger seat. She looked rough, even to me, black makeup pooled in the hollows around her eyes, the remains of a crudely drawn red liner sketching the shape of her mouth. I sidestepped Denz, yanking at the door.

What you doin?

The inside of the car was warm, but the skin on Chrissy's legs was raised up in tight, hard goosebumps, a thin denim jacket hanging loose from her shoulders. She didn't answer, just pursed a cigarette between her lips, jabbed the button of the car lighter.

D'you want a lift somewhere, Neef? Denz asked me, an uneasiness in his voice that I wasn't used to.

I took a step back, looked at him carefully. Nah. You're all right, ta.

He shifted uncomfortably. You seen Danny lately?

Yeah.

He doin all right?

I s'pose he'd tell yer, I said, my eyes narrowed. If he wanted you to know.

Denz looked down at the ground then. I shot Chrissy a disgusted look, walked away from the two of them as fast as I could, turning back in the direction I'd come from.

By the time I got to Danny's, my jaw was sore from clenching it. As soon as he opened the door I greeted him with my whole self. Pushed my mouth against his, slid my hands roughly under the fabric of his T-shirt, like the sight of Denz and Chrissy together had awakened something urgent in me.

He didn't pull away. He kissed me back, placed the warmth of his palm around the base of my neck. There was a moment, then, when everything fell into place. The fit of the two of us together, the light and the joy and the sweetness. The sense of exactness, of all the hurt and heartache and anger leading to this. This this this.

And then it was as though Danny remembered, suddenly, who I was, looked at me questioningly, but I didn't let myself think, pulled him close, felt him swell against me, his hands moving over my body.

Me nana's due back in a minute, he murmured as I tugged at the waistband of his trackies.

It's fine, I insisted, but he moved my hand away gently.

Nah. Come on. Let's go somewhere else. Let's go up to Devil's Claw.

I winced, recoiling. It's all right, forget it—

Nah, nah, come on, Neef, he said, excited now, apologetic almost. I want to, I do want to. Come on, we'll go up to Devil's. No one ever goes up there. No one except me and you.

I HADN'T BEEN THERE SINCE THAT NIGHT. I TOLD MYSELF IT didn't matter, it was just a place, nothing more than a patch of earth, it could have been anywhere really. All that mattered was that I was there with Danny. The time before had meant nothing, I couldn't even remember it after all. It didn't matter, it didn't matter. It didn't happen, it wasn't real. All that mattered was the here and now, Danny's body and mine, me on my back in the grass, Danny and I pressing ourselves against each other, into each other, the thistles unyielding against our skin, all of it heightened and sharp and bold. I squeezed my eyes shut, but in the darkness I felt them again, the weight of those faceless boys, and I gasped, stared up, the branches above my head mocking me, laughing at me. *We know what you did. We know what you are.*

When it was over, Danny rolled onto his back beside me, reached for my hand, but already I was getting to my feet. He pulled himself up so that he was leaning on one elbow, looked at me strangely.

What's up?

Nowt.

What you in such a rush fer then?

I'm not, I just . . . need to get out of here.

A look of bewilderment passed over his face and he sat up, pulled his trackies back on self-consciously. Didn't you like it?

What? No . . . no, it int that; it's just . . . I'm cold, that's all.

All right. He nodded, taking my hand and smiling at me uncertainly. All right.

AFTER THAT DAY, DESPITE ALL ITS COMPLEXITIES, ALL ITS CON-fusions, it felt as though a fog had lifted; our whole way of being simplified to the understanding that I was for him and he was for me, that Danny and I together could be a source of mind-emptying bliss. The hours spent lying innocently in the grass beside one another, or riding Danny's bike through the streets, disappeared. Instead we would find ourselves entwined at every opportunity, starving, ravenous, filled up only by one another.

Mary knew something had changed between us. She pulled me up on it first, a long time before she even mentioned it to Danny. He and I had been upstairs in my room, my bed, most of the afternoon, the threat of being caught only adding to the thrill. We'd managed to get Danny in and out with a stealth operation of back doors, all fours and skin-of-our-teeth timings, waiting for hours to make sure Barry and Mary were both occupied with something at the exact same moment, so that we could execute our plan. And it had worked, to some extent. Mary only cornered me as I was walking back inside the pub, once we'd thieved our last fumble behind the safety of the beer-garden wall. She caught me by the sleeve as I tried to sneak past the kitchen door. It was only when I looked down at her hand on my arm that I realized the jumper I had on was Danny's.

A word, please, lady, she said sternly, steering me into the kitchen and closing the door behind us.

What? I said, my eyes inflated with fake innocence.

How come you've been avoidin me?

I've not.

Mary crossed her arms over her chest, looked me square in the face. I tried to hold her stare but I was the first to look away. The silence stretched between us and I wondered if she was waiting for me to speak, although now I think she was looking for the right words, that the discomfort was as palpable for her as it was for me.

Look, love, she said eventually. You and Danny, you've been glued at the hip since you moved into this pub a couple years back. And don't get me wrong, it's been a good thing. Fer t'most part. There's been times when I don't know what our Danny would've done without yer. She stopped then and I took a step back toward the door, my heart sinking at the look in her eyes, a sadness I hadn't expected to see.

I know you're both gettin older. I'm not daft. You're a nice-lookin girl, and Danny's . . . well, Danny is who he is. And I've been around long enough to know what happens at your age. But, Neef, I'm saying this fer your sake, not his. You be bloody careful.

We haven't slept together, I blurted out, my mouth seeming to form the shape of the lie without ever making any sort of deal with my brain. Straight away I felt my cheeks flame, my eyes clamp shut, not knowing where to look.

I don't want to know the ins and outs, love, Mary said after a pause. Just remember what I said. She picked up a dish from the drying rack and began wiping it with a tea towel, making it clear the conversation was over. As I scurried upstairs out of sight, I heard her begin to cough.

32

Mostly Danny and I spent our days in the little jungle behind Mary's house, and before long we were spending our nights together too. Danny gave me a key to the back door and I'd sneak in after Mary had gone to bed, no one at the pub ever thinking to check if I was there.

Now and again we'd go adventuring, rambling for hours and ending up in the types of places I never knew existed. We were lying together in Danny's bed one night when he told me about a well in a town not far from us, where the water turned everything it touched to stone. When I said I didn't believe him, he promised to show me.

We'll go tomorra, you'll see!

At the first sign of light we set off, creeping down the stairs, sliding the latch silently off the door. As soon as we got outside our eyes were shining, kids on the cusp of adulthood, ready for anything. It was almost ten miles from where we lived, but we didn't care. We were never happier than when it was just us two. We played games on the long stretches of road—Eye Spy and Yellow Car and Numberplate Words—and when we tired of that, Danny took my hand, promising me shortcuts that never materialized. Climbing fences, trudging across fields and farms. Pulling faces at jittery sheep and melancholy cows that eyed us skeptically, stopping every now and again to admire some tree or flower or mushroom that Danny spotted along the way.

By lunchtime we were almost there, and it was then that Danny remembered the lido.

It's ace, he said to me, all excited. I went there once with me dad, there's a beach and an ice-cream shop and all sorts.

I thought you were gonna show me a magic well, Dan, I ribbed him.

He grinned. Later, later. This is better. You'll love it, Neef, I promise.

We had to ask for directions twice, once from an old bloke who I swear told us the wrong way just to spite us, and a second time from a tired-looking mam pushing a double buggy, who gazed at us wistfully and told us she remembered what it felt like to be young and carefree. She pointed us in the direction of the caravan park, and as soon as Danny saw it, he knew we were on the right track.

I remember beggin me dad to stay here fer t'night, he said. But you can't. They're all privately owned or summat.

The sight of the lido made me less sore about missing out on the magic well. It was even prettier than Danny had described it, sitting on a little gorge at the bottom of the park, a stretch of grass and sandy beach leading onto a calm sweep of river between two weirs. On the far side, the bank stood thick with trees, their leaves dipping into the current as a waterwheel turned idly. A little boy stood in the shallows, flying a kite as his mum watched on, an orange ice lolly melting in her hand.

Danny lay down on the grass and I nestled into him, my feet aching from the walk, snoozing on his chest until he grew restless.

C'mon, he said, let's go in t'water.

It was spring, and although the sun had shone all day, the afternoon was growing late.

Will it not turn me to stone? I murmured.

Danny laughed, wriggling free. Why don't you go and find out?

I looked up at him, the mischievous smile on his face, daring me. I didn't need asking twice. Jumping to my feet, I ripped off my trackies and T-shirt, running ahead in just my knickers and bra until the river reached my knees.

Come on! I yelled, turning around to face Danny, who was sitting up straight now, his face creased with laughter. It's lovely in here!

The water was ice cold, the kind of bitter that empties your lungs. Danny ran toward me and I kicked my leg up in the air, a gasp rising from his throat as the droplets hit his chest. He bent down, scooping his hands through the current, and I tried to duck away, but my heel caught on the slippery surface of a rock. I keeled backward, sinking with a splash as Danny moved toward me, arm outstretched, breathless with laughter and cold. I lifted my hand as though to take his, but as soon as he was close enough I hooked my ankle around his knee, making him lose his balance, fall down with me. We were giggling and splashing and playing like two little kids, and then his hands were on my waist, firm, tender, pulling me in, in, in. It felt, then, like we were the only two people in the world, both of us overwhelmed by the type of innocent love that only happens once. We kissed for a long time, for as long as we could stand it, until at last it got too much. I took Danny's hand, led him back to the shore, our skin blue and pimpled.

Danny gave me his T-shirt to dry off with, but it wasn't much use. The damp had sunk into our bones, the sun already setting. Neither of us had any idea how we were going to get home.

Mebbe there's a bus, Danny tried hopefully.

Mebbe. You got any change?

Danny checked his pockets, shook his head woefully. I laced my fingers in his, pressed his icy knuckles to my lips. It didn't matter how we got home. When. If. We were to-gether. That was enough.

The beach had grown deserted, the little boy and his kite long gone. A bloke walking a scrawny terrier along the river passed us by, then disappeared round the bend. The park, too, was quiet. Rows of static caravans standing dark and silent as the night began to draw in.

Mary'll be wonderin where we are, I murmured. Danny didn't say anything back.

We set off up the path to the main road, our arms wrapped tight around one another, the blisters on the backs of our heels slowing us down. I ran through the options in my head. Beg our way onto a bus. Try and jump a taxi. Barry would probably come for us, if I called, but he'd be pissed by now. I didn't fancy his chances on all them country roads. A thought came to me then, and I tugged Danny off the path toward the back of the caravan park.

What you doin?

Shh, just come with me.

We were almost at the fence perimeter when I saw what I'd been hoping for.

Jackpot.

At the very edge of the park stood a dilapidated caravan that looked like no one had taken an interest in it for a while. The wooden slats at the base were showing signs of rot, paint peeling from the steps. I squeezed Danny's hand, nodded my chin toward the window at the side. Danny saw it too then, the way it had been left open a crack.

Gimme a leg up, I whispered.

Neef, I dunno . . .

Come on, Dan. We won't do it any harm. Didn't you say you always wanted to stay in one of these?

I tiptoed over, slid the pane of glass across. Danny hesitated, then locked his hands together and I climbed onto them, levering myself up. The space was tight, but I was small enough to squeeze through it, just about.

Neither of us had ever been inside a caravan before. The electricity was working, but we didn't dare turn on the lights, feeling our way around the place in the half dark. It was old, but clean, cozy. A place for everything, and everything in its place.

It's like havin our own little home fer t'night, Dan. I grinned, pottering around, opening a cupboard here, a drawer there.

Danny hung back, smiling uncertainly, his hands deep in his pockets. I found an old kettle and a tub of dusty teabags above the sink, made us both a cuppa, ignoring the rumbling in our bellies. There was no bedding anywhere, but there was a pile of blankets stashed in a cabinet next to the bathroom and we nestled into them, holding on to each other to keep warm.

It didn't take long for Danny to drift off. The day, the walk, our cold-water swim had worn us both out, but somehow sleep evaded me. I watched Danny's eyes fall closed, traced the bones of his jaw, the scars of our laughter in the tiny creases next to his eyes. A fine layer of sand still covered the back of one of his hands and I brushed it away, ran my fingers along the lines of his palm, the moon crescent of his nails. And I thought about how flawless this was. How happy we were. How this was all we would ever need.

The next morning before we set off for home, Danny folded the blankets, rinsed our mugs in the sink. Then he crept outside, picked a bunch of wildflowers from the grass sprouting up behind the caravan. I arranged them in a little plastic beaker that I found in a cupboard, left it there as a thank-you for all the memories we'd get to keep.

33

Chrissy left for good two weeks before I turned fifteen. I'd been with Danny the night it happened, lying together in his bed for as long as we dared, creeping out before dawn so that Mary wouldn't catch on. Danny walked me back to the pub, his hand in mine.

It was still dark when he left me there that morning, trailing his fingers along the length of my arm in goodbye, both of us too distracted by thoughts of sleep to speak. I remember feeling glad to find that someone had left the back door open, the pocket where my keys had once been now empty, turned inside out when I'd pulled my jeans off hurriedly and left them in a pile on Danny's floor.

I woke up much later to the sound of slamming, Barry's footsteps pounding across the apartment and up and down the stairs, raised voices somewhere in the pub. Danny's scent rose up from my skin like a vapor and I dragged myself to the shower, turning it on full and sitting on the floor of the bath, so that the hot water pounded onto the back of my neck. The hammering on the door brought me round again, someone yelling my name.

My full name.

I stood quickly, my head rushing and my feet slipping on the ceramic base as I grabbed a towel, wrapped it around myself, the air so thick with steam that I could barely see.

What? I said, pulling the door ajar. Barry was standing there, his big cheeks damp and his eyes red-raw. Behind him stood Mary, her face ashen.

What's goin on? said Barry, his voice hoarse and cracking.

I stared at him blankly. What you on about?

Chrissy. Where the bloody hell is Chrissy?

SHE'D DISAPPEARED SOMEWHERE BETWEEN LAST ORDERS THE night before and early that morning, taken everything. All her clothes, makeup, jewelry. She must have waited until Barry was pissed enough not to notice her packing it all up. Or maybe she'd been doing it bit by bit, planning it over the course of a few weeks, months. I didn't want to believe that, it hurt less to lie to myself, to tell myself she'd done it on a whim without ever really thinking it through.

She hadn't said a word to anyone, not even so much as left a note. When Barry told me that, I ran to my room, searched the bedside table, the bed, the floor, got down on my hands and knees to check underneath. But he was right. She'd left nothing.

Barry thought I knew more than I was letting on, insisting that Chrissy must have said something to me, I must know where she'd buggered off to, and if she thought she could do this—just swan off for a few weeks and then waltz back in, whenever she felt like it—she had another think coming; he wouldn't hear of it, he'd be damned if he'd let her make this much of a fool out of him. And on and on and on.

I sat there on the sofa, my hair still wet from the shower, listening to him, letting him bellow then sob like a child, then bellow again. I knew she wouldn't be back. Not in a few weeks, not ever. Despite everything, I knew Chrissy. She always left me a note.

THE PUB STAYED CLOSED THAT WHOLE DAY, EVEN THOUGH IT WAS a Sunday. I couldn't be there, though, couldn't listen to Barry and his desperate search for answers. I wanted Danny, wanted to crawl back into bed beside him, let his body distract me from my head. But as I crept out of the back door, I came to see that he was the last person I could go to. Although I'd never have said it out loud, in my gut I knew who Chrissy was with. Danny's face was too close to the one I hated most.

Instead I put my head down and walked right out of the town toward the main road, only letting myself catch a breath when I reached the hard shoulder where the long-distance lorry drivers sometimes pulled over for a kip. I hadn't planned on stopping there but then it started to rain and one of them saw me out of the window, shouted my name. I recognized him from the pub, a Geordie fella who came in for breakfast sometimes on his way to London. He told me to get inside, get out of the wet. I didn't want to, but it was pissing it down by then and I hadn't brought a jacket and I didn't have anywhere else to go.

He poured me a cup of coffee out of his flask, and even though I didn't drink coffee—still hate it to this day—I swallowed it thirstily, letting it burn my tongue and my throat. I don't remember what we talked about, or even if we talked. But I was there a while, longer than I should have been. I remember leaning back against the headrest, letting my eyes fall half closed, listening to him laugh at something. I remember I laughed along, even though I didn't know why. Then his hand was on my leg, the big thick knuckles, the sprouting of wiry hair, and I looked up at him, saw that look, that hunger that I'd seen cast on Chrissy so many times. The niggling fear that I had been trying to ignore for months rose up in my throat. Of being so cheap that anyone could afford to touch me. Of becoming just like my mam. I sat up straight in the seat, fumbling for the door handle, climbing, falling out onto the dirt below and then stumbling away, the bitter, dirty coffee rising in my throat.

IT WAS THREE DAYS BEFORE I SAW DANNY AGAIN, AND ALTHOUGH I craved him, a part of me was glad not to have to look at his face. When he finally showed up he seemed sheepish, said his nana had told him what had gone on and he figured I might want a bit of space. I knew he was lying, but the relief of his nearness made me pretend I didn't.

She'll be all right, you know, he said, leaning against the windowsill in Barry's front room. She'll probably be back in a few days, you know what she's like. Probably just sleepin off a bender.

I didn't react, stared at my feet curled up beside me. It felt too hard to look him in the eyes.

D'you wanna go round mine? Have a smoke? When I didn't respond, he moved toward me, placed an arm around my shoulders. Come on, Neef. I'm tellin yer. She'll be all right.

My hand moved to his calf without me thinking, tracing the three fluorescent stripes that were sewn down the length of his trackies with the tips of my fingers. I knew where Chrissy was. We both did. But neither of us seemed able to say Denz's name out loud, too frightened that putting the words into the air in front of us might sever the thing that was solely ours.

Danny slid down from the arm of the sofa, kissed the top of my head, and I sank into his chest, wondered if perhaps I might cry, but instead I moved my lips to the base of his neck, let them linger there against his collarbone. His hands found the hem of my T-shirt, sliding underneath, drawing me closer to him, our bodies working together intuitively. He drew me to my feet and we moved wordlessly into my little-girl bedroom, although we didn't make it to the princess bed. Instead I pressed Danny's frame against the door, pulling at his shoulder blades as though trying to split him open, his body releasing something in mine that was beyond my years, making me pour all the love I had for Chrissy into Danny, but making me pour in all the hate too. Because hating Danny felt like hating Denz, and in that moment we were all the same, it was all the same. I loved and I hated and I knew then, with absolute certainty, that I would never, ever be able to live without Danny.

. . .

WHEN DANNY LEFT THAT AFTERNOON I CAUGHT THREE BUSES TO Denz's house, stood on the front step ringing the bell for so long that the neighbor across the way started bawling at me from her top window, threatening to call the police. Still no one answered, although I swear blind that I saw someone moving around inside. In the end I gave up, headed back the way I'd come and went straight to Danny's. I didn't tell him where I'd been, just undressed silently, tore and thrust against him with all the lostness in my heart.

Only once, when Chrissy had been gone weeks, did I broach the subject of Denz.

You heard owt from yer dad then? I asked him casually as we lay together in his bed.

He's workin away, Danny answered without looking at me, standing abruptly to pull on his pants, making it clear the conversation was done before it had even begun.

34

Chrissy leaving tore Barry up into so many pieces that a few of the locals ran a bet on the sly to see how long it would be before he lost the pub. But he didn't, not while I was living there at least. He probably would have if it hadn't been for Mary holding everything together, despite the fact that her own body was quietly failing her by then.

Barry begged me constantly to tell him where Chrissy was, why she had left, what he could do to get her back. I didn't have the words he wanted to hear and so I retreated, stayed out of his way as much as I could. But he took my coldness for complicity, convinced that I was hiding something from him, protecting her. Most days as I tried to slip out of the back door unseen I'd catch sight of him, slumped over the side of the bar that didn't belong to him, drowning in wine and whisky and anything else going from morning until night, falling asleep with his cheek on the cold wood in a puddle of drool and spirit-tears. One night I got back late, watched as a couple of the locals heaved him upstairs to bed, a dark, stinking patch of piss staining the front of his trousers as he slurred at me over his shoulder, demanding that I tell him where she was, goddammit; tell him where the dirty slapper was hiding, tell him why she'd left, why he deserved to be treated like this, humiliated like this.

Tell me, you little cunt.

It didn't help that the older I got, the more I looked like my mam. Barry saw it too, I sensed it in the way his eyes would stay on me longer than they should, how he'd watch me sometimes moving around the apartment, the bar, telling me often that I was the mirror image of her, even calling me by her name a few times. I told myself he was nothing more than a harmless old fool, but in the pit of my gut I felt unnerved.

One night I got back to the pub late, tipsy but not drunk. It was empty in there except for a couple of locals and Barry. I'd gone upstairs without even saying hello, fallen into bed with my clothes still on. I don't know how long I'd been asleep but when I opened my eyes, I could see the shape of him standing in the dark, his body casting a shadow over me, his hand on the zip of my hoodie. I shirked back, gasped. Barry looked confused, like he didn't know what he was doing, didn't even know he was there, and then he turned, stumbled out without saying a word.

I lay awake the whole night after that, dreading the next day. But when I saw him, he acted like nothing had happened. I wondered if he'd forgotten, if he'd been too drunk to remember. Or if perhaps it was innocent, that he'd seen me in my clothes, thought it best to help me take them off. But that thought turned my stomach, made me want to vomit. The thought of Barry undressing me.

After that I slept with a chair propped against the back of the door so that it couldn't be opened from the outside. Whether Barry noticed or not, I'll never know. But Mary did. She'd come upstairs one morning in an attempt to get me up for school, tried the handle, found it stuck. She didn't say anything then, just banged on the door, told me to get a bloody move on. That evening she suggested brusquely that it might be an idea for me to stay at hers a bit more often, while Barry got his head around everything that had been going on.

When Danny asked me what had brought on that about-turn from his nana, I played dumb. I don't know why. Maybe I was protecting Danny, maybe Barry. Either way, we weren't going to argue, the both of us bobbing our heads like a pair of nodding dogs as Mary set the ground rules. She wasn't giving us her blessing, she said. Far from it. I could have Danny's bed but he was to stay downstairs on the sofa. We were sure we could get around her, but Mary stayed true to form. It was like she'd had the whole of the staircase sensored—the minute Danny would so much as step a foot out of that living room, she'd be there in her long white nightgown, her hair wild, sending him back off to his quarters. It did our heads in then, but looking back, it only added to the thrill.

CHRISSY HAD BEEN GONE OVER A MONTH WHEN MISS BELL turned up at the pub. I'd been due to start my final year at

Boroughford that September, but it was a few weeks into the term by then and I hadn't shown up once. I certainly didn't miss the school, the sneery girls, the sense of being somewhere I wasn't supposed to be. And yet there was a part of me, a tiny shard, that wondered sometimes about what I might have achieved if things had been different.

It was a pointless thing to think, stupid. A place like that could never have worked out for someone like me. I wouldn't let my head stay in the thought for long, filling my days with so much of Danny that there wasn't room for anything else.

Miss Bell was sitting in the main bar, looking uncomfortable, when I saw her, a blouse buttoned up to her neck and an untouched drink on the table in front of her. I was only ducking in to pick up some clothes. I could have avoided her if I'd chosen to. But instead I made my way toward where she sat.

At the sight of me she beamed, her eyes all eager and pathetic. Jennifer, she said, getting to her feet. I was hoping I'd bump into you.

What you doin here?

She gestured to the chair across from her. Why don't you sit down?

I swore under my breath, but I did as she asked.

There was no one else in the main bar; the pub was often empty by then. I was glad not to have an audience, knew how everyone would gawp and stare at the outsider on home turf. Miss Bell watched me closely as I toyed with a beer mat, worrying the corners until they frayed.

How are you, Jennifer? she asked gently. Something in the way she said it made my throat hurt.

Fine, ta.

She nodded, pensive. We've missed you at Boroughford. I know Mrs. Herrington's been trying to get in touch.

There's been a death in t'family.

Another one? She gave a conspiratorial smile, one eyebrow raised as though we were in on a joke together. I wanted to hate her but I didn't.

I'm sorry to turn up like this, she said, leaning forward in her seat. It's not protocol, really. Not "the done thing." I'd probably get in trouble if anyone found out—

I snorted. Calm down, Miss Bell.

To my surprise, she gave a little laugh. I know! Quite the rebel!

I smiled then, despite myself, and something between us thawed.

Listen, Jennifer . . . I know you don't think much of Boroughford, or of me, for that matter. But regardless of that, there is a genuine concern for your welfare. You've missed so much school and I can't bear to see you waste all your potential . . .

That word again. I rolled my eyes and Miss Bell sat up straight.

I mean it, Jennifer. You're one of the most talented writers I've ever taught, you could achieve so much, if only you'd—

Barry chose that very moment to stumble in through the front door, his lip curling at the sight of us sitting there. He looked from her to me and then back again. What's goin on ere then? he barked. I could tell he didn't recognize Miss Bell.

It's me teacher, I muttered, my cheeks flushing. You've met before.

Barry folded his arms over his chest, rocked back on his

heels unsteadily. Oh, aye? School fees goin t'wards home visits now, are they?

Miss Bell cleared her throat. Well, no. Actually, it's sort of an unofficial visit. But I know the school have been trying to get hold of you both. You and Jennifer's mother—

Barry let out a harsh laugh. Well, good luck on that front, love. You can pass on a few words from me, if yer manage it.

I'm sorry?

Not as sorry as I am. Has she not mentioned it? he said, nodding at me. The silly cow's buggered off. Washed er ands of us both, left me to raise er bloody kid wi'out a word of warnin.

Miss Bell was staring at me now but I couldn't look at her, kept my eyes to the floor as the shame crept up my neck. Jennifer, she said. I had no idea.

It's none of your business, I snapped.

That's right, said Barry. That's right, it int. Comin ere, stickin yer nose in where it int wanted. Well, you can bugger off—you and all yer money-grabbin teacher pals.

I can assure you—

I got to my feet then, got right up in her face. You heard him, I hissed at her. Just fuck off.

Miss Bell looked at me as though she had been slapped and I swallowed hard, hating myself.

Jennifer—

Have we not med ourselves clear enough, eh? Barry spat, his voice raised now.

Miss Bell bit her lip, her cheeks pink, her arms limp by her sides. I willed her not to cry, saw how her hands shook as she reached down to retrieve her sensible little handbag from the stool by the table. She didn't look at us again. Kept her head bowed as she made her way out of the deserted pub.

After she left I stood there silently, watching the dust motes float in a patch of cheerless sunlight filtering through the mucky windows. Barry made his way behind the bar.

You can go to t'high school, just like everyone else, he said as he pulled himself a pint. You're no more special than every other kid round ere, y'know. You and yer sly bitch of a mother've done me out of enough money to last . . .

His words trailed off into nothingness as I pushed open the door.

35

It was Danny who suggested that we run away. He'd said it when he'd first moved back from Denz's around six months before, and the thought had stirred up a feeling in me, a sensation from long ago. A notebook in my waistband, a favorite childhood game. Dreams of another life. But I'd shaken my head firmly, told him I couldn't leave my mam, and I remember the way he looked at me, his eyes full of pity. How naïve I'd been.

What about yer nana? I asked him when he brought it up a second time, not long after Chrissy had left.

She'll be glad to see t'back of me. All I ever do is stress her out, make her sick.

That int true, I said, even though we both knew it was. Since Danny had come back, the tension between him and Mary had thickened, Mary moving around Danny warily whenever he walked into a room, Danny never quite meeting her eye. And Denz? I said, testing the water.

Danny didn't look at me. Denz only cares about himself.

Chrissy being gone gave me all the more ammunition to want to run away. I imagined her turning up at the pub one day, full of sorrow and regret, desperate to get me back, only to find I'd disappeared. I wanted her to feel just some of the hurt that I did.

Before long it became the only thing we thought about, talked about. We'd go to London, Danny said. Stay with Lewis, or near him at least. Brixton was sick, it wouldn't be like that little town, all bigots and small-mindedness. Danny would get a job at those botanical gardens he'd been reading about, maybe start out by mowing the lawns, then work his way up. And you could write stories, he said. Or poems, or both. Make a name fer yerself with one of them big fancy publishers, they'd be fallin over themselves to work with you once they read yer stuff.

Danny made it all sound so possible and I wanted to believe it. But still the doubts niggled at the back of my mind. We need money, I'd say. We can't just go down there without any money.

Yeah, yeah, Danny would nod, taking another draw of his spliff. We'll figure that out.

OUR PLANS SLOWED WHEN MARY AND BARRY BOTH GOT LETTERS in the post, threatening them with a court summons if we didn't start going to school. There'd been a hoo-ha with the government inspectors at the start of the year and they were cracking down on attendances. Neither of us would have paid it much heed, but it was bad enough now that Miss Bell knew Chrissy was gone; the last thing we needed was the council snooping around. Next thing there'd be social services involved and I'd be shipped off into care. No doubt Barry would jump at the chance to have me taken off his remit.

I had wanted to go to Danny's school ever since we'd moved to the pub, but by the time I got there it meant nothing to either of us. We started going just to keep the world off our backs, although neither of us achieved anything by being there. I felt invisible in a whole new sort of way at the high school; there were no Miss Bell types breathing down my neck, no one who cared in the slightest about my words. I thought of her often, not that I'd ever have admitted it.

Most of the kids we'd knocked about with a few months before went to the same school as us, but I kept myself to myself, turning in the opposite direction whenever I saw anyone who knew my name. Ste had finished up there the previous summer, being in the year above Danny and me. I was glad not to run the risk of bumping into him each day, although he still spent most of his days loitering near the school grounds. Now and again I'd see him skulking out from the back of the new Portakabins where all the kids gathered for a smoke, and he'd smirk at me in a way that rattled me senseless. I was sure he knew how dirty I was, the things I'd done.

Danny wound up sitting outside the head teacher's office whether he kept himself in check or not; he was going in stoned most days just to get through the boredom of it. I'd walk past any chance I got, hungry for a glimpse of him, spinning a pen in his fingers or with his feet up on the desk, flashing me a grin, a little wink.

We avoided Mary as much as we could, heading up to Devil's Claw if we knew she wasn't on shift at the pub, knowing that bumping into her meant rows, nagging. Accusations and slammed doors. But then one evening she came home earlier than we'd expected, said she wasn't feeling good. Danny and I weren't doing anything wrong, sitting together on the sofa watching telly, but the look she gave us made it feel like we were.

I'm havin an early night, she said, glaring. Turn that bloody thing down.

Danny ignored her, his jaw clenching, but halfway up the stairs we heard her pause, her whole body racking with coughs. He turned the telly off.

The sound of yelling woke me up the next morning, although I couldn't make out what was going on until I got downstairs. The kitchen was a mess, one of the drawers upended on the floor. I looked from one to the other, unsure who was the angrier of the two.

Well? Mary snapped. Do you know owt about it?

What?

Me purse. Me purse, with a week's worth of wages in it.

What you on about?

It's gone. It's bloody well gone.

She slammed out of the house, her heavy walk more wearied than usual, the sound of her coughing and phlegming carrying halfway down the street. I watched Danny carefully as he poured himself a bowl of cornflakes, set it on the table so heavily that the milk splashed over the sides, never once meeting my eyes.

You think I took it, don't yer? he said to me later as we walked to school.

I swallowed. Did yer?

He stopped in his tracks. Don't really matter, does it? What matters is you think I did.

I didn't see Danny for the rest of the day, and when I went round to Mary's that night he wasn't there.

I've not seen him, she said, her lips tight. I've got no bloody idea where he is.

Well, if you do, tell him I'll be at t'pub.

I was about to leave when I caught sight of her handbag there on the kitchen side, the corner of her purse peering out of the top. You found it then, I said to her, pointing.

She glanced back. Oh. Yeah. Turns out I left it at work.

I LOOKED ALL OVER FOR DANNY, FOUND HIM DOWN BY THE RIVER in the end, an out-of-the-way spot at the far side of the car park. He was leaning up against the trunk of a tree and I sat across from him, slid my knees between his.

I'm sorry. I just thought . . . well. I know we've been tryin to think of a way to get hold of some money.

Danny looked at me hard. You think I'd do that to me nana?

I shook my head, lowered my eyes from his.

I could've turned it on you, y'know. Could've said to her, why don't you ask Neef? Could've asked you meself, later. Except I know you well enough to know you wouldn't do summat like that. Not these days, any rate.

I stayed quiet and he leaned forward, tipped my chin up with his fingers so that we were looking at each other again. Then he let go, resting the back of his head against the tree. Funny, innit? How she assumed it were me straight away. How it never crossed her mind to question you.

I frowned. But it weren't me.

That int the point, Neef.

She found it anyway. I shrugged. She'd left it at the pub.

Danny raised his eyebrows, then nodded slowly like it all made sense. I toyed with his shoelace, trying to think of something to say, but he spoke first. Did you ever ask yer mum what it's like?

I frowned. What?

You know . . . gettin on it. What she takes.

What you askin me that fer?

No reason . . . well, you must wonder. She's yer mum, int she?

Pins and needles of anxiety bristled at my fingertips and I stretched out my arms, lying down on the grass so that Danny couldn't see my face. I tried it, y'know, I said quietly.

What?

I twisted onto my side, propped my head up on my elbow, my heart racing. I tried it. Me mam's stuff.

He studied me carefully and I waited for the lecture. Hoped for it, I think. Did she give it yer?

What does that matter?

He shrugged. What were it like?

All right. Good, actually. Yeah, pretty good.

I wanted him to call me an idiot. Shake his head at me, be disappointed. But instead he just nodded again. We need to get out of here, he said.

36

More than a week has passed since Denz and I spoke at Brixton Market, and yet still everything swirls around and around in my head.

He was angry when I couldn't answer him, when he asked me if I thought Danny was in London and I looked at him like a deer in traffic, stuttering over my words. But Denz doesn't understand what it means to put that idea into the air. All the things it brings up. The confusion, the long-buried hope. The years and years I have spent, blocking all of it from my thoughts.

You're not the only one with a past, Ali had said to me in the days that followed. *Find a way to get unstuck from it.* His words battle with Denz's, taking turns to circle my brain. Ali is right. I am stuck. But perhaps the only way to change that is to answer Denz's question.

. . .

THE MAP ON MY PHONE TELLS ME IT IS JUST OVER AN HOUR FROM the caff to Richmond, but the journey takes me the best part of the morning. I don't let myself think about what it is I'm doing and so I count all the way to Streatham Hill station, fill my brain with numbers on the first ten-minute train ride. By the time we pull into Clapham Junction my head pounds with the effort, my eyes swimming as I tread the platform.

For a while I walk in circles around the inside of the station, try to steady my nerves. I think about going into one of the overpriced chain cafés, their menus as long as my arm, but a strange sense of loyalty to Fionnoula and Ali stops me and instead I head out onto the high street, pace up and down, tell myself I'm being ridiculous.

Eventually I pull myself together, stand shivering on Platform 6, but still I let two trains pass me by before I force myself to get on. I haven't told Denz what I'm doing. Don't even want to admit it to my own mind. I'm just having a little day out, that's all. I've never been to Kew Gardens before.

Richmond smells like money, like people with second homes and personalized number plates and flat-faced dogs that cost more than I earn in three months. The gardens are a fifteen-minute walk from the station, and as I pass through the streets I let myself daydream a little, the way I used to when I was a kid. What would it be like to stand in front of the organic grocer's, squeezing avocados with one neatly manicured hand while the other distractedly rocks a designer pram? To call in at a hair boutique for a dip-dye job that they're calling something fancy and French-sounding these days, or to while away an hour clad in pastel leisurewear, meditating on a yoga mat inside one of the chi-chi studios? A familiar feeling comes to me then, an itch in my fingers for the grip of a pen, the long-ago yearning for my notebook, and the shock of it brings me to a stop in the middle of the street. I pull the wall down on my thoughts, start to count again, to fill up my head.

The lady at the entrance to the gardens smiles at me distractedly, watches me scrabble through my bag for every last penny. The price of the ticket works out at a couple of hours' worth of my wages, and I kick myself for not checking my purse before I set off. In the end I am short, but not by much. For a moment I think she will turn me away, but she sighs, waves me through. The shame of it bites my tongue, stops me from explaining to her why I'm here, what it is I'm looking for. I walk away quickly, unsure where to begin now that I've arrived.

I wander aimlessly, my eyes seeking out someone who might be able to help me. It is winter still and the gardens are quiet, but there are people I could ask, if I had the nerve. An older man pushing a wheelbarrow a few yards ahead, a figure crouched down near some flowerbeds. I walk a little further and cross paths with a salt-and-pepper-haired lady wearing a fleece and a name-badge, so close that I could touch her. I realize I am staring when she smiles at me questioningly, but I bottle it, look away.

The chill numbs my hands, stains the beds of my nails violet, and I seek out the warmth of the glasshouses. This is stupid. A stupid plan. Not even a plan in fact, because what am I doing here? What is it I'm looking for? Chasing a long-lost dream, a half-hatched idea that Danny and I used to fantasize about when we were stoned out of our teenage minds? The gardens are enormous, over three hundred acres, one poster tells me. What am I going to do: just wander around them all day, hoping I might find answers, when I don't even know what the question is? I shouldn't be here, this is all Denz's fault. I'm going backward. I need to forget again.

I'm not looking where I'm going, don't notice the hosepipe trailing on the floor in front of me until it is too late. I trip, fall, scuffing the heels of my hands. A man wearing a navy-blue T-shirt branded with the garden's logo and a name-badge that says "Graham" helps me to my feet. He is apologetic, checking if I'm all right, if I'm hurt. I brush my palms off on my thighs, insist that I'm fine. Just embarrassed if anything, I say with a fake little laugh.

Are you sure? he says. Your hand's bleeding.

No, really I'm . . . Something about the kindness in the man's voice makes me brave and I take a deep breath, let the words tumble out too fast. I'mlookingforsomeone.

Oh?

Yeah. A friend of mine. I thought maybe he might work here.

The man nods amiably. He is short, only an inch or so taller than me, his hair thinning, combed over to one side. What's his name?

Daniel, I say. Daniel Campbell.

The feeling of Danny's full name on my tongue changes the taste in my mouth, and when I meet the man's eyes, I see that he is looking at me strangely. He parts his lips as if to speak, but then turns away, bending to gather the hosepipe. It's a big place, Kew Gardens. There's—ooh, gosh—close to eight or nine hundred people work here, see.

He might go by Danny, I try again.

The man stands, studies me intently. I shift my weight, brush my hair out of my eyes, awkward under his gaze. Sorry I couldn't be more help, he says at last.

There is a look on his face that I can't read, suspicion or pity, or maybe both. Is there anywhere else I could try? I ask hopefully.

He turns the hosepipe another loop over his arm before answering. Up to you, love. He shrugs.

I nod, defeated. At the door of the glasshouse I glance back over my shoulder, see the man still standing there, watching me.

I TRUDGE BACK ALONG THE PATH, PRESSING MY BLEEDING HAND against the lining of my coat pocket, trying to ignore its sting. Part of me wants to give up, shove my head back in the sand. But there is something about the way the man stared at me, the strange look on his face, that I can't shake. It's almost a surprise when I find I am outside the administration office, as if I have delivered myself there on autopilot. Pushing open the door, I step inside before I can change my mind.

The girl behind the desk is flustered by my presence, my questions. She is busy, too busy to try to understand what it is I want, her eyes darting around the room as she speaks. I'm sorry, she is saying. But I can't disclose information about our employees. It goes against our company policy and, apart from anything, it's actually illegal—

Right, yeah. I nod. Don't worry about it. I turn to leave, but as I do so she sighs.

I can pass your details on to someone in HR, if you like, she says, pushing her glasses back into her hair and rubbing at her eyes as though the thought of it has given her a headache. But I can't promise they'll be in touch.

She waves a pad of sticky notes at me and I smile at her with as much gratitude as I can muster, scribble down my number, slide it back across the desk. Thanks, I say flatly. I know I won't hear from them again.

I walk back to the station in a daze, dizzied by the frenzy and movement around me, the sense of everyone being too swallowed up by their own shit to stop and ask you anything about yours. Hours later I find myself standing across the road from Brixton station, watching face after face stream out of the Underground and into the street. Men in expensive suits and oversized headphones weaving their way through the drunk and the lost and the lonely. Harassed-looking women dragging whining schoolchildren by the hand, dodging the wild-eyed preacher on his soapbox. Pixie dreamgirls puffing on sugary vapes as they skip toward the Academy. Bewildered locals who look like they no longer recognize the streets they once called their own.

Every age and color and shape and sort, but not a single face I know.

37

The weekend that followed the mess over Mary's purse, Danny and I set about pruning the branches of the plants he'd been secretly growing at the bottom of the greenhouse. Back then I took it as a given that Danny knew all there was to know about everything, and yet the years that followed taught us plenty. The plants he'd grown weren't ready for drying; the weed still too young and sticky to make for a decent smoke. But we didn't think about any of that, all we cared about was getting away from that dead-end town.

I'd managed to avoid Ste properly for months up until the day Danny led me behind the Portakabins at the far end of the school grounds. A few of the kids we used to knock about with down the park were congregated there, Ste at the center, their self-appointed leader. A sly smile spread over his face at the sight of us. Look what the cat coughed up. He sneered.

I hung back, didn't make eye contact with anyone, let Danny do the talking. No one seemed interested in buying off him, mind. Ste made sure of that, prodding at the contents of the baggy Danny let him take a look at, then throwing it back with a sneer.

We're all right, ta, he said, speaking for all of them. He took a step toward us, his eyes narrowed. This what you been doin all this time then, sittin in on yer own, tryin to smoke this shite? You used to be a good laugh, yous two. Don't you ever feel like havin a bit of fun?

Danny bristled, twisting his tongue between the gap in his teeth. Depends what you call fun.

Yeah, I s'pose it does. Ste cocked his head at me then, a glint in his eye. You and me got a friend in common, I hear.

Oh yeah? I mumbled, my voice small.

Yeah. He nodded. Jody.

I bit the inside of my lip, aware of Ste's minions behind him, their eyes on stalks. Danny was looking at me too, I could feel it.

He wouldn't take kindly, I don't think, to hear you're tryin to shift on his patch.

Jody sells whizz, Ste, I said then, finding my voice.

Ste took a drag of his cig, blew out the smoke slowly. I'd watch yer mouth if I were you.

As we walked away from them toward the main road, I slipped my hand into the crook of Danny's elbow. He stiffened.

Who's this Jody then? he asked.

I tossed my hair over my shoulder. A mate of Chrissy's.

You never mentioned him.

You never asked.

Despite Ste, Danny managed to shift everything he had to a bunch of clueless kids in the lower school; but all we got to show for it was fifty quid. I could have lifted some money from the till easy enough, except I knew Danny would never stand for it. We'd just have to think of something else.

WE WERE ASLEEP UPSTAIRS TOGETHER WHEN THE POLICE TURNED up a few days later. Mary hadn't been as onto us recently; she'd started taking sleeping pills or painkillers, or maybe both by then, not that Danny or I ever thought to ask why. They were pounding on the door, yelling for us to open it, that they'd break it down if we didn't, even though they knew it was Mary's house. It was four in the morning and Danny jumped out of bed in his boxers, ran down the stairs and I followed him, stopped in my tracks at the sight of Mary across the hall in her nightie, creases on her face from the pillows, her lungs creaking.

They must have had a warrant, although I don't remember anyone showing us it. They were all over that house in minutes. The three of us sat on the sofa under the watch of one of the officers, a young lad not much older than us. They let me put a dressing gown on over my underwear, but Danny was still sat there in his boxers. None of us spoke— I can't remember if they told us not to. I kept looking over at Mary, her gray skin, the terror in her eyes, and Danny next to me, his leg jiggling up and down, his jaw tense.

They didn't find anything, other than a couple of sad-looking plants, their branches picked bare. It must have been a disappointment to them, all those resources, all that fuss. Still, they made the most of it, putting Danny in cuffs in front of his nana, making her cry. He kept calm until it became apparent that they were going to arrest me too. Then he started kicking off, shouting and swearing, calling them all a bunch of bent bastards. In the end they didn't even let him put any clothes on, took him down the station just like that.

They made us go separately, Danny in the van, and me in the patrol car driven by the young lad who'd taken pleasure in marching us out of the house as the whole street woke up to the sight. He kept making eyes at me in the rearview mirror, passing little digs. You could do a lot better, love. He smirked. Nothin good will come of him, I'll tell you that fer nowt.

They put me in a holding cell and one of the policewomen brought me a cup of tea in a Styrofoam cup, asked me if there was anyone she could call on my behalf. I gave her Chrissy's mobile number, even though I knew it was long dead. The tea tasted like shit and I poured it down the steel hole in the corner of the cell, ripped the cup into little pieces, spelled out our names with the torn shreds. N-E-E-F, then D-A-N-N-Y, rearranging the letters over and over again.

After a while they unlocked the door, took me to a stuffy gray box of an interview room lit with bright strips that cast ugly shadows on the officers' faces. It was the same one who'd been driving the car and another bloke, older, fatter, with an accent that wasn't from round there. They told me they'd not been able to get hold of Chrissy, asked me if I wanted another adult to come and sit with me while we had a chat. I said no and they seemed pleased with that. I stumbled over their questions: my name, where I lived, how I knew Danny. They wanted to know how long we'd been seeing each other and I remember feeling confused, not knowing how to answer that question, not understanding why that had anything to do with the reason I was there. Since we were kids, I said, and they eyed me strangely, exchanged a look but moved on.

What were those plants in the greenhouse, Jennifer?

I dunno.

Were they marijuana plants?

I dunno.

Has Daniel Campbell been cultivating marijuana?

No.

Does he sell drugs, Jennifer?

No.

Eventually they turned me loose, leading me out into the waiting area of the station where Mary sat, her chest rattling. Where's Danny? I asked. The officer raised his eyebrows, grimaced.

We've got a few more questions we need to ask him yet, love.

I made a move as though to sit beside Mary but she looked at me with a face set hard as stone, told me to get my arse out of there, get back to the pub.

Barry was waiting for me in the back bar; someone must have let him know what had gone on. He didn't say much. Just looked at me in the same way Mary had, barked at me to go upstairs and sort myself out, I'd be working the kitchen today, seein as his cook was "required elsewhere."

THE PIGS DIDN'T HAVE EVIDENCE TO CHARGE DANNY WITH ANY-thing, but he was expelled from school all the same. He'd been on his final warning, they'd made that very clear, they said. Daniel knew fine well the school had zero tolerance on drugs; there were no more chances. The police would be notified immediately if he so much as tried to step foot anywhere near there again. Mary stopped speaking to us for a long while after that.

A few days after the arrest we were sitting around at Mary's, doing not much of anything, when we heard a noise like the flat of someone's palm banging against the PVC door. My first thought was that the pigs had come back, but then we heard the voice, hollering for Danny to open up.

Danny didn't move at first, and when he did it was slowly, as though he were wading through water. He twisted the latch, then took a step back, the visitor's shadow darkening the hallway.

I hadn't seen Denz since before Chrissy disappeared. Half expected that the next time he showed up it would be with my mam on his arm, trotting her around like a trophy, like the rest of them always had. I wanted to go to the window, run past Denz out of the door, see if she was sitting there in the passenger seat of his car. But the stillness of Danny and Denz bearing down on each other cemented me in my place.

A moment passed before Danny walked back into the living room. Denz followed behind him, uninvited. At the sight of me, he stiffened.

I didn't know you had company.

Danny was taller than his dad now, slimmer too, although the two of them were so undeniably alike. Better she's here than stuck on her own at t'pub with that old pisshead. He sneered.

Denz swallowed, refusing to take any bait. Come on then. Let's hear it.

What?

All this bother you been gettin into wi t'police.

I don't have to explain meself to you.

Oh yeah? Why's that?

Danny puffed his cheeks out, blew the air through his lips in disbelief. You think I owe you honesty? After all the shite you've fed me?

I don't know what you're talkin about, Danny.

I held my breath as Denz took a step forward, reaching out as though to place a hand on his son's shoulder, but Danny shirked away.

Danny, Denz tried again, his voice softer now. I aren't here to judge you. I know what the pigs are like. I just need to know . . . He glanced at me and then back again. You're only sixteen, Danny. I don't want you to ruin your life over all this. I need to know how far you're into it.

Danny frowned. What?

You look skinny, man. Denz turned, angling himself so that his back was toward me. You . . . you don't look good.

What you on about?

You been takin summat? Denz asked warily. You on gear?

Danny let out a laugh like a bark. Recognize the signs, do yer? he jeered. You'd know all about that, wouldn't yer? You'd only have to look at yer girlfriend.

Denz stood back as though he'd been struck, and I heard myself speaking as though from very far away.

You seen owt of me mam, Denz?

Both of them stared at me then. Not for time, Denz replied eventually.

You were shaggin her, though, weren't yer?

Danny flinched, but Denz held my glare. You shouldn't talk that way about your mother, he said, then paused, licking his lips as though readying his mouth to say more. I thought, he said slowly, I thought it might've done you a favor, her leavin. Thought without her around, you might be better off. Might sort yourself out. But I can see now I got that wrong, eh? The apple don't fall all that far from the tree, does it, Neef?

I felt my body tense. He had no right to speak about my mam that way, to look down his nose at her, at me. I wanted to stand up, scream in his face, but something kept me still in my seat. Perhaps it was the truth in his words.

Danny took a step toward me. What's that supposed to mean? he growled.

It means, Denz said carefully, that if you know what's good for you, you'll steer clear of her. He gestured at me with a nod, but he didn't look at me. And when you do, you know where I am.

My eyes stung from the sharpness of Denz's words. I wanted to ask him more, make him tell me where Chrissy was. But he was gone before the words could form in my mouth, the pair of us watching in silence through the window as he climbed into his car and pulled away.

DANNY MUST HAVE GONE OUT TO THE GREENHOUSE AFTER THAT, because I remember sitting in Mary's front room by myself for a long time. We couldn't avoid the truth anymore. We both knew that Denz had plenty to do with Chrissy disappearing.

When Danny came back in I was all geared up to confront him, for the pair of us to understand what all of it might mean.

You were talkin about me mam, before, weren't yer? I asked him, my voice weaker than I wanted it to be. When you said Denz had a girlfriend?

Danny didn't react, perching across from me on Mary's coffee table.

Danny—I tried again, but he stopped me, waving his hand like it didn't matter.

Don't worry about all that, he said, a strange look on his face. He put his hands on my knees, his eyes glittering. Let's get fucked up, Neef.

What?

Let's go see Ste, you and me, and get summat. Get mad fucked up.

I frowned, confused. D'you mean, like . . .

Yeah. He was grinning now. Might as well, everyone thinks we're on it, as it is. Might as well, eh?

38

Danny and I didn't have any money but Ste let us score a couple of pills on tick, said he'd heard we'd been in a bit of bother, it was understandable we needed cheering up. I wanted to snipe back that I wasn't surprised he'd heard, that it was funny how the police had come round to Danny's only a few days after we'd seen Ste round the back of the high school. But as soon as I opened my mouth, Danny dug me in the ribs like he knew I was about to start something I shouldn't.

After we swallowed them we walked over to a spot by the river that none of the other kids ever bothered with, sat there quietly with our backs against the viaduct, waiting to feel something. It was only when I turned to Danny to tell him that Ste was as much of a dickhead as I'd thought, giving us a pair of duds, that I felt it. The rush.

Your pupils are massive.

Yours are.

Can you feel that?

Yeah. Yeah, yeah.

I don't know who came up with the idea to go on a bike ride, whose bike it was. But before I knew it, that's what we were doing, our skin tingling as we flew, soaring through a wonderland of streets and fields and pathways that felt brand new, even though we knew them like the back of our hands. Danny was shouting something to me over his shoulder but I couldn't hear because of the wind rushing in my ears, the drizzling rain like stars on my skin and my hair flying behind me like electricity. But I was nodding and grinning, and grinning and nodding anyway.

Doesn't it?

What?

Doesn't it feel good, doesn't it feel so *good*?

Yeah, man. Yeah.

We rode all the way to the far end of the old railway track, dumped the bike at the edge of the castle ruins, lay down on our backs in the long grass, hidden by the old stone walls. Both of us talking, talking like our jaws were running on motors. Big plans, big dreams, because anything was possible. And it did, it felt so good, better than anything I'd ever done with Chrissy. The minutes sped past us, staining the sky navy until I had the sense of the magic slipping away from us and I shivered. Danny pulled me in close and then his lips were on mine, and mine on his, like we were starving for each other and I loved him I loved him. I love him so much.

· · ·

IT'S NOT AS THOUGH DANNY AND I WENT OFF THE RAILS AFTER that first taste of ecstasy. It was a now-and-again thing, we kept a lid on it mostly. We still had plenty of dreams, big ideas. We still believed we'd run away.

Danny was keen to start working, reckoned he'd make enough for the pair of us to get to London within a couple of months. He started applying for all sorts as soon as he got kicked out of school, but none of them ever came to anything. Mary still wasn't speaking to him, other than to call him work-shy, lazy, turning-out-just-like-you-know-who, that was her favorite one. Then one day, seemingly out of the blue, Craig from two doors down knocked on the door, told Danny he was looking for an apprentice and would he be keen?

Mary denied it, but I'd put money on her having a hand in setting it up. Craig had been at school with Danny's mum, had a thing for her by all accounts, although he'd never said more than two words to Danny. He had his own landscape-gardening business, but Danny never bothered to ask him about a job, he'd always had the feeling Craig didn't like him. Nothing he could put his finger on, he said. Just got that vibe.

Well, you must've got it wrong. He wouldn't ask you if he didn't like you, would he?

I aren't bothered if he likes me or not. Danny shrugged. It's money, innit? It'll get us out of here at least. And any rate, it's gardenin. I'll be good at this.

Despite what Danny said, I knew he wanted to impress Craig. It embarrassed him, to be doing what he'd always said he wouldn't—going nowhere like everybody else. But it was bad from the very first day. He didn't need to tell me, I could see it in the dull of his eyes each evening, could hear it in the grunt of the few words he spoke. Only much later did he admit to me all that went on, Craig's attempts to humiliate him, make him feel stupid, acting as though Danny would have struggled under the simplest of instructions, even though he could have done that job with his eyes shut. Danny was ten times the gardener Craig was.

He was supposed to finish at half past five every day, but always Craig made him stay on after all the other lads had gone home so that he could do an inventory of his tools, just to check nothing had been left behind on the job, he said. He'd make Danny trail behind him with a clipboard and pen, ticking everything off his list, eyeing him suspiciously as though Danny might have stuck a hedge-trimmer up the sleeve of his jumper.

Once, when the two of them had gone to pick up some stuff from the suppliers and Danny had been sent off to load bags of soil into the back of the van, he'd watched from behind a stack of pallets as Craig laughed and joked with the bloke who owned the place, his body curved over and his arms swinging, ape-like, as he repeated, slack-jawed, a question Danny had asked him earlier in the day.

Less than a month into the job, the pair of them were lowering the lawnmower out of the back of Craig's van and somehow it slipped, cracking one of the side panels. Craig roared at Danny, showing him up in front of the woman whose house it was. But it was the words he muttered under his breath that made Danny's fists swing.

The woman called the police, had Danny arrested on the spot, made this big long speech to the officer about what a lovely fella Craig was, how he'd been doing her garden for nearly two years, how Danny had attacked him, unprovoked.

Danny didn't say anything, didn't tell them how Craig had riled him. What would have been the point? he said flatly when I asked him about it later. They're all the same.

I was helping Mary at the pub with the food service, running plates of sandwiches and bowls of soup and microwaved pasta dishes in and out and in and out, when the call from the station came. The phone rang for ages before anyone got round to answering it; we were short-staffed that day, as we often were. Barry had never bothered getting anyone in to cover Chrissy's shifts.

One of the locals picked it up in the end. Neef, love, he said, waving me over to him. It's Danny. Think he might be down t'cop shop. When I answered the phone, he didn't sound scared or angry. He didn't sound anything. Just blank, like none of it made him feel anymore.

I'm at the station, he said. Need someone to come and sign me out.

Who, me?

He laughed then. Nah, man. A guardian. Because I'm only sixteen.

So, yer nana?

A pause. Yeah. Can you tell her?

Mary was in the kitchen, shuffling around. She'd been coughing all morning, having to stop every few minutes to clear her lungs, then nipping outside to calm down with a cig. I dreaded going in there. She knew straight away there was something wrong. What you doin, skulkin about? she said when she saw me hovering by the door. What's up with yer?

Danny's been arrested, I mumbled. He's there now, at the station. But you can go and pick him up, they said.

She went off on one then, swearing and cursing, about

Danny and Denz and *here we effin go* and *this is just the start* and *mark my words, I'll string him up before I'm six feet under,* and on and on and on. I wanted to go with her but I didn't dare ask, stood there dumbly as she chucked her apron on the floor and limped toward the door. A coughing fit overtook her as she neared it, making her lean against the frame while her whole body shook. I couldn't watch, stared instead at the orders Blu-tacked to the shelf and took over where she'd left off, spooning out mashed potatoes and mixing gravy granules into the pot.

WHEN DANNY TOLD MARY WHAT HAD GONE ON WITH CRAIG, SHE stared at him in disbelief. Sticks and stones, what have I always taught you? Sticks and bloody stones.

What's that s'posed to mean?

It's words, Danny, only bloody words! You've got to grow a tougher skin, lad, you can't be losin every job you get just because someone calls you summat you don't like.

I hadn't dared look at Danny in that moment. Heard the door slam behind him as he left.

Two weeks later, someone put through the front windows of Craig's house and the police came looking for Danny again. There wasn't enough evidence to charge him, but they made it clear they were biding their time. We've got our eye on you, lad.

It seemed to me they were waiting for Danny to lose his footing. Danny said it was because of how he looked, but I told him it was more to do with him being Denz's son; they'd never liked Denz. I didn't understand what he meant when he said it was one and the same thing.

Mary couldn't let it rest. Yer mother would be ashamed of

you, she'd say. She'd be turning in her grave at what a mess you've become. Look at yer. You're nowt but a common thug. You're going to end up just like *him,* she'd rant. Just you watch. That pieceofshitofasocalledfather.

It would push Danny so far that in the end he'd storm out of the house in silence, his eyes wild, and I'd know, then, that there would be trouble. A run-in, a fight, an outlet for him to unleash his fury elsewhere. And so the cycle would go on, Danny's springs uncoiling further and further while the chasm of Mary's fear stretched until it tore.

39

For a time everyone seemed to be in denial about how poorly Mary was. We told ourselves not to notice the gray-green tinge to her skin, the labored rattle of her breath. The incessant cough that had plagued her for months.

She'd survived cancer twice before: once when Kim was a teenager, another time when Danny was in primary school. There was a solidity, an assuredness to Mary that gave the impression of something indestructible, but we carried on the charade of ignorance for far too long. When she finally got round to seeing the doctor it had spread too far for them to do anything, and yet still she insisted she knew better. Scaremongerin, that's what them doctors like to do, she'd say as we stood by and watched her shrink.

Mary only stopped working when she could barely stand anymore, and even then she kept telling everyone she'd be going back soon. I tried to play along with her. It's only fer a few weeks, I'd say, reassuring us both. You'll be back there before you know it, once you're feelin better.

It's nowt to do with feelin better! she snapped one afternoon after I'd trilled off the same old lines. It's you bastard kids I've got to keep an eye on. She coughed so much then that I had to run to get her a bowl to be sick in, thick like tar and streaked with blood.

Mary worried that the pub would fall apart without her there—all those years of grind had given her a sense of responsibility about the place. I tried to tell her that it would be all right, that we'd all pull together, but I don't think she trusted what came out of my mouth. As much as I couldn't bear being around Barry, I did my best to cover her shifts, impossible as it was to keep on top of that kitchen, all the cooking and cleaning.

Three months had passed since the incident with Craig. It was coming to the end of my final year at school, but I'd paid no attention to my exams. Most days after the last bell I'd walk round to do Mary and Danny's tea. She was too done in by then to argue, although it was probably pointless me being there. Nobody would eat much. It hurt Mary to swallow and so I started puréeing hers, turning sausage and mash, cottage pies, fish and chips into strange sorts of soups.

By then Danny was smoking so much that a conversation about Mary being ill felt impossible. Almost everything was broken between the two of them, but she was still his nana. I know it terrified him, to see her fade. I know that's why we stopped talking about leaving.

They looked as bad as each other at one point. Mary with the skin hanging off her bones, her shuffling walk, and

Danny with his yellowed hue, his red, hooded eyes. I needed to keep busy, keep cooking, anything to fend off the sensation of creeping terror; the fear that Mary might be gone soon. Worse still, what that might do to Danny.

Don't think, Mary said thinly one day when the three of us were sitting round the table, Danny with his head bent low, almost as though he were half asleep. Don't think I don't know what's going on under this roof.

I tried to fill the silence. A nervous laugh, a clattering of plates. What d'you mean, Mary, me and Danny? Not till we're married, I've told you that before, ha-ha. But even when she was poorly, she still had that steely gaze that could stop me dead in my tracks, make me feel like a little kid again.

Don't talk soft, she snapped, lifting a gnarled finger and jabbing it at Danny. I know what you're up to. Sellin that crap, workin fer that bastard.

He turned his face toward her slowly, his eyes dark. Workin fer what bastard?

Don't gimme that, Danny. That piece of shit, the same evil that saw yer mother six feet under, that's what bastard. Draggin you into all sorts, givin you big ideas, tellin you the police have got it in f'yer and then gettin you involved in all his doings—

Danny jerked upward then, his knees clattering against the table as he stood, his voice laced with resentment. You don't know what you're talkin about, all right? You leave me dad out of it. I know what you are—I've always known. I know why you don't like him, why you don't like me. I aren't daft, I can see right through yer—

Danny, stop. Stop—

He turned on me then. Shut yer mouth, Neef, he spat. It's

got nowt to do with you, it never has. You've never under-stood.

He stormed out, knocking his plate off the table as he left. When I looked at Mary, her eyes were filled with tears, her hands trembling. I stood to clear the mess and she began to cough, so bad I started to think that was it, she was going to choke on her own phlegm and I'd be left there, scraping puréed roast potatoes off the kitchen floor. I put out my hand to comfort her but she shrugged me off, the coughs slowing down until all that was left was the death-rattle in her chest. When she spoke, she was quiet and bitter, almost as though she were talking to herself and not me.

He's gettin more and more like him every day. You watch, once I'm gone, he'll turn into him.

40

Over a year had passed since Chrissy left. I'd limped across the finish line of school without a qualification to my name, turning sixteen without ceremony. Winter was already darkening the skies by midafternoon. Barry and I barely exchanged two words anymore, even though I was working at the pub all the time by then. He'd found some loophole that meant I could serve on the bar even though I was underage. One night I'd heard him talking to one of the few remaining locals. I hadn't been eavesdropping, he was saying it for my benefit.

No wonder this place is goin down t'pan, he'd griped. First that slapper upstairs sleeps with half the punters, then her kid gets caught up in all sorts and the police start breathin down me neck. No wonder everyone stays away from here these days. They're a bloody curse, them women, I should never have opened up me home to them.

If the pub had begun on its downward spiral after Chrissy left, once Mary stopped working there it went to the dogs. It must have broken Barry's heart to see all the old fellas who'd lined the bar every night for god knows how many years dip their heads and cross the street when they saw him coming. He wasn't daft. He knew they all drank up the road these days, at the flashy new place owned by one of the breweries.

Danny said Barry was taking the piss, how he never paid me on time. When it eventually came, it was always under at least twenty quid, never mind all the extra I put in. I didn't bring it up, felt like I owed it to Barry after what Chrissy had put him through. And I felt like I owed it to Mary too.

I NEVER TOLD DANNY ABOUT THE NIGHT MARY DIED. I WOULD have, if he'd asked. My shifts were meant to be supervised, but Barry didn't pay any heed to that, left me there on my own while he was upstairs, doing the books. It was midweek and he'd come down just before ten to tell me I could lock up, no point staying open when it was dead in there.

She was on the sofa when I got to theirs and it struck me as odd straight away, because by then she was spending most of her time in bed. It was too much for her to be traipsing up and down the stairs, she needed to be near the bathroom on the landing. At first I thought she was asleep, could hear the rattle of her chest with each breath, shallow and labored but consistent, steady almost. But when I leaned down next to her, I saw the packet of painkillers lying empty by her side, the purple skin around her eyes, cheeks hollowed out like two sunken pits. I don't know if she knew I was there. I tried to talk to her, said her name over and over, squeezed her hand, but she didn't respond, didn't even flicker her eyes in acknowledgment.

I called Danny before I called the ambulance. Three, four, maybe five times but he didn't pick up and I couldn't wait any longer, even though I knew she'd hate me for what I was about to do.

There was a fella who used to come down the pub—Jim, I think they called him. Before his wife got poorly he'd be there every Sunday at opening for a pint. Mary always had time for him. She'd sidle out and say hello, ask after his wife, Sheila.

Sheila got diagnosed with cancer around Halloween one year, and by Christmas she was dead. They took her into a hospice three weeks before she died and after that Jim started coming in the pub most days. Mary never spoke to him anymore, not really. After a while I pulled her up on it, asked her why she had such a problem with him. At first she acted like she didn't know what I was talking about, but finally she came out with it, said she couldn't believe that he'd let her die like that, away from the place where she felt safe, where she'd lived for all that time. The woman deserved dignity. She should have been allowed to go in her own home.

Mary never regained consciousness in the hospital. The doctors said it was unlikely she was aware of her surroundings, but I could feel it in my heart that she knew. She took her last breath two days later, lying in a hard green hospital cot bathed in the smell of antiseptic.

Danny never came. I veered from fury to fear, left messages, called everyone I could think of. But he was off the grid, disappearing into thin air just like Denz.

They sent me home with a carrier bag full of Mary's things, and Barry and I drove back to her house in silence, a feeling in the air like we were waiting to wake up from a bad dream. I asked Barry if he wanted to come in and he looked at me like something he'd stepped in. It's not your home to be invitin me into, he said, and I lowered my head with shame.

Danny showed up late that afternoon, walked into the front room where I sat on the sofa like an intruder, a thief who had robbed Mary of her last wishes. I could tell by his face he knew. Neither of us could think of the words to say and for a while I just watched him walk around, trailing his fingers over the furniture, the kitchen counter, the back of the chair where Mary used to sit, pausing at a single strand of hair, a silver scar on worn velvet. He didn't cry and neither did I. Eventually he sat down in the corner of the sofa. I climbed onto his lap wordlessly.

The pair of us moved through the days that followed in a daze, not knowing where one ended and another began. It was Barry who organized the funeral. He tried to involve Danny in the planning but eventually he gave up, pushed a note through the door with the details of the service at the church and the do planned afterward at the pub. I stuck it on the fridge as though it were an invitation to a wedding of someone we vaguely knew. When the date came round, I woke up to find the space in the bed next to me empty, Danny's suit hanging like a hollowed skin on the outside of the wardrobe.

He was downstairs on the back step, an ashtray and a half-drunk cup of tea beside him. It starts at eleven, I said dully and he nodded.

I know.

I trudged back upstairs, stood under the shower until the water grew tepid. When I came out of the bathroom, Danny was gone, the hanger where his suit had been now cast aside on top of the unmade bed. It hit me like a kick, that he would have left without me. That he wouldn't have wanted us to be by one another's side on that day, of all days.

The walk to the church was the loneliest I could remember. I half wondered if word might have got to Chrissy, if she might show up unannounced. As I neared the crowd gathered outside I found myself scanning it for a flash of bleach-blond hair, that scrawny little silhouette, but there was no sign of her and no sign of him.

Slowly everyone began to move inside, Barry standing greeting the mourners at the door like a grieving husband, and it struck me as sad, in that moment, that that wasn't who he'd been. I waited for Danny for as long as I could, smoking my cigs to the filter, one after the other, as the last person filed in. It was ten minutes past the time the service was supposed to begin when the vicar came out and told me they couldn't wait any longer.

But her grandson— I started and he nodded at me with understanding.

I realize he's not here and I'm terribly sorry, but we have to adhere to the schedule as closely as possible. We have another funeral here later today.

The vicar led me inside and I slid into a pew at the back, so that I could watch the door. Halfway through the service I saw him come in and my heart leaped, but my eyes were playing tricks on me and instead of Danny there was Denz. He didn't sit, stood at the back on the opposite side of the church, his head bowed. I wanted to go to him, to ask him if he knew where Danny was, but as the congregation sang the last hymn I looked over and saw that he'd slipped away.

On the way to the wake, I stopped by Mary's house but no one was there and so I left, carried on alone. The pub was heaving for once, it seemed like the whole of the town had shown up to say their goodbyes. I remember wondering who had done the buffet, thinking how pathetic it all looked, compared to if Mary had been in charge. I didn't want to speak to anyone and yet all the time I fielded questions. Where's Danny? We've not seen him yet, how's he gettin on, where is he, love?

Most of the kids from down the park were there but I stood alone in the back bar, watching them all drift off one by one. None of them said goodbye. I stayed late to help Barry get cleaned up, although he didn't do much himself, he was well gone by then. When the pub eventually closed, I went back to Mary's, fell asleep on the sofa, my face swollen with all the tears I didn't know how to cry.

Danny was standing over me when I woke up. I could tell he hadn't been to sleep. He sat down beside me, put his head in his hands. Please, Neef, he said. And I understood.

His feet led us to Devil's Claw without words, our fingers laced together. Danny didn't notice me freeze there at the bottom of the bank, carried on, disappearing into the undergrowth. By the time I reached him he was lying on the grass, flat out on his back.

I couldn't face it, he said, his eyes staring up at a patch of colorless sky.

I sat beside him, chewing at the skin around my nails, not wanting to think of the arms and knees that had pinned me to that ground. Denz were there, I said.

He turned on his side to look at me and for once I couldn't tell what he was thinking. I wanted to leave that place, wanted to be away from its smell and its taste and its memories. But I didn't have the words, didn't know how to say any of it. I leaned forward, touched my forehead to his, circled the back of his neck into the crooks of my elbows and pulled myself close so that we were wrapped up, entangled, alone.

t is a terrible thing to say, to think even, that someone's death could make things better for those still living. Especially someone you thought you cared about. The truth of it was, though, Mary dying did just that. For a time, at least. We both grieved, in our own way. But despite my worries about what might become of Danny once his nana was gone, it felt like a weight had been lifted. The house wasn't filled with animosity anymore. With tension and disappointment and judgment. Instead it was filled with us.

It took weeks to sort everything out after she died. At first we kept it as it was, all the little doilies and dishes of potpourri, the thousand photo frames filled with memories that didn't belong to either of us. But slowly, gradually, guiltily, we began to erase Mary from the space. China ornaments of ducks in bonnets and cats dancing jigs were laid flat in cardboard boxes. Chenille cushion covers in dusty shades of mauve and moss were folded into plastic bags, then carted off down the road to the Oxfam shop. Barry's words about it not being my home rang in my ears with every change we made, but we did a good job of pretending it was ours.

Mary had been dead for over a month when I came back from the pub and found Danny sitting next to the cupboard underneath the stairs, a half-torn box between his legs, exercise books, notepads, pieces of paper in plastic sleeves scattered on the floor. I knelt down beside him and picked up a worksheet, saw writing that I understood to be Danny's at first, but when I looked closer I realized it was different, somehow. There was a cursivity, a femininity to it that I didn't recognize.

She wrote a bit like me, he said and smiled. Except she could spell.

I saw then, the name on the front of one of the books. Kim's homework planner, dated in what must have been her last year at school, the year she had Danny. I picked it up, opened it to the back page, filled with scribbles and doodles and practiced signatures. Denz's name was everywhere, his initials wrapped in love-hearts, her name melded with his. *Kim 4 Denz. I heart DC. Mrs. Kim Campbell.* Danny reached over to take it from me, his fingers tracing the lines drawn by Kim's pen.

Mad, innit? he said. Proper mad.

We thought, after that, about going into Mary's room, hopeful that perhaps there might be more of Kim in there, hiding in drawers and pockets and the folds of Mary's old clothes. But neither of us could face it. It felt like trespass to sit there going through her knicker drawer and stripping her bed. So we left it as it was.

We threw a lot out, but we held on to every photo of Kim.

And even though we tried to part with them, we couldn't bring ourselves to say goodbye to Mary's hoard of garden gnomes, rearranging them instead around the rockery that Danny made to remember his nana, right outside the kitchen window, so that we'd see them staring back at us every time one of us stood at the sink, washing pots.

THAT LITTLE GARDEN BEHIND THE HOUSE WAS LIKE A BAROMETER for the state of our lives. Danny had left it alone for months after the police smashed it up, as though they'd broken a spell somehow, destroying something that had once been sacrosanct. But after the funeral, something sprang within him again and I watched him slowly cast his magic, coaxing out the wild and the beautiful. We didn't have the money to spruce it up, so instead we'd go up the garden center, shove bulbs in the front pocket of our hoodies, casting sidelong looks at each other, glints in our eyes.

I thought you didn't like pinchin, I whispered to him as we sidled through the aisles, hand-in-hand.

I don't remember sayin that. He grinned. And besides, this int pinchin, not really. We're doin a Philibert Commerson.

When I asked him what he was on about, Danny pulled me in close, murmured in my ear. He'd been a French botanist, he told me. The best plant-hunter the world had ever seen. Got his start stealing from the university garden for his collection. He had a sidekick as well. A lass he was in love with, who he used to dress up as a fella to go on their adventures on the high seas together.

Mebbe I should try that with you. He smiled, ribbing me with his elbow as I slid a packet of seeds into the waistband of my jeans.

. . .

IT USED TO LIGHT ME UP, THE WAY DANNY WAS IN THAT GARDEN.
Bringing things to life, sparking his brain. When he talked
about it, about the plants, nature, biology, he was so animated,
so happy. I remember him explaining to me once, how he
could visualize the seasons. He had a picture, he said, a clear
picture of how things looked now and then again in three
months' time, the quiet of winter rolling into a kaleidoscope
of spring behind his eyes. I'd skin up and we'd share the spliff
while he talked, his hands flying, pacing, pointing at this
patch, that area, this crevice.

We began to plan again, to talk of our escape. Just as soon
as we had enough money we'd leave town, make our way
down to Brixton. Danny reckoned Lewis would put us up for
a bit until we found our feet, till Danny made a name for
himself at the royal gardens. We'd stick around for a year,
maybe two. But after that we'd be free to go wherever we
pleased, to travel the world, live out all the fantasies I'd put
on paper so long ago.

I hadn't written a word since that night up at Devil's Claw.
Danny had been on my case about it, wanting to know why
I'd stopped. I'd fob him off, tell him I didn't have anything to
say. But in that dreamlike time after Mary's death, that time
of sharp and painful happiness, I found my words again.
Just musings, really. Poems, I suppose you'd call them.
About us, our life, watching Danny from the window. Sometimes he'd call out to me, ask me what I was doing, and I'd
answer that I was washing or ironing or some other chore;
in those days I reveled in the newfound domesticity of our
lives. But often I was writing, not ready to tell him yet. And
then one morning he came in and I didn't hear him, only

realized he was there when I felt his hand on the back of my head, locking his fingers into my hair in that way he used to. It made me jump, cover my paper with my hand. He asked me if he could see, but I shook my head and he didn't push it, just smiled, ran his hands from my crown down to my jaw, cupping my chin in his palm before leaving again.

For some reason I felt brave then and I walked out after him, circled his waist with my arms, whispered the words I'd written into his ear. And it was different, that story. Because for once we weren't other people, we weren't living a make-believe life. We were us. It was a story about us and all that we were, and all that we had and all that we hoped for.

I remember the intrigue in Danny's eyes when he looked at me, as though he was seeing me anew. After that he started to ask me to read to him, to write for him whenever we were out in the garden, so that it became almost the only place I could put words down with any truth. Sometimes he'd carry on with what he was doing, on his knees, hands thrust into the earth, one ear tilted toward me. Other times he'd come and sit in the doorway or lie out on the grass beside me. Two little urchins pouring our hearts out in different ways, cradled inside Danny's jungle.

42

Even though Danny and I had a home of our own, we'd often still sneak out at night in search of adventure, creeping silently along thistle-lined trails, crawling through undergrowth and scrambling up muddy slopes, lying together on the damp ground to gaze up at the stars.

It felt like no one in the world had ever felt the aliveness, the untamed thrill of togetherness that we did. Everything glowed, but never more so than when we were high. Mostly we smoked weed, but now and again we'd score some pills or a bit of molly, the pink crystals glimmering like sherbet inside the wrap. We didn't need it, although it made things more interesting. Sharpened them, opened them up. We played at being grown-ups, but we were just kids without adults.

Danny still hadn't found another job, but we made do

with the money I earned at the pub. Whenever I had a day off we'd fill up a rucksack with crisps and pop, get on a bus with the vague aim of making our way down to London, except we never got that far. It's only now that I wonder why.

We went to plenty of other places, though. Ate chips in the rain on a beach in Whitby, walked the length of the medieval walls in York. Went to a rave in a field filled with coconut-scented gorse bushes, and made friends with a bunch of old-timers from Manchester, woke up two days later in a tiny little village somewhere over east called the Land of Nod.

We'd been too skint to go anywhere for a few weeks when Danny won twenty quid on a scratchie and announced he was taking me somewhere special. We caught a bus and then another one, but by the time we got to the third I was panicking, my palms sweating. I recognized the route. We were headed toward Denz's house.

I sat on my hands so that Danny wouldn't see them trembling, wondered what we would find when we got there, if we would rock up on the doorstep to see my mam and his dad standing on the welcome mat, ready to greet us both with open arms. But before we reached Denz's stop, Danny tugged at my elbow, pulled me to my feet.

Me dad used to take me here all the time when I were a kid, he told me, leading me across the road toward the entrance to the indoor wildlife park. I slid my hand into his, knew then that he was hurting too.

We shared a jay behind the building, then spent hours floating around inside, the dreamy fug of marijuana transforming that series of interconnected greenhouses on the outskirts of Leeds into some sort of enchanted realm. I remember now so clearly the color and the heat and the taste of magic, Danny leading me past groups of squealing school kids and ducking under the elbows of mums pressing sticky-fingered toddlers up against the glass. Together we gawped at scorpions writhing in tiny cages, dodged butterflies the size of our faces, stood under a rainforest canopy, silenced by the largeness, the possibility of the world.

Look deep inside nature and then you'll understand everythin better.

The tone of Danny's voice cracked through my daze and I rubbed at my eyes. You what?

Einstein said that.

I followed Danny's gaze into the plants below us, trying to make out what he was talking about, but I found nothing, just a tangle of damp and branches and leaves. What you on about, Dan?

It means, he said, that Denz were full of shit.

About what?

All of it. All that shit he were always spoutin about what drugs are good and what's bad. Because it all comes from the earth, one way or another. You know a quarter of all medicines start off in t'rainforest? Every drug on this planet pretty much comes out the ground. You got yer coca leaves, yer agave. Penicillin. Friggin aspirin. Smack, even smack—all it is is a poppy, man. Nowt but a fragile little flower.

I pulled at the fabric of my T-shirt, the cloy of the sham forest making it cling to my skin. What you gettin at?

He looked at me then, as though only just remembering that I was there. Nowt, he said. Only that I should never have trusted him. Me dad.

t's afternoon and the lunch lot have cleared off, leaving only Sandy and me in the caff. I haven't seen Denz for over a week, both of us steeped in our anger. He thinks I'm keeping something from him, but it's him that has all the secrets.

I move around the tables with a dishcloth, collect empty mugs and plates with one hand and wipe things down with the other. The telly is on, as it always is. I have no idea what is playing. Sandy is sitting at his usual spot, tucked away in the corner furthest toward the back. I want him to stay, don't want him to shuffle out just before closing and leave me here with nothing but my thoughts.

Slowly I cross the caff to where he sits, fuss around the table across from him. Only after I've wiped the surface for the third time do I find the courage to speak.

Can I get you anything else, Sandy? I ask quietly.

He looks up at me in surprise, his eyes the color of clay, the skin around them craggy and worn. Sluggishly, he shakes his head and I turn away, the guts sinking out of me. Only then does he speak, his voice gruff and thickly Glaswegian.

You naw that's nae me name, dinnae you?

I let my eyes meet his again. I don't know your name.

No, he says, not breaking my gaze. D'yer naw how that feels, eh? For not one single person to naw yer name?

The ground feels unsteady suddenly under my feet and I breathe in sharply. More than you'd think, I mumble.

THAT NIGHT I DREAM OF A FIRE, AN ALARM. WE ARE BACK IN THE flats, Chrissy and me, but I have lost sight of her and I can't remember the way out and I am stumbling, searching, hitting a dead end at every turn and still it doesn't stop, ringing and ringing until I wake with a start, my breath catching in my throat.

It is late, dark, and I stagger around, searching for a light. The ringing is coming from downstairs, the phone in the caff. My robe is hanging on the back of the door and I pull it on roughly, shove my feet into a pair of running shoes. By the time I reach it the ringing has stopped, but just as quickly it starts again and I lift the receiver, press it to my ear.

Hello?

Neef, it's Denz.

Do you know what time it is?

Sorry, I—

It's nearly two in the morning.

I know, I'm sorry.

Are you drunk?

He doesn't speak but there is a noise at the end of the line and, although it is muffled, I realize with horror that he is crying.

You're right, he says at last. I owe you an explanation. About Chrissy.

oward the end of that first summer after Mary died, I got a letter in the post. Danny brought it out to me while I was sitting in the garden, having a cup of tea and a cig. It had my name on the front, but Mary's address, and the top had already been ripped open.

What's this?

He looked at me, his eyes nervous but a smile playing on his lips. Don't be pissed off. I only did it cos I know you're so good.

I frowned, took the letter from him, scanning my eyes over it quickly and then again, more slowly. It was from the editor of a local paper, the big one that went all over Yorkshire. Something to do with a poetry competition, congratulations, an invitation to submit for the next round. I looked up at Danny and he was smiling wider now, his teeth shining.

I sent some of yer stuff off, what you wrote, he gabbled, his words coming out too quickly. I know I should've said summat, but you wouldn't've let me if I did. I know what you're like. And anyway they liked it, see. I knew they would. You've been shortlisted, they want to see more of yer work. You'll get it published if you win, it'll be in a proper book, Neef. You're not pissed off, are yer?

I sat there quietly for a minute, processing what Danny had told me. No, I'm not angry. I leaned forward, ran my thumb along his jaw. Thank you.

Danny helped me choose the poem for the paper, said it was no contest, that it was the best thing he'd ever read of mine—of anyone's in fact. I wasn't so sure, it felt a bit daft to me. But still, I let him send it. I didn't give it much thought after that, I only had room in my head for him.

It didn't occur to Danny or me to think about bills or keeping a roof over our heads. Once the summer ended, we stopped taking as many trips out, curling up together in front of the telly instead. September was bitterly cold that year and the thought of sleeping outside lost its appeal. We'd leave soon, of course we would. But London wasn't going anywhere and neither was the rest of the world, so we might as well wait until we'd saved up a bit.

Money only started to become an issue when the leccy meter ran out a week before I was due to get paid; we'd never thought to put extra aside so we could make sure it stayed on. We scrabbled down the back of every sofa cushion but still only had enough to keep it going for another day or two. Danny started looking for work properly again then, although nothing ever seemed to come together. I told him he should sign on but he refused, too proud to even entertain the idea. In the end they took him on at one of the factories on the industrial estate near the high school. He said it made his brain feel like it was dying, but it would be worth it when the money started coming in. We promised each other we'd start saving properly, maybe even open a bank account, put a bit away every month. But when Danny's payslip arrived, there was a mistake. Surely that wasn't right—all those hours he put in, all that dead-end time. He took it to his manager, who glanced over it, taking pleasure in telling him that was all Danny was owed.

The mood in the house took a dip after that. Each day after his shift Danny would come home more beaten down than the one before, drawing back inside himself again, spending more time hunched over the coffee table building spliffs, less and less time outside bringing things to life.

I asked Barry for a few more shifts at the pub, to try and make ends meet, and he agreed. I was cheap labor after all. Business was picking up, but the clientele had changed. Ste seemed to be in there almost every day, graduating from the kids behind the Portakabins to knocking about full-time with Jody and his whizzhead crew. I knew he was selling a fair bit, he was never short of a bob or two. How's Danny gettin on at the factory? He'd smirk, unrolling the notes from a wad in his pocket as he paid for his double Jack Daniel's and Cokes.

I tried to ignore him, did my best to stay out of his way. But Ste never was easy to shake off. One evening after my shift he caught me by the freezer near the kitchen, ramming bread rolls and bags of chips into my bag. What you doin with that? he asked me. I didn't answer, shoved my way past him out the back door.

The next day he sidled over to me in the car park when I was chucking out empties. I know yer hard up, Neef, he said, fake sincerity veneering his words. I'll let you in on it, you only have to ask.

I never intended to say yes. But then one morning before work I had no choice but to slide a packet of tampons into my bag at the Co-op without paying. When I turned round I saw the girl behind the counter watching me. She didn't say a word, just smiled at me with a face full of wretched pity, and the shame knocked me sick.

A few hours later I was following Ste upstairs to his bedroom, hating myself for doing it. He told me to sit on the bed but I shook my head. Nah, I'm all right here, I said, leaning against the closed door.

What, you think I'm after a piece? Get over yerself, Neef. He sneered.

I stared down at the floor, felt my cheeks scalding as he knelt, slid out the drawer from under his bed, rifling through the clothes and socks and pants, before pulling out a large oblong package wrapped up in brown paper like an old-fashioned Christmas present. He held it out to me but I didn't take it, and so he dropped it onto the bed. Two hundred pingers, he said with a half smile. Need em shiftin fer four quid a pop.

I sat down, pulled back the paper and ran my hand along the clear plastic, tracing the shape of the pills with the tips of my fingers. Don't tell Danny, I said.

wasn't going to keep it a secret forever. Just until the first lot of money came in, so I could show him what it could do. It didn't take long for word to get round. Whenever I was on shift at the pub they'd come crawling in, all those caved-in faces crowding round the back bar, ready for me to slip them a side of narcotics with their blue WKD. I told myself it wasn't all that bad, it was nothing harder than Danny or me would take ourselves. When I spread the notes out on Mary's coffee table a few weeks later, Danny stared at them for a long time.

I take it Ste had summat to do with this?

I shrugged vaguely and Danny stood, walked outside. We didn't talk for the rest of the night. The next day he left the house early and didn't come back until it was well past dark.

I wanted to cheer him up and so I went shopping to a big

discount place on the edge of Leeds. I don't know why I thought doing that would make him happy; we'd never been into labels, not the way most of the kids round our way were. But that day I bought all sorts. Trainers and jackets and bags and caps. A great big padded coat for Danny with a huge hood that hid most of his face, and one for me, white with fur trimming the color of honey. As the numbers flashed up on the till, I half expected that I'd need to turn round and do a runner with the loot, but instead I pulled out the roll of cash from my pocket, counted off the notes like it was no big deal. When I got back that night I laid out all the presents on the sofa ceremoniously, grinning at Danny as he looked at each one.

Cheers, he said flatly, and I grinned even harder, pretended not to see the revulsion in his eyes.

That night, after I'd cooked our tea, I made vodka cocktails with a packet mix that tasted like melted sweets. I wanted us to talk like we used to, wanted to unearth all of Danny's forgotten dreams. London, the royal gardens, our new life in Brixton. Jungle-covered mountains, cloud forests, propeller planes. Canoeing through tangled rivers, adventuring through the unknown. Sumatra and Indonesia and Borneo and the Philippines. All the places we would go, the things we would do.

It'll happen, Dan, you'll see.

Yeah, he said, the plate of food lying untouched in front of him, the cocktail curdling on the table. Yeah, all right, Neef.

DANNY NEVER ASKED ME TO STOP SELLING AND SO I PRETENDED like everything was fine. But there was a tension between us that was tight and new.

I'd been at it for a couple of months when he finally con-
fronted me. The sun was out at last after months of cold and
I was in a good mood, sitting on the floor in the bedroom
straightening my hair, singing along to the radio blasting
out.

D'you get a kick out of it then?

Jesus, you made me jump, I laughed, standing up to turn
the volume down. Danny was leaning against the doorframe,
the curl of his mouth turning me cold. What's up with you?

Nowt. I just asked you a question, s'all.

I ignored him, knelt back onto the floor.

D'you like it? he said, taking a step into the room so that
his shadow fell across me. The thrill of it? Workin with Ste?

What sort of a question's that?

A pretty fair one, I'd say. You seem in a chipper mood
since you started. And it got me thinkin. Must be that that's
makin you so happy.

I'm doin it fer us, Dan.

He snorted. You keep tellin yerself that, Neef.

WHEN I GOT DOWNSTAIRS DANNY WAS ON HIS WAY OUT. WHERE
you goin? I snapped, our argument still bitter on my tongue.

He crouched to tie his shoelace. Off to see me dad.

I stared at him, winded. I didn't know you were talkin to
him.

Now and again.

Why didn't you tell me?

You never asked.

The anger surged in my chest and I bit down on the inside
of my cheek, tasted copper. When will you be back?

He shrugged. Later on.

I craved a drink or a smoke or something—something—rubbing at my eyes with the heels of my hands. More than a year and a half had passed since I'd last seen my mam.

Does he ever say owt about Chrissy?

Jesus, Neef, Danny barked. When are you gonna get it through yer thick head? No one gives a shit about her anymore.

46

Denz takes a deep breath before he speaks again, the static crackling on the phone line. The slowness of his memories grates on my nerves: the first day he saw Chrissy, how she stumbled into the pub as he played pool with Lewis. How her drunkenness had irritated him, when she could see his kid was sitting right there. And how he realized, just by looking at the two of us, that her kid was right there too.

So you fancied her, I cut in impatiently.

Nah, not really.

I frown. Why not?

She weren't my type. And besides. She were with Barry.

You hated Barry.

Barry hated *me*. And what I mean is, if she were the type to be with someone like him, well. She weren't my type.

I lean back against the wall of the kitchen, then sink to the floor, wrap the phone cord around my wrist so that the skin bubbles between each twirl, mottled pink and white.

Go on, I say, and Denz does as I ask, tells me how he made an effort to stay away from the pub, how he always knew they had a problem with him in there and he couldn't be doing with it, didn't need the aggro. Then one day he was walking through town, on his way to see Danny. He'd parked his car by the supermarket; if he left it near Mary's, she'd only give Danny grief about letting Denz in her house. That's when he saw Chrissy coming toward him across the car park, dressed up to the nines in the middle of the day, waving at him and then linking his arm like she'd known him for years, even though they'd only met for five minutes down the pub that time. At first he was off with her, didn't want anything to do with folk from that town. But she kept chatting away about this and that and, in the end, he warmed to her a bit. He felt sorry for her, he said. Even though she was flirty, too flirty, there was something sad about her. Something lonely.

She walked with him nearly all the way to Mary's, not seeming to care that anyone might see her—he knew how they liked to gossip round there. But he quite liked it, that she didn't care. At the top of Mary's street he told her she'd better go, that he was going to meet Danny, and Chrissy grinned, stood up on her tiptoes and kissed his cheek, and he'd thought yeah, all right, she's not a bad girl after all. But just as she'd been about to leave, she whispered in his ear.

Got any gear?

He'd stiffened, standing up straight and taking a step back from her. What makes you ask that?

Well, have yer?

No, he'd said. No.

She'd shrugged then. All right, she'd chirped, turning on her heel and waving at him over her shoulder. Bye.

It made him uneasy, after that, the way Danny would talk about me all the time. Denz knew Chrissy's type, knew that anyone mixed up with her could only mean trouble. He didn't want Danny falling into the wrong crowd, but he wasn't around enough to make sure he didn't.

Where were you then?

I were workin, sometimes, he says. But other times, it's like I said. I weren't well, Neef. I weren't up to bein a dad.

So you weren't in the nick then?

The *nick*?

That's what I always thought.

Denz lets out a laugh on the other end of the phone. Nah, man. Not in the nick. I mean, they tried their hardest. But no, I never went down. Easy to make assumptions, though, innit? he says, and I am glad then that he can't see me.

The next time Denz saw Chrissy he asked for her number and he could tell that made her giddy, but it was only because he wanted to keep an eye on her. On me. He wanted to know the people around Danny; could tell there was something between his kid and hers.

He rang her every week or two, and after a while she started to confide in him. At first it was just over the phone, but then he got into the habit of picking her up, taking her for little drives before he'd go and see Danny. Then one day he took her to his house and once she knew where he lived, that was it, Chrissy started showing up there whenever she felt like it without a word of warning. He'd grown to like her company by then, and besides, no one wants to see anyone as unhappy as she was. Somehow they ended up sleeping together—

Somehow? What's that supposed to mean, "somehow"?

I aren't sayin I'm perfect, Neef.

So why did you do it? I snap. Did you care about her? Did you love her?

Denz pauses, chooses his words carefully. Not at first, he says. I aren't gonna lie. It were just . . . I needed to keep her close. But then it kept happenin and yeah, maybe my feelings changed. I felt sorry for her—

You slept with her because you felt *sorry* for her?

No. I dunno. It's hard to explain. I thought I could help her. I thought I could sort her out. Then Danny started gettin in trouble, police on his case all the time. I needed to get him out of that town; he were old enough by then that Mary didn't have a say in it, and that's when he moved in with me. I cut things off with Chrissy, I couldn't give her what she needed and, besides, Danny needed me more. She took it badly, though, started turnin up at me house again at all hours, always off her nut.

I rest my forehead on my knees, listening.

One night Danny woke up, came downstairs to see what all the noise was about and found Chrissy half naked in the hallway. I tried to lie me way out of it, but Danny weren't stupid. He couldn't understand what I were playin at and I didn't have the words to explain. By then Chrissy were in a bad state, I couldn't turn her away. I didn't know what she might do to herself if I weren't there to listen.

Denz pauses.

It's not because I loved her, owt like that, it's just . . . I didn't want . . . It's complicated, Neef.

Keep going, I hear myself say.

Denz clears his throat, does as I ask, his voice slow, measured. The third time she turned up there, Danny packed his bags, called me a hypocrite. All those years I'd preached to him about morals and respect, and now I was sleeping with someone like Chrissy—Chrissy who had a fella and still put it about, who were off her head on all sorts, who couldn't even look after her own kid— He catches himself. I'm sorry, Neef. I know it int nice to hear them things. I'm just . . .

Go on.

He lets out a long sigh before speaking again.

Danny said he didn't want to see me anymore, moved back in with his nana that same day, and I knew then what a mess I'd made of everything. I'd wanted to keep Danny away from that town, away from Chrissy, from . . . from you. And instead I'd pushed him further into it.

So I came up with a plan, a stupid, flawed plan. If I couldn't keep Danny close, then at least I could keep Chrissy away from him. I told meself I were doin you a favor too, that you'd be better off without a mam than one like Chrissy.

When I told Chrissy to leave Barry, she laughed out loud, said it weren't as easy as that, she had nowhere to go. So I told her I'd look after her. That I'd help her sort herself out.

And me? I ask.

Denz doesn't respond.

Well? I say quietly. Didn't she ever say, What about Neef?

The sound of his breath hisses in my ear. I told her, he says, that you were all right where you were. That you were happy there. That it would be better for you. And besides, Chrissy had . . . She needed to sort herself out.

I press my skull hard against my kneecaps. Denz told Chrissy to leave me. He was the one to convince her it was a good idea, that she'd be better off without me around. But the truth of it—the cold, hard, bitter fact—is that she listened. My mam chose to leave me behind.

I aren't proud of what I did, Neef, I hear Denz saying. I thought it were for the best.

Who were you to decide that?

A silence falls but I need to know it all.

And after that? I whisper hoarsely.

She stayed with me. For a bit. But she couldn't change. I told her I wouldn't stand for it, I wouldn't have any of that shit under my roof. I warned her the first time, gave her three chances in t'end. But she didn't listen, she kept on doin it. And so I lost patience, realized I couldn't help someone who don't want to be helped. Kicked her out, told her she needed to look after herself.

I frown, confused. But what if she had sorted herself out? What if she'd stopped using there and then? Would you have made a go of it? Would the four of us all have lived together, playing Happy Families? And wouldn't that have defeated the whole point, wouldn't that mean Danny would be around the both of us even more than he already was?

There is a long silence before Denz speaks again. I always knew she wouldn't stop, he says quietly. She weren't the type.

I suck in my breath sharply. You tricked her.

Nah, no, that int true—

She thought she was leaving Barry to be with you. She thought you'd look after her. But you never had any intention of being with her.

She needed to look after herself. You both did.

You're a piece of shit.

You're not the first to say that.

I take a deep breath. Another. Another. I am furious with Denz for what he did to my mam. Furious with her for falling for it. For all the lies, the countless let-downs. But there is still a part of all this that I don't understand.

Why didn't Danny tell me?

Denz is quiet for so long that I wonder if he's hung up. Probably he were ashamed of me, he says at last. He held it against me, you know, all these years.

Did you hear from her? After that?

Yeah. Yeah, now and again. She went off the rails good and proper for a bit, got mixed up in all sorts. And then a few years ago she got in touch. She lives in Ireland now, apparently. Married to a fella out there—somethin O'Leary, I think. Seems to be doin all right, by the looks of it.

Chrissy. Married. I can't imagine it.

Why didn't she ever come back for me? I murmur, maybe more to myself than to Denz.

I dunno, Neef. Denz lets out a long sigh. She were a mess for a bit. I reckon she had some sort of breakdown for a while there. And then a few years later, you'd disappeared yourself. She might've been looking for you all this time. I am sorry, you know, Neef. I thought I had no choice, I did it for—

For Danny.

He pauses. Yeah.

I pick up a paper napkin lying forgotten on the kitchen floor, shred it with my fingers, let the material disintegrate like snow.

You've got to understand, Neef, Denz says eventually. You've got to understand what it were like.

What?

For Danny. For me. I were only tryin to protect him, I know I went the wrong way about it, I can see that now. But back then, I thought I were doin the right thing.

But what about me?

With all due respect, he says, his voice thick with sorrow, you weren't my kid.

called Ste purely out of spite after Danny stormed out to see his dad. He knew I'd never stopped caring about my mam. He'd chosen his words to hurt me.

Ste didn't need asking twice to come round to Mary's. Him and a bunch of his bootlickers were still there and half out of it when Danny got back late that night.

Danny gave me a dirty look as he walked through the door but I pretended not to see it, slunk upstairs to get a hoodie. When I came down again, Ste was leaning over Mary's coffee table rolling a cig, while Danny stood glowering in the far corner of the room.

That's where the proper money is, see, Ste was saying. I been hearin about it, these lads over in Bradford. They're smart, man. Know how to get around the law. They tape the shit under a pool table, or leave it in old pop cans in t'gutter, and after the money's been exchanged, they tell the junky where to find the can, or which boozer the table's in. Means the pigs can't pin it to anyone, so it's risk-free, yeah?

Danny took a swig from a bottle of something in his hand, his foot tapping, eyes hard. I willed Ste to shut up, but I never said it out loud. Just leaned against the wall, picking at the chapped skin on my lips.

Key wi that stuff, Ste ranted, is just to push it. Not to take any yerself, but to find those that want to. Know what I'm sayin?

Nah, Ste, Danny growled. I don't know what you're sayin, pal. Elaborate fer us, will yer?

Ste's face was smug and he leaned forward conspiratorially, as though he were making some big revelation. Smackheads, man. That's where the cash is. That's how yer lass can put some proper bread on t'table.

The room itself seemed to hold its breath then. There was a line, even if no one had ever said as much. But now Ste had crossed it.

You know owt about that stuff, Ste?

Ste looked up at Danny again. I know what I need to, mate, he scoffed.

Danny nodded slowly in a way that reminded me of Denz. *Papaver somniferum,* he said. You know what that is?

You what?

The flower of joy. It comes from the mountains. Miles and miles from here. And when the flowers bloom, they're bright, bright red.

Ste scratched the back of his neck then looked back down at the table, carried on with what he'd been doing like he'd lost interest in the conversation. But Danny's eyes stayed fixed on him with an intensity that made me pull the collar of my hoodie up over my chin.

When the petals fall away, they leave behind a pod, a little pod in the shape of an egg, Danny said. We were all watching him by now, but no one spoke, no one sure where this was going. That's where you'll find it, inside that pod. Dreams of the damned.

Ste sat up straight in the armchair, put the cig he'd been rolling to his lips, but he didn't light it.

As the sap oozes out, Danny carried on, taking a step further into the room, it turns thick and dark. A black, sticky gum that seeps from the pod. They mix it up then. Mix it with all sorts of chemicals and shit—stuff that'll rot yer insides, eat away at yer brain and yer body. They turn it into a fluffy white powder, pack it into bricks and sell it on fer someone else to mix with a load of other shit, and then someone else and someone else again. Until eventually it reaches some poor fool, someone who's got nowt else to live fer, and they pump it into their veins and ruin their whole fuckin lives. Next thing you know . . .

He lifted his fist, brought it down hard on the table.

. . . BOOM! You're dead.

I gasped and Danny cackled, a manic laugh that didn't reach his eyes. He looked at me for a second before turning, leaving through the back door.

He's off his rocker, that one, Ste muttered.

But the room didn't feel the same after that.

NOT LONG AFTER THAT NIGHT, STE ASKED ME TO GO ON A PICKUP with him, pulled up next to me in his chavvy little Corsa when I was dragging my feet back to Mary's at the end of my shift. I hesitated, wanting to say no, but not wanting to face Danny, either.

Danny and I had been bickering constantly. If he wasn't stoned out of his mind, he'd be in a bad mood about the factory, looking for a row, getting on my case about every tiny little thing. It wound me up something rotten, but mostly I just bit my tongue. Danny was all I had, I didn't know who I was without him. I wanted to pull it back, fix us. But it wore me down, the way he'd snap and snarl and scowl at me, like all the bad things were my fault.

Are you comin or what? Ste bawled through the crack in the window.

I pulled open the passenger door, climbed in beside him.

The stereo was broken and neither of us had a right lot to say. Instead I stared out of the window as we drove away from the town toward Bradford, a place of Gothic, looming cathedrals and the shut eyes of abandoned mills. Past a football club, a train station, turning off behind a row of narrow terraces.

Ste squeezed my thigh, too high, too hard, winked at me. He climbed out of the car and I followed him, walking quickly with my head bent low. A bunch of kids were playing in the street, two girls in tracksuits pushing prams, a man in a gray salwar kameez hurrying up the road. We stopped outside an unremarkable little house, the paint on the windowsills chipped, no number on the door. Ste knocked, but no one came and so he tried again, louder this time. A few minutes passed before a girl of no more than twelve or thirteen peered out, a curtain of dark hair hanging over her face. A look of recognition flitted in her eyes at the sight of

Ste and she opened the door just wide enough to let us pass. I watched as she closed it firmly behind us, securing it with a chain, her little hand a pocketful of bones.

Inside, the air smelt like vinegar but sweeter somehow, the room almost empty of furniture. An upturned box was being used as a makeshift table, littered with torn-up bits of foil, papers, a couple of burnt spoons. In the corner stood a scruffy armchair occupied by a fella who I could barely make out in the half light.

Now then, Ste, he said, his voice coarse and cracked. I took a step toward the wall, my legs Bambi-like as I rested up against it, trying to bring the room into focus.

You all right, love? He leaned forward into the light and his eyes slithered along the length of me. I saw then his misshapen nose, the front tooth split in half. A face that looked as though it had met its fair share of fists. You look like you're gonna keel over. Why don't you take a seat? he rasped.

I'm not stoppin.

The man laughed. What, you don't like it here? He nodded at Ste then. This yer bird, is it?

Ste smirked. Summat like that.

My eyes darted to him furiously but I kept my mouth shut. The man laughed again, then got to his feet and Ste followed him wordlessly out of the room. The door fell closed behind them and the young girl stood up silently from where she'd been kneeling on the dirty floor, her movements sluggish. I edged toward the sofa, perching on the arm, and from there I could see through the doorway into a sparse-looking kitchen where two other girls stood, one playing on a mobile phone, the other staring vacantly into space.

The young girl was leaning over the makeshift table now, her hair still covering most of her face. She was laying out objects. Foil, a lighter, a small straw-like tube. I watched transfixed as she folded over, head bent, the room so quiet that I could hear the crinkling of the foil, the flick of the flint, the sucking intake of breath. After a moment or two she slumped back against the wall, her face dead, her shoulders sagged forward. I tried not to think about how old she was.

When Ste came back, he didn't speak, gestured at me with a nod to get up, get out. It was dark by then and I kept my eyes fixed on the tail lights of the cars in front of us—see how fast they go, see how they blur, look at the shapes they make in the darkness. Block out all that I had just seen, fill my head with thoughts of nothingness. Silent and blank.

WE PULLED UP OUTSIDE MARY'S HOUSE AND I REACHED OVER TO unhook my belt, but as I did so, Ste lunged forward, hooked a hand around the back of my neck. He tugged me toward him, pressing his mouth on mine so hard that I felt the edges of his teeth on my lips.

What you doin? I hissed, rearing back in disgust.

Come on, Neef, it's only a bit of fun. He grinned, leaning in toward me again.

I climbed out of the car as quick as I could, slammed the door behind me, almost running toward the house. But the other door slammed too. Ste was following me.

What the fuck are you doin?

He smiled. Just comin in to see Danny.

. . .

DANNY WAS IN THE FRONT ROOM, THE TELLY ON MUTE. WHERE you been?

Nowhere, I lied. Just at t'pub.

Ste still had that stupid smirk smeared across his mug, sat himself down on the opposite side of the sofa from Danny, who was eyeing us both warily, tapping his fingers against the can in his hand.

Oh, I meant to say, Neef, Ste said casually, lifting his feet to rest on the coffee table. I saw an old mate of yours today.

I didn't say anything back, just looked at him coldly.

Shaun, he carried on. Shaun McAlister.

Never heard of him.

You have. Course you have! Shauny Mac, you remember him.

I cleared my throat, got to my feet. Anyone want a brew? I asked, my voice sounding strange. Too chirpy, too high-pitched.

You were sick in the back of his brother's car, remember? That night. When you took em all off fer a little adventure.

I froze then, my body tensing.

Yeah, Ste sniggered. I thought you'd remember.

Danny was staring at me too now, his face a question, but Ste wasn't done.

Funny, innit? he said, helping himself to a can from the six-pack on the table, snapping back the ring-pull so that the lager fizzed over his hands, dripping onto Mary's sofa. You two. Playin house.

Is it? Danny said, an edge in his voice.

Yeah. Ste flicked his hand, spraying amber droplets onto

the carpet. Yeah, I never thought. I dunno. Just didn't think you'd end up together properly, you pair.

Why's that then?

Well. You always had an eye fer t'ladies, Dan, let's be honest now. And Neef. He paused, sucking the froth from the top of the can and looking at me in a way that made my lungs tighten. She were a wild one.

Danny narrowed his eyes. Hardly, mate.

I willed Ste to stop, my heart pounding against my ribs, but he knew he had the floor now, knew he had something on me that Danny didn't. Well, if you don't call what she got up to with all them lads out in t'lap of nature *wild*, pal, then I don't know what to tell yer.

The air sucked out of the room and I felt myself begin to tremble, didn't dare look at Danny, stared down at my feet instead. What? I heard him say.

Neef, Ste answered. Back in t'day. You must've heard. Everyone were talkin about it. She were a little firecracker, by all accounts.

It weren't like that, I said, but so quietly that no one could have heard.

Anyways. Ste smirked. All a long time ago, though, innit? Only got eyes fer each other these days, eh?

I knew Danny was still staring at me but my head was too heavy to lift, to meet his gaze. There was a roar in my ears, and the next thing I knew, Ste was standing, saying something about leaving us to it, that it didn't seem like we were in the mood for company tonight. As he left he reached out, ruffled my hair. See yer later, sexy. He grinned.

. . .

THE ROOM STAYED SILENT AFTER STE HAD GONE, THE PAIR OF US sitting there in the half dark, our faces illuminated by the glow of the muted telly.

What were he talkin about, Neef?

It weren't like that, I said again. I put my head in my hands, squeezed my eyes shut, my fingers rubbing at my scalp, remembering how it had hurt. It were ages ago. Before you and me ever . . . I thought you were with Donna and . . . I were drunk, I never—

Who were they?

I don't know. I never knew.

You never knew?

Some lads. I dunno. They were older, we were all drunk.

What happened? Where did you go?

It don't matter.

It matters to me. All this time, I thought I were the only one you ever . . .

You are, you are. They didn't count.

Danny leaned forward in his chair, rubbed his face with his palms. Course they counted, Neef. Course they fuckin counted.

I pressed the heels of my palms against my eyes, tried to stop them seeing. When I looked up, I saw that Danny was watching me.

When did it happen? Where?

Ages ago. You were livin with Denz.

What did Ste mean? About nature, about an adventure?

I shook my head, didn't want to think about it, didn't want to remember.

Where were yer?

It don't matter.

Where, Neef?

I swallowed, met his gaze as the room closed in on us. Devil's, I whispered.

It took a moment for the word to sink in, but once it did, Danny's face, the way he looked at me, changed.

I waited and I looked and I hoped. But for all the time I knew him, it never changed back.

anny didn't say another word about me and those boys in our special place. I wanted to hope he'd forgotten, but I knew we both felt their shadows, lurking in corners, crawling into bed, slipping between our sheets. It never occurred to me to try and explain to him that that night had been taken from me. That it wasn't what I wanted, that I never said yes. Back then I wasn't even sure if that was true, or if it mattered either way. The belief that I'd let it happen hung like a noose around my neck.

We'd been sharing a bed for the best part of three years, but it felt like a lifetime had passed since we'd stretched out in the wildflowers imagining our new life in London and everything that would come after that. My words had dried up again too, I had nothing left to say. We'd stopped talking about our dreams, our promises for a future. We'd lost the ability to see that far.

It seemed as though our whole world was spiraling, like the plug had been pulled out from underneath us, leaving Danny and me with nothing to hold on to as we spun into oblivion. I couldn't get a handle on what was happening, or why. It was money, it was drugs. It was Denz taking away my mam. But perhaps it was everything. All the broken pieces of our lives, of the lives that had come before us. The faceless fathers, the absent mothers. The bigots and the braggarts, the heavy-handed men who had taken what wasn't theirs. Hurt and hate and abandonment, passed from one generation to the next, landing on the shoulders of Danny and me, pushing us down, waiting for us to go under.

More and more people came to know Mary's for what it had become. A place where just about anyone could drop in, pick up, have a sniff, a smoke, bring round a new bird that they didn't know where else to take, ask if they could stop on the sofa for a night, maybe two. Once, someone asked me where I'd got the nickname Neef. I looked at Danny, my heart lifting at the memory. He shrugged, told them he couldn't remember.

Danny's frustrations seemed to rise with each passing day: with me, with work, with life; the acidity of them spilling out through the windows and the doors, tangling the leaves and choking the flowers and turning the grass thin and brown. He'd stopped taking pride in the garden, letting people chuck out their empty cans, leave old bottles lying in the bushes, not batting an eyelid when they'd stumble out of the back door to take a piss in Mary's rockery.

Most of them we knew from round and about, but there were others too. Adult men with sharp eyes and curling smiles whose custom I told myself I couldn't afford to turn away. They'd fill up the room with their grown-upness, getting a kick out of intimidating us. All right, Danny lad, all right, kid, they'd sneer, making the air taste bad even after they'd left.

Where before we'd hungered for the other's touch, now getting off our heads became the only thing that held any interest for us. I convinced myself we were managing it, there was nothing wrong with the hours we kept, sleeping most of the day, then waking up when it was time for me to go work the night shift at the pub, coming home late to get pissed or high or stoned. We could have stopped, if we'd wanted to. We just didn't have anything to stop for.

At some point Danny packed in his shifts at the factory. Rumors about him and me went flying about that town, the stories carrying like wildfire so that every time either of us stepped out of the door you'd hear a new one. That was the way of that place, like a pack of sheep, they were. You enjoyin yourselves up there, at Mary's house? they'd snarl, their questions barbed, their eyes narrowed, looking down their noses at us. Got it sorted, haven't yer, you pair? Free house, free everythin. Got it made.

Barry stayed silent most of the time, but once he'd had a drink, the vitriol would drip from him. There's a waitin list long as me arm fer them houses, he'd rant, his lips purple from red wine. Hard-workin folk in need, and you two just waltz in, turnin it into a dosshouse, actin like it's yer god-given right.

I was never on time for work anymore, but one weekend me and Danny and a whole load of others whose names I can't even remember got carried away with ourselves and I ended up missing two shifts back-to-back. I've no idea where all those lost hours went, only that at one point I realized Danny was gone.

Where is he? I asked Ste. He sneered.

Outside talkin to t'trees. I'm tellin yer, he's too far gone, that one.

I found Danny in the garden, pacing, pacing, staring up at the sky. Slowly, I walked up behind him, placed a hand on his shoulder. When he looked at me, his eyes had turned animal, the whites barely there.

They're cuttin em all down, man. They're just goin in there with their tools and shit and choppin it all down, all those ancient forests and woods and that. Gone. Dead. Carnage, man.

What you talkin about, Dan?

Danny's lion-eyes bulged as he brought himself to his full height, his fists clenched. I know. *I know.* You think I don't know. He shoved me in the shoulder, hard enough that I stumbled back. All the shit they're puttin in t'ground. The farmers, the government, man. They're putting chemicals in our soil, in our vegetables, in our meat. That's what's poisonin us, Neef, can't you see that? Can't you *see?* They're all lyin to us, you can't trust owt they say. You can't trust me, either, Neef. *I know.*

He raged out of the back gate, wild, untethered, and I was glad he wasn't near me anymore. I don't know where he went but when I finally came round, he was asleep downstairs on the sofa and there was a message on Mary's answering machine from Barry telling me not to bother coming in again. There wasn't work for me at the pub anymore.

I deleted his voice, turned off the machine and lost a few more days, I don't remember, never knew how many. Danny and I were paranoid, edgy, always on a comedown, only ever made better by another this or that or something else. We didn't realize how far we'd gnawed into the stash that Ste had given me to sell until it was too late. And the more we took, the more I had to chase my tail, trying to shift as much as possible, buffering up the little baggies with half teaspoons of bicarb to make up for what we'd sniffed. Until in the end people started going elsewhere, because the stuff I had was shit, they said.

We were tearing at the seams, and when I looked at Danny—my perfect, clever Danny—all I could see was the mess of myself. The way our fingers shook, the disquiet of our minds, how every time I'd try to sleep, I'd roll over and see his eyes, open too. His paranoia grew worse and so in turn did my need for him, the two things feeding off of each other like parasites.

Why you so clingy, what's wrong with you, what is it you think I've done, what is it you think I'm hiding?

Why don't you want to be near me, what's wrong with me, what have I done, why don't you look at me like you used to?

On and on and round and round, another line, another drink, another smoke, until eventually the circles and echoes of our quarrels would cut Danny loose, wild-eyed and slamming doors as I rotted, high and desperate in the fug of that house.

As the customers fell away, the debts crept in and eventually Ste stopped letting me have anything on tick. I'd lost a handle on how much money I owed, but he hadn't. No one bothered coming round to the house anymore. The ruin of us both must have scared them off.

Danny tried to get his job back at the factory but they

wouldn't have him, he looked a state by then. The house was freezing, the leccy meter had gone off again in the midst of all those lost weeks and in the end we just got used to it, the pitch-black, the cold, as miserable inside as it was out.

Letters piled up on the mat by the door, all of them still in Mary's name. Bills, probably. Notices from the council too, although we didn't realize that until it was too late. Neither of us opened anything, waiting until the stack got so big that we'd trip over it when we reached the bottom of the stairs and then scoop up a handful, tearing the hardier ones into strips to make roaches for our spliffs, shoving the rest in the bin under the sink.

IT NEVER CROSSED OUR MINDS THAT WE MIGHT NOT BE ABLE TO stay there, in Mary's house. Except it wasn't Mary's house, it belonged to the council, but no one seemed to join the dots for a while, the bloke in the Births and Deaths department forgetting to fax the right paperwork over to the girl in Housing to say that Mary no longer required her home. By the time the council caught up with themselves, Danny and I had been on our own in there for a few months and of course they sent letter after letter, but we never bothered opening them.

The social worker finally turned up on our doorstep after Mary had been dead more than a year. She was outside when we spotted her, eyeing the house up and down, scribbling something into a little notebook and then slipping it back into the fake-leather handbag slung over her shoulder. We both exchanged a look when we heard her rapping on the front door, but it was Danny that got up to open it.

Her name was Jane or Janet or something, said she'd been assigned to Danny's case because he was a minor. He told her he'd turned eighteen six months before, and that seemed to throw her a bit.

Oh, she said, and I heard the rustle of papers, imagined her fussing around in her bag to check her notes. Right. Well. I just wanted to have a quick chat, if you've got a minute. Do you mind if I pop in?

Immediately I jumped up, tried to make the place look a bit more presentable, sweeping little bits of paper and tobacco off the surface of the coffee table into my hand, hoping it didn't smell too bad in there. I could tell Danny was attempting to fob her off, but she wasn't backing down.

We've sent you letters, a number of letters. It's my job to look into your living situation, to assess whether or not you're getting the support you need. I'd really appreciate it if you could let me in.

Now's not a good time, that's all.

Mr. Campbell. Are you aware that your eviction from this property is imminent?

Jane or Janet, or whoever she was, walked into the sitting room ahead of Danny, her face full of judgment, catching herself quickly when she saw me there and forcing her lips up into a stiff smile. Danny hung back, scratching his arms, and I stood up to offer her a drink, remembering a packet of biscuits I'd nicked from the Co-op that I could maybe lay out on a little plate if I could find one. But Jane or Janet told me she was fine, she didn't need anything, thanks. Just a quick chat with Mr. Campbell about his living situation.

What were that you said about bein evicted?

The social worker turned to where Danny loitered in the

doorway. Yes. I'm afraid so. We've sent you numerous letters, Mr. Campbell. Daniel. Do you mind if I call you Daniel? There was a bit of a mix-up, I think, with the paperwork. After your grandmother died. I mean, really, you should have notified us of the change in your living arrangements, but that's by the by now—

There ain't been no change in me livin arrangements. I've always lived here.

Yes, I understand that. But it's a council property, as I'm sure you're aware. And when a tenant dies, there's a succession plan, of course. But this is a family home, it's not suited to someone in your . . . situation. We will of course look to rehouse you, we'll do everything we can to help, but—

Hang on a minute. Danny stepped forward then, cutting her off with a wave of his hands. This int on. You can't just come in here and take away me house. I've got rights, like everyone else.

Yes. Of course you have rights. But there has been correspondence from the council, a number of letters sent, let's see . . . She pulled out her notebook then, licking her thumb and forefinger in that way Danny always said was unhygienic as she leafed through her papers, handing them to him one by one. He stared at them blankly while she listed off dates, requests for payment, final reminders and, eventually, a notice of eviction. You still have a month, I heard her saying. Plenty of time to get everything in order. There's still a *whole* month.

If we'd had a few more years behind us we'd have known better, looked into getting a lawyer perhaps. Investigated these rights that Danny seemed to think we had. But there was a feeling by then in both of us of having been defeated.

Fuck it, Danny said once she had left. We'll leave.

And go where?

London. Go see Lewis, like we always said. Fer starters, at least.

We both knew we had about as much chance of getting to London as we did to Madagascar or the Kibale Forest by then, but neither of us would say it out loud. We didn't have a penny between us, barely knew what day of the week it was, couldn't even make it out of the front door most of the time. The social worker came round once or twice after that first visit, but we made her job impossible. We didn't want to be interfered with, we'd sort ourselves out, it was none of her business, until in the end she gave up. There's only so much you can help those who don't want it.

49

Danny would never have let on how much it hurt to
lose that house, but I know it shattered him. The
only home he'd known, his mother's, his nana's, slipping
right through his fingers. It was different for me. I'd never
thought of any of the places I'd lived in as my own.

In those last weeks I wandered around in a daze, trying
not to think about where we'd live as I threw our belongings
into plastic bin liners, a sense of déjà vu flitting at the back
of my mind. I was up in the bedroom, staring into space,
when Danny came in with the letter.

This were fer you. In that pile at the bottom of the stairs.

I glanced at it, confused. It seemed familiar somehow,
although I couldn't quite place why. The seal peeled open
without ripping the envelope, the letter inside a thick, creamy
stock that only ever comes with good news. My eyes scanned

over the words and I sat down on the bed with a thud. It's from the paper, I said quietly.

Danny took a step closer. What does it say?

It says . . . it says I came third. Highly commended. Says they'd like to publish me poem in t'book. There's an awards ceremony, they want to present summat to me onstage. Take a picture that they can put in there, next to me name.

I looked up at Danny, full of hope. The old us would have been jumping up and down on the bed together at that news. We'd have gone straight to the offie and got ourselves a bottle of fizzy wine to celebrate, giddy at the thought of a fancy night out, a free dinner, my picture in a book, right there, next to my name. But Danny just frowned at me.

When is it?

March twentieth.

That were two weeks ago, Neef.

Were it?

Yeah. It were.

Oh, I said. Oh. I blinked twice, trying to focus. Well. It don't matter. I'll still be in t'book, still have me name in there.

Mmm, Danny said flatly. Yeah.

THE PROSPECT OF OUR EVICTION HUNG IN THE AIR LIKE A GHOUL, an unspoken fact that neither of us dared look in the eye until it was only a few days away.

Where will we take our stuff? I said to Danny as I watched him drag a battered suitcase to the bottom of the stairs. He kept his back to me, knelt down and started fiddling with the lock, muttered something I couldn't make out.

What?

I said . . . He paused. I said mebbe we should do our own thing fer a bit.

I frowned, confused. Our own thing like what?

Like . . . I dunno. You could stay at the pub fer a while and I'll . . . I'll just sort meself out.

He stood, walked past me toward the kitchen, but still he wouldn't look at me, opening a cupboard, closing it again. Sliding out a drawer. I wanted to go to him, to take his face in my hands and make him look at me, but my feet kept me still, rooted to the spot. I thought we were goin to see Lewis, I said quietly.

Danny rolled his eyes with a sigh, then picked up a discarded bin bag from the floor, started chucking things in it randomly.

Danny, I tried again, but he was already halfway out of the room.

I kept waiting for him to tell me he hadn't meant it, that he hadn't been thinking straight. But the words never came, his eyes never meeting mine. We shared a bed, still, but always his back would be turned to me, unyielding as I pawed at him.

DENZ TURNED UP AT THE HOUSE THE MORNING BEFORE OUR final day. I shouldn't have been surprised, yet the sight of him floored me. I looked at Danny, my eyes full of accusation, and for once he looked back.

Where else could I have gone, Neef?

Fuck you, I said to him. Fuck you.

I ran upstairs then, sat on the edge of the bed listening to the two of them load Danny's things into the boot of Denz's car. At the sound of the engine starting, bile rose up in my throat, but within seconds it had cut again. Somewhere a door slammed, Danny's footsteps on the stairs. When I looked up, he was standing there, watching me.

In that moment, all of it, everything fell away and we were two kids again, twelve and thirteen, our eyes locking through the open window of a beat-up old BMW, an understanding of each other that went beyond words. Remember? I wanted to say to him. Remember us? Wishing, willing him to cover the ground between us, to fix it, to put it all back together again.

I turned from him. Just go.

Danny stayed where he was for a few seconds longer, but then I heard the door close behind him, footsteps descending, the engine coming back to life. I drew the blinds across the window, couldn't bear to watch him climb into the passenger seat. But even in the darkness with my eyes squeezed shut, I could see him, his every movement so familiar to me.

I stayed there on the bed for a long time, digging my nails into the soft flesh of my inner arm. And then on impulse I stood, snatched up every one of my notebooks and threw them into one of the leftover bin liners. Pulling on a pair of trainers, I paced down to the river, the weight of my words a burden in my arms. When I reached the bridge, I tipped the contents out into the water, ignoring the shouts and yells of disgruntled passersby, letting every single one of my poems and stories wash away. After that I walked over to Ste's, told him to come over to Mary's that night, to bring everyone he knew. We'd go out with a bang, have a party. A leaving do, I called it, the phrase making me think of another time, another life. An empty cigarette pack blowing across a car park, Chrissy dancing to a beat no one else could hear and, again, that feeling. Of me becoming her.

THEY STARTED TURNING UP BEFORE IT HAD EVEN GOT DARK, familiar faces at first, kids from round and about. All I could think of was getting wasted, getting so fucked up that I'd forget everything, all of it. I wasn't interested in talking to anyone, went outside on my own, sank down against the side wall next to the bins. Two girls were round the back, chatting on while one of them went for a piss behind a tree.

I had a bit of a thing with him, years back, one of them was saying. He weren't bad-lookin then. If yer into that sorta thing.

Proper thick, though, her mate joined in, rustling her knickers back up her legs. Couldn't even write his own name, someone told me.

Yeah, but she weren't much better. Both right skanky. Been on and off with him since they were kids, pretty much.

Bet he were puttin it about still. He were a dirty bastard like that.

Terrible what he were doin to his poor nana, as well. After she raised him all them years. Took advantage of her, I heard. All a bit off how she died so fast, weren't it?

I know. Me mum said the same thing happened with his mum years ago—summat to do with his dad apparently, big gangster-type fella from t'wrong ender Leeds. No wonder Danny turned out like that.

Scum, really. Mucky scum—

As they walked back toward the house, one of them glanced in my direction, her eyes bulging like a fish at the sight of me. All right, Neef? She smiled, the pair of them exchanging a look they thought I didn't see.

All right, I said, helping myself to a cig from the packet she shook at me.

Sorry to hear about you and Danny.

Are yer?

Lucky escape, if you ask me.

I didn't.

The other girl standing beside her sucked her lips in between her teeth, and I felt their eyes follow me as I stood up and made my way back inside the house. Fuck you, I thought. Fuck all of you. I burrowed into my purse, pulled out another pill, gulped it down with a can of something I was clutching in my hand. There were more people now, throngs of people everywhere, all of them feeling unfamiliar to me, spilling into the garden and the pavement out the front as I moved through the house. Sharp eyes and twisted smiles and faces that made the acid rise to my throat.

The police showed up early on, apparently. It had been a warning, telling us to shut off the music, scaring away the few people who cared about getting into trouble. I didn't see them, too busy getting out of it to notice, chemicals and alcohol coursing through my veins, the music pulsating in my face, my eyelids, doing whatever I could to blot out my ability to feel. Maybe it was just a bad pill or maybe it was everything that was going on, but I remember the jarring uneasiness, the sense of unrest building, of wanting so much to be near Danny, wanting him to pull it all back together again. At some point I lost my head, not knowing what was real and what wasn't anymore. I searched for the shape of Danny in the kitchen, the front room, pushing past the mob toward the stairs only to find them overflowing with limbs, bodies, mouths pressed against mouths so that I had to force my way through, squeezing myself flat against the wall and then under an arm, over a leg, until eventually I found space, air, an empty square at the top of the stairs. And yet still I had the feeling of being unable to breathe.

All of a sudden there was a flurry of activity and I felt something thrust against my lower back so that my legs buckled, and then an elbow or perhaps a knee in my temple. I clawed at the wall, trying to stand. Someone was yelling, dragging at my wrist, then a realization that they had the wrong hand, the wrong arm.

I ended up back in the front room, pushing and elbowing my way in. There was a fight, or maybe a few different ones, it was hard to tell. One of the kitchen windows had been put through, Mary's old coffee table upended on the floor. A lad with a shaved head had a younger kid pinned up against the wall, although most of the action seemed to have cleared out into the garden now. Ste was on the grass, the sinews in his neck popping, yelling, fists swinging. From somewhere I heard glass splintering, a revving of engines and then police cars pulling up outside the house, crowds of kids scattering, jumping over walls, under hedges, sprinting through neighbors' gardens and out of sight. The officers swooped in and down on the remaining gaggles, scooping up those too out of it to make a quick enough getaway, pulling apart others who had been so absorbed in the brawl that they hadn't heard the sirens cutting through the night sky. I was calling Danny's name into the darkness and the next thing I knew Ste was dragging me by the elbow, pulling me away from the house and into the back of a car.

Danny's not here, Neef, what you on about? Danny's not here.

I yelled at him to get off me, reaching for the door handle, but he was in my way, blocking my arm.

The lad driving the car, Lee I think he was called, took us to a terrace a couple of streets away, his sister's place, he said. She opened the door in her dressing gown, her hair scraped back from her face and her eyes heavy with sleep. For a minute I thought she wouldn't let us in, but then she did, giving us an earful about the police all over the estate tonight and how she didn't want trouble coming to her door.

I recognize you, she said, thrusting her chin at me. You're the lass that used to live down at the Lion, aren't yer? I gave a half nod and looked away, but not before I saw her shake her head, grimace in disgust. You best be gone by the time I wake up, the lot of yer.

STE AND LEE FELL ASLEEP ON THE SOFA, BUT I STAYED AWAKE until it was light, then crept back to Mary's house. I could see from the other side of the street that it was trashed. Someone had kicked one of the panels in the front door so hard that the wood had cracked and splintered, and there were windows broken at the front and back of the house. Drops of blood and a pool of vomit had congealed on the pavement outside, and out in the garden piles of beer cans and cider-bottle bongs lay abandoned among the souls of Danny's plants.

The back door was still open. My feet stuck to the floor as I made my way through the debris of the rooms, the surfaces wet with spilled drinks, the sofa cushions speckled with hot rock burns. I crept up the stairs, following the tracks of muddy footprints trampled into the carpets. Pushed the door of Mary's room open.

For a long time I just stood there in the doorway trying to

sense her, to feel her. But the room smelt of damp, a light-gray mold crawling up the corners of the walls, the edges of the curtains punctured by the teeth of hungry moths. I took a step back, pulling the door closed. There was nothing of Mary there anymore. Nothing of him or me.

enz has called me countless times, sent message after message since the night he told me the truth about Chrissy. He's stopped short of actually turning up at the caff. I don't know what I'd say to him, what I'd do, if he did.

I always knew he had plenty to do with Chrissy leaving. But there was so much of it I didn't know, didn't understand, and now it's like I'm looking back at our lives through a different prism, the picture fragmented. Maybe he's right, maybe he did need to take Danny from me. But he didn't need to take my mam.

I'M IN THE BACK KITCHEN SCRUBBING THE WORK SURFACES, waiting for Fionnoula and Ali to disappear so that I can be alone. I don't want to risk tainting them with all the pent-up feelings that Denz is drawing out of me.

The caff has been closed for at least an hour, but neither is showing any sign of leaving. Fionnoula is pottering around, wiping something here, rearranging something there. Ali is sitting at the little table that we use for peeling veg, yesterday's paper spread in front of him, the crossword pages open. Every so often he calls out a clue.

Two down. Dregs in a cup. Six letters then seven.

Ooooh. Dregs in a cup . . . *dregsinacup* . . . hmmm . . . Fionnoula's head appears from the depths of a cupboard and she lifts her chin, frowns. Stain? She tries. Tea stain?

Ali shakes his head. Six letters then seven, Fionnoula. *Six*. Then *seven*.

All right, all right, let me think. Fionnoula places a hand on the kitchen bench, eases herself to standing. She taps a knuckle against her cheek, purses her lips. Six then seven. Leftovers? Would leftovers work?

Ali mutters something in Farsi and rustles the paper with irritation. I glance over his shoulder on my way to the sink. Seventh letter G, eighth letter R. He sees me looking.

Well then, Jenny *joon*. Give it your best shot.

I barely have any energy to think, to speak, but Ali is looking at me expectantly. Umm . . . something *grounds*? I try. Maybe . . . maybe *coffee grounds*?

He narrows his eyes dubiously before counting the letters off in the grid, penciling the letters in lightly.

She's a genius, he exclaims, raising his hands aloft. Our girl is a genius! *Yallah*, Jennifer. Come and help me with this. No use asking Mrs. Can't-Count over there, it's you I need, of course it's you.

Fionnoula bustles over to where we stand, leaning over the paper. You never told me the other letters, ye daft beggar! she says, flicking him with a tea towel. Settin me up for a fall, you were!

Oh now, don't give me that. Let's not pretend that would have helped, *aziz-am*. Ali grins, wiggles his eyebrows at me. Do you hear this, Jenny, eh?

Fionnoula goes to flick him again and Ali cowers in mock fear. Don't you try and get her onside, ye wee conniver. Needs to learn what side his bread's buttered on, isn't that right, Jen? she says, winking at me. Needs to understand that us girls stick together.

Never mind, never mind. Ali waves his hand at Fionnoula, gesturing at me to sit down with the other. *Yallah,* Jenny *joon*. Come and help old Ali.

For a moment I hesitate, but the warmth of Ali's voice, the eager look on Fionnoula's face draw me in. I let the dishcloth fall into the sink, move over to sit beside Ali. We bend our heads over the crossword, close-close, studying the words, the clues. Fionnoula comes to stand behind us, a hand on each of our shoulders, and the firmness of it there, of sitting between the two, is like cool water on hot coals, tempering the tumult in my brain.

The moment is interrupted by the sound of my phone behind us, its vibrations carrying it across the kitchen surface with a metallic buzzing that makes Ali's head whip round with an air of annoyance. Fionnoula reaches across to pass it to me.

Don't, I say. It's okay. It'll only be Denz.

The pair of them turn to look at me, concern etched on their faces.

Is he bothering you, love? says Fionnoula.

I yearn, then, to tell Fionnoula and Ali everything. To get unstuck, to pour it out. My thumb hovers over the screen, but when I look down, it isn't Denz's number I see.

Hello?

Oh, hello there. A woman's voice. Well-spoken, groomed, foreign to me. Am I speaking with Jennifer?

Who's this?

Oh. My name's Sandra, I'm calling from the Royal Botanic Gardens at Kew?

I can feel Fionnoula's and Ali's eyes on me, the heat of their worry. I stand, crossing the kitchen in two strides to the back door.

Hello? Hello, are you there?

Um . . . yeah. I'm here.

Sorry, I'm . . . I'm not sure if I have the right number? I believe you came in a few weeks ago, looking for a friend of yours? Is that right?

Yeah. I did. Danny. Daniel Campbell.

Oh good, yes, that's the one. Now I must apologize for taking so long to get back to you, I've been on holiday, you see. And then of course I came back to an absolute mountain of emails, not to mention a million other bits and bobs . . .

I will the woman to hurry up, to get to the point. *Come on, come on, come on.*

Now, as I think was explained to you, we're not really meant to disclose information about our employees. But my colleague, Graham, one of the horticulturists here, he's been quite insistent about it all. Been to my office to chase it up twice in fact. I gather he bumped into you in the Temperate House, is that right?

I think back to that day at Kew Gardens, the man helping me to my feet. Yes, I say. Yeah, I remember him.

Right. Well, it turns out he worked quite closely with this Daniel and . . .

My legs feel unsteady suddenly, and I lean back against the wall for support. So he does work there?

Yes. Well, that's to say, he did. I don't believe I've met him personally, but Graham spoke very highly of him indeed! An incredibly talented gardener, by all accounts. Very knowledgeable, very intelligent.

Come on. Comeoncomeoncomeon.

He was with us for a year or so, but unfortunately he's gone on to pastures new now.

No, I want to scream. No, no. Please no.

Where did he go? I croak.

Well, that's the thing, you see. We're not entirely sure, although Graham was quite adamant that we should update you with whatever we knew. He seemed a little upset, you see, that he hadn't been more honest with you in the first place. He's terribly loyal, Graham. Not one to break another's confidences, I'd imagine, unless he's quite certain—

I cut in abruptly. So is there nothing else? Nothing more you can tell me?

Sandra clears her throat. Not much, unfortunately, she says, her tone a little terser. There was some mention of an old girlfriend, someone he had reconnected with or perhaps was looking to reconnect with?

I understand, I hear myself say, except it's a lie, because I don't. I don't understand at all.

I did ask around, and a couple of other people were under the impression he was going traveling, some far-flung place overseas, although no one was entirely sure where, I'm afraid.

Oh.

Funny thing is, no one's heard a word from him since. Which is rather worrying, I suppose. I'm terribly sorry I can't be more helpful. I do hope everything's all right?

51

After the party at Mary's house, it felt like I didn't have any choice but to seek out Ste. I knew he'd get a kick out of me crawling to him. But there was nowhere else for me to go.

He'd taken a job of sorts a couple of months before, up at the hotel near the roundabout, staff accommodation to boot. It was an ugly, rundown building just off the exit to the motorway, a one-night stop-off for people on their way to somewhere else. Everyone around the town looked down on them that worked there, worse than they used to on me and Danny. I knew a few of them, knew they were the type that were good for Ste's business.

The accommodation was at the very back of the hotel, the side closest to the traffic. Two squat breezeblock structures, adjacent to one another like the outbuildings of a prison. Ste said I could stay there for a few nights, even though I owed him a shit-ton of money by then. It was the last place I wanted to be, hated the feel of his hardness pressing into the small of my back night after night. But it's not like I had a right lot of choice.

The hotel manager was a lad called Scouse Gary. He was mates with Jody, been down the pub a couple of times before Chrissy left. Gary thought he was something special, thought he'd really made it, managing that seedy hotel, mincing around in shirts so thin you could see the outline of his nipples, fluoro ties done right up to his Adam's apple, rubbing against the greasy little mound whenever he spoke.

Ste told me that if I put on a short skirt and went to see Gary, I'd be bound to walk out of there with a job and so I did as he suggested, tottering through the main entrance in a pair of Chrissy's old shoes and too much makeup weighing down my face. The girl at reception smirked at me when I asked to see the manager, then picked up the phone and turned away to murmur something into the receiver, giggling before hanging up.

Scouse Gary appeared a couple of minutes later, gave me a look like the sight of me made him bored and hungry all at the same time. He told me to come to his office and made me walk in front of him, didn't bother to look at my face as he sat down at his desk, started tapping at his computer as though he'd forgotten I was there.

What can I do you for? he said at last, his eyes still on the screen. I didn't answer straight away. I was waiting for him to face me, trying to pull some of the power back. Eventually he turned his head in my direction. I flashed him the kind of smile that Chrissy would have been proud of.

I'm after a job.

Oh yeah? What kinda job?

Well, I said, leaning forward slightly, I can pull a decent pint.

He ran the tip of his tongue along his teeth before asking me how old I was. I told him I was eighteen. It was only a half lie; my birthday was just a few months away. It didn't matter anyway—there were no vacancies in the bar. None in the restaurant, either.

There's housekeepin, though, he said, a smirk creeping across his face. If you don't mind scrubbin bogs.

I don't. But I need a place to stop.

He sat back, his eyes on my chest. I thought you were Ste's bird?

I looked at him squarely. No. I'm not.

I WAS IN LUCK, IF THAT'S WHAT YOU WANT TO CALL IT. A LAD who'd been staying in the block next to Ste's had done a runner a few nights back, got himself into a bit of a fix with someone apparently. The rent was cheap, Gary would take it out of my wages every month before he paid me, but if there was any trouble I'd be out on my ear, he bleated, reeling off a list of house rules as we crossed the car park. I nodded along, barely listening. Gary drummed on the door three times before a bloke with acne scars all over his face opened it, looked me up and down with a leer.

Who's this then?

Gary answered for me. This, he said, is your new house-mate.

The building was identical to Ste's, except my room was

on the ground floor, right at the end of a narrow hallway and next to the shared bathroom. I pushed the door open with my toe, taking in the cracked bath panel, the toilet with no seat, an empty bog-roll hook hanging half off the wall. When's the last time that got cleaned? I asked quietly.

Gary grinned. You can see to that now.

There were four bedrooms in total, plus the bathroom and a kitchen. The rooms were rented out to the foreign employees mostly. Eastern Europeans, Irish, the odd French or Spanish bloke. No one stuck it out for long. Still, there were always people around, mingling between the two buildings, hunched over the tables in the filthy kitchens, loitering outside the grotty little bathrooms.

I didn't want any part of it, barely came out of my room at the start. I ignored the attempts at chat from the other housekeeping girls until they stopped bothering with me, whispering when I walked past them in their little gaggles having their cig breaks round the back.

Scouse Gary cornered me in a room on the top floor within the first week of me working there, doubled over on my knees, scrubbing the base of the bath. I heard the door click, thought it was maybe the girl I'd been on shift with, coming back to help me. She'd gone out for a cig two or three rooms ago and I hadn't seen her since. I stood up straight away, ready to have it out with her, tell her it wasn't on, buggering off to leave me to do all the graft on my own. But then I saw that it was Gary, leaning against the doorframe, fingering a keychain that hung from his pocket.

Workin hard?

He was watching me in the mirror, his eyes on my reflection but never on my face. It made my stomach twist, the way he couldn't make eye contact. Even when you were talking right at him, he'd find somewhere else to look, some other little spot to busy his attentions with. Yeah, I answered. I need to get past, though.

He moved his body to the side but stayed within the narrow doorframe, leaving enough space for me to squeeze through, but not enough that I wouldn't have to smear myself up against the length of him. I rolled my eyes and turned to the sink instead. He took a step closer to me, clearing the doorway, and I walked past into the bedroom, Gary following close behind.

Were there summat you needed?

He was standing no more than a foot away from me, his eyes resting on my stomach. Just wanted to check you were settlin in.

I'm fine, I said, giving him a tight smile. Thanks.

He nodded, then gestured to the window behind me, overlooking the staff accommodation. How's it down there then?

S'all right.

The lads not givin you any bother?

Nowt I can't handle.

Gary smirked again. Bet you've handled a fair bit in your time.

I didn't reply, ripping open the poppers of the thin polyester duvet cover, gutting the insides into a pile on the bed.

You gonna tell me how come you don't wanna stop with Ste then? He was watching me still, the fabric around the long bones of his fingers sheening in the pocket of his cheap suit.

He's just a mate.

Oh yeah? You gorra fella then, do yer?

I picked up the clean sheet, unfolding it carefully on the bed. Yeah.

Gary made a noise like a laugh, high-pitched and nasal, closing the gap between us with another step, his breath hot against my neck.

Were there anythin else? I asked, my body stiff, my eyes staring straight ahead at the wall on the other side of the room. For a moment he was quiet, and then he took a step back. I sidestepped him quickly, moved to the other end of the bed.

He sniffed, drawing his whole nose up into the action. You wanna get a move on. There's still a whole floor to get through here.

hated every moment of working in that hotel. The dingy rooms, the stench of sweat and stale smoke that clung to everything, no matter how many cans of air freshener I emptied. The leering eyes of the grubby customers, the deadbeat, soulless staff. I would have walked out on my first day, had it not been for Danny.

For the first few weeks I put everything I had into that job. I was determined to be good at something, however paltry it might have been. I told myself that if I worked hard, kept clean, then I could win Danny back. I was for him, and he was for me, we both knew that. We'd just lost our way a little bit, that was all. And I could fix that. I just needed to show him that I was still me, still Neef. Prove to him that I was capable of earning a living the proper way. That I wasn't a druggy, a skank. That I was different from my mam.

I didn't touch a thing that first month, steered clear of Ste, despite his constant goading. *What's up with yer? What you actin all prissy with me fer, eh?* he'd chide. *No point trying to pretend you're summat you're not, Neef. I know you too well fer all that.*

There were plenty of nights when I almost cracked, when the miserable truth of what my life had become threatened to steamroll me. I missed the feeling of being off my head, of being able to block it all out. But there was gold at the end of the rainbow, I was sure of it. Every abstinence brought me closer to Danny.

The day I got my first pay packet you couldn't have wiped the grin off my chops. I practically skipped into Gary's office to pick it up. *I'm here fer me wages,* I said, standing in front of his desk like a kid.

He leaned back in his chair, sensing my keenness, my pathetic eagerness for that meager little envelope.

Oh yeah?

Yeah. I nodded, holding out my hand. He didn't move, just sat there with a sick little smile on his face. *Can I have em then?*

Gary licked his lips, then made a big show of reaching into his drawer, pulling out the thin brown packet. I stepped forward to take it from him and he drew back his hand.

Ah-ah-ah, he said, waving his finger at me. *Ask nicely now.*

I resisted the urge to roll my eyes, played along, even though it made my stomach reel. *Please can I have me wages, Mr. Gary, sir?* I simpered.

He grinned, dropping the envelope into my hand. *There's a good girl now. Off you go.*

After that I got the bus straight up to the garden center, a fizzing in my chest, the sights and the sounds and the smells of the place reminding me of Danny with such force that twice I found myself turning to him, only to remember that he wasn't there.

I wanted to buy him something, a gift so that he could see how well I was doing. I'd save the receipt and all, show him I didn't need to help myself from there anymore. I had a job now, my own place to live, sort of. Danny would be proud of me. I could picture him, scrambling to show Denz that he had me all wrong. In the end I picked out a lush little plant in a terra-cotta pot, its leaves striped in all different shades of green. The lady next to me told me it was called a calathea.

It's got a special meaning, she said, reaching forward and caressing the stems with her knotted fingers, each of them clad in chunky rings that matched her silver hair. Means "to turn over a new leaf."

I burst out laughing then, told her it was perfect, and she smiled at me sagely, touched my hand, wished me good luck.

On my way back to the hotel I stopped at the pay phone, dialed Danny's number, the digits ingrained in my brain. I was being silly, not calling him off my own phone. He'd have answered, of course he would. But still . . .

When he picked up, the sound of his voice made my own catch in my throat, so that he had to say hello over and over again.

Danny. It's me.

A beat passed. You all right? he said eventually, his tone gruff.

Yeah. You?

Yeah.

My reason for calling vanished from my mind and then just as suddenly reappeared, so that the words came tumbling out of my mouth too quickly. I were wonderin. If you wanted to meet up. If you wanted to see me.

Danny let out a breath. I dunno, Neef—

Please, Dan, I cut in, hating the sound of the whine in my voice. I just . . . I'm doin really well, see, and . . . I wanted to show you. That's all, that's it. I . . . I really fuckin miss you.

There was a noise on the other end of the line, a shuffling, a changing of position. I could picture every line of him. The slouch of his shoulders, the curve of his neck, the way he'd press the phone between his shoulder and ear. All right, he said falteringly. Okay. Yeah.

We arranged to meet the next day by the viaduct, and I walked all the way from the hotel with the plant clutched to my chest, a forest of dappled leaves blocking my view. I was dizzy, giddy with excitement, ignoring the fears that niggled at the edges of my mind. The coldness of his tone. After all, I was doing so well now. I hadn't been using, hadn't been shifting. So it would be fine. It could go back to how it was—it would all be fine.

I got there early but Danny was late, so late that I began to doubt he would turn up at all. When he eventually did, the sound of his footsteps startled me, making me pick up my keys and clutch them between my fingers, the way girls are taught to.

We stared at one another, his face confused as I grinned up at him. Something switched on in his eyes, and then just as quickly turned off. Y'all right? he frowned.

For a moment I was speechless, taking him in, all of him. His hair had grown over the past six weeks and he'd put on weight. It scared me, to see him changing. Already he was less of the boy he'd been, more of the man I would never see him become.

You look fit, I said eventually and a flicker of annoyance passed over his face. I'd wanted to make him laugh, but I could see it hadn't worked and so I cleared my throat awkwardly, thrust the plant toward him. I brought you this. Fer . . . I trailed off, my reason escaping me now, the stupidness of the situation, of my pitiful idea, crawling across my skin.

Ta. He nodded, taking it, glancing over his shoulder nervously, then back in my direction without meeting my eyes.

It's called a cally . . . calla . . . I can't remember now exactly, but it's written there on t'label, see? There! Calathea, I said, my voice too manic, too high. There were this woman in there, proper hippy she were, had all this long gray hair down to her arse. She told me it means summat special. Turnin over a new leaf, she said.

New beginnings, said Danny quietly. That's what it means.

Right! Yeah! Exactly. I grinned. That's good then, innit? That's like . . . fittin. Don't you think, Dan?

He nodded, still not looking at me.

Aren't you gonna sit down then? I said, gesturing to the space beside me.

Danny sniffed, wiped his nose with the back of his hand. I can't stay long. I got a lift here. Me dad . . . he mumbled, gesturing vaguely in the direction of the car park.

Yer dad's here?

Yeah.

Does he know you're seein me?

Yeah.

We were quiet then, me looking up at Danny expectantly, him staring down at the ground.

It's just . . . he began.

What?

Danny rubbed a hand over his face. I've got to be somewhere.

Where?

I'm meetin someone.

You're meetin me.

Neef—

How old are you, Dan? I snapped. You runnin off because yer dad's told you to stay away from me?

Neef.

Jesus, Danny. Grow a pair, why don't yer?

Danny looked at me properly then, our eyes locking. You know it int like that.

I know fuck-all.

Yeah, he said after a while. Yeah, you're probably right.

He turned then, heading back down the path, still holding the plant. I didn't call out to him, just watched him disappear.

THAT NIGHT I FOUND MYSELF OUT THERE WITH THE OTHERS. IN that dirty kitchen, smoking cigs and sniffing lines of whatever was going, off the surface of the grimy tabletop. And it wasn't so bad, you know, because after all, who was I to complain? I should count my lucky stars I had a roof over my head, people who knew my name.

There was all sorts of stuff knocking around the hotel by

then, most of it thanks to Ste. Gary was in on it too, I came to work that out pretty quick. He had to have been, the amount everyone was off their heads in that place. Often I'd see the two of them standing by the outbuildings, both of them looking shifty. Other times I'd watch from one of the hotel windows: Ste in his Corsa, pulling away from the hotel and onto the main road, then slowing at the corner and the passenger door opening, a lanky figure slithering inside, suit trousers shining.

Before long I couldn't even remember what had been the point of that job. I became slovenly, half making beds, giving scum-ringed baths a cursory rinse with a showerhead, piling trays of plates one on top of the other and then leaving them for someone else to find. Five minutes before the end of my shift I'd abandon my trolley outside the cleaning cupboard so that I could avoid the other girls, their narrowed eyes watching to make sure I put every spray and wipe and bloody bucket back in its hole.

When I was younger, the locals at the pub used to tell me to stay away from the people who worked at the hotel. They're up to no good, they'd say. Dangerous. I knew better than to judge, but still I'd been wary of them. Later, when they started coming round to Mary's to pick up, I could see that the locals had been right, even though I was a lowlife myself by then. Nothing compared, though, to what I was in the hotel. There, I was one of them. A parasite whose rotting skin and empty eyes made other people's skin crawl.

I thought time had turned upside down in those last few months at Mary's house, but the inside-outness of that place was far worse. The strange shifts, the odd hours. I tried to fool myself, tell myself this was what it was like, this industry. I'd got the staff wrong before, I hadn't understood. People had to adapt, hospitality has its own rules.

Ste had been waiting for me to drop my knickers for years, and in the end his time came. We'd been drinking in the kitchen all night, and all he kept banging on about was how much money I owed him, asking how I was planning to pay him back. I kept trying to change the conversation, to move onto something else, but before long I was in his bed, flat on my back. I don't remember much of it, just limbs and sweat. Hot breath and stink. The sensation of someone inside me, although in that moment I couldn't remember who. Waking in the morning tangled in his dirty sheets, feeling sickened by the thought of what I'd done, but more sickened by the thought of being on my own.

I don't know if he was keeping tabs on it, crossing off a debt every time we entered into one of those empty, feeling-less transactions. But I found myself there with him often.

53

'd been at the hotel for what felt like forever the morning
Danny showed up there. It could have been weeks or
months—like I say, time didn't work the same way in that
place. I'd been up most of the night in the kitchen with Ste
and a couple of Albanian waiters. One of them had left his
wife for an English girl he'd met in a chatroom, who had
failed to tell him she was already married with two kids. The
other didn't like to talk about what had brought him there. I
don't remember it being fun for anyone. It was just something to do.

Danny was sitting outside on the wall near the bedsits,
smoking, his back curved over and his elbows on his knees.
I saw him as I came out of the side door, my arms piled high
with plastic laundry bags full of mucky sheets. The sight of
him stopped me in my tracks and I stood watching him, as

though he were an apparition that might vanish with the slightest movement. He must have sensed me there, though, because he looked up, his eyes locking with mine until eventually he nodded his head back, that familiar gesture, drawing me toward him. I couldn't move, wanting with every part of myself to go to him and with every part of myself to run in the direction that I'd come from. But in the end the shape of him won out and I dumped the bags there on the floor, walked over, sat down a couple of feet away, stared at a line of ants crawling near my feet.

Neef, he said after a while, and I felt the tips of his fingers on my jaw, a jolt of electricity down my spine. I shivered, turned to look at him, the sight of him filling me up as it always had. Jesus, Neef, he said, like the look of me made him sick. He drew his hand away, rubbed at the back of his neck.

I put my fingers to my mouth, trying to cover the sores around my nose and lips. I knew I looked like shit. I didn't need him to tell me. What d'you want? I asked, my voice a rasp.

Just. To see yer, he said gently. See how you're doin.

The silence fell between us then, awkward, uncomfortable, not the way our silences had ever been before.

Will you show me where you're stayin? he asked.

You after a shag?

Danny whipped his head around to face me. What?

I laughed but the sound fell flat. You heard.

He was staring at me but I didn't dare look up to meet his eyes, afraid of what I would see there. You know, he said eventually, his voice measured, you know that's not why I'm here.

I shrugged, got to my feet, let him follow me to the front

door, regretting it as soon as we walked in. The stench of old food and unwashed bodies curled up into my nose as we stepped into the kitchen, the squalor and the dirt and the grubbiness making the whites of Danny's eyes turn blood-shot.

This is where you're livin? he asked, looking around.

I ignored him. You got any cigs?

Danny pulled a full pack from his pocket, handed them to me. I ripped the top of the carton open greedily, pulled one out, leaned over to light it on the greasy hob.

Will you come fer a walk with me?

There was a dried stain on the countertop where someone had spilled food and I scratched at it with my thumbnail, the flakes settling on my skin. A walk?

He nodded. Yeah, just a walk. I've . . . I've got summat to show yer.

Outside the house I heard the sound of laughter, crude and deep. Men's voices. The front door opened and Ste appeared, still in his grubby kitchen whites, one of the caretakers close behind. Ste paused for the briefest of seconds at the sight of Danny there. My beautiful Danny in that dirty, rotten place. Then he walked in, slapped me hard on the arse, slung a scabby arm around my shoulders.

All right, stranger. He sneered, a humorless grin smeared across his pockmarked face. Danny surveyed him levelly, then looked back to me.

You comin, Neef?

Ste snorted. Oh aye, takin him fer a ride, are we, Neef? Mucky little madam, this one. Ooh, the stories I could tell yer, Danny, lad. Mind you, you've probably got a few yerself, ain't yer?

The caretaker guffawed and the two of them fell about laughing—inane, idiotic laughter that filled me with hot shame. Ste collapsed down onto a kitchen stool. Go on then, Neef, love. Go and gi'im what he came fer before he fucks off back to his dad's.

Neef, Danny tried again but I ignored him, Ste's words roiling inside me. I moved over to where Ste was sitting, perched myself on his lap. Only then did I turn to Danny, the pain of his abandonment tearing open like a fresh wound.

Nah, I said, screwing up my nose. Not today, ta. I'm all right.

For a moment we just looked at one another and I felt something crack inside my heart. Danny nodded slowly, stood up straight. From his back pocket he pulled out a thin paperback, its cover sleek and maroon, dropped it onto the table without looking at me. Then he left.

IT WAS AN ANTHOLOGY OF POETRY, PUBLISHED ONLY WEEKS before by the local paper. I didn't have to look far to find my lines, my words. There was no photo or bio, but my name was there. My full and proper name, printed in black and white. That night in my room, I let my fingertips trace the outline of each letter, over and over until I couldn't see them anymore, the page buckling with my tears.

n the weeks that followed I put so much shit inside me
that it was no wonder my body decided to turn itself inside
out. I woke in the night, fighting to make myself small, ball
up around the fire in my stomach, and yet my body riled
against my efforts, stretching itself, attempting to empty itself
of anything and everything within me. I crawled from the
bed and out into the draft of the hallway, the filth of the bathroom, retching, gagging, vomiting into the toilet bowl with
such aggression that it splashed back out, streaking my face
and neck with acid. It wasn't the first time it had happened,
although it was the most violent. I'd been throwing up for
close on three weeks, sending me into a state of panic that
had made me sicker still, staggering down the road to the
chemist and peeing on a stick in the public toilets near the
Methodist church. I'd celebrated with a line of speed and

half a bottle of flat cava left over from a wedding at the hotel when the test came back negative.

I begged the lads at the bedsits to call me an ambulance but none of them would, said it wouldn't be a good idea to have them sniffing around. A good idea for who? I'd tried to ask, but all that came out was a croak.

There was a new bloke staying there; he was from Wales, I think. He made me lie down on my side in case I choked, drink small sips of water through a straw, left a bowl by the bed for when it started happening again. Which it did, over and over. When the morning came, he borrowed someone's car to drive me to the clinic near Mary's house. It felt strange being up that way, passing buildings and faces and bends in the road that had once been a part of my every day.

The doctor said it was an ulcer, that the lining of my stomach was so inflamed there wasn't enough room for food to pass through. Lots of reasons why it can happen, he said, peering over the top of his glasses at me. Although you're a bit young.

What sort of reasons? I asked, bent double with the pain.

He leaned back in his chair, eyeing me warily. Stress, he said. Over-consumption of alcohol. Excessive use of aspirin. Recreational drugs. He set his eyes squarely on me then. Would any of these apply to you, Jennifer?

Yeah— I started, but then caught myself. Yeah. I get a lot of headaches. Too much aspirin, probably, I'd say.

The doctor looked at me hard, then nodded, unconvinced. I see, he grimaced. Well, I can certainly write you a prescription. Although it obviously won't do you any good, if your lifestyle is . . . incompatible.

In the car on the way back to the hotel I'd laughed at his

choice of words. Lifestyle. Life*style*. *Life*style. He made it
sound so fancy. The lad from Wales didn't get the joke, told
me to stop acting so fucking weird.

The medication stopped me throwing up, but it didn't fix
me. Something had burrowed inside me, made my insides
its nest: dread in the form of a creature that festered in the
darkest part of me. Still now, when I wake up each morning,
I feel it, niggling and scratching and biting. That's why I do
all the things I do, the blocking out, the counting, anything
to fill up my head. I want to quash it, to suffocate it. And it
works, for the most part. Nothing can grow if you don't let it
breathe.

55

The day after I'd been to the doctor I went to see Scouse Gary, told him I needed a bit of time off. He didn't even look up from his screen, just said that if I wasn't back by the weekend they'd kick me out, but I was past caring by then. Ste came to find me that evening, his shadow falling across where I sat at the kitchen table, staring into nothing.

What you mopin about like such a misery fer? he snarled.

I'd been avoiding Ste. Despite how messed up I'd been getting, I hadn't let him put his hands on me since the day Danny had dropped my book off at the hotel.

What d'you want? I muttered, uncurling my fingers from a cup of long-cold tea.

He took a step toward me. Just come to see if you were finished hankerin after that Danny yet.

I edged my chair toward the wall, rubbing the heaviness

from the corners of my eyes. Something in the way Ste was looking at me made me nervous.

Come on, get yer shit together, he said tersely. I'm off out fer a drink with Gary—you can come.

Nah, I'm all right.

Come on. It'll be a laugh.

I'm poorly, Ste. I feel like shit.

He stepped forward, wrenching at my arm. Get up, yer daft bitch.

Gary was already in the car when we got there. I didn't bother asking where we were going, knew they wouldn't answer me. We drove the back way, barely passing another car until we hit Leeds and pulled up outside a derelict cluster of tower blocks. Ste got out and I closed my eyes, sank back into the headrest, hoped that maybe I'd be able to fall asleep.

Wakey-wakey!

I hadn't realized Gary was still there, leering at me from the passenger seat. I turned my face away, hated to be alone with him, but he reached backward, grabbed the inside of my thigh with his long fingers, making me yelp out in pain, and shock.

He laughed. Relax, girly. Me and Ste'll soon have you feelin better.

It was a while before Ste reappeared. The two of them strode ahead of me and I skulked a few feet behind, like a child. At the top of the street stood a rundown old pub that reminded me of being a kid in the flats. Metal bars were fixed across the two lower windows, a grubby flag of St. George pinned up to one of them.

Inside it was dark, a scrawny lad in a worn-out tracksuit playing on the nudgies and an old bloke half asleep on the bar. I followed Ste and Gary to a table in the corner next to a window covered in a layer of white scum, distorting the view outside so that it looked like someone had wiped their palm across a chalk drawing. Ste went to the bar without asking what I wanted, came back and pushed a glass of warm, sour wine across the table at me. I fiddled with the beer mat, tearing it into shreds and dropping them onto the dirty carpet.

A thank-you might be nice.

Ta, I mumbled. The two of them got up to play pool and I hoped perhaps they'd leave me alone for a bit. I sipped the wine slowly, but before I could finish it, there was another drink in front of me, and then another and another. Malibu and Cokes, bottles filled with bubblegum fizz, a bright-red shot that made me gag just from the smell.

I told you we'd have a laugh tonight. Ste grinned. I smiled at him tightly as Gary handed me a pool cue.

Come on then. Let's see what all them years livin at the boozer did for yer.

I didn't want to move, but I could tell by his face he wasn't going to let it go and so I stood, stumbling slightly. We played and I lost, knew I was drunk by then. I could nail almost anyone at pool. And then we were outside, round the back with a spliff.

We're goin now, Ste was saying.

Where?

The hotel—where d'you think? We'll have a little party, how does that sound?

I shook my head. Nah, nah. I don't want to.

The two of them laughed, but I didn't know what was funny.

By the time we got back it was pitch-black. I lurched out

of the car, a wave of nausea washing over me, sat down on the tarmac of the car park. Ste tried to make me stand but I pushed him away, elbowing him in the shin hard enough for him to jump back, swear, call me a silly slut.

We ended up in Gary's office and I remember looking down, seeing that I had a mug in my hand, but it was empty and I wasn't sure if I'd drunk from it or if it had never been full. There was music playing and Ste and Gary were bent over the desk, sniffing lines of something, waving the rolled-up note in my direction. The room wouldn't stay still, and I had the sense somehow that Danny was there, that I was saying his name, but I don't know whether anything came out of my mouth or if it was just in my head, and when I looked at Gary and Ste again, I saw they were laughing.

I tried to bring their features into focus but something had happened to my eyes, my ears. I brought the mug to my lips again, then remembered it was empty, but I'd got it wrong somehow because in fact it was full, and it wasn't a mug but a plastic cup. There was a cigarette between my fingers, or maybe something else, and I suddenly felt cold. Only then did I realize I didn't have any clothes on. I must have tried to stand, because the next thing I knew I was on my knees on the floor, someone's hands on my back.

You've always been a lively one, haven't yer?

You might not be as fit as yer mam, but you're plenty like her in other ways.

Come on then, come on, there's a good girl, that's it, that's it.

And then I am on the ground, and Gary is above me, his features all stretched out and distorted, like the Joker. He is flicking water in my face and I am trying to sit up, and now

Ste is there too and there is a weight on me, in me, pressing me down, and then there is no more laughing but there is hot breath and hands and heat and spit and I am back there, on my back at Devil's Claw, and I want them to stop but I don't have the words and I asked for this and I led them on and at some point there is no more music, no more stench of sweat and bodies, and when I wake up again the next morning I am alone and I know. I know I let it happen again.

Everything after that is ruptured, disjointed, like when you get dirt in your eye and the more you rub it, the more painful it gets, and the less you can see.

Ste came to see me at some point, let himself into my room without knocking. I kept my back to him, curled up in a ball on the mattress. Didn't have to look at him to see the sneer smeared across his face.

You know how to have fun, don't yer? Proper little goer when you want to be.

He came again the next day, and the one after that. I hadn't moved from the bed. At first he was light, jokey, but as time wore on, his mood changed.

I don't know what you're bein so mardy about it fer. You sore or summat? You need to get yer shit together, you do.

By the fourth day he started getting scared. Come on,

Neef. It were just a bit of a laugh. You liked it at the time, you were up fer it. Don't you remember?

At some point I must have got up, got dressed, because the next thing I remember is flagging down a cab on the high street, giving the driver an address a few streets away from where Denz lived. When the taxi got near, I opened the door and jumped out onto the curb, then ran as fast as I could toward the park, while the driver yelled after me to pay him his bloody fare. I hid in the bushes until it felt safe enough to come out, pulling my hood over my head as I hurried down the street, my body bent low.

It was dark when I arrived—inside Denz's house as well as out. I remember standing on the doorstep, looking for the bell, not being able to find it and knocking instead, bouncing from foot to foot. Everything itched and I rubbed at my face, my arms, wishing I could tear off my skin with my nails. Knocking and knocking, but no one came and so I banged. I banged and banged and banged and maybe I yelled, shouted, called out Danny's name, Denz's too. Eventually there were noises inside. Voices. A light being switched on then off, then on again. And another noise, an animal perhaps . . . a dog. No. A baby. A baby crying.

I banged harder, harder, until finally someone was there, a key turning in the lock on the other side of the door and a face peering out from the open crack, the chain still attached. Dark lashes and full lips, a flash of gold. A brief moment of lucidity. The girl blinked then turned and said something over her shoulder. A voice, deeper than hers, and the door closing, opening again without the chain. The girl took a step backward to where Danny stood, rested her hand gently on his shoulder before taking a round-cheeked baby, its nose wet with snot, from his arms. Three pairs of eyes anchored me to the spot before the baby's face crumpled, a shrill cry escaping from the black hole of its mouth.

I took a step back, the blood rushing in my head. Needed to sit, to lie, to not see what I'd seen. I stumbled, felt cold metal against my arm. A car. A great, dark hulk of a car. Denz's car. Denz.

A fury took hold of me then and I lost it, lashing out. Kicking and hitting and punching. Going at that cold, hard lump of metal and glass with all my strength. Pounding and thrashing and booting until I felt hands on my arms, someone pulling me, dragging me away, a palm clamped over my mouth, and only then did I realize how loud I'd been screaming.

Danny hauled me down the street, his fingers pressing hard into my skin, a pain that was better than anything I'd felt in months. By the time he let go we'd come off the road and into a park, dimly lit but recognizable still. We used to go there together in the summer, Danny and me, in the days when I was still something close to welcome at Denz's. The pair of us would lie out on the grass, watching early-morning dog walkers give way to mams pushing buggies, shoving elevenses into fat little hands that thrust out from beneath pram hoods. Once the sun climbed to its highest point we'd go and find a spot of shade in the woods that encircled the park, watch the runners arrive, lithe and slender, headphones clamped over ears, light rings of sweat smiling from the underarms of their designer sports vests. In the darkness I could still make out the lake at the bottom of the hill that Danny and I had swum the length of, years before. Afterward we'd sat on the bank, both of us sharing one ninety-nine, because we only had a quid between us. Danny let me have the flake to myself, told me he didn't like them, but I knew it wasn't true. I ate it all the same, though.

I lay on the wet grass now, flat on my back, as Danny paced up and down in front of me. I didn't want to think anymore, just wanted to be, and so I closed my eyes, arranged my arms over my face. Danny dragged them off me, yanked at my shoulder, making me cry out, forcing me to sit. His nose was only inches from mine, his eyes furious, hard. I stared back at him, watched his face soften. He sighed, collapsed down beside me.

What were that all about, Neef?

The image of the baby in Danny's arms played over again in my head, the girl's hand on him. I needed a cig, a drink. Something.

You can't do shit like that, man. Can't just turn up, shoutin yer mouth off. You're lucky Rina didn't call the police—

Rina.

Yeah. Rina. That's her house too—

So you're livin together. My voice was dull, a monotone.

Yeah. We all live there. Denz. Rina. The baby, Nia.

Didn't take you long, did it?

What?

I looked at him, trying to hide the hurt in my face, my voice, with a twist of disgust. A baby, Danny? A fuckin baby?

Danny frowned. What you on about, Neef? That's me sister. Nia. Well, half sister . . . Rina's her mum, so . . . hang on, you thought . . . He laughed then, a laugh of confusion and disbelief. Do the maths, man. Nia's not far off a year old. We only moved out of me nana's nine months ago—how would that even have worked?

I rubbed my eyes. Nine months. Had it really only been nine months?

Neef, Danny said softly. What's happened to yer?

I stayed quiet, rocked back and forth, my arms wrapped around my knees. Danny knitted his fingers together at the back of his head, let out a long breath through his lips.

That hotel, man. That place. You need to get out of there.

And go where?

Anywhere.

Let's go to London, Dan. You and me. Let's go to stay with Lewis fer a bit, like we always said we would.

Danny stayed silent, staring down toward the lake. Did you read it? he asked after a while. The book?

I tried to speak, but when I opened my mouth, no words came. A noise rose out of my throat, guttural, animal-like.

Jesus, Neef.

He put an arm around my shoulder, pulled me in close to him, his face buried in my matted hair until the shaking stopped. I tilted my chin, my lips meeting his, and in that moment everything felt okay again. He kissed me back. I had started it but he did, he kissed me. My hands wandered, searching, tugging at the fabric of his clothing, sliding them below his T-shirt, feeling the warmth of him, his skin, my skin. I wanted him so much, I wanted all of him.

But then he pulled away, stopped me in my tracks. Neef, don't, he said. Don't.

He got to his feet, lifted me to standing. I didn't want to go, but I let him lead me, mesmerized by the feeling of my hand in his. We made our way out of the park, back down the street toward Denz's house. I didn't question it, didn't know where I would end up, only that Danny was there, and that meant it would all be all right now.

. . .

AS WE REACHED DENZ'S HOUSE, DANNY SLOWED. THE LIGHTS were on inside and there was a figure in the driveway, kneeling down, inspecting the car. I remembered then what I'd done. That blind rage, that painful fury. The figure stood, his outline silhouetted against the light from the front room. Denz.

Go inside, Danny.

I waited for Danny to argue, to tell his dad no, but he barely paused. He squeezed my hand, let it go, then walked toward the house without looking back. I began to shake all over again, my whole body trembling, my breath catching in my throat. Denz was watching me but I didn't care, let him do whatever he wanted. Nothing could hurt like Danny walking away. In the end, he just sighed. Get in the car, Neef.

I don't know why I did as he asked. Maybe I thought it would make Danny happy. Maybe I was too worn down to do anything else.

The car was as I remembered it, but different too: the sound system a toned-down version of the one he'd had before; a baby's chair fitted in the backseat, a pink-and-green mobile rainbowed over the top of it, and a rattle in the shape of a smiling star cast aside on the cushion. We drove in silence along the dual carriageway. The rain had started again, sheets of water flying off the sides of the glass as the wipers fought against them, swinging frenziedly backward and forward. Denz pressed his foot on the accelerator, dodging and weaving through the traffic, cutting sharply across the lanes, in such a hurry to be rid of me. Only when we slid onto the exit toward the town did he speak again.

You can't do that again, Neef. D'you hear me?

I ignored him, wrapped a section of hair around my finger, yanked at it from its root.

Neef, I'm serious. Danny's tryin to sort himself out. He were . . . well, he were a lot like you are now when he came to stay with me. And I know I'm not perfect, I've made mistakes too. But he's doin good, man. He's on a course at college, he's got a job doin gardens. He don't need all this . . . this . . . shit.

Danny loves me.

Denz let out a long sigh. No, Neef, he said. No. He don't.

enz dropped me on the outskirts of the town but it was morning by the time I made my way back to the hotel. When I got there the door to my room was locked, black bin bags of my belongings dumped outside it, for the third time in my life. Ste was lurking in the hallway in his boxers, his face the same mushroomy shade as the walls. Gary wants you out, he said.

Out where?

He looked at me like I was stupid. Out of here, Neef. You ain't shown up fer work in days. And look at yer. D'you think anyone'd want their rooms cleaned by you, the state you're in?

I stared at the bags at my feet for a while then looked up at him, smiled serenely. Okay.

Ste narrowed his eyes, confused. D'you want a lift somewhere?

Yes, please. Could you take me to the park? The big one up at Roundhay?

The park?

Yeah.

Ste shrugged, started walking toward his car, and I floated behind him. As he pulled open the driver's door he turned, looked at me strangely. D'you not want yer stuff?

Nah, I heard myself say. Nah.

WE DIDN'T SPEAK THE WHOLE WAY THERE, BUT AS WE PULLED UP to the park, Ste cleared his throat. Listen, Neef . . . no hard feelins, yeah? It just got a bit out of hand, the other night, and me and Gary—well, you always seem up fer a bit of fun and that, we thought you were enjoyin it . . .

I opened the car door, drifted away without closing it behind me. I didn't need to hear it. Everything was about to work itself out. It was summer time and warm, the flowers not yet wilted, the colors hyper-bright. Lying down on the grass, I stared up at the clouds, pointing out the shapes to Danny. Look. A little girl with a balloon! A bear! A donkey wearin a hat! I didn't mind that he never said anything back.

After a while I got to my feet, gliding through strangers' gardens, under hedgerows and around cars parked in driveways. Occasionally I would hear someone holler, yell, but it didn't matter. I was invisible, after all.

I didn't want to bother Danny, didn't want to bother anyone. I wasn't trying to make a nuisance of myself, I just wanted to see him. There was a bus stop opposite Denz's house and I sat there for a long time, waiting for someone to come out, but nobody did and so I crept over the road, pressed my face against the window into the living room. It looked different from how I remembered it. The artwork was still there, but the weights had been replaced by a baby walker, a playmat. A pair of women's boots lay discarded on a thick rug by the sofa, toys strewn around the space.

I slid along the brickwork toward the kitchen, where there was music playing, somebody moving around. The girl, Rina. I could see her. The baby too, gurgling in her highchair, a rusk in her hand. Rina was swaying to the music, dancing, making the baby laugh. I wanted to go inside, to crawl inside Rina's body, be her, be part of that picture. Suddenly her head swung toward the window, the music stopping abruptly as I ducked, slinking along the hedgerow to the back of the garden. Danny's touch was everywhere—how beautiful it had begun to look. I crouched in the bushes, near a little herb garden he'd carved into the earth, feeling closer to him there than I had in months.

BY EVENING I WAS IN LUCK. THE FOUR OF THEM WERE OUT ON THE decking, the baby bouncing on Denz's knee, Rina pouring wine. I crouched out of view, watching, watching. They were too far away for me to hear what they spoke about, but every now and again one of them would laugh and it would warm me up inside, like I was part of it too. And was it my imagination or did Danny turn in my direction every now and again, glancing at the bushes with a curious look on his face, like he could sense me there?

Eventually they drifted inside and I took that as my cue to leave. I didn't want to be a bother after all. Back at the park, I fell asleep under one of the benches near the lake, and the next morning I woke with the pockets of my trackies turned inside out.

My body rattled and shook with each day that passed, my routine always the same. Sometimes I wouldn't see them at all. Sometimes just Rina and Denz. The best days were when it was only Danny, sitting out there on his own on the back step, his elbows on his knees, a spliff or a mug in his hand. How I loved to watch him. How I longed to crawl from my hiding place, lay my head in his lap. It took every part of me not to go to him. I needed time. Needed a plan.

58

Fionnoula thinks there's something wrong with me. I mean, more wrong with me than she'd thought before. Like I'm sick, or coming down with something, or on the verge of slipping off the edge of a precipice that I've been teetering on since the day we met. I think, perhaps, she's right.

I'm struggling, right now, to separate the days from the nights. To remember what I did yesterday, this morning, an hour ago. All these years I've been hiding from the past and now my memory is pinned so far back I've forgotten what it means to live in the present day.

Last week I slept in late, left the customers standing out in the cold until most of them turned round and made their way to the big Starbucks at the bottom of the hill, where the tea costs three times the price but at least you know someone will remember to open the bloody door. Fionnoula let it go, laughed it off and said she hoped whatever it was that had kept me up half the night was worth her caff going down the pan. But then it happened again this morning.

She's been watching me like a hawk all day, biding her time, waiting for a lull in the endless serving of teas and coffees and bacon butties so that she can corner me. I've been doing all I can to stay out of her way, and as my shift draws to an end I slink across the caff, keep my head bent low as if that might help. But Fionnoula won't let me escape that easily, pulling me up in the passageway between the kitchen and the little pantry at the back.

What's going on with you? she says.

I try to keep my face blank, tell her I don't know what she means. She crosses her arms over her chest, gives a deep sigh, and in that moment I have the sense of Fionnoula and Mary's lines blurring together so that I'm no longer sure who I'm talking to, which life I'm in, which version of myself I am. I put out a hand to steady myself against the wall, try to herd my thoughts, the plaster against my palm belonging to both the caff and the pub all at once. Someone is saying my name, a singsong lilt, and then a hand is under my elbow, Fionnoula's touch bringing me back together, pulling me into the present day. I frown her face into focus, see the worry lines creasing around her mouth.

Come and sit down, love. Take it easy for five minutes, will you? she says, leading me out to one of the tables, maneuvering me onto a chair. And for goodness' sake, tell me what is going on.

In the background Ali makes us a pot of tea, carries it through on a tray and places it gently in front of us. I smile my thanks and he squeezes my shoulder, looks on me with his kind eyes before walking back into the kitchen. Fionnoula turns to me again.

Is there something I can help with, love? Anything at all?

I shake my head, reach for the cup, but the tremble in my hand makes the tea slosh onto the tabletop and then on my thighs, burning through the cheap fabric of my trousers.

Oh dear, oh dear. Fionnoula starts flapping about, dabbing at the mess with a damp dishcloth that only serves to make everything soggier than it already is. I hope that might be enough to distract her, but then she carries on.

You know, she is saying, you've been off for a while now, ever since that fella came in, I swear it is. What's his name? He did tell me . . . D-something. Daniel, is it?

I look up at her sharply. Not Daniel, I say. It's Denz.

Denz, that's it! Denz. Well, it's ever since he's been around, there's been something different with you, love. And, you know, you know I'm not one to pry. But I can't help but worry; it's not like you, all this forgetfulness and sleeping in and never quite knowing if you're coming or going. I mean, you've always had your quirks, Jen love. But it's more than that now, isn't it? She pauses, laying her warm hand tenderly over mine. You know, Ali and I are so fond of you. But this is our livelihood too, we have to look after it. And if you think that the early starts are getting to be too much, if you've maybe been staying out late or seeing this Denz fella—

How many times? I snap. I'm not seeing Denz, not like that. I've not been going out, I just . . .

Just what, love? Fionnoula takes my hand in both of hers, the warmth of the gesture making me want to curl up in a ball.

I'm sorry, Fi, ignore me, I say quietly. I shouldn't have spoken to you like that. You don't need all this. I shouldn't be making your life difficult.

Oh, Jen, she says, edging her chair closer to me now, circling an arm around my shoulder. Don't be daft. You make our life better—I hope you know that. I don't know what we'd do without you, love.

I want time to slow, to stay here in the safety of this moment. To lean into Fionnoula, trust her with all the truth that I've buried. And I want to believe that she would listen, that it wouldn't make her turn on me. I want to believe it so much.

t was especially hot the day I saw Rina and the baby out in Denz's garden all alone. I'd gone in the lake for a dip, dumped my clothes on the side and waded in, in just my underwear, then lay out in the sun waiting for it to dry, my pale skin blistering in the heat. I lost track of time, panicking when I woke that I might have missed them, but in fact when I got there it was much earlier than I had thought, nowhere near time for Denz or Danny to be home.

Rina was out there with the pram, rocking the baby backward and forward absentmindedly, flicking through a magazine on her lap. The baby fussed, resisting sleep, but eventually she quietened and I could see Rina relax. There was a noise then, piercing and loud, cutting through the air. A phone ringing inside, threatening the serenity, and Rina jumped to her feet, disappearing through the screen door to silence it.

She mustn't have realized that she hadn't put the brake on, or maybe she knocked it off by accident when she stood. She didn't see the pram rolling slowly down toward the bottom of the garden. Couldn't have heard the baby wake again and let out a little whimper. The pram was picking up speed—it would have tipped over, had I not caught it. I was only trying to help, I only wanted to make sure she didn't get hurt. I didn't mean to pick up the baby, I hadn't been thinking. I only did it because I heard her cry, I only wanted to comfort her. I was just going to show her Danny's herbs, that's all. I was going to crouch down and show her, let her smell them. But when I looked at her little rosebud mouth, the clear, dark depth of her eyes staring up at me, I didn't know how to put her down again. I only wanted to show her the flowers in the park, how beautiful they were, how Danny and I had always loved to look at those things. I wasn't hiding, when I took her into the woods. I only wanted to show her the trees. I didn't hear anyone screaming, anyone looking, the sirens filling the air. I didn't. I would have taken her right back if I'd thought anyone was upset. I only wanted to show her. I only wanted to hold her. I only wanted to be held.

IT WAS DARK BY THE TIME DANNY APPEARED IN THE CLEARING of the woods. I wasn't surprised to see him, gazed up at him with a smile like I'd been expecting him the whole time. He crept toward me slowly, quietly, like someone might approach a wild animal. Can I have her, Neef? he whispered.

I frowned at him. No! Shh! Don't disturb her, I whispered back. I've only just got her settled.

Danny sat down beside me, his breathing heavy, his face damp with sweat.

I need to take her, Neef.

The baby was sucking on my knuckle, her eyes heavy with sleep. Softly I began to sing to her, a melody from long ago, scratched CDs in Barry's front room.

Remember when we were kids, Dan?

Yeah, he said gently. Yeah, I remember.

It were good, weren't it? Bein a kid. I never used to think it were, back then. But it were better than I thought.

Yeah, Neef. It were better.

Chrissy said I were a good baby, I murmured. Like this. Said I hardly ever cried. Said people used to moan and whinge about the baby stage, but it were never bad, fer her. It only gets hard when they get an opinion, she used to say.

Danny nodded, the fear in his face softening. You heard from her? Chrissy?

No. I thought fer a long time . . . I really thought she'd be with Denz. But . . .

Yeah. Well. He's got Rina now.

The baby let out a little sigh as I lifted my knuckle from her mouth. I thought mebbe she'd write to me, y'know. She used to write me notes. Poems and that. She were a good writer.

Like you, Danny said.

I shook my head. Not anymore. I'm no good at anythin anymore, Dan. I've messed it up, ruined it all.

My arms began to tremble and Nia's eyes snapped open, her bottom lip curling.

Neef, that int true. I know you, know what you can do. Danny reached across, laid a palm on my knee, gentle, tentative.

I looked at him. You still think that?

Danny nodded, inching closer to me. Remember what you wrote, Neef? Remember the poem, in the book?

The clouds in my head parted just a crack. It were about us, I whispered.

I know, he said softly. I know. I understood it. I understood every word. He touched my cheek with the tips of his fingers. And it were right, what you said. That when other people see us, they only see the bits above the ground. They can't see the rest, the roots, the stuff that's made us who we are. And some people, their roots are strong. They've had someone lookin after em all this time, givin em food and water and sunlight and that. But others, they've had it all messed up. The soil underneath them is loose and full of old shit that people've ground down on top of em. They ain't had anyone takin care of em, makin sure they grow and flourish. And then sometimes it's too late, sometimes you can't fix that. But sometimes you can.

The rims of Danny's eyes were red, locked with mine. I loosened my grip on Nia, stroked the little curls next to her ear.

I know you, Neef. You can get better. I can help yer.

Denz wants to keep you away from me.

He smiled, rested a hand on mine. I'll always be able to find you.

I let him take Nia then. Let him take me too, lift me by

the crook of the elbow, help me out of the woods. I hardly had any strength left, my legs buckling as I walked, Danny half carrying me out of there. Only then did I see the lights. The police cars. The ambulance. All of them waiting to take me away.

only ever had one visitor in that unit they took me to. My heart leaped when I saw the name on the list. D. Campbell. But even as I sat there wanting Danny, a nurse hovering nervously in the corner, I knew it would be someone else I'd see.

Denz took a seat across from me in the sterile little lounge that they'd tried to dress up with unbreakable vases and flowers made from shiny plastic. I couldn't look at him, wishing he wasn't there, wishing I knew how to explain.

They been takin care of you? he said after a while. I nodded, pinched hard on the inside of my forearm, twisting the skin between my finger and my thumb. You feelin any better? he tried again.

Yeah, I said quietly. Yeah.

He let out a breath, long and low and hard. I wondered if he hated being there too. Wondered why he had come at all.

It int easy. Seein you like this. Int easy for me, so . . . so I don't know what it would do to Danny.

At the mention of his name I had the urge to scream, squeezed my eyes shut, concentrated on the colors behind my lids.

But still. I think it's right. I think it's the right place for you to be, for now. You need . . . support. You know that, don't you?

I said nothing, hugged my knees to my chest, my eyes still shut.

You won't be here forever. You'll get better. Soon, I bet. You'll be able to start again, but . . . that's why I'm here, see, Neef. There's summat I need to say.

I opened my eyes then, looked at Denz properly for the first time. His face was pained and he was leaning forward with his elbows on his knees, his body taking a shape that reminded me so much of his son.

I don't know how much you know about me and Kim. Danny's mum.

Nowt, I said quietly. Only that you took her to a party one Christmas and she died.

A nerve in Denz's jaw twitched. Yeah. Well. I should've known, the day I met her, that it wouldn't be easy. Should've read the signs. But love's blind, innit? Or it's meant to be.

He looked at me expectantly but I had nothing to say, and so he turned to the window, began to speak almost as though I weren't there. He told me how he used to meet Kim off the school bus every morning, how they used to chat about anything and everything. Denz's family back in Jamaica, the auntie that he was living with in Leeds. Kim told him things too, about her life, her family. Her mum. How it was just the two of them, how close they were since her dad had left when she was too little to remember.

One morning when I got off the school bus, she were nowhere to be seen, Denz said, his tone changing. At lunchtime I waited for her where I always did but she never showed up, and so I went lookin for her at the end of school. Soon as I see her, her eyes light up. But then it's like she remembers summat bad, carries on walkin.

I follow her, ask her where she's been and she goes: here. At school. And that hurt me, see. So I stopped and she slows down, looks at me like she's embarrassed. Says she's sorry. Says her mum, Mary, had seen me, the day before, when I walked her home. So what? I say. Kim looked like she wanted the ground to swallow her, kept glancin over her shoulder for a reason to get away. And then she comes out with it. That's just what me mum said. That she didn't like it. The look of you.

I knew straight away what she meant by that, so I turned around, walked away from her. After that I told meself to let it go. However much I liked Kim, I weren't gonna let Mary or anyone shame me, look down on me just for bein the person I was.

Denz looked up at me then. But it int always that easy, is it? There was already summat between us—that pull. And it won out in t'end.

Kim came to find Denz a few days later, told him she was sorry and that she loved her mum but she could be daft sometimes, she was old-fashioned, Kim was all she had. Mary was just over-protective, that's all. Denz wanted to tell Kim where to go but the way he felt for her overruled everything. And so they carried on, in secret at first, sneaking off up to the woods, down to the river. Even to Kim's house, when Mary was out at work.

The thing with Kim was, she were special. Real special, Denz said. It were like she put a spell on me, I swear. When she got excited about summat, her whole body came alive. She were so clever, I've never known anyone be able to store so much information in their head. Until Danny came along, that is.

He let out a sigh and for a moment I thought that was all he was prepared to say. But then he spoke again.

See, he said, she might've been clever. But she were wild too. And I know you won't believe this, Neef, but I weren't like that. I were a good kid, me auntie were strict. She promised me mum she'd take care of me and she tried, she did her best. Chose that school for the pure reason that it were out of the city, she thought it would keep me away from trouble. She were a god-fearin woman, and her standards, her expectations, were high; good grades, hard work, no distractions. She drummed it into me time and time again that nowt in my life would come easy.

Kim, though. She were the opposite, never needed to prove her place in the world. She knew the streets she danced down belonged to her. And I loved that freedom about her. But it terrified me too. When she started knockin about down the park with her mates, gettin so drunk she could barely stand, it would be me who would carry her home, me who made sure she reached her front door safely, despite the fact that whenever Mary would see me, she would treat me like a piece of shit. Her eyes could only see in black and white and that meant I were the bad guy, and what could I do but take it? If I'd answered back, I'd only have been provin her right.

I only brought Kim home to me family once, for lunch. She barely touched a mouthful, pushed the food round her plate for the whole time she were there, and you ain't never tasted a cookin like me auntie's. I should have been embarrassed of her, but instead, it were me that felt ashamed that day. Of the mad colors me auntie wore, the way she spoke, the mad beats she played on the record player. That day, I'd wished I were someone else. But when Kim said to me, later, when she looked at me with that grin of hers and said, I didn't realize your lot were so *foreign,* I understood what me auntie meant, about mebbe bein better off with someone more like me.

We broke up not long after Kim's sixteenth birthday, before I knew she were pregnant, Denz said, leaning back in his chair. I'd had enough. We were too different. She were a party girl, I weren't like that. Couldn't have been even if I'd wanted; me auntie would have thrown me out on t'streets if I'd started comin home in the states Kim did. And besides, I wanted to go to uni, needed to keep on top of me grades, and that were hard enough as it were, because no matter how hard I tried, how many hours I poured into study, I still could barely keep me head above water, impress the teachers or that school.

Denz looked straight at me then and I saw the worry etched on his face. I don't want you to think I'm slating her, mind, he said. It int like that. I'm just sayin, Kim had choices. But it weren't the same for me, we weren't the same.

He turned to the window again, gazing out at the perfect lawn, its edges encircled by a wall topped with wire.

Kim cried when we broke up, he said. But I knew it were the right thing to do. I knew we couldn't be together, that we'd end up ruinin each other's lives. And I know you'll judge me for sayin this and I don't blame you, Neef. But sometimes I think to meself, mebbe it were a good thing that she died. Because if she hadn't, if we'd stayed in each other's lives, who knows what would have happened to us all?

Denz's mouth set in a way that told me he was finished and I looked at him, confused. But that's not it, I said. That's not the end of the story.

What d'you mean?

Well, what about Danny? What about when Kim died?

That's not the point, he said vehemently. That's not what I came here to tell you.

But—

Denz cut me off, his eyes shining. See, Neef, he said, leaning forward. We aren't all that different, you and me. I know what it's like, for your head to get all messed up. But the only thing I care about—really care about—is that Danny gets to live the life he deserves. And he'll never do that if you're in it.

Danny can make me better.

No, Neef.

The nurse behind me cleared her throat at the volume of Denz's voice and I saw him glance at her, take a breath. No, he said again, quieter this time. I been thinkin about this for a while now. I been wantin to get Danny away from you, from that town and everythin in it for as long as I could re-member. When he came to stay with me, I said to Rina that it were time to move on, to give Danny a fresh start. But she wouldn't hear of it, didn't want to leave her life behind. And so I put it to one side for a while, because I could see you and Danny were leavin each other alone. But then you showed up again. Pulled that shit with Nia. And that were enough to persuade Rina I were right. What I'm tryin to say, Neef, is that I can't let you see Danny again. I won't let you drag him down.

I put my hands over my ears, not wanting to hear any more, but Denz leaned in closer, carried on.

Don't try to get in touch, we won't be where we used to be anymore. After today, you won't see any of us again. I hope you get better, Neef. But you'll have to do it on your own.

didn't believe that Denz would be able to keep us apart. What Danny and I had was different, special, impossible for anyone else to understand. I couldn't let go of what he'd said to me that day in the woods. He'd always be able to find me.

His words were the only memory I let in after Denz visited me in that place. All the others were like razors against my skin, slicing my brain into so many ribbons. I needed a way to stop them, to block them out. It started with counting—counting everything I saw. My steps, my blinks, the shutting of doors. So many complicated patterns, so much filling of the space in my skull.

Funny thing is, it seemed to convince the nurses. My mind was always so busy, so full of nothing, that it kept me quiet, focused. There were no more outbursts, no more smashing of mirrors, no more shouting my mouth off in the common room. Instead I kept myself to myself. Counting, blocking, numbing, quietening. I learned to answer their questions with my mouth without engaging my heart, giving them what they wanted while, behind my eyes, I disappeared.

I can't remember how long it was before they decided I was normal. Can't believe, still, that anyone could have drawn that conclusion. Perhaps it was more to do with needing the bed, funding cuts. Perhaps I really was becoming Chrissy, a master of putting on a show.

I was lucky, they said, as they prepared to discharge me. Lucky the family were so understanding, lucky that I'd got help. Who knows what might have happened to me otherwise?

Yes, I replied. I'm lucky. So fortunate, so very, very blessed.

The caseworker smiled tightly. I see you still have the ability for sarcasm, she said, tapping something away into her computer, her eyebrows raised.

They found me a place in an assisted-living facility, just until I got back on my feet. I'd still have access to support, would need to report in regularly.

That all seems manageable, I said, nodding, and she looked at me again with uncertainty, but something in my face must have won her over because she smiled more kindly this time.

They arranged for a taxi to take me there, but I never had any intention of going inside. Instead I sat on the wall outside the building where the driver dropped me off, gave him my sanest grin and a thumbs-up. He eyed me nervously for a moment before driving off. He'd done what he was told, I wasn't his problem now.

The main road was only a short walk from the hostel, I'd

already looked it up on an old map I found in the scant library at the nuthouse. I walked quickly, glancing over my shoulder, thinking someone must be following me, must be making sure I was doing what I'd been told. But the street behind me stayed empty. When I got to the busiest intersection I stuck my thumb out like I'd seen someone do on an American film that me and Danny watched once. Within ten minutes, a lorry had picked me up.

The driver dropped me off near Birmingham. It took three more rides before I arrived in London. I saw Danny everywhere: catching glimpses of him in the reflections of the shop windows, watching him slip just out of reach on the escalator at the Tube. Every day I'd cross another part of the city, zigzagging from the north all the way down to the south, toward Brixton. For the first week I slept in doorways and on the back of buses, without any idea of what I might do next, only that this was where I needed to be. Danny would know how to find me here.

By the time I followed Sandy into the caff that day, I only had enough money for a cup of tea and I nursed it for hours, counting a pattern of tiny squares on the tablecloth, smaller then larger, then smaller again. I kept losing track and every time I did, I'd make myself go back to the beginning, start again.

At some point Ali brought me over another tea, but when I tried to tell him no, I couldn't pay, he waved my hand away. And then closing time came and Fionnoula bustled over, thrust a cheese sandwich wrapped in clingfilm into my hands, told me they were shutting up shop for the day. I trudged back down the hill after that, searching face after face after face, wondering when Danny's would appear.

In the end, I fell asleep on a bench near the markets, dreamed of Danny mowing lawns in the royal gardens, my name on the front of a book. And then I found myself back at the caff again. I liked the noise in there, the clatter and the din. It must have gone on like that for a week or so, until one day Fionnoula told me enough was enough, she couldn't keep feeding me cheese sandwiches and tea for the rest of her life. I nodded mutely, stood up to leave, but she stopped me, put her hand on my shoulder. You'll help me in the kitchen, she said. Do a bit of washing up, a bit of chopping and peeling too, p'raps. She smiled then, leaning in closer to me with a wink. I'll pay you in tea and cheese sandwiches, if you like.

There was something about Fionnoula that made me trust her, a humanity I hadn't seen in anyone for a long time. When she asked me my name, I answered honestly.

My name is Jennifer.

At first, I'd just show up each morning, wait for Ali to arrive with his keys and let me in. Scurry off into the back and get on with things. There was a telly in the kitchen and one out the front, and on the counter there was always a radio blaring. That old saying: too loud to hear myself think. It was true and it was perfect for me.

I chopped, peeled, did the washing up. They still kept me in tea and cheese sandwiches, but they paid me too, enough so that I always had a bed in one of the hostels down the road. When my shift was finished I'd walk all the way to Brixton, wander the streets and search the faces, hope against hope that someone was searching for mine too.

Over time, Ali and Fi came to trust me. Ali had an extra set of keys cut and the pair of them would let me open up now and again. And then Fionnoula's back started playing up. She didn't like to be on her feet all day and so they asked me, would I mind taking on a bit more, managing things up front, meeting the customers, that sort of thing? I was scared to do it but I said yes, they had been so kind to me. And then Fionnoula said, well, it doesn't make much sense you always tottering off at the end of every day, so why don't you stay upstairs, there's a little room up there you could have, it's not much but it's just sitting empty, you might as well.

I waited for Danny for a long time but he didn't keep his promise. As the years passed I taught myself to forget. It hurt too much to think he'd never been looking.

haven't left the little room above the caff in days, although I can't remember when I last slept. Fionnoula has been at my door countless times, trying to coax me out with promises of shepherd's pies and tea, and that show we both like on the telly. Mostly I ignore her. Every now and again I croak back that I'm poorly, better left alone. The visits are starting to dwindle now, although I still hear her footsteps on the stairs. At the end of each day, I open my door to find a stack of Tupperwares filled with hot food.

I know I should feel ashamed at all the ways I've let Fionnoula and Ali down, but it's like I can't think straight, can't get out of my head. I still haven't spoken to Denz, although he hasn't stopped calling. My phone was on silent but I couldn't figure out a way to turn off vibrate, and so I flung it across the room just to shut it up. For hours its

mosquito-whine cut through my thoughts but I haven't
heard it in a while. It must be long dead by now.

I NEED TO GET OUT OF THIS ROOM, THIS BOX. NEED TO BREATHE,
to run, to expel my thoughts. The caff has been closed
for hours but still I creep downstairs, afraid of bumping
into every shadow. I leave through the front door, walking
quickly. I'm halfway down the street when I see him there.
Denz.

At the sight of me, he picks up his pace. I want to turn,
run back inside, but in the same breath I am angry, seething. How dare he hound me like this. Lurking on street
corners, trying to catch me out. It's then that I realize he is
not alone.

It takes me a few moments before I recognize the other
man's face. He is taller than Denz, skinnier too. His hair is
cut short, a whisper of gray at the temples, and the skin
around his eyes creases as he lifts his hand in a half wave.

Y'all right, kid? Lewis says with a hesitant smile.

I steady myself against the wall, dizzy. Yeah, I'm all right.
Been a while.

Yeah.

Lewis looks at me curiously. I only live round the corner.
But you already knew that, didn't you?

I don't say anything to that, and Denz nods with an air of
smugness that makes me want to smack him in the face.

So you remember him now, Neef?

What are you doing here?

Denz holds a plastic orange Sainsbury's bag toward me. I
came in the caff earlier. Been comin in a bit, actually. But

your woman in there said you were poorly, so I just wanted to drop off a few bits.

I don't take the bag, leave it hanging clumsily from his hand. So you've been skulking around, waiting for me to show my face?

Denz laughs uncomfortably. Naaaah. No. Actually, it were good timin, he lies. We were . . . we were round this way and . . . well, it were a coincidence.

I narrow my eyes, and Denz shifts his weight from one foot to the other.

Listen, Neef. I know it's a lot, seein me, bringin up all these old memories. But I've been worried about you. Since I told you all that stuff about Chrissy.

I snort. Really?

Yeah, he says. And if I didn't know him better, I'd almost believe him. Yeah, I've been worried. And I'm sorry, Neef. About your mum. I am sorry.

I rub my eyes, try to wish him away. It was ages ago, Denz. I don't want to keep talking about it.

Okay, he says. Okay.

The three of us stand there awkwardly for a minute, before Denz speaks again. I'm not going to keep harassin you, Neef. Jen. If that's what you're worried about. But I just . . . I wanted to ask you, one more time, if you'd thought any more, if you had any idea about . . .

I look up at him, the phone call with Sandra playing on my mind. I don't think we're going to find him, Denz.

He holds my gaze. You sure, Neef? You sure there's nowt you can tell me?

I shake my head, even though I can see how much he is hurting. His shoulders slump and I watch the hope drain out of him. I wait for him to say something else, but no words come and I wonder if it is because he doesn't trust himself to speak. Another beat passes before he looks down at the ground, turns back in the direction he came. For a moment Lewis hangs back and I see that he is watching me, a strange look in his eyes. But then he goes after Denz.

I've lost interest in going anywhere, slump back against the wall. It's only then that I realize Denz has left the orange carrier bag on the ground. I take it with me back to the caff, tip the contents out on one of the tables inside. A trashy magazine, a plastic box of cookies, a lip balm, Strepsils, a jumbo packet of paracetamol. It almost makes me laugh to think of Denz—Denz who could never stand the sight of me, who hated me all those years ago—wandering around a supermarket choosing things to make me feel better.

I leave the stuff on the table, go out the back for a cig. I've taken to smoking a lot again lately. I am standing in the side passage of the caff when I hear the voice.

Got a light?

It makes me jump, gasp out loud. Lewis is on the main road, just by the entrance to the alleyway, and I swear under my breath at the sight of him.

Sorry, he says. I didn't mean to scare you.

He moves toward me, his hands held up as though in surrender. Hey, chill, Neef. I aren't here to do anythin other than talk.

Where's Denz?

He's gone back to the flat. I told him I was meetin a mate.

But you're not.

No.

He gestures to the unlit cigarette in his hand, and I fish the light out of my pocket. He takes it, sparks up, lets out a stream of smoke before speaking again.

Must be mad, seein Denz, he says at last. Must mess with your mind.

I don't respond, toy with the keys to the caff in my pocket.

Man's got a lot of demons. Got a lot he wants to put right.

He thinks I can fix it for him, I say. Thinks I can put things right between him and Danny. But I can't. I have no idea where he is.

Lewis shakes his head. Nah. This int about findin Danny.

What?

This, he says, waving his hand vaguely in my direction. All this, with you. Nah. This is about regret. This is about him sayin sorry, for what he did.

I don't think so.

Lewis shrugs. Trust me. He knows he made a lot of mistakes, knows he screwed you over. He can't live with the guilt, man. Danny piled it on him for years. Denz knows as well as I do that Danny int lost.

What do you mean?

He looks at me thoughtfully. If Danny wanted to see Denz, he knows where to find him. But Denz hurt that kid too many times, hurt too many people that Danny loved. He int lost, he just don't want to be found.

I twist my neck to look down the alleyway, half expecting to see Denz standing there, listening. I need to get back inside, I say, but Lewis cuts me off.

You didn't really disappear, did you, Neef?

Lewis's words stop me dead in my tracks. What?

You came to South London for a reason. Because you and

Danny had always planned it. You knew that if you came here, Danny would know where to find you.

I thought I'd forgotten, I hear myself say.

But you hadn't.

So why didn't he find me then?

Lewis takes a long drag of his cigarette, his eyes trained on me. Maybe he did, he says.

didn't know you smoked.

The vaguely familiar voice cracks through my daze and I look up, startled. It is early, barely even light outside. I haven't slept since I saw Lewis the night before. I'm in the corner shop, standing at the counter. The old lady with the scarred face and the limp who comes into the caff is looking at me strangely.

I—I don't . . . I stutter as she places the carton of cigarettes in front of me. I haven't . . . I used to, I mean. A long time ago. But I quit. Years ago.

The lady raises her eyebrows, pulls her lips into a half grimace, half smile.

Bad habit to get back into, love. Expensive one and all.

Yeah . . . I nod, confused. Yeah.

I'm an ex-smoker meself, y'know. That's how I got these

scars, see. She gestures to the puckered skin on her cheek. Fell asleep with a dart in me hand, woke up to the blinkin sofa on fire. She laughs good-naturedly. I quit after that. But I still fancy one, now and again. Once a smoker, always a smoker, eh? she says with a wink.

I stare at her. I didn't know that.

What?

About your face. The scars. I've served you breakfast every day for years and I never knew what had happened.

The old lady looks taken aback. Well, no. We've never really chatted. It's always so busy in there, isn't it?

You've never spoken to me before.

She laughs again, more awkwardly this time. You've never spoken to *me* before, love. Never seemed keen to, in fact. I was just making conversation, that's all. I didn't mean to pry, if that's what you mean. None of my business if you smoke or not.

She takes a step back and I rub at my temples. Sorry, no, I didn't mean that . . .

Never mind, love, never mind. How're Fionnoula and Ali doing anyways? Poor old Ali looked done in when I saw him last. I told him he should take it easy—

What?

Ali, the woman says irritably. Ali from the caff? I were just saying. He's not been looking too well—

I don't hear the rest of the sentence. I've already left the shop.

ALI IS TURNING THE SIGN ON THE DOOR TO OPEN WHEN I GET back to the caff. His face flushes with something like relief at the sight of me and he grips my shoulders in his hands, squeezes tight. I can barely look at him, shame washing over me. The old lady was right. Ali looks exhausted.

Fionnoula blanches when she sees me, but she doesn't pry, just passes me the order pad, carries on as though I've never been away. I can feel her watching me for the rest of the day, but there is no interrogation, no recrimination, even though that is what I deserve.

At the end of my shift I head out to get some air, leave Fi and Ali to lock up. The sky has been low and pregnant with storms all day but I need to stretch, to move, to keep my brain busy. I can't work out what Lewis meant, what he was trying to say. And I can't figure out what matters, the past or here and now.

On my third lap of the common the rain begins, fat drops that hit the ground and then bounce back up, as though wanting another chance at life. I turn, make my way back to the caff. Fionnoula's van is missing from its spot in the side street when I get there, but the lights are still on inside. Ali must have stayed late to prep for tomorrow; they can't count on me to do that anymore.

The caff feels off-kilter as soon as I walk in, something in the air not tasting quite right. I move toward the kitchen and it is then that I hear the noise, a sound like a wounded animal. My heart thumps as I call out Ali's name, hear it again and quicken my step, banging my hip on the counter, the kitchen door swinging behind me. A figure is heaped on the floor, bent almost double on his side. Ali. Ali, lying there on the ground, his face pale, contorted.

Jesus Christ.

I drop to my knees, take his hand in mine. It feels cold,

clammy, the pulse in his wrist weak. Ali, I say. Ali, can you hear me, but no words come, just a groan. My hands shake as I punch the numbers into the phone. Ambulance, I hear myself plead. Please. Quickly. Send an ambulance.

It arrives within minutes, although it feels much longer, Ali's grip in my palm growing weaker with every second that passes. Paramedics rush in, sirens and stretchers and words, language flying around, terms I don't understand. Everything is happening so fast, a machine on his chest, an electric current into his heart, the sight of it, the noise making me cover my mouth with my hands to strangle a sob. Ali, Ali. Sweet, kind Ali.

A female paramedic with a rope of long blond hair asks me what my relationship is to the patient and I tell her he is my boss. She nods, says I've done the right thing in calling them, lifts him onto a stretcher and closes the back doors. Can't I come with him? I ask, but nobody hears me.

The ambulance drives away screaming, as I stand trembling, watching the lights disappear into the night. It only occurs to me after they leave that I should have said, should have explained. He's not my boss, he isn't just my boss. He means so much to me.

Fionnoula doesn't pick up her phone and so I scrawl her a note, leave it in the middle of the counter, run outside to flag down a cab. We pull up to the hospital and I shove a handful of notes into the driver's hand, don't bother to check if I've given him too much or not enough.

Inside it is chaos, or maybe it isn't, maybe it feels like that in my head because I don't know where Ali is, don't know where to go or who to ask. Eventually I find my way to the information desk, try to explain to the woman sitting there.

She looks at me sympathetically, nods, listens. But I can't give you any information, she says. I'm so sorry. Not unless you're family.

I walk away, pace up and down for a while then try again. You don't understand, please. He's important to me, I need to see him, need to know he's okay. The woman exchanges a look with her colleague, who shakes his head but doesn't meet my eye. I want to cry with frustration, want to reach across and push them out of the way, type his name into the computer myself, but then I hear a voice.

Jen!

Fionnoula is rushing down the corridor, her cheeks flushed, panic in her eyes. A nurse follows close behind, a concerned look on her face as Fionnoula grabs me in her arms, holds me tight to her chest.

Oh, Jen love. Thank god you're here, thank god. They're taking me to see him now, come, come—

The woman at the counter gets to her feet. I'm sorry, she is saying, I'm sorry but it's family only. She's not—

Fionnoula turns to her sharply. What the devil are you talking about. Of course she's family! Of course she is.

64

We wait for days before the doctors tell us Ali will get better, although he will need to stay in hospital for a little while. It was touch and go there, they say. You called us just in time.

Thank god you got back when you did, Jen, Fionnoula says to me, gripping my hand in hers, but I know I am to blame. He shouldn't have been there, shouldn't have had to work late. He was doing my job, packing in all those extra hours because I was too consumed by my own selfishness, my stupid fucking ghost-hunt, my past life.

I'm so sorry, I tell them. So, so sorry. But every time I say it, every time I crumple at the thought of what I've put them through, I am held, reassured. Put back together again.

That afternoon, after I have found out that Ali will make it, I call Denz. Tell him about the phone call with Sandra from Kew Gardens. He is quiet for a long time and I have no idea what he is thinking, feeling. In the end all he does is ask me if I'd like to go for a walk sometime.

I visit the hospital every day, armed with sustenance from the caff. Ali won't touch the food the nurses bring, the plastic trays congealing beside him until someone takes the hint to clear them away. Fionnoula is always there, fussing, plumping his pillows and straightening his cover and making sure his pajamas are fresh. Only when I arrive does she allow herself a break, nipping out to use the facilities or grab yet another stewed tea from the vending machine.

She's driving me up the wall, this *zaneh*, Ali says to me, throwing his hands up to the sky as soon as Fionnoula is out of the door. It makes me laugh.

She's only looking after you, Ali. You have just had a bloody heart attack.

I'm fine, he insists. Absolutely fine. All a lot of commotion over nothing. What I need is to get back to work. It's too much to run that place all by yourself.

I tell Fionnoula that I'll be able to manage the caff on my own while Ali gets better and at first she says no, but eventually she relents. I'm so busy that I barely have time to think about Denz and Danny and everything that has occupied my head all these weeks.

I lose count of how many people ask after Ali and Fionnoula, my heart filling with all the ways they show their love for them. The greengrocer with his crates of fruit dropped off at the back door, the florist who brings fresh cuts of rainbow-colored bouquets wrapped in brown paper. Casseroles and cakes and hotpots and lasagnas, card after card after card, a pile of pastel envelopes teetering on the worktop by the end of every shift. I chat with the customers more in those weeks than I ever have, matching names to faces that I've known for years. Esther, Mo, Colin. Turns out Sandy's real name is Greg, although he doesn't like to go by that anymore.

Belongs to another life, he tells me, and I nod.

I know what you mean.

65

Y ou still write, Neef?

It is a Sunday afternoon and I am back from the hospital. I've been so busy with visiting Ali and keeping the caff afloat that I'm only now taking Denz up on his invitation of a walk. We are strolling along Streatham Common together, the sharpness of winter slowly easing, the taste of spring in the air.

I shake my head. Not for years and years. I wouldn't know how to anymore.

I'm sure that int true.

I don't know what to say to that and so I stay quiet.

Danny used to talk about your writin all the time, y'know. Used to tell me how talented you were, how he bet you'd get published one day.

Neither of us has mentioned Danny up until now. Instead

we've let the shape of him root itself into the ground between us, both of us skirting around it, pretending it isn't there.

Do you miss him, Neef?

The directness of Denz's question throws me. I think for a while before I open my mouth.

I never let myself. I thought the only way I could handle it was to forget.

You still think that?

I dunno. Maybe not.

Denz nods slowly, like my answer has satisfied him, and we walk a little further in silence.

Lewis reckons Danny knew where you were, Denz says after a while, and I know he is doing his best not to look at me. Reckons he might've been keepin an eye on you.

I don't think that's true.

Why?

Because . . . because if he knew where I was, why didn't he come see me? If he'd gone to all the bother of tracking me down, finding out where I lived, where I worked . . .

Maybe he just needed to know you were all right.

But I'm not all right, Denz. I've never been all right.

Denz lets out a low laugh. Come on, Neef. Look how far you've come.

We get to the bench where we sat together all those months ago, pause there without discussion.

Remember when I came to visit you? he says. In that place—that institute?

Yeah. I remember.

I told you about Kim.

You only ever told me half the story.

Denz's eyes cloud over with thought. Would it help, d'you think? If you knew the rest?

I look at him carefully. I don't know, I say.

He takes a breath, starts to talk, although it's a while before he begins making any sense. The story stops and starts, jumping from one thing to the next as he fumbles for the right words, only finding his flow when he gets to the part about Kim telling him she was pregnant with Danny. How when his auntie got wind of it, she gave him a month to find a job and somewhere to live. Denz took out a lease on a little flat the next day. Upped his shifts at the supermarket, stacking shelves all night, then getting up for college the next morning. Kim came to live with him, the pair of them crammed in his shoebox room, her belly swelling bigger every day. But they rowed like cat and dog, couldn't seem to find a single thing they agreed on. They were miserable, trapped, skint, and in the end it was too much. Kim packed her bags, took a taxi back to Mary's.

When Danny were born, I'd go over and see him as much as I could, Denz says. But you know Mary never liked me. Whenever I'd go round there, Kim would be sleepin off a big night or gettin ready to go out, or in a bad mood because she'd been stuck at home all day, all week, with a baby, by herself. I wanted to see Danny, but Mary wouldn't have it and so I told them I'd be gettin legal advice. It shook them up enough that they invited me over for Christmas. Plan were that I'd go over the day before, stay the night and have the whole of Christmas Day with Danny, at Mary's house. Course it weren't anywhere near what I wanted. But I figured I'd play nice, for Danny's sake at least.

Denz leans forward so that his elbows rest on his knees, and I see that his legs are trembling.

Five p.m. I turn up, he says. I've got a whole sackload of presents for Danny, a bottle of fancy champagne for Mary.

Kim were done up all nice, and I thought for a minute it were for me, daft bastard that I was. But next thing she says she's goin out, and Mary's fumin. *I ain't got no desire to sit in all night with him,* she says, like I aren't even in the room. And *I aren't havin you hungover all Christmas Day.* But Kim wouldn't back down, carryin on about it bein her Christmas too, how all she ever did were make sacrifices for everyone else.

I looked at her properly then, saw that mebbe she didn't look so good after all. Her skin all messed up, her eyes too deep in their sockets. Danny started cryin and I picked him up, tried to soothe him, but Mary and Kim were proper goin at it by then and so I stepped in, offered to drive Kim to the party, make sure she got home safe, at a decent hour. I remember Kim givin me this funny look. It won't be your sort of thing, she goes, and I laughed, told her she were probably right.

THE PARTY WAS OVER AT A HOUSE IN LEEDS, ON THE OTHER SIDE of town from where Denz lived. He had a bad feeling about it as soon as he walked in, didn't like the vibe in there, the dead eyes and the caved-in faces, the way no one looked like they were having fun. Kim disappeared almost as soon as they arrived, and although he sought her out a few times, in the end he gave up, went outside to sit in the car and listen to music and have a smoke. He only realized he'd drifted off when he heard the sirens, saw the ambulance pulling up outside, two police cars behind it. He jumped out of the car, tried to get back inside the house, but they wouldn't let him past and he lost his temper, pushed one of the officers out of the way. Denz felt the hands on him then, grabbing him from behind, flipping him onto his front on the bonnet of a squad car, slapping cuffs on his wrists, and all the while he was writhing, twisting, trying to catch sight of the door, trying to make out the shape of the figure being carried out on a stretcher, seeing the red sheen of her hair as it caught in the lights.

When they took him down to the station, they found nothing on him but a tiny bag of weed and traces of marijuana in his urine. Still, they kept Denz all night and into the next day, Christmas Day, and not one of them would tell him what had happened to Kim. It was only when they led him into the interview room the next morning, after he'd sat there wide awake all night, thinking of Danny without his mum or dad on Christmas morning, that they told him they'd need to ask him a few questions in connection with Kimberly Morris's death.

I'M SORRY, DENZ, I SAY QUIETLY, BUT HE DOESN'T LOOK AT ME.

They let me go in t'end, he says. No charges, no nothin. But it didn't matter. Everyone had already made up their minds that I were guilty. No smoke without fire, and all that shite. People said I'd sold it to Kim, said I'd pumped it straight into her veins. Didn't matter that I'd never touched filth like that in me life, didn't matter that I weren't even at the fuckin party. Murderer, scumbag, smack dealer. I heard it all.

I didn't . . . Danny never—

Denz cuts me off, his voice hard.

You know what they did to me the next time I set foot in that town, the next time I tried to go and see my *son*? They jumped me. Behind your precious pub, a whole pack of em. And that cretin Barry turned a blind eye, let them kick ten shades of shit outta me, like I weren't even human. How you think I got this, here? He jabs at the scar across his cheekbone.

I wipe at my eyes, shake my head, because none of the words I can think of are good enough. Denz sighs.

See, Neef, he says. I had to fight for Danny, his whole life I had to fight for him. I had to battle tooth and nail for every scrap of a visit I could get with that kid. If I ever breathed a bad word about Mary to him, she'd have pulled the rug out from under me feet quicker than I could have caught a breath. I didn't see Danny for close on three years after Kim died. Three *years*. It killed me. I tried to get a lawyer involved, get access, but they all told me I didn't have a strong enough case. In the end I went to Danny's school, picked him up and took him home. I'd been worried that he wouldn't come to me, but the minute he saw my face at the classroom door he got up and ran straight into me arms, like he'd seen me just the day before. Course the police turned up at my place within a couple of hours and took him back, arrested me for kidnap or some bollocks, but Mary didn't press charges. She were that terrified of it happenin again that she backed down, but only half an inch. Said I could see him one Sunday every month, so long as I promised never to try and take Danny from her again. And despite everything, I felt so bad for her. She had nowt—no one else. So I agreed.

He takes a deep breath, sits up. So that's how it were, how it always were, all them years. And I always said, it'll be different when he's older, I'll explain it to Danny. But then you came along and, look . . . forgive me for sayin this, Neef, but . . . I were scared. I thought you were gonna ruin his life, drag him down a road he'd never have come back from.

It wasn't like that. I loved Danny. I never would have done anything to—

It don't matter, Denz cuts in abruptly. You still don't get it, do you? You don't know how dangerous you were to a kid like Danny. I could see it a mile off. I'd been there before, remember? I'd been there with Kim. I had no choice but to get him away from you, surely you can understand that now? I never meant to do that to Nia. I wasn't going to hurt her. It weren't about Nia, Neef. Yeah, all right, that were some crazy shit and it were clear you needed help by then. But even if that hadn't happened, I would've got Danny away from you, one way or another. You're rememberin it all wrong, like Danny was your savior or summat. But that's you puttin yourself at the center of everyone else's story, Neef. It weren't as easy for a kid like Danny to fall and get back up. You could do things that he couldn't and still come back and pick up your life. And that's what you did, even if you can't see it for yourself. It wouldn't have been the same for him. There would have been no goin back.

THE EVENING IS WARM AND YET I SHIVER ALL THE WAY BACK TO the caff, the hair on my arms rising up to standing. By the time I reach the corner it is growing dark, the street illuminated by lamplight. A memory comes to me and I let the reel play out in my mind's eye. Danny and me, dancing in matching Reeboks down a street, the orange glow of the lamp posts catching on his smile. How many hours we spent, how many days and weeks it must have added up to, the pair of us lying together, talking about the future. And they were beautiful, those times. They were golden. But it's only now I can see the picture in full, see the ways in which mine and Danny's worlds differed. How blinkered I was. How little I understood.

Almost two weeks pass before Ali is discharged from the hospital, and not long after that Fionnoula starts coming to the caff most days. He's driving me bonkers, always under me feet, he is, she says. Silly old beggar won't bloody well sit still.

I smile, count every one of my lucky stars that he's on the mend.

Perhaps we should throw him a welcome-home party, I say, and at first Fionnoula looks at me like I've gone stark raving mad, but then her face splits into a grin.

What an idea, she says with glee, clapping her hands. What a bloody great idea, Jen.

We tell all the regulars, put a little flyer on the counter with the details. Fionnoula invites a few friends, the delivery boy from the grocer's, one or two of the suppliers. She asks me if there is anyone I'd like to include, and I know she means Denz. For a moment I consider it, but in the end I tell her no.

On the day of the party we set to getting the caff ready as soon as the lunch rush has cleared, stringing up bunting and filling buckets with ice and water, stacking up beers and wine and even a few bottles of bubbles that Fionnoula got cheap from a girl she's friendly with at the offie.

Feels like we've got a lot to celebrate, doesn't it, Jenny? she says as she covers the little Formica tables in brightly colored paper cloths. We're so lucky, aren't we, love?

There is a moment when the word jars, when it feels so at odds with my idea of myself. I turn it over in my head. Lucky. *Lucky.* When I look up, I see that Fionnoula is watching me, her eyes shining. I smile. Yeah, Fi, I say. Yeah. We are.

That night the caff fills quickly, a harmony of laughter and chat that carries up the stairwell and floats through the cracks of my door. It doesn't surprise me, to hear it. I've come to learn how much the caff means to people.

At the back of my wardrobe I find a dress that Fionnoula bought me a few years back. She'd seen it in the window of a charity shop, thought it would be perfect for me, although I've never had occasion to wear it. I pull it over my head, cinch it in around the waist with a velvet ribbon left over from some Christmas wrapping. In the drawer of the little dressing table next to my bed I unearth an old mascara, almost dried out now, and a lipstick the color of plums.

My reflection in the dresser mirror is tired, but there is more to it than that. The skin around my eyes has begun to crease, lines forming where once there were none. I'm not the kid lost in my memories, not even the girl who walked into the caff all those years ago. It hits me that I must be older now than Chrissy was when she left. She was so young.

Once I'm ready, I make my way to the top of the stairs, stand there for a long time before taking the first step down. The ebb and flow of the party drags at me like a tide and I walk slowly along the narrow hallway that leads past the kitchen and into the caff, take a deep breath before pushing open the door. There is a swell of warmth and light and noise and faces, so many faces, all of them lit up, like the gray drudgery of their everyday has been left at the door. I scan the room and my eyes fall on Ali, propped up in a chair at one of the tables, his face pale and worn. He looks up as though he can sense me, breaking into a smile as he beckons me toward him. I step into the buzz of the tiny space and feel a hand on my arm, a warm cheek against mine.

Oh, hello, Jen love, we were wondering when you'd join us.

It is Esther, the old lady with the scarred face and the limp who works down the corner shop, and beside her stands Mo, the night cleaner, pushing a plate of food toward me. Eat, eat, he is saying. There's plenty of food!

That's right, eat! And drink! Enjoy! A hand on my shoulder: Colin, the shy musician with the long, graying dreads; and beside him Sandy, nodding ferociously, still in that long brown coat.

Always so quiet, meek as a little mouse, scurryin aboot wi yer plates and yer dishes. But not tonight. Tonight we party! He lifts a can of beer in the air, and I cheers him with a paper cup that someone hands me.

The party carries me along, carries all of us. Music and laughter and snatched pieces of conversation. Every so often

I catch Fionnoula's or Ali's eye and we grin at one another at the fun we are having. The feeling that, tonight at least, we are all exactly where we are supposed to be.

Halfway through the evening I feel Ali's hand on my arm, the same warmth but the grip weaker than it once was. I turn to him, concerned. Are you okay, Ali? Everything okay?

He smiles, nods. Yes, yes. I just need a little air, Jenny *joon*. Do you think you could help me outside for a moment?

Of course, I say, easing him to his feet, leading him out toward the back door. In the half dark I scramble around, trying to find somewhere for him to sit, but by the time I turn around Ali has made himself comfortable, beaming up at me from his perch on a wooden crate against the wall.

I'm okay, Jen, he says, amused. You don't need to worry about me.

I sit down beside him, feel the jutting bones of his thin knees against mine. But I do worry, Ali.

There's no need—

You don't understand, I cut in. That night when I came back to the caff, when I found you, the stuff that went through my head, I couldn't stand it if . . .

He waves the thought away, then reaches for my hand, squeezes it gently. I'm fine, Jen. I'm fine.

There is so much I want to say, so much I want to explain. I want to tell him how much he and Fionnoula mean to me, how grateful I am to them for all they have done. How glad I am to be here, to have them. But the words catch in my throat and all I can do is squeeze his hand back.

You know, he says gently after a while. Me and Fionnoula. We just want you to be happy, Jen. *Doret begardam,* you see? You're the closest either of us has to a daughter.

His words make my heart hurt. Perhaps this is what it feels like to be part of a family. Thank you, I say quietly.

I can see a change in you, Jenny *joon*. But trust me when I say this, because I speak from experience. You can't be happy, you can't move on, if you don't make peace with the past. Do you know what it is I'm saying to you?

But that's what I've been trying to do, all these years, Ali. I've been trying to forget, to block it out—

No, he stops me, shaking his head. That's not what I'm saying. You can't forget about it, can't bury it. You have to make peace with it, Jenny. It's the only way. Every single one of us on this earth has things that have happened to them, he says. Things that they've done or had done to them that they would rather forget about. But forgetting isn't the answer, it's not possible, see? You have to make peace with it. You have to let it all go. Do you think you can do that?

I look at him uncertainly and our eyes lock. I'll go slow, Ali, I smile. But I won't stop.

A few days after the party I see Denz for what I know is the last time. He comes to the caff just before closing, hovering in the doorway like he did on that day all those months ago. I meet his gaze. You coming in then or what?

He finds a seat right at the back, his eyes glued to the screen of his phone until he sees me turn the sign on the door. We are the only two people in there now.

I'm sorry if I upset you, when I saw you the other day.

I pull out the chair across from him, sit down slowly. They were things I needed to hear, I say.

Denz looks at the table. We're thinking of leavin London. Me and Lewis. Mebbe go up north for a bit. Or Spain.

I swallow, not sure how to feel. And Danny? I say.

He takes a breath, shakes his head slowly. He int lost.

We say our goodbyes at the door, but we don't hug. Just

before he leaves, Denz hands me a piece of paper with a name scrawled on it that I don't recognize. Christine O'Leary.

Some people want to be found, some people don't. You know what I'm sayin, Neef?

I smile. It's Jen, I tell him.

IT TAKES ME ALMOST A WEEK BEFORE I BUILD THE NERVE TO TYPE the name on that scrap of paper into the little blue app on my phone. There are hundreds of Christine O'Learys, it turns out. I nearly shut it down there and then, but a photo catches my eye. Or a photo of a photo, I should say. Two girls, almost like sisters, posing on a sofa, both of them wearing Christmas-cracker crowns. Blurry and old, taken years and years ago now. A memory captured with a cardboard camera. In that moment it's like I can see my mam clearly.

There was a conversation that I overheard between Chrissy and Barry once, when they first got together. I'd been sitting at the top of the stairs waiting for them to come up, like I often did in those very early days. It was late, the pub was closed, but they were in the back bar, pissed. Barry especially. He kept telling her how much he loved her, how beautiful she was, how grateful he was that she'd come into his life, but with every compliment, every lavished praise, I'd hear Chrissy say the same thing. And Jen, she'd say, and Jen? You love her too? You're grateful fer her too? And he'd reply, yes, of course, I love that little lass, what a little gem, what a treasure, thank you fer bringin her to me, Chrissy, thankyouthankyou.

At the time, all I'd wanted was for Chrissy to shut up and come upstairs, to stop asking him for all that inane reassurance, but now I think maybe she was testing Barry, seeing if he could give me what she couldn't. Perhaps it was always part of her plan to leave. Before Denz, before Barry, before we even left the flats. Maybe since I'd been tiny. Everyone thought she was a shit mam, but maybe they got it all wrong. Maybe she'd just been looking for a home for me, somewhere I would be settled. Somewhere that she could leave me, hoping that I'd be better off.

I stare at the photo for a long time, think about sending her a message. But in the end I slide my phone under my pillow, make my way downstairs to set up for the day ahead. Flick all the switches. Oven. Kettle. Coffee machine. Toaster. Butter bread, lay out bacon. Crack eggs. Sauces on the table, red and brown. Salt and pepper. Napkins. Cutlery. The pattern of it soothes me and I drag the black bag from under the sink, cart it toward the back door. The key is in my apron and, as I pull it from my pocket, it slips from my fingers, drops down on the floor.

It is only when I bend to pick it up that I see the envelope there. It is white, nondescript, and the front of it is blank, save for four letters scrawled in blue biro, the stroke of the script stirring a memory from long ago:

Neef

Inside there is a plastic bag no bigger than the size of my palm, filled with tiny black seeds. I turn it over in my hand and see the label, written in that same familiar stroke:

Calathea
For new beginnings.

ACKNOWLEDGMENTS

After so many years of procrastination, I'm still slightly in shock to find I've written a novel! I owe thanks to so many, but first and foremost to my agent Millie Hoskins at United Literary Agency, who believed in this story from the get go, and always has my back. Millie, I feel so incredibly fortunate to have found you!

Thank you to Hannah Westland for picking up my manuscript in the midst of a bout of COVID, and seeing enough in it to allow Neef and Danny to come to life. Thank you to the wonderful team at Serpent's Tail—in particular Mehar Anaokar, Luke Brown, Emily Frisella and Drew Jerrison. Thank you also to the forensic eyes of SJ Forder and Mandy Green.

Huge thanks to Molly Friedrich and Hannah Brattesani at The Friedrich Agency for taking *Wild Ground* on its journey stateside. Thank you to the team at Penguin Random House USA—Clio Seraphim, your love and enthusiasm for this story has blown me away. I am so grateful to you! Thank you also to Rachel Parker, Madison Dettlinger, Caitlin McKenna, Leila Tejani, Windy Dorresteyn, Maria Braeckel and the many, many others behind the scenes who have breathed life into *Wild Ground*.

Putting pen to paper with any sort of real intention has always been my downfall, and it is only thanks to the discipline and structure afforded to me by the Year of the Novel course at Writing Center NSW that I was able to finally get my words on a page. Thank you, therefore, to my teacher, mentor and friend, Emily Maguire, and my writing comrades Clare Fletcher and Sarah Percival. *Wild Ground* would never have got started, let alone finished, without you!

Britain is a multicultural country, and it's important to me that my writing reflects this. As such, this story includes characters from a diverse range of backgrounds. Whilst I can never claim to fully understand the complexities of prejudice and discrimination faced by those outside of my own lived experience, I hope I have done my due diligence in listening, reading and educating myself, and that my exploration of these issues has been done with sensitivity. I am especially grateful to Desiree Reynolds and Daryoush Haj Najafi for your thoughtfulness, generosity and guidance. Thank you also to my long-time friend Helen Early for your insights into psychiatric care in the UK.

This is a story about first love, and it would be remiss of me not to acknowledge the first person I ever felt for, SB. Although you're no longer with us, I thought of you often when writing this. Keep smiling up there. You are not forgotten.

Huge big thanks to my boy tribe, Sonny, Rafferty and Jesse, for allowing me many a weekend and evening of reprieve from wrestling and trampoline-jumping so that I could hide away in a quiet room and scribble down words. Everything I do is for you.

And of course, to Andy. You have always been my champion, my confidence and my confidant. Thank you for believing in me. I love you.

ABOUT THE AUTHOR

Emily Usher grew up in West Yorkshire, and lived in Salford, Sheffield, and London before relocating to Australia. She is an author, award-winning short story writer, and freelance writer specializing in the not-for-profit sector. Usher has also taught creative writing in prisons both in Australia and in the UK. *Wild Ground* is her first novel.

emilyroseusher.com